STANDING OUTSIDE
THE LAW

STANDING OUTSIDE
THE LAW
S.J. Smith

Standing Outside The Law, © 2009, Shira Smith

A note to old friends:
This is a work of fiction and any resemblance between the characters and persons living or dead is purely coincidental. I labored for years to be sure that my characters are of my own making. They are not meant in any way to be representations of anyone I used to know.

ISBN: 978-0-578-01262-9

Contents

*This book is dedicated to all those
who went before,
to those who were there at the time,
and to those yet to come.*

*Also to good friends who patiently
read earlier drafts and made many
helpful comments.*

This land is your land.

*"Memories are neither true nor false.
They're only more or less vivid."*

*Overheard on the porch one evening at
Joaquin Murrieta Mountain Celebration XIII*

I.

The Garden

The morning in 1969 when things boiled over between Coleman and Jesse, things that were never patched up completely, started like so many others had that sweaty Texas summer, over strong coffee, poppy-seed kolaches, and discussion of the morning news around the worn wooden kitchen table. "Anybody remember when it became so goddamn popular to smirk like this?" Raz held up our local paper, the *Denton Record-Chronicle*. On the cover was a rising conservative Houston politician grinning on one side of his face.

"Trying to look like James Dean, I guess," Jesse mumbled over his cup, brushing his shoulder length brown hair away from his face and drying his droopy moustache with the back of his hand. The groupie from Dallas who'd followed him home nodded and smiled in agreement. He hadn't introduced her, so we assumed we wouldn't be seeing her again tomorrow.

Raz turned to me. Neither his native stubbornness nor his need to argue early in the day would allow him to let the idea go lightly. "Got to be more to it than that. Troy, you remember?" I shook my head no, preferring to listen rather than talk.

"I thought it was always part of the macho Texan look," Duncan said as he headed for the fridge. "Man, whose turn was it to fill the ice trays?"

"Yours, so no complaining. Actually, it is a relatively new look. My dad's friend Mack goes on about this all the time." R.E. was standing by the sink, still braiding her hair, a time-consuming chore since it fell in a red-gold wave to her thighs. She cracked her neck, adjusted her shoulders, and dropped her voice to a soft growl as she strode across the floor, imitating him. "Just irritates the hell out of me. Texans never did that before and now all the rich little daddy's boys who ever saw Giant pose like that. Goddamned spoiled brats wouldn't last a day doin' real work." Duncan, still staring at the empty ice bin, looked around, his baby blues at their most pleading. After receiving neither sympathy nor assistance, he slowly started filling the metal trays.

Raz kept at it. "So, it's just an imitation of a movie star? A pose?" Amanda, Raz's Rubenesque blond girlfriend, began cleaning up the crumbs from the table, in the conversation as usual only by virtue of eye contact and head nodding.

But that was as far as it got. Coleman, who had been listening from the other room, leapt to the door frame and started doing pull-ups, kicking his feet higher every time until he could thump the ceiling. We ignored him until he dropped to the floor: pale blue eyes frosted with a cocaine glaze, black hair pulled into a high ponytail, Mongol-style, his slim frame shivering from the exertion. "Never underestimate the value of a good pose," he whispered.

The phone rang and Jesse stepped out to answer it. Coleman made his move, taking the little groupie by the elbow. "You and me. How 'bout it?" He led her into the living room and towards the stairs. The rest of us locked eyes one by one then followed them silently. Coleman had crossed a line he'd never crossed before and he'd done it three ways: hit on someone already with one of us, done it right in front of R.E., and in our home.

Jesse caught them out of the corner of his eye and hung up the phone mid-sentence. "Cole," he said in a low, even voice, "She came over to see me, not you, so back off."

"Then why don't you already have her upstairs?" He clicked his tongue. "Such bad timing for a musician."

Stiff-arming the girl to keep her between them, Coleman never took his eyes off Jesse as he started backing up the stairs, "Please allow me to introduce myself, I'm a man of wealth and taste," he sang softly into her ear, smiling with his mouth but not his shiny eyes.

"Damn you, Cole, leave her alone," Jesse growled as he stomped towards them. Yanking her away, he whispered, "Leave it where it is." The voices had been low enough, but the vibes sent ripples of chicken skin from ankle to neck. Jesse and the girl turned to walk away, but Coleman jumped over the railing and bounded in front of them in one move. As he slid one foot behind the other and drew his right fist back slightly, he whispered, "Come on. Winner takes all."

I caught a flash of denim and calico from the corner of my eyes as R.E. dashed from a shadow and grabbed Coleman's cocked elbow from behind. Startled, he almost lost his balance. "Fuckin' stay outta this," he yelled, turning on her.

Jesse saw Coleman's right coming around and stepped into the swing, blocking it and shoving R.E. away with one foot. They wrestled briefly for balance. Then he half turned and mule-kicked Coleman's shin so hard he fell back onto the floor with a heavy thud. He lay there breathing hard, not moving at first. As he propped himself up on his elbows, he shook his head. Bracing himself, he flipped back onto his feet without taking his eyes off Jesse.

"Drop it, Cole. It ain't worth it. There's only one way to finish this, and I don't want it to come to that."

"I'm sure you don't, since you don't have a chance in hell of winning." He bared his teeth in a chilling smile and took a step towards Jesse.

I spoke up. "You can't fight us all, Cole."

We'd been friends since grade school and in all that time, I'd never confronted him when he was in a rage. But now I stood shoulder to shoulder with the rest of the household as we circled in Jesse's defense. Coleman glanced from face to face and tried to smile again. Fight was not an option; only flight remained. He threw his head back and howled in anger, the fury of it raising the hairs on my neck. Bounding to the door, he flew out of the Palace. We heard his Mustang rev ferociously and smelled the baked dry dirt being spun up in the yard as he gunned it down the path that led to the highway.

Jesse, R.E., and I went outside to the yard. The black car was just a speck dropping over the horizon. R.E. broke the silence. "He's so hard to reach when he's high like this."

"I don't get it. Why do you even try?" Jesse kicked an unoffending rock as far as he could down the road.

"I have to do what I can."

"No one can help him, R.E. It can't be done."

She started to speak, thought about it, and finally said, "There are some things. They take a lot of energy, though."

Jesse shook his head and didn't say anything else. He kept staring at R.E. as though there were something between them that had been said before: a silent told-you-so. Once back upstairs in my room, I sat by my window, watching the heat dance on the distant highway, the violent scene like a bad dream, one you remember vividly and can't shower away. Only a short few months ago, we'd all found this place and started what we hoped would be a real home.

***

It all began one brisk March morning earlier that same year, in the back yard of the place in Fort Worth where Jesse was crashing. He and I were reading the ads in the *Record-Chronicle* about places to rent in Denton. Coleman was reading an article from *The Rag*, Austin's *Village Voice*. "If we could only find something big enough for all of us, we could do this, too."

"Do what?" Jesse asked.

"You know, live in a commune like this one. All of us." Coleman spread the paper out for us to see: beautiful women in long dresses in a big kitchen, waiting on guys sitting around a table heaped with hippie delights: stoned contentment. You could almost smell the incense. "Think about it. A real home." He smiled and nudged the paper closer so we could both see the photos.

Jesse asked, "You honestly think it would work? You, me, all the rest of us, under one roof? One set of rules?"

Coleman smiled. "Could be interesting, depending on the rules. Why not? I've got plenty of cash right now."

That was nothing new. He always had money. We were never sure where he got it from, but we were never rude enough to ask either.

It was that moment I saw an ad and read it aloud: "Hey, listen to this. Six bedroom, two bath house, $125 a month, utilities not included. Offered as-is." We piled in Jesse's van and took off. As soon as we drove up, we knew it was perfect. Two stories and a lofty attic, just outside of Denton city limits, far enough for privacy but close enough for water and lights, it was actually little more than a rambling, added-on-to, wooden firetrap. Small wonder the rent was so low. The absentee Dallas landlord drove out that afternoon. He said if we paid the rent on time and didn't burn the place down, he didn't mind what we did or how many people lived there. Coleman and Jesse went back to Fort Worth to gather our meager things. I stayed at the new digs, soaking up the vibes. I wanted to see the afternoon sun come in from every window, starting upstairs in the smallest room, the one that looked out onto the roof. Then working my way from space to space, I ended up in the huge, empty downstairs. As I sat down in the quiet and smiled, I knew I was home for the first time in my life. Coleman and Jesse returned after a while and flopped down beside me. "Our place, my brothers, our house," Cole whispered. "Home."

The days and weeks that followed were the sweetest spring I can remember, rich with lilac and irises everywhere, clear skies and cool breezes, and the promise of a commune of our own. Coleman was a blur of action the first week, lugging in the few chunks of furniture necessary for elevating our lives above refugee status, food and a fridge and stove, a new stereo and stacks of albums. I'd never seen him so upbeat, positive, and happy. He could be a pretty decent guy when the mood took him. He was equally capable of being a violent drunk and even more volatile demon when he was coked up. You rarely knew which Coleman would come through the door. But for that short season, he was the best he was capable of being. He had to be in order to populate our little Utopia as we'd planned that first evening in the house.

Duncan, a musician friend of Jesse's and current band-mate, was the first to be invited. He had a small inheritance and lots of connections to local marijuana growers to add to our collective riches, so he was voted in as the first member. He was a frugal guy, even though he always had access to his trust fund. He kept cash and stash both in an old military cartridge box in his room. "Just a little private bank, fireproof and waterproof." Of course he didn't keep so much on hand that being ripped off would end a friendship. It would end trust, though, and he always made that very clear to us.

Another of Jesse's friends from a short-lived day-gig on a construction site was elected next. His real name was Morgan but we called him Raz, short for Rasputin, because of his pale, thoughtful face, long black hair, and scraggly beard. He was a carpenter's assistant and could fix just about anything. Given the "as-is" conditions we had already accepted, he had his work cut out for him. He would also be the house banker. Son of second- generation free thinkers from Big Sur, he'd learned early on how to manage money since neither his parents nor his grandparents were really interested in the material side of life. The only small hang-up had been that his girlfriend Amanda would come along with his luggage. But she was reluctant to be the only female presence in the house. Coleman smiled and said casually, "Then I guess it's time to ask R.E. to move in, too. She can take the roof room." He'd met her earlier in the year but had gone to great lengths to keep his feelings about her hidden, only mentioning her in passing now and then. I was the only one who knew how smitten he really was. And even though he'd said she'd have her own room, we all knew that she'd spend more time in his.

Coleman first saw her at The Corner Room, a local diner where she worked for Eddie, a Beatnik guy who'd been in town for a couple of years. The early winter morning they met, we'd been looking over the menu purely out of habit. It never changed, but reading it was part of the ritual of waking up. The waitress approached and asked, "Coffee?" We nodded then a slender arm reached across the table. Three silver bracelets jingled on her wrist as she filled our mugs. I glanced at Coleman and saw his pupils spread as though to swallow her up in one gulp. She was tall and long-legged, with coppery-tan skin and hazel eyes shot through with gray, green and blue streaks, eyes that could look right into you, right down to the bone. Since it was cold that morning, she was wearing a long dark green skirt, a long-sleeved lilac calico shirt, and brown leather boots. Her red-gold hair was in a thick braid curling over her shoulders, the end swinging about mid-thigh. "What'll you gents have this morning?"

"Whatever the lady recommends." He took her free hand and kissed it lightly, never taking his eyes off hers.

She paused for a second and then laughed, "Two specials, it is." The whiskey sound of it warmed me better than the coffee. Just over her shoulder, I could see that Eddie was watching the interaction carefully. For a second, I thought he would come out from behind the counter, but she was already heading to the next table. As we left, Coleman glanced back to see her watching us. She smiled and he said softly as we turned to go out the door, "She's mine."

The spring day she moved in, I was doing my best to be invisible in the darkest corner of the still-empty downstairs room. The Snake, the palsy I've wrestled with since my memories began, rode me hard, pulling my left shoulder up and back, taking my chin and the rest of my head along for the ride. I struggled to keep my arm from going with it, grimacing from the effort. The arm I could usually control, but of course, not that day. I could see from the window that looked onto the porch that R.E. was wearing the lilac shirt and boots I remembered but this time with jeans. Jesse answered the door. She was about to say hello when Coleman slid up alongside him and whispered, "Welcome home." He opened the screen door and leaned out, kissing R.E. longer than necessary. She pulled back, looking him straight in the eyes as she narrowed hers with a slight smile. Walking past him into the room, she patted Jesse' arm in greeting then looked up and around. "Man, I love the morning light in here. It's absolutely delicious."

Amanda came in from the kitchen. It was baking day and she'd been busy since sunrise. She held out her hands to R.E. and they hugged lightly, just long enough to leave traces of flour on R.E.'s hands and shoulders.

"Are you making kolaches? Which fillings?" R.E. noticed her hands and wiped them off on the legs of her jeans, leaving behind wisps of white.

"The usual. Poppy seed, cottage cheese, apricot."

"Oh, I'm glad you made the poppy seed ones. They're my favorites."

Amanda nodded.

Coleman had had enough. He dusted off R.E.'s shoulders. "Let's get your stuff up to your room. And then we can go to mine." He smiled as he leaned out the door to pick up her suitcase. "Troy, can you bring her trunk?" He knew better than to ask Jesse.

As I tried to slip by, R.E. stopped me and held out her hand to draw me into a quick friend-hug. I noticed how warm and smooth her skin was. She wore no artificial scent of any kind, but there was one thing that lingered: her cotton clothes, sun-warmed and just washed. She looked me in the eyes and for a moment, I flashed back and forward in time all-at-once. She nodded in return. Coleman cleared his throat.

Then good servant me, I dragged the trunk from the porch and followed them up the stairs to the roof room, the first I'd explored the day we moved in. We'd started calling it that since it was the only one with easy access to a nice sitting place partially shaded by tree limbs, perfect for sunning and stargazing both. R.E.'s setting up involved setting down the two pieces of luggage. The downstairs radio had been tuned to a local station. You could barely hear the announcer, "And now an old favorite, the *Port Arthur Waltz*." Cole bowed, R.E. returned with a curtsey. Then they started dancing around the room. I'd never seen him move like that before. Sure, we all threw ourselves around to rock, but this was something different from him: stately, practiced, done with straight-backed, almost arrogant ease. As the song wound down, he waltzed her towards the hall and his room. His door slammed shut like an exclamation point and there was little else to do except go downstairs. It was that or listen to the sounds soon to be coming from Cole's floor. And walls.

And so our little family was gathered. We named our home the Palace, after the flophouse in *Cannery Row*. It operated on basic communal rules: everyone added to "Money In", or "MI", as best we could. Cole always had cash to throw in. The bands brought in a little, but their day-gigs brought more. Raz always contributed from his construction jobs and Amanda worked a little too, various part time jobs around town. I pitched in almost all of my government disability check after Raz cashed it for me, and sometimes a little extra from odd jobs, but those were few and far between. "Money Out After Rent and Bills", "MOARB", was agreed on by all and kept to a minimum. That part of our mutual agreement sailed along smoothly, especially with Raz in charge.

Work was a slightly different story. At first, we just sat back, living Coleman's dream of guys being waited on, the story he'd seen in *The Rag*. But R.E., and then Amanda in her quiet way, put their feet down about chores by the end of the second week. Grudgingly, we fell in line and started taking turns with cleaning (as much as we ever did), cooking (still mainly up to Amanda and R.E., since they were so good at it), washing dishes, dealing with the trash, and hauling dirty clothes to the Laundromat in town. We became fairly righteous about checking off the tasks written beside our names on the big chart on the back wall of the kitchen. Coleman, however, cheated the most by conning young hangers-on and groupies into taking care of his work for him.

Towards the end of spring, he started cheating in another way. He would disappear from time to time, tomcatting around after other women. I couldn't understand why he would do that, given how happy he said he was. I asked him about it one day when R.E. was at work. We were in her room, me on the windowsill and him on her mattress, fooling around with one of her bracelets. He shrugged and said, "We have an arrangement. I let her know when I'm getting some strange."

"And she doesn't mind?"

"Does she seem like she minds?" he smiled.

"Well, no. I just--ah, fuck it."

"That's the seminal--as it were--word, oh my brother. Fucking. She knows I couldn't be sexually faithful to one woman if my life depended on it. I explained all that before she moved in and she accepts me as I am. That's one reason why she has her own space here. Besides, R.E. does things for me no one else can. Or will."

Even if half his stories were true, he'd had more done to and for him than the rest of us combined. "You are one lucky son of a bitch, Coleman."

His gaze went cloudy as it turned inward. "You think?" Then he bounded to his feet and out the door. I could hear him at the well, pulling up a bucket of spring water, heard it splashing on the concrete inside the latticed, vine-covered well house that surrounded it. We had tap water but we preferred the well's mineral rich taste and had the good sense to know it was best used for ritual cleansings and deep thirsts, deep enough to ease your soul.

All the rest of that spring and summer, most of us worked and some of us went to classes at North Texas State University, all of us danced and partied and created our art: baked and stewed, jazzed and R&Bed, painted and written. We argued politics and culture, literature and music, history and science. The Flick, our favorite movie theater, provided an alternative to the drive-ins and regular film fare. Plus, after hours, there were more private viewings of the racier sort of film. After all, it was aptly named; the folks who ran the place painted the "L" and the "I" deliberately close together so that at a distance THE FLICK resembled another word entirely. City fathers would go up on the roof and paint the base of the "L" to appear shorter, and later we'd paint it closer again. Small rebellions such as this kept us all amused.

Less amusing was our generation's dark cloud: the war. For us though, it was a distant threat. Selective Service had blown past us. Jesse had been busted for something as a teenager, he'd never said for what exactly, but being a "criminal" made him a last-chance pick by Uncle Sam. I was more bullet proof with the Snake rattling me around. The musicians moved so many times, the "Your ass is mine" letter would have had to bounce around a lot to find them. Duncan's bad eyesight made him a poor choice and Raz's childhood asthma, now outgrown for the most part, was his protection. We never knew why Coleman wasn't worried, but he wasn't. Mostly, we loved our lives and each other as much as any group of crazies could in those times and in that place. And then, that one day, it all damn near went to hell when Coleman and Jesse finally had the face-off they'd been building up to since R.E. moved in.

A couple of days after that head-on had gone down, with Coleman still missing, R.E. and I were smoking a joint on the front steps. A cold front had been teasing us all day, its low line of inky clouds bunched on the horizon, a classic blue Norther. But it wouldn't commit and push on past the Red River. Still and hot, it was as humid as it can get without raining. She was quiet and thoughtful; I was worried. Coleman had really crossed the line this time. We'd always accepted him as he was, our pale and moody brother, the catalyst of many all-male adventures, untouched as catalysts always are after the chemical reactions occur. We knew he was driven by demons, but that was accepted along with the rest: our Red Loki, our Coyote. But we hadn't seen his kinder side for weeks and for the first time, his rage had been turned on one of us.

Not the first for others outside the Palace, though: we'd all been at a roadhouse one New Year's Eve when some stray redneck had the bad sense and worse timing to hit on a girl Coleman was with. By the time we got them separated, blood, shit, and bone were flying and the poor bastard was stumbling into the night, his hemorrhaging mess of a nose bleeding into his hands. We thought that had been the worst of it, but when he had turned on Jesse with that same chilling smile, I knew it wouldn't be much longer until R.E. became a target.

"Has Coleman ever mentioned the bar fight he got into last year?"

She nodded.

I bit my lip lightly before speaking, unsure about the thickness of the friendship ice I was skating on. "Why are you with someone who can be so violent? What do you see in him?"

She held the hit and whispered, "Well, he is one of the most attractive men I've ever known. Charming, too, when he wants to be."

"That's it?"

"People rarely do anything for just one reason." Exhaling, she watched the smoke curl away. "Deep down, there's something good in Coleman. Energy, creativity. If I could just help him get to that core and stay focused on the positive, he could bring so much to the world." Then we heard his car on the highway. He drove up slowly and for him, quietly. After he parked, he sat in the car watching us for a moment. Then he got out and walked up to R.E., his footsteps making no sound at all. She put her hand on my knee, asking by gesture for me to remain.

Coleman saw that and said, "I just want to talk to you, R.E."

"So talk."

"I'm sorry." That was the first time I had ever heard those words come out of Coleman's mouth. "I've been under a lot of pressure lately. There's been something going on that I can't talk about just yet, not even with you, not until it's finished. I was way out of line the other day. I know that. But I got no other place to be, other than this place. No other woman can stand me for long and there's sure as hell no one else who can--you know--help me like you do. Don't shut me out, R.E. Please." In the distance, low thunder hollered from far away and the first hint of cool air danced across the yard.

She squeezed my knee lightly without taking her eyes off him. I got up and turned to go inside but before I left, I said, "Coleman, you have to know how close you came yesterday to being on the outside for good, man. You don't trespass like that, especially not right in front of R.E., and you sure as hell don't fight with one of us like you were going to. Jesse's no redneck stranger. Outside, you do what you do, but not here. Not in our home."

He looked up at me, eyes wide. To tell the truth, I was a little surprised myself. I was the least likely to lay down house law on anyone. Then he ducked his head and said softly, "I know. I know that. But, Troy, you don't know just how far outside I already am."

I had seen him do the wounded poet, the lost soul before, but this time did seem sincere. As far as I knew, Coleman really didn't have any other home. I knew that he had always gone somewhere in the same direction as me after classes ended in grade school, but I never knew to what, because he always walked away alone and I was never invited to join him. I suppose I understood because it was the same for me; my aunt Pearl's house had never been home in any way. He had mentioned once that he had a sister, but other than that, we had never used the word "family" in any real sense, not until we had one. And now he was trying to get back in.

R.E. stood up. He walked up to her and stayed on the lower steps. She reached out and took him in her arms. "You still have to work it out with Jesse."

"I know." She smoothed the way somewhat by coming back inside arm in arm with him. He walked over to Jesse and held out his hand. "Peace, man. Too much coke. You know. Won't happen again." Jesse stared at him for a long minute before he reached out and shook. They didn't say anything, and neither did anyone else. But, for better or worse Coleman was back within the fold. An uneasy truce settled over the house. Hot and cold, violent and peaceful: the vibes ebbed and flowed, mixing like the thunderstorm air building outside.

***

The last member of our household joined us a couple of months later on an autumn Sunday morning. We were all hanging out on the porch, soaking up the light and the warmth of the sun, listening to Jesse and Vance, the newest musician in town, as they practiced scales and harmonic pings. Then they started taking requests. I asked for *Embryonic Journey* and they both smiled as they went right into it. We drank coffee and ate the warm kolaches Amanda had just made. The taste of poppy seed filling on sweet yeast dough, the smell of distant burning leaves and flannel recently fished out of mothballs and cedar: the moment is tattooed in my memory because that's when R.E. drove up to the Palace with Claire. They got out of the truck and walked up softly speaking French to each other.

She was a little thing and waif-slim. Her black hair was very short and straight, razored neatly to points in front of her ears. Dark skin, dark eyes: she wore black knee high boots and electric blue tights, a very short black skirt, and a close fitting blue sweater the same color as the tights. And where the hell did R.E. learn to speak French? They were doing those vowel sounds, that *oo* sound that can make you a little crazy. We were culture-starved hippies and suddenly, it was Paris and I don't mean the one most directly east of us. Jesse and Vance almost tumbled into each other trying to make room for her to sit down and Raz rushed off to provide pastry and coffee. Duncan just stared. R.E. introduced her, "This is Claire. We met at the cafe. She, as you can tell, is from France. She said she wanted to meet some 'ippies','" she teased, "and so--here they are."

"'Allo," she said shyly as she sat cross-legged on the porch and the skirt rode up to there. Coleman all but devoured her with his eyes. It seemed she did and didn't know the effect that she was having on us guys. We were in lust, smitten like deer in her headlights.

She could speak English after all, but she didn't have to speak much because she had this way of asking "'ow you say?" even when she seemed to know very well "how you say"; everyone jumped in with the words for her. She was faced with the full display of male courting behavior at that point. Being human and a male myself, I was also interested, but I was under the full attack of the Snake that morning. The palsy had been riding me hard ever since Coleman had started changing. The stress was also taking a toll on R.E.; she looked a little thinner and there were circles under her eyes some mornings. She pulled away from the porch gradually as soon as she was sure that Claire was settled, and slipped away to her truck. No one else turned to look when she started it up, so she drove away with a secretive smile. As I passed the crowd on the way back inside, Claire looked up and smiled at me. The Snake jerked me hard and I went inside, through the empty, echoing house and out to the well. Pulling up a bucket, I lingered for a while, studying the face some previous tenant had carved into the wood, a man peering out of a mask of leaves. Then I took off walking.

Some time later, I found myself on one of the back roads, once two-lane blacktop, now mostly dirt, the trail that connected our place to Denton. As I was about to round a bend, I looked up and saw R.E.'s truck and a black '55 Buick stopped on the road. The motors were running and she was talking to someone in the other car: Eddie. At first, I thought it was a chance meeting, two people cruising on a Sunday, passing each other in transit. Eddie said something. R.E. leaned her head on the steering wheel for a moment then shook her head no. He nodded. She reached her hand out the window to him and he responded. They held fingers lightly for just a heartbeat, smiled at each other, and then pulled away and drove on. I stepped back into the thicket as Eddie passed me. He didn't see me but I noticed that he looked thoughtful, and there was just the trace of a smile.

I stayed out all day, pondering the mystery of that meeting. I knew that Eddie was a really decent guy. He was about ten, fifteen years older than us but he wasn't "some old guy." His Beatnik style and mysterious Big City background added to his general cool. R.E. had said that she could talk to him about lots of things she couldn't with any of us, since he'd been so many places and had had so many experiences. I really admired him and his equally hip business partners Stan and Moe, having always looked up to the Beats and read just about everything written during that era. They helped me out with the occasional dishwashing gig and paid me in cash, no questions asked. I'd always thought that R.E.'s relationship with Eddie was also that of hero worship. But the intimacy of that hand-touch and a sudden shiver of insight made me wonder if their friendship was developing into something deeper and more dangerous for them both.

When I returned about suppertime, R.E. was on kitchen duty and the hordes were lying in wait while exotic smells filled the Palace: curry night. She was always trying something new and different, full of spice and garlic, strange herbs and tastes. It was also a little celebration. Duncan had taken his virgin dose of LSD the night before and was to be presented with his Mercury dime. It was a house ritual. The wings on the god's helmet represented the flight of the mind. Jesse had decided the moment called for some sitar-like sounds so he and Vance were fooling around with the wah-wah pedal and the amps. Hot Tuna howls and Jimi-inspired flourishes began to careen off the walls while the meal was being set up.

Claire had made something she called couscous. I'd never heard of the stuff before but I felt a shiver when she bowed her mouth to say the name. The steaming, brownish grain was piled onto the biggest platter in the house and around it were dishes of vegetables: okra, beans, potatoes, carrots, onions, mushrooms, and squash. There was also a bowl of roasted chicken bits for the die-hard carnivores. The gravy boat was filled to the brim with a yellow-red curry sauce. There were also bowls of toppings: fruit, coconut, peanuts, yogurt, green onions, and raisins. On the side were stacks of flat, tan bread that Amanda made by rolling the dough thin and grilling it in a skillet. You were supposed to eat this stuff with your hands after a ceremonial wash-up. There was a basin and a soap dish on one side of the sink. R.E. had filled it with warm water and rose petals. First, you soaped and rinsed in the basin. Then you swished your hands around in the rose water. Then Claire dried you off on with a bright yellow towel. I was last, and by the time she took my hands, everyone else was already eating. She held them for an extra second and looked me in the eyes. She asked, "Where have you been all day? I haven't had a chance to talk to you yet." She pouted a little.

At first, I couldn't speak but finally, I said, "Later. We'll talk later." She smiled. Everyone was digging in, making vegetable sundaes on the couscous, covering them with the toppings and digging in, sopping up the juices with the bread. It was great. The sauce had an amazing way of staining your hands and mouth and shirt fronts so we all looked like we'd been water-colored by Cezanne by the time we finished: warm yellow tones that matched the mood of the day and the soft yellow light of the kitchen.

It was Duncan's turn to do the dishes, but it was his Mercury Night, so we all pitched in and in no time, the kitchen was cleaned up. Then Jesse waved his hands for silence. He produced a little matchbox from his jeans and cleared his throat, "For Duncan." He rattled the box and opened it enough for us to see the dime shining inside. "He took his dose and sailed like a man. For the most part. There was that one crying jag but he recovered." Duncan blushed and accepted the hoots and hugs and his dime. Then a couple of dessert joints, and we adjourned to the big room. Time for music from our house bands.

Duncan now fronted his own jazz group called Cloud Shadow. Jesse and a new guy, Vance were the powerhouse in the more blues-oriented Texas Weather. This didn't mean that they didn't all jam together now and then in different mixes. They were still friends who shared equipment and the Palace practice room, arguing amicably over which musical form had the most potential. Duncan said blues bass wasn't challenging enough for him anymore and he rarely played it, although he did experiment sometimes with a fret-less bass. Jesse thought it was only because he couldn't keep up with Vance. It wasn't easy. Vance had been playing since he was twelve and was already head and shoulders above the competition in both Denton and Austin.

Duncan was in a North African mood due to the food and started some undulating sounds on a wooden flute. Claire startled us all by making that sound we had heard only in desert movies, a back of the throat trill.

"Whoa!" Duncan grinned. "What was that?"

"I'm not sure if it's the same word in English, but we say ululation." She rounded her lips on the u sounds and stressed the last part of the word.

Coleman whispered, "Where did you learn how to do that?"

She explained, "It's part of my culture. We make this sound for many reasons. My mother, she is from Algeria, she taught me. She taught me to sing, too. She was a cafe singer when she was a young woman." Then she noticed one of Duncan's drums. It was flat and thin, no more than a skin stretched across a wooden hoop. "She taught me how to play the tambour also. Like that one."

"Show us," Duncan asked.

She took a low stool from the corner and sat on the edge of it with her pelvis tilted forward slightly and her knees close to the floor. She gestured with one slim hand for the drum, which Duncan fetched. Then she sat with it held between her knees, leaning it back towards her so she could reach over the edge. She started by tapping the edge of the skin with her fingertips, then alternating patting or slapping the center of the skin with her palms. Then she started to sing in Arabic. After the initial beat was laid down, she nodded to Duncan and he responded with a riff on the flute. Vance couldn't resist and came in on acoustic guitar, a fast Flamenco lick. The three of them fell into such an instant sync it blew everyone away with its speed and its intensity. It was a telepathy that verged on the erotic. I began to feel a little embarrassed watching them, like I was peeking into a bedroom window. Claire carried the melody, changing the speed and the key now and then, and even though Vance and Duncan had to hang in there and follow her moods, they kept up so well that none of them wanted to stop. The song went on and on, changing tone and pitch until it just wound down and ended. The room was silent, shocked for a second then everyone put their hands together and begged for more. Claire was part of Duncan's band from that moment on.

He told me later that evening that he had rarely felt such an instant sync when jamming with someone for the first time, and he'd never felt it before with a woman. Sure, there were chick singers. Some bands had them. But Claire was a musician. The only question now was, where was she going to sleep that night? I wasn't in the mood to watch the jockeying for position, so I headed out to the porch. The night was chilly and clear enough for the stars to sparkle. I pulled a small one from my stash bag and lit up, leaning against the porch rail. R.E. came out and we smoked in silence. She asked, "So, have you had a chance to talk to Claire yet?"

"Not really."

"You ought to. She said she thought you were really sweet."

I frowned, "I haven't said two words to her."

"She also said..."

"Look, there's no way someone like her is going to be interested in a shaky freak like me, so let's just drop it, okay?"

She fell silent for a moment. Then lightly touching my arm, she smiled, "You really underestimate yourself, you know that?"

Time to change to subject. "Was that Eddie you were talking to on the road today?"

She nodded, puzzled.

"I was out walking and saw you guys."

"He was just asking if things were okay."

That explained her shaking her head no, but not much else about the conversation. Then Claire quietly joined us, asking with her eyebrows for a hit off the joint. R.E. slid away gracefully, smiling at both of us. I froze, unable to speak.

"So, you are Troy."

"Yeah."

"I like that name. Like the city. I've been there. Where they say it was."

I nodded for her to go on as we exchanged hits.

"It is something, I can't really say in English, to stand in a place so ancient, to feel so many ages piled one on the other. That's why I like the name."

"I like your name, too, but I can't say it right. It's that damned r."

She laughed at that, "I'm used to it. As close as you can get is okay." She was standing very close to me. I had seen her at the same distance with everyone else that night, though, so I couldn't tell if it was a culture thing or if she was flirting. Then she came even closer. I could smell her skin, a musky clean smell. Was it patchouli or was it her? It sent the hairs on my neck up. She looked me straight in the eyes.

"Your eyes are the most incredible color of blue. I have never seen such a color before. It's so pure." Her lips pursed on the u sound and I did something I had never done before; I made the first move. Dropping the cold roach to the porch, I took her shoulders, drew her in close, and kissed her. And she kissed me back, long, slow and tender. Placing her hands on my chest, she leaned in to kiss my throat.

Coleman and Jesse were at the screen door and I could hear them saying, "I don't believe it." Too bad: they had had all the luck so far, and now it was my turn. I pretended that I didn't see or hear them and they finally drifted away. Claire and I sat down on the porch to talk but it was getting really cold, so we went around back through the kitchen and up to my room. Talk and smoke continued. She told me about being a half-breed in southern France, how it was and wasn't okay, that it was easier than being "colored" in Paris. I found myself talking to her about the Snake, the same way I talked to R.E. about it. Then she talked about her family. In the summer, they would go to her grandparents' house in the mountains around Auvergne and she and her mother would sit in the thyme meadow behind the place, drumming and singing in Arabic and French. I asked her, "What is it like to speak so many languages?"

"Nothing special. Everyone I know does."

"It's special here."

"I know," she frowned. "I must speak English all the time. It's a little boring."

"We're still a baby culture. Give us a chance."

She smiled. We kissed. Then we talked some more. I was in no hurry and she didn't seem to be, either. And to tell the truth, I was more than a little nervous. I wasn't a virgin, but I'd only been with a woman twice before. It was over with so fast I wasn't sure if I'd even done it right: making strange for them more than making love. Talk, smoke, kissing, silences, and then to bed. Claire assured me the next morning that I knew what I was doing. That was nice to know since we had done so much.

We were still under the covers and I was about to ask for another go-round when a car pulled up in front of the house. It was the purr of an expensive diesel, different from the engine sounds we usually heard. Then I heard footsteps on the porch and a heavy, insistent knock on the front door. Heart pounding, I grabbed my jeans and tossed Claire an extra pair, figuring it would take too long for her to get into her tights. "Put your sweater and your boots on, now," I whispered as I scooped the stash bag together.

"What?" she whispered back, "What is it?"

"I don't know." We slipped out into the hall and ran into R.E. coming out of the roof room, pulling on a sweater and skirt, barefoot, her hair wild. Voices downstairs and then Jesse loped up the stairs two at a time naked, carrying a pair of jeans. "Straights in suits downstairs. They want to see Cole," he reported, trying to balance on one leg, get dressed, and pound on Coleman's door at the same time.

He jerked it open, also naked, as he grumbled, "What?"

"Some guys downstairs to see you, man. They said they had to talk to you right away about your father. They said it was urgent."

I calmed down a little bit. Every second that passed reassured me a little more. Narcs and other cops either kick the door in and drag your ass and your stash out or something else happens because it isn't a bust.

Cole turned back, went over to his window, and glanced out at the car. Then he let out a loud howl of triumph. "Finally!" He combed his hair back with his fingers and stretched, smiling, "Tell 'em I'll be down in ten minutes or so." He was the only one who didn't seem in a hurry to cover himself.

"Coleman..."

"Just tell 'em." Then he said to R.E., "He's dead. Those are his lawyers. I told you there's been something going on, something I didn't want to talk about until it happened, and now it finally has. That old bastard is dead and now I'm gonna be the richest son of a son of a bitch in Texas."

"II. ... Besides, it is well known, that all the Claudii
... were always of the patrician party, as well as
great sticklers for the honor and power of that order;
and so violent and obstinate in their opposition to
the plebeians, that not one of them, even in the case
of a trial for life by the people, would ever
condescend to put on mourning, according to
custom, or make any supplication to them for favor;
and some of them in their contests, have even
proceeded to lay hands on the tribunes of
the people.

III. From this family Tiberius Caesar is
descended..."

C. Suetonius Tranquillus,
Tiberius Nero Caesar (Tiberius),
The Lives Of The Twelve Caesars, Volume 3

II.

The Machine

Coleman walked to the door frame, placed his back flat against it and pressed, his muscles flexing and stretching as he scratched between his shoulders: shedding the old skin. "Ah, yeah, dead. At last."

Jesse shrugged, buttoned his jeans, and went back downstairs. Coleman said to R.E., "I want you to come to Fort Worth with me until this is over. You, too, Troy."

I looked at Claire. She said, "I have to stay with my host family tonight, anyway. They are okay about me staying out now and then, but, you know. I will see you again when you get back."

Sure. Damn you, Coleman. "Why?"

"I need help with this. Will you do it?"

I nodded, "Yeah, I guess so."

R.E. said, "I can't. I work."

"Work? You call that hash slinging work? You don't get it, R.E. I'm a rich man now."

"So what? I'm not rich."

"You're my old lady. You don't have to work. Not anymore. And especially not at that hole in the wall for that old loser. I need you with me for this. I gotta bury my f-f-f-." He shut his eyes and shivered. The stress-stammer was something I hadn't seen him do since childhood. "Father. And I gotta see all the other families again. All of them. And deal with the lawyers. I need your magic, R.E. I need you." He was still trembling slightly, but he was too flushed to be cold.

They locked glances. She sighed, shut her eyes, and nodded yes. Coleman held out his hand and R.E. took it. They looked at each other silently then walked back into his room. His door shut quietly.

"I will be here when you get back, Troy," Claire said as we went back to my room. "There is something special about you. You are a, I don't know how to say."

"A freak."

"What?"

I shook for her.

"So what's that? You shake. It's the--the--vehicle. I interest myself in the driver. That is how R.E. says it, yes? Vehicle? Driver? Damn language! You know what I mean. You do not know how beautiful you are."

I didn't believe her, but it was nice to hear. I smiled and said, "Right."

"You are. I will show you one day."

"Okay, yeah." I had no idea what the hell she was talking about, beautiful, so I changed the subject. "I don't know how long this will take. Something heavy's going on with Coleman."

"So it appears to me as well. Here's my host family's phone number. Please call. Call me from wherever you are, okay?"

I kissed her and took the number, folding it carefully and slipping it into my wallet. No need: I had memorized it on the spot. It was the first time a woman had ever asked me for a second date. But I was no fool. I was afraid this time would be the last, so I asked, "Would you take those jeans off? They're my only other pair."

"Is that the only reason you would like me to take them off?"

I laughed as she slowly slid out of them.

Later, as we stood in the hall, she said, "Goodbye for now." I smiled at that and she asked, "Why? Is that funny?"

"Sounds formal."

"There are many ways to say goodbye in French. I'm never sure how to say it exactly in English. Some mean for a little while, some for longer. Some forever."

"Say the little while one for me."

She said something I couldn't understand, sounded like "a bent toe." I was pretty sure it meant something good from her smile.

By the time I got downstairs, Coleman had dressed and was out on the porch talking to the men in suits. He was in jeans, boots, a white Renaissance style shirt, fringed leather jacket, and concha belt, his hair loose around his face. They were going through thick sheaves of papers, one by one. Then he nodded and they walked back to the car, got in, and drove away. He came back in, said "51 percent" to no one in particular and went back upstairs.

R.E. was at the kitchen table with Jesse, drinking coffee, rubbing her forehead with her long, slender fingers. I stood back in the shadows in the hall, unseen. I wanted to watch the hall in case Coleman came sneaking up in his silent way and to give Jesse a little space to talk her into staying.

"How long you think you'll be gone, Zelda?" He'd started calling her that recently, though not when Coleman was around.

"I don't know. However long it takes to
get through this."

"What about your job? You just going to walk away from that, too?"

"I'll have to tell Eddie today."

"And you know what he'll say. Don't do it. Don't go with him."

"I already said I would."

"You get a look at those guys? They're bad news. And what was all that about Cole being the richest son of a bitch in Texas? What was all that crap? Him? With money?" He frowned. "Being able to feed his habits is the last thing he needs."

"But if he has come into big money, he'll really need me to help him stay sane. I can't explain it right now, there's not enough time. But, I owe it to him to at least help him through the funeral. Otherwise, he'll just go off the deep end for good."

"So what? You don't owe him shit. What has he ever done for you? He's been screwing around on you since you moved in! Goddamn it, I don't understand you!" Jesse snorted in disgust and stood up to walk away.

She looked up at him. "You don't have to understand. We had an agreement about how things were going to be before I moved in so if there's been any hurt, I brought it on myself. I said I'd help him and I will."

"And then?"

"I don't know. It depends on him. I've invested a lot in this, Jesse. A lot of time and a lot of work. And there's something to Cole, something that could be good if he could learn to control all that energy and to direct it. And I seem to be the only one who can bring it out."

"You can't fix him. It can't be done."

"So I shouldn't even try?"

"No. You shouldn't."

"Well, I'm going to." Her mouth was set in a straight line.

He shook his head and glared at her from under clenched eyebrows.

"Yeah, yeah. I know," she nodded. "But look. If things get too strange, I'll leave. I'm not a fool. I'm not going to let him hurt me."

"If he even tries, I'll kill him. I mean it."

"I know you do. But I don't think it would ever come to that. He does love me."

"As much as he can love anyone," Jesse sighed. "Okay. You know you can come back here anytime you want to." He walked over to her and she stood up. He glanced back over his shoulder then abruptly hugged her close and whispered, "Watch your back, Zelda. And come home soon."

***

R.E. and I drove over to the Corner Room. Eddie was in his office, going over the books. "What's up? You two are out and about early." He leaned back in the chair, balancing against the wall and folding his arms behind his head. I was always reminded how skinny we all seemed compared to his working man self.

She started to speak. Then she sat down and sobbed so hard that Eddie and I just froze. Clenching her fists, struggling for control, R.E. said, "I have to leave for a while."

"What?" He clanged the chair to the ground as it hit him: Coleman. "Why? What has that son of a bitch said or done now?"

"His father died. He has to go to Fort Worth. Bunch of legal stuff. His old man was rich. Really rich." The tears had stopped but she was still having trouble talking.

"Great. He's rich now." He stood up and paced, stood with his back to us, arms folded, tapping his fingers angrily. He spoke slowly, evenly, softly, with his back still to her. "So you're going along, leaving your own life and tagging along with him because he says he needs you? He'll use you, R.E. you know that. And he'll hurt you." When he turned around, his dark eyes seemed shiny.

I wanted to leave but I couldn't.

She stood up, wiping her eyes, her voice more even. "I told him I would help him through this. Promise made, promise to keep."

He sighed. "So, how long you think you'll be gone?"

"Just for a little while. I have no interest in living in some mansion."

He made direct eye contact with her for the first time in several minutes. R.E. smiled. He didn't return it but he nodded and sighed again.

"What about your shift?" he finally asked.

"Amanda can cover for me. She's a natural."

"Have you asked her?"

"I will. Don't worry. If she can't, I'll find someone else who can or I won't go right away. I'm not going to leave you hung out to dry over this. Please, Eddie. Don't make this any harder for me than it already is." She had done something amazing; she had been able to keep talking and to stop crying.

Eddie said, "Okay." Then he wrote something down on a piece of paper. "I might be at these numbers if I'm not home or here. If you need me, you call me, hear? Anytime. Day or night. If someone else answers, just go ahead and ask for me."

"Okay. Thanks, Eddie."

There was nothing else to say so we turned to leave. He asked, "Say, what the hell does R.E. stand for, anyway?"

"I'll only tell you my first name. Rachel."

He smiled. "I like it. Mind if I call you that?"

She grinned, "You and my dad are the only ones who can. Troy, you never heard it, okay?"

I nodded.

"Good," Eddie said, "I have a semi-exclusive. See you when you get back. Rachel."

She walked out and he turned to me. "You going, too?"

"Yeah."

He nodded. "Good. I would have asked you to, anyway. Keep an eye on things. She's too close to the situation to see it for what it is, but you and I both know she's jumping into the deep end."

"I know. Can someone cover my shift?"

"Sure."

"I mean, it's just pearl diving. Doesn't take any special talent."

"Shouldn't underestimate yourself."

"Second time in the last couple of days I heard that."

"Well, listen to the universe." He ran his hand back through his Kerouac wave of black hair. I noticed that he wasn't using as much grease on it as usual. "Seriously, take care of our girl."

He nodded again and I left.

Amanda agreed to cover for R.E. Always practical, she said that she could use the money. Most of us were downstairs in the big room. In one of those moments when everyone else was quiet, Duncan asked Coleman, "So, who was your old man?"

Cole smiled and said, "The Dutchman."

"Jake van der Veer?" I asked.

R.E. went pale. "What did you say?"

We all knew who he was talking about. The Dutchman's legend was built on womanizing, multiple families, and scandal. The van der Veers lived on the edge of Fort Worth in a huge layered mansion surrounded by oaks as old as their money: land rich, oil rich, history rich. They had been part of north Texas since there was such a thing as Texas. Even longer than that, really: the first of them had come over from Holland about 1800 and got the family fortune started by stealing land and cattle from the Spanish. When Mexico took the territory over from Spain, shady arms deals endeared them to that government and they received protection and land grants in return; gambling and blackmail kept them on top of the other "Texican" settlers back in the days of the Republic. They had so many politicians on both sides of the slave issue in their pocket by the time of the Civil War that they came out richer in 1864 than they had been before it started, and Reconstruction only gave them more opportunities to turn everyone else's sorrow into cash. And of course, there were the boom days of the 1880s and 90s: cattle, railroads. As the century turned, they roared along with the times and discovered how much oil was under all the land they owned. The family fortune was so vast by the 30s that the Depression was just a little rain on their picnic. Jake was the sole heir by that point, so he dusted himself off and waited for his newest acquisitions, the helicopter and airplane plants, to churn out profits in the 40s, 50s, and 60s: on and on, money upon money, Bob's *Masters of War*. No disaster occurred without giving the van der Veers a chance to make a hefty profit. His most recent acquisitions had been a hefty parcel of AT&T and an even larger one of IBM. He'd been quoted in the paper as having said that he already owned the land and everything under it: "It's time to put my brand on what's whizzin' around over it."

Jake van der Veer was in his 70s the last time anyone checked, but he didn't look it, and he certainly didn't act it. He bulled around town, getting a different pretty young women pregnant every ten years or so and re-writing his will, keeping the gossip columns busy with speculation about who would finally wind up with his loot. He kept all his families dancing to his mean old tune. We had all read about him at one time or another in the papers. He was both creator and creature of the Texas mythos of excess and greed which held that everything was not enough and that nothing was beyond contempt. And so, Coleman, our crazy brother, was apparently the next one in that long line to take control of all that dark and bloody money.

"I thought your last name was Jackson," R.E. whispered.

"That was my mother's name. I don't want to go into it now. Time to go."

R.E. was still stunned as we went upstairs to get our things together. I was throwing some stuff into a paper sack when she came in with her own small bag. I asked her, "You okay with this?"

She whispered, "What have I gotten myself into? The van der Veers. Damn it to hell, my father will never forgive me. Oh, man." She was shaking, her face pale. Then she managed a thin smile. "At least it's going to Jake's funeral. Some grave dancing is in order."

"What are you talking about?"

She breathed in hard, held it for a long time, and then let it go in a shuddery blast. Coleman walked in before she could answer. "Ready?" We glanced at each other and nodded. After brief goodbyes to everyone downstairs, the three of us squeezed into Coleman's Mustang and drove away from the Palace. He didn't look back.

***

The walled grounds of the estate loomed above us as we drove up to the massive wrought iron gate. R.E. said, "I think I saw this in Citizen Kane."

Coleman smiled. "Where do you think he copped the idea from? Never was that original." He leaned out the window and pressed a button inside a small metal recess. A reedy voice from somewhere said, "May I ask who is calling?"

"It's me, Ev." The gates swung open silently. We traveled down the immaculate tree-lined white gravel road for what seemed like a long time until we reached the front of the house. Coleman stretched as he got out, smiled as he looked around. A guy in a dark gray uniform walked up and Coleman tossed him the keys. He nodded and without a word, got in, and drove the car away. Coleman smiled, "Let's go see if the old motherfucker is really dead or if he's just yanking our chains again."

We stepped up towards the thick front doors and another guy in the same dark gray uniform swung them open. The entryway was a long narrow hall with a dark gray rug running the entire length of its white marble floor, gold VDVs woven in strips down the middle. A row of chandeliers hung from the vaulted ceiling. Long tables lined one side of the hall, loaded with expensive looking white vases overflowing with white Calla lilies. The only dark note was a black wooden stand on our right as we came in. It held a big open book with a brass lamp over it and a black pen in a black stone holder beside it. The pages were filled with names. Coleman skimmed through them quickly. The air smelled cool and clean, like a museum or a bank. Slow church music came from somewhere in the walls. A girl a little younger than us came from a room at the far end of the hall and slowly walked towards Coleman. She was dark haired like Coleman, rail-thin, pale, with huge dark eyes, full lips, and the shoulders of a whipped pup. Her dress was black but the skirt was short and the cut made her look childish. "Hello, Coleman," she said when she finally reached us. It seemed like it took at least five minutes, the hall was so long and she was walking so slowly.

"R.E., Troy, this is my sister. Mazie, this is my old lady, R.E., and my friend Troy."

"He was asking for you at the last."

"So?"

"He just wanted to see you, Coleman. I wish you'd come earlier. I've been trying to find out where you were for days. I had to arrange all this by myself." Then she stepped a little closer and hugged Coleman around the neck.

He allowed the embrace for a few seconds and then pushed her away lightly saying, "Yeah. Well, I didn't want to see him. Not 'til he was cold." He swept his hands back through his hair and pulled it high and hard into his Mongol ponytail, slowly tying it off with a leather thong. From out of nowhere came an old white man in the same gray suit. The only difference was that he was wearing a black armband. He asked, "Would you like me to take your jacket, Mister Coleman?"

"No, Everett. You have to dress right for every occasion." He walked down the hall; Mazie snuffled a little and followed. Everett stared at R.E. for a split second as though he knew her. Then he slipped the blank servant-mask on again and walked down the hall in the same direction. R.E. and I shrugged at each other and followed him towards the sound of voices.

There were dozens of people in the big room at the end. It was as white and austere as the entryway and had the same high ceilings. One wall was nothing but three picture windows going from ceiling to floor, framed like a triptych in white wood trimmed with gold. The white curtains were pulled all the way open and held at the walls with gold cords. Outside you could see the grounds. It seemed like they went on forever: manicured, green, and perfect. Bookcases lined the other side of the room, all the volumes bound in dark red-brown leather with the titles in gold. R.E. and I glanced at each other, mouths slightly open. Then we looked around at the crowd.

Everyone was dressed in very expensive, very straight clothes. I was in jeans, an old sweater, a blue-jean jacket, and scuffed boots. R.E. was too, but she was wearing all her silver bracelets like shields, her braid tied loosely with a tri-color yarn ribbon, red, white, and black. A Blue Jay feather and a green bead dangled from the end. As

I glanced at it, I suddenly thought that I should have brought along my own medicine bag for spiritual armor. The ones closest to the door turned to stare at us, but they didn't look for long. Cole was working his way through the crowd, parting it with a couple of words or a silent gesture, going though it like juicy news through a small town. A bubble of silence before and around him, the buzz of gossip behind him as soon as he was out of range: everyone focused on him one by one as he headed for the centerpiece at the far end of the room.

The silver and gold casket was on a blue satin-draped bier in front of a white marble fireplace as outsized as everything else we'd seen that day, flanked with dozens of the same Calla lilies we'd seen in the hall. Cole stood with his legs slightly apart, balancing himself, his arms behind his back, hands clasped loosely as he looked down into the front of it for some time. Finally, he turned around and surveyed the room. His face was blank, not a flicker of emotion that could be read. Everyone found an excuse not to meet his eyes directly as he studied them one by one.

It was at that moment a guy in a black suit came up to Coleman and smiled at him, some guy who worked in the funeral business. I'm not really sure why I knew that's what he did. Maybe it was that fatal attempt to console. He reached out and patted Cole's shoulder. Cole turned to him very slowly, a wolfish smile growing on his lips. There were so many people talking that I couldn't hear what was being said at first. The crowd wasn't talking loudly, because there was a dead man in the room, but there were just so many of them that the sheer number of voices made for a constant buzz. Then Cole's voice rose above it all and I heard him say, "You call this a suit? You get it off the rack at J.C. Penney's?" He thumped something inside the coffin, maybe the dead man's chest from the hollow sound. "Do it over again by tomorrow morning and do it right this time or you'll never bury another goddamned stiff in this state as long as you live, do you understand me?" The guy went pale, no small trick given the fact that he was almost translucent. Maybe it was being around formaldehyde all the time. He nodded and tried to say something several times, but Cole kept on his ass so he had no choice but to keep nodding and smiling. Cole found fault with the hair, the makeup, even the way the teeth looked. Everyone in the room had long since stopped talking.

Cole turned back to the crowd and said, "Get out. The funeral won't be until tomorrow and you've already signed in so I'll know who was here and who wasn't. Just get out." They did, one by one, whispering and gossiping, but they all began to leave. They knew who the new bull in the pen was. You could hear dogs baying in the distance when the front doors opened, but not when they were shut. Cole walked back towards where we were standing by the door. I kept looking around the room. What I could see of the floor was shiny black polished marble. Most of it was covered by an enormous Persian rug. Everything in the place was immaculate. Except the rug: I got a closer look at it as the crowd thinned. There were a few splashy stains on part of it near the window and some small, deep dents around them like heavy furniture had been placed over the dark spots to conceal them and only moved out today to accommodate the mob.

Then it was just me, R.E., Mazie, Cole, the old man in the box, and the old man in the gray suit with the black band on his arm. Cole stretched and said, "Everett, open up the Deco Suite right away and send up some food and champagne. Set the Pedernales Room up for my friend. Cut that damn church music off. And get somebody to either shut those dogs up or shoot 'em, one or the other."

Everett said, "Right away, Mister Coleman," bowing his head slightly as he left.

Cole whispered to Mazie, "Home again, home again. Jiggedy jig."

She looked stunned. Cole took her arm and whispered something quietly into her ear. She nodded, confused. Then he patted her behind and said, "Go take a nap or something, and lay off the Valium. I'll take over from here. That's a good girl." She bit her lip and looked at him doubtfully. Then she nodded yes and wandered away, humming softly along with the churchy music that was still seeping out of the walls. A few seconds after she disappeared, it stopped.

R.E. was looking around the walls, avoiding the end of the room with the casket. Cole said, "Come on, you two. I want to introduce you to someone."

"Oh, no," she protested.

"Come on. He's dead. I checked. He won't bite."

"Coleman, please don't."

"Come with me," he insisted.

We walked over to the box, our steps making little padding sounds in the silent, empty room. But about halfway, Cole began to lose it. He started shaking. R.E. reached out and took his arm, bracing him. "Come on, Cole. Leave it for now."

"No," he managed to say between clenched teeth. Somehow, he finished his long walk and we stood beside him and stared at the opalescent face lying stone still on the dark blue satin pillow. I looked at the nose and forehead and mouth for a while, studying it. It was the first corpse I'd seen since my mother's, but I'd been only six at the time and that was a long time ago. I remember being forced to kiss her goodbye: Southern custom. Now, I stood looking at another set of remains. I couldn't see much resemblance between what was in the box and my crazy brother. I glanced at Cole. His features were trembling with rage and hate and fear all mixing like fast-running river water. "Damn you, damn you, damn you, old man. I'm gonna bury you so goddamn deep they'll think it's raining caskets in China."

Then he turned abruptly, still shuddering, and looked out the window. And he screamed, the same rage-filled sound that he'd made the day of the fight between him and Jesse at the Palace. Somehow it didn't seem as out of place in that mansion.

We went slowly up a couple of flights of stairs after Cole had regained his composure and found a flurry of maids and more guys in gray suits leaving a room at the end of one of the halls. Everett was at the door. He said, "Everything is ready, Mister Coleman." He nodded absently then the old man walked away, his gait somewhere between dignified and arthritic. We went inside and I realized why Cole had called this the Deco Suite. I felt like I'd walked into a 1920s film. Everything was silver and black and white, with curved lines running up the walls and sweeping across the high ceiling. The curtains and all the furniture were the same three colors, except the stuff on the bed. It looked like a giant black sleigh and it was covered with sheets, quilts, and lots of pillows in a dozen shades of purple running from dark to pale. A wrought iron table with a glass top stood in the middle of the room, loaded with food and lots of bottles of champagne in silver ice buckets. Cole opened one bottle, poured us all a round into expensive looking glasses. I handled mine carefully. He held his out and we all touched rims. "To outliving him." The stuff was dry and fizzy. It tasted like sudden wealth.

He walked around, relaxing somewhat, taking off his jacket and tossing it onto a chair. Then we settled down around the table. There were glass plates and silver platters full of fancy roasted birds and French cheeses and breads and mustards and all sorts of things I had read about but never tasted before. We smoked and toasted the old man's death again and again, R.E. and I pretending to sip when those rounds came around. I picked at the food and R.E. didn't eat at all, but Cole put it away like he was starving. He alternated between rambling at top speed about what he was going to do with the money, changing his story every time he started it again, and sitting in a wordless stupor. R.E. monitored him carefully, either nodding like she understood what he was talking about or watching him talk to me, exhaustion etching the circles under her eyes deeper and darker as the day and then the night wore on. Cole called for more champagne about two in the morning then he opened the windows after it arrived and stood in the draft, watching the limbs of the oaks creak and groan just inches away as they bent to the steady north wind. Someone had indeed silenced the dogs. I found myself hoping suddenly that they hadn't been shot. R.E. stood up and said, "Cole, I'm worn out. I want to crash."

He held out his hand to her. She went over and he swept her up in his arms, swinging her around in slow circles. Her hair, now loose and blown by the icy wind wrapped around them both. "Troy, take the rest of the bubbly out to the sitting room while I put her to bed."

I slipped the stash and papers into my pocket, pulled the bottles out of the ice, and walked into the adjoining room. It was as big as the bedroom and just as cold. When I turned back to close the doors, Cole was taking his shirt off and R.E. was on the bed, looking at him, her face pale. At least the walls and the closed door were thick enough I couldn't hear what would be going on. I remembered Alice's trip down the rabbit hole as I arranged wood and kindling in yet another cavernous fireplace and settled in, feeling very small.

An hour or so, Coleman joined me, wearing a long gold and black bathrobe cut like a smoking jacket, his wet hair still pulled into the ponytail, tugging his eyes back hard, making him look like a half-breed Chinese gangster from an early film noir. There were two antique armchairs against the wall. He picked them up one at a time and placed them in front of the fire. I'd been sitting on the rug.

"Have a seat, man. Be comfortable."

"They looked too expensive to sit in."

"No, no, it's just the semi-precious stuff." He popped one of the bottles and drank straight from it. "This is too warm. You should've brought the ice out, too."

"What? It's freezing in here. How do you stand it?"

"High tolerance for cold," he smiled. "Skewed blood chemistry runs in the family." He sank into one of the chairs and I sat gingerly in the other. He took another long pull on the champagne and said, "Hand me a joint."

I had rolled a few in advance, so I gave him one. He opened the other bottle of champagne and set it beside me. We smoked one each without passing and drank in silence for some time. Then Coleman shut his eyes, leaned back, and started to talk. "Do you know, can you feel, how strange it was to grow up as part of this family? Maybe you can start to understand why I'm--like I am." He drank deep and I waited.

He continued, "This is the second time I've been back here since..." He stopped and then went on, "I want to explain it, all of it, to you. I've never talked about it before, not even to R.E. I think she knew something was screwy about me, my family. Maybe that's one of the reasons she's put up with my bullshit for so long. But I have to talk about it, get it out of my system before tomorrow or I won't be able to handle everything. And everyone."

I nodded, "Go on, man. Say what you have to say."

He sighed and took two deep hits. Then he began. "Mazie and I are the old man's third legitimate litter of kids. There are five official families, couple more around town but they won't come into any of this. His first marriage was back in the 20s, another in the 30s, my mom in the late 40s, one in the 50s, and the last one just a few years ago. The kids from the first two are dead, car and horseback riding accidents and wars and bar fights, all except one, and he's locked up in an institution. Even though he was the old man's favorite, he was violent, vicious, totally untreatable. When he realized that there was no way Sonny Boy could be fixed, my old man got divorce number two then married my mom. But Sonny Boy wasn't going quietly. He kept coming around the house. The doctors tried everything, electro-shock, pills, you name it, nothing helped. Then one day he went wild and tried to kill the old man, my mom, and me. I vaguely remember him. I must have been about three. The old man had a mental hospital built out in El Paso. The deal with the city was that they could accept as many patients as they wanted, but they could never, ever let Sonny Boy loose. I think he may even still be alive. The 50s and 60s wives and offspring are definitely alive and well, though. They'll try to contest the will, but they can't. It looks like he set it up airtight. He even bribed the probate judge in advance. I'm not sure why he made it so easy and so fast for me to come into all this." He stopped for a moment, took another long drink, belched, and took a hit. Then he shut his eyes and continued, "I was always afraid of him. He used to beat me and Mazie and my mother and Everett and even the dogs. Bam! Whenever he was in a mood, he just took your arm and twisted it 'till the joint or the bone popped or he slapped you so hard your teeth rattled or knocked you down and kicked you senseless. I can't count the times he punched me out." He let me digest that revelation for a moment. I recalled his many unexplained absences from school and the healing bruises I'd seen. It didn't seem surprising to me at the time, since I was also frequently covered with them. Then he went on, "I had broken bones and loose teeth and black eyes and concussions. But no one, not a single teacher or doctor, had the guts to put any of it on record. They knew better. He owned so many boards and so many people it would have been like signing their jobs and their lives away. He was especially bad after..." Several minutes passed. "Mazie and I were playing outside one day. The hunting game." He paused to relight the number and take several slow, deep hits.

It was his favorite pastime as a kid. We played it all though our grade school years. Even at the Palace, we'd all indulge him once in a while when he needed to let off steam. The game was a combination of hide-and-seek, chase, and war: disappear, pursue, pounce. We would play for hours as kids, shorter amounts of time at the Palace, and he always won. You'd be walking along, thinking you were back safe at whatever we had designated as home base, and then he'd jump you out of nowhere.

He went on. "I'd been following Mazie. Wasn't much of a game with her. She's so easy to predict. Most people are. Always follow the same path, more or less. I'd already jumped her a couple of times and was just running on my own. I came up to the window just as it happened. My mother and the old man were looking at each other, standing in the middle of the room. He asked her something and she shook her head no. He went really pale and turned away. That was when she cocked the pistol she was holding and pointed it towards her thigh, right at the femoral artery." He flinched horribly and I did too as I remembered the stains on that rug. "I don't think he knew that she even had a gun. He grabbed her hand just as it went off." He shut his eyes. "I still don't why she did it. He never said and no one else could ever find out because he burned all her letters and papers that night."

I didn't know what to do or say, so I just sat there and took another hit and a very hard pull on the champagne.

He went on. "We were allowed to be around just long enough for him to knock someone else up. Then, we got shipped off to live with that family on the North Side. They weren't kin to us. It was just a financial arrangement. They had to keep us until we were both out of high school. He told them to enroll us under our--under Jackson. There never was any official paperwork that changed anything. It was just his way of distancing himself from us. Especially from me. The male heir. I don't know if he blamed me for what she did or not. I never knew. The family that took care of us was okay. They were scared of him, so they did what I told them to. I think he paid them pretty well. It was like a cheap boarding school. We were just parked there."

I remembered the first day Coleman came into class in the third grade. Due to the tyranny of the alphabet, he and I, Jackson and Jacobson, were always next to each other in classes from that day forward. He took one look at me and said at recess, "You're as weird as I am. We might as well be friends."

He continued. "It seems the last two families didn't work out very well. The 50s wife was caught screwing around. That put her four brats' heritage into question, and she was gone. The 60s one was real young. She had three kids in three years. He was really freaked out by those babies. I heard from Mazie that all of them were severely brain damaged at birth. No one could figure out if it was her genes or his, but after the last one, he dropped her like a rock and sent the kiddies away, probably to the same place where Sonny Boy is. He got Mazie to move back in about then. I think he was screwing her. He said one time that there was nothing he couldn't do to anyone. He even had something to that effect put on his tombstone. He already had the damn thing ordered. The ultimate last word. I haven't seen it yet. All they had to do was carve in the year of death. He was very specific about how he wants his funeral to go. His show, all the way, right up to the end. It's all in the papers he left. He had just taken up with a new girlfriend when he had a heart attack trying to carry her up the stairs."

We sat for almost fifteen minutes then without saying anything. When he spoke again it startled me, but he had his eyes shut and didn't notice. "I came back here once when I was eighteen. To kill him. I'd made up my mind. I came in the back way. Everett let me in. I said he'd asked to see me. That wasn't so strange. He'd invite all the wifeys and kiddies over, at different times or the same, just for fun, dangle the money in front of them, see how far they'd go to stay on his good side. I had never come over for one of those visits, but it wasn't a surprise for anyone to see me here. I guess they all thought I'd finally given in. Anyway, I went up to the study and got his old 30-30 out of the case and loaded it. Then I walked down the hall. You know the song," he smiled. For a blink of a second, Jim Morrison was sitting there beside me, and then, just as suddenly, it was Coleman again. "He was at his desk. He told me he didn't think I had the balls to do it. Then I put one into his chest. I could have sworn I'd killed him. I threw the gun down and ran out. No one stopped me. They were all too busy running up the stairs to see what the noise was. I knew that was it. I was going to jail but it was okay. He was dead. The next morning, I read in the papers that he'd come close, but that he would make it. Seems his heart wasn't exactly where it is in most humans. His was farther to the right than normal."

"Oh, you're bullshitting me! That's impossible!" The whole tale was growing so strange and I was getting so loaded that I was having trouble understanding it all.

He shrugged. "Stranger things than misplaced organs have happened in this family. It's not that uncommon. We're all approximations on a norm that no one matches completely. Some match it more, some less."

Some a lot less: I mulled that one over for a moment and then asked, "And you never got in trouble?"

"No. All the papers said was there had been an accident. Nothing happened. And nothing changed. That's our way. Handle things in-house."

After a long, long silence, I finally said, "Why do you think he left it all to you if you tried to kill him?"

"Not sure completely. All I know is what was in the letter. It was in those papers they brought out, damn, was it just this morning? It was from him." He took it out of the pocket of the bathrobe. "It says, 'Take it. Use it. Ruin it for all I care. You are the only seed I have sown that has produced a being as ruthless as I am, and that's saying something. 51 percent, boy. The rest is divvied up between your sister and the rest of them. If you live long enough, you may understand how corrupt it is possible to be.'" After a long pause, he asked, "Ever read anything about Tiberius?"

I nodded. I had read some histories, but mostly about another emperor, Claudius. We had both been afflicted by what I suspected were similar Snakes.

"He hated Augustus and his mother Livia for forcing him to be emperor and he hated being emperor because everyone hated him. Oh, he enjoyed having power alright. He and the old man were a lot alike in that way. So, just before he died, he handed it all over to the one person he was sure would destroy the Empire. Caligula. Maybe I'm his Caligula, his ultimate fuck-you to the world. Just one thing, though. I might not screw up. There just might be a whole new dawn for this damned, in the literal sense of that word damned, family." Cole undid his hair and shook it out. Then he gripped it in both hands and pulled it back away from his face, pulling the corners of his eyes back even more tightly. "A new dawn," he repeated softly as he turned to me. "I don't know what will happen now, but I can already feel myself changing."

It was true. If I hadn't known him for so long, I wouldn't have recognized him. His features seemed fluid. Maybe that was just the hour, the booze and the smoke, though. It was getting light outside. I nodded and shut my eyes. I vaguely remember him taking the joint out of my fingers. Then it was all darkness and someone else's bad dreams.

I woke up gasping in a huge bed in another movie set of a room filled with heavy wooden furniture. I had no idea where I was or if I was even still in the mansion. The walls were adobe and the windows were framed in dark wood and covered with black wrought iron grille work. Expensive looking Navajo rugs covered the tiled floor. Someone knocked and a small-boned Mexican girl in a colorful blouse and skirt came in with a tray loaded with steaming bowls of food. She smiled at me. "Su desayuno."

"Gracias," I answered. She set everything up for me on the table by the window and left. I was still in last night's clothes, but that was okay. I dug into the food, as Mexican as the room: crisp pieces of fried tortillas and eggs and cheese scrambled together with fresh hot sauce on the side, potatoes fried together with onions and chilies, hot tortillas, Mexican sausage, juice, fruit, and coffee, hot, black and sweet with brown sugar and cinnamon. I usually didn't like it sweet, but it was full of precious caffeine, so I drained the pot and gulped the food. I was starving. Suddenly I realized that I hadn't really eaten much since curry night. Another knock: I went over and opened the door. It was R.E. She was in jeans and boots and a sweater.

"Okay?" I asked.

She nodded and came in, whistling low at the room. "Can you believe this place? God, all these rooms are different. I've been wandering around. There's a Chinese one and a French one, like Louis the 14th French, all museum pieces, and an African one. The last one is pitiful. It's full of animal heads and rugs. Real ones. Someone really liked to hunt."

I whispered, "I can't believe anything about any of this. It seems like a bad dream. I don't think Coleman is going to be able to handle it, R.E."

"I'm more afraid it's going to handle him."

Before I could ask her what that meant, he came in wearing all black: boots, jeans, turtleneck, and a simple tailored jacket that looked expensive. His hair was pulled back hard again. He glanced at the tray and the remains of the food. "Good. I told them Mexican style. Fits the old Pedernales Room, don't you think? Finish up. It's going to be a long day. The deal goes down at four and it's almost eleven now. He had it all laid out in his final papers how he wanted it done and I'm not missing a beat."

He called Everett in from the hall and told him to find me a suit. "Have Neiman's send out the dress and shoes I told you about, too." The old man glanced up and down at both of us, nodded, and left.

"Why can't we go like this?" R.E. asked.

"Because they expect us to." He started to walk away and then he added, "And you're going to look especially elegant. Now, just go and look after Mazie. Don't let her dip into that Valium bottle." He walked away quickly. All you could hear was the ticking of a previously unnoticed clock.

Back in the Deco Suite, I eased gingerly into a chair, still self-conscious around such nice things. R.E. stretched her back against the wall as she sat down on the floor near the fireplace. Mazie flopped beside her, and laid her head in R.E.'s lap. "You know the strangest part of it all," Mazie said in her reedy little girl voice, "is that I was always the one who did everything just like I was supposed to and Cole always did the exact opposite of what he was supposed to but he's the one who gets control. I did everything Daddy told me to do, just like he wanted me to do it, and I only get 15 percent. That's nothing. I could throw in with the others, but even all together, we're only 49 percent. And we won't go in together on anything, I know. It doesn't work that way. He knows that, too. He just set us all up to lose our money in court, arguing through lawyers." She cried a little and then she asked, "Is Coleman good to you?"

"Yes."

"Really? Do you fight?"

"Sometimes. With words."

She pursed her lips and looked right through R.E., her eyes focused somewhere way beyond. "Has he ever smiled at you in the middle of a fight?"

R.E. shook her head no.

"Well," Mazie said in her tiny little voice, "just watch out if he ever does."

At fifteen until four, R.E. and I were as ready as we were going to be. She wore a form-fitting green dress with long sleeves and a V-shaped neckline, black high heels, and an extravagant emerald and diamond necklace. She begged him not to make her wear it, but he insisted. I was in black like him: boots, dress pants and jacket, simple shirt and tie. Mazie wore a white Chanel suit trimmed in black. She fussed when Coleman placed a Jackie-like matching pillbox on her head. "I hate hats."

"I don't care. It's part of my tableaux."

The wind laid and even the sun seemed to pause for a moment as we walked up the smooth gravel path that led to the cemetery on the hill. The oldest headstones on the east side were mossy yellow lumps and the newer ones were white marble in various stages of aging. The crowd was arrayed around a freshly dug, flower-covered grave crowned by a huge block of white marble with standing room reserved around it, apparently for Coleman and Mazie, but he walked to the opposite side and motioned for her to remain directly across from him. The same motions were made towards us to indicate we were to flank her. The same damned lilies Jake seemed to favor were carved on both sides of the headstone and a rather well endowed pink marble angel lay draped across the top of it, an earthy smile on her lips. In the center, carved in plain deep letters was the following:

Jacob van der Veer
The Dutchman
1896 - 1970
He did whatever the
Hell he wanted to.

All the details had been carried out as Jake had said they should be. Coleman was covered legally, braced, and ready to take the first step as head of the house of van der Veer. He pulled an old watch on a chain from one pocket and said, "Four o'clock." The crowd swayed and parted to allow a preacher to walk through. Squaring his shoulders, Coleman nodded and the service began.

"Jacob van der Veer was not a chapter and verse kind of Christian. No, sir. He knew that the Lord God Jehovah was the only God and that the King James Bible was the only word of that God. So I won't quote from the Holy Scriptures today. No sir, I'll just say that Jacob was a Christian man. He knew it was a sin to covet and a sin to kill and he knew that it is better to give than to receive." He shot Cole a covert glance at this, but Cole was studying the crowd. He went on, listing virtues then denying any wish of the old man's to be recognized for them. Then after about ten minutes, he wrapped it up. "And lastly, I will not speak for long, for Jacob van der Veer was a man of few words. They were said honestly, plainly, and with a mind to the greater service of the Lord."

I was wondering what the hell he meant by the last bit when I slid out of my body for the first time in my life. Not the last, but it was the first and it damn near scared me to death. One moment I was just standing there, watching Coleman and the next, "I" seemed to fold up and become small inside my body. The spine slowly unlocked bone by bone and "I" slipped out like a hand coming out of a glove. I could see my own head down below, my body still standing straight and still. Then "I" floated towards Coleman and looked out through very different eyes.

Okay, scan time. That one is weak and easy. Look at how light the colors are, so soft. The cousin, he's dangerous, all jagged and red around the belly. Another dark one over there, too. All in all, they look edible. The preacher's scared. Piss yellow all over him, trying to be mental. Hello, that one, yeah. Bright clear orange. Get her phone number. Ah, a liar! Green flash coming out of the shoulder at that unmistakable 45 degree angle. Check the eyes. Typical. No direct contact. Cowards. Most of 'em look like they got pudding for auras, milky, cloudy, usable. Couple of clear reds with black--mm--R.E. so fine so strong and clear those colors like stained glass high and vivid. Nothing coming from the ground. You are dead after all you old--hello--someone else--.

I gasped and looked out my own eyes again to see Cole staring at me. He shifted around and balanced himself, his legs slightly apart and his hands clasped in front of him. The preacher said, "Let us all offer up a moment of silent prayer for the peaceful rest of the soul of Jacob van der Veer."

Everyone except the main players bowed their heads. An elegantly dressed young blond stared at R.E.'s necklace. Coleman took notice of that and also of two young blond men looking straight at him. He bared his teeth in the same smile he'd shown when he was going for Jesse that day at the Palace. They returned it in kind. I glanced at R.E. Her skin seemed opaque, the emeralds glowing against her neck and chest. Then the preacher raised his head and started up a song, one of those songs they sing in church, a dirge-like droning march. We didn't sing; we kept our eyes on Coleman. He nodded slightly and when it was over, he held out his hands to us. Mazie and R.E. walked around the grave to stand beside him and I followed along. He directed R.E. to his right and I stood on his left by Mazie who clung to my arm so tightly my hand went numb after a while. One by one, the people around the grave filed by. The blond was talking to a couple of older folks, parents maybe, and they all nodded to Cole as they walked away. He nodded back. No one offered to shake his hand and by the way he stood, still clasping his hands together in front of him, it was clear he didn't want to be touched.

That evening we crashed early for us, about one. When I woke up in the Pedernales room just before sunup the next day, I floated out of my body again and drifted somewhere else.

They were standing at the grave. Coleman seemed calm; R.E. looked drained. He turned to her just as the sun came up and said, "R.E., take off your clothes."

"Why?"

"Something I want to do, something I've dreamed of doing ever since I can remember dreaming." She silently did as he asked. The morning breeze lifted her loose hair away from her white shoulders. Cole came up to her and took two hands full of the glorious redness, rubbing them over her breasts and belly then rubbing his face and chest with the thick strands. Then he stripped too, and pulled her down onto the mound of flowers on top of the grave. I floated above them as he rolled her around and around, copulating on his father's grave as though his life depended on it. Then he straightened them both up into a seated embrace, legs around each other. "Do it," he whispered, eyes shut. She nodded and began working her hands up his spine slowly, one bone at a time, whispering something about a "frame", her eyes also shut. When she reached the top of his head, they lightly touched foreheads. Waves of color seemed to shoot up from their bodies and swirl around them. I gasped as I fell away, back into my body, back into the Mexican bed. When I was able to, I left quickly and quietly. It wasn't that hard to get a ride back home once I was on the highway. The first car that passed was a friend of Vance's. I guess I'd done so much dharma in the last two days that the gods owed me one.

"A person in danger should not try
to escape at one stroke
...be satisfied with small gains, which will come by creative
adaptation."

R.G.H. Siu, *The Portable Dragon:*

A Western Man's Guide

to the I Ching

III.

The Crossroads

A manda took over R.E.'s shift and I continued to work in the back washing dishes. I often stayed after closing, since it gave me a chance to hang out with Eddie and his friends, Stan and Moe, talking about jazz, books, and history, past and being made. Moe, short for Mohammed, was a fast-talking, fair-skinned Irish-Moroccan mix from the Jersey shore; Stan was the witty Black bookend to the unlikely pair, the one who closed the dialogue with perfect one-liners after one of Moe's speed-induced raps. My inclusion in their triangular conversations and their acceptance of the Snake and my spotty self-education honored me in a way that both touched and amused them. Sure of themselves and their place in the world, they couldn't understand why something they took so for granted would be seen as such a gift. Maybe that's what comes of being grownups in the world of hip rather than children, as we were. So I redoubled my efforts to keep up with my reading and with the news.

One morning while skimming the Fort Worth *Star-Telegram* or as we usually referred to it, the *Startle-Gram*, I read the daily body counts from the latest battles in Vietnam and recalled Nixon's now-empty promise that his "first priority" would be to end the war. The usual supportive, conservative columnists beat the war drums and condemned the "Peace-niks." Disgusted, I paged on through, looking for relief in the funnies. That was when I ran across the local society pages. A picture of Mazie and Coleman jumped into my attention. She was wearing sunglasses and he was helping her out of a limousine. From the camera angle in the picture, I couldn't tell if he was wearing the Chinese tail or if he had cut his hair short. He was wearing sunglasses, too, and a different suit, looking like an Italian movie star. The blond from the funeral was standing beside him. It gave her name in the caption below the photo along with Coleman's and Mazie's, a name that was on street signs and big buildings all over Fort Worth and Dallas. The other few sentences under the photo said, "Due to the strain of the recent death of her father, Jake "The Dutchman" van der Veer, Miss Mazie van der Veer is going on retreat to the Wellness Institute of Big Sur, California for an indefinite period of time. Her brother, Mr. Coleman van der Veer, heir to the family estate, will be in charge of her affairs while she is away. Family and friends are asked to refrain from contacting her while she is recuperating." The first time you see someone you know or have known in the news is diminishing. Once three-dimensional, now the person is suddenly only two in grainy black and white. I laid the paper aside for the next person to read and went on with my shift, wondering whether or not Mazie would ever see the light of day again or whether she, like their crazy older half-brother, Sonny Boy, was now behind very expensive brick walls for good. At least hers were in Big Sur, not El Paso.

Days melted into weeks and before long it was February: our discontented winter, so gray without R.E.'s sunny presence. To add to the dismal funk, Amanda had come down sick with what we thought was the flu. It had been two weeks now and she still couldn't seem to shake it. I was wiping down tables one late afternoon when she came in for her shift, looking especially pale. She smelled the onions hit the grill and bolted for the back. I followed her. She came out of the bathroom, now green on white. Eddie came in. "Okay, what's up?"

She looked at him then at me. "Do you have a number where I could reach R.E.?"

I nodded. I knew it was probably unlisted, so I'd memorized it while I was there.

"Eddie, can I call Fort Worth? I'll pay you back."

"It's a freebie. Say hello for us all. Come on, Troy, let's get those orders out. Braid that mane and put on an apron."

I'd never worked the grill before. He showed me how to put the patties and everything on so they'd cook at the same time and how to slip potatoes into the grease slowly so I didn't get spattered. He handled the orders and tables, I handled the food and we got through the dinner rush. I was surprised at how well I did. When we hit a lull, we went back into the office. Amanda was still sitting there, sipping on a glass of water and eating a slice of bread.

"Well?"

"She says hello and sends her love to all. It was a short call. I've just been trying to avoid the smells."

Eddie asked, "You okay?"

"As okay as you get when you're pregnant."

He whistled. "Is this a good thing?"

"It's a natural thing."

"Have you told Raz?"

"Yeah. This morning."

"What are you going to do?"

"I don't know yet. That's why I wanted to talk to RE. She said she'd come see me as soon as she could, but she wasn't sure when she could get away. Couple of days, maybe."

"Well, if it's contacts you need. Of any kind."

"Maybe. I want to talk to her and to Raz some more before I make any decision. Thanks, Eddie. I was going to ask. I thought if anyone knew about, well, you know, you would."

"The woman's good. She's helped a couple of friends out before. She's safe and she doesn't charge much. I'll introduce you, if that's what you decide. In the meantime, can you handle the rest of your shift?"

"Yeah, I feel a little better now. It was just those onions." She shuddered.

He smiled, "I could take them off the menu for awhile."

"No, no. If they're ordered, they're ordered. Besides, it's not just them. I'll just have to figure out a way to deal with all of this."

Later, I walked home with Amanda, me shadowing her calm deliberate steps. I asked, "How did R.E. sound?"

"Like she was real far away. Bad connection, maybe."

Maybe.

***

The next afternoon, Claire came over for some quick sex. Her host family had been cracking down on her hanging around The Palace.

I'd fallen asleep afterwards and when I woke, R.E. was standing by the window, arms folded, the fading daylight soft around her. She looked thinner than I remembered. At first, I though I was dreaming then she turned and smiled at me. I was so glad to see her I jumped out of bed still naked.

"I'm glad to see you, too."

"Oh, right." I grabbed my jeans and a sweater as she sat down and started to roll a joint. "So, talk to me. How are you and how is Cole and how is that scene?"

She shook her head. "Well, all you guys were right on about one thing. I'm in way over my head. I feel like I've fallen into some dark fairy tale. You wouldn't believe how much Coleman has changed. I can't believe some of the things he's been saying. And doing. His politics, everything. It's like the Dutchman has taken over the Cole we knew. Or maybe it's that place. Or the money. Maybe it's his real self, one that he kept hidden. I don't know. But the person he's become is way too unbalanced and too conservative for me to be around much longer." She paused then added in a whisper, "And it's really dangerous being there. Things have been happening. Someone tried to kill him the other night."

"Ah, Jesus! Are you okay? Is he?"

"Yeah, yeah. We were in the study. One of those vicious guys from the funeral, remember? It all happened so fast. He bashed his way in and got off a couple of wild shots. Then, he ran out and down the steps with Cole right on his tail, blasting away at him. I thought he kept missing but he told me later he didn't want to kill him on the property. He only wanted to chase him out. He wants to wait until later and have someone get him on the street one night so it won't be tied to him." She started shaking. "He's been packing a gun day and night. He even sleeps with it."

"What are you going to do?"

"I'm going to get out of there in a way that doesn't get me or anyone else hurt."

"Is it that bad?"

"It's worse than you can imagine."

We finished the number in silence. Her hands shook each time she passed to me, but gradually she began to calm down. I gave her the space and the quiet that she seemed to need, knowing that when she was ready to talk, she would. But curiosity won out on one count so I asked, "What the hell is the Wellness Institute?"

She laughed, shaken out of her reverie. "So, you saw that story? It's just what you probably thought it is. A very discrete loony bin, very expensive, tucked away somewhere down in Big Sur. Mazie almost ODed on Valium a couple of days after the funeral, so Coleman had her sign her share of the estate over to him and then he put her away. Poor kid. She just kept regressing further and further. That last morning, she was actually sucking her thumb."

"And the blond in the picture?"

She frowned, "Some rich bitch. I never know these days." She took a deep hit and flopped back on my mattress. "I just try to stay out of his way as much as possible. Troy, he's completely out of control. There's no one anymore who can keep him in line. He's got access to money and power and connections. And what effort he'd been putting into keeping a lid on his excesses is a thing of the past. I had no idea how crazy he really was until it was too late. I'm scared to death of him. I don't want to do anything to piss him off. There's no telling what he would to do to me or to all of you if I tried to leave him. He claims he loves me, and who knows, maybe he does. But it's a kind of love I can live without."

"But why would he let you come up here alone if he's that possessive?"

"He's in Big Sur for a couple of days. With Mazie." She frowned. "I was given permission to come up to talk to Amanda while he's gone. I'm so glad she called. The timing was perfect." She looked out the window. "But, screw all that for now. He's gone for a few days. And I get a little break from trying to heal him."

"What do you mean, heal him?"

She shrugged. "It's hard to explain. I'll tell you some other time." She paused again, looking out the window into the cold, growing darkness. "I'm glad to be back home, even if it's only for a little while."

"Man, you have got to get out of there."

She shrugged. "I know. But right now I don't want to think about him or talk about him anymore. Tell me some good things, things that are going on here."

"Well, Jesse and Vance got a gig tomorrow at Bonnie's, that new club in East Austin. There's a rehearsal party tonight."

"I could use a party." She finished the joint. "Well, I can't talk to Amanda yet since she's not here, so let's go see Eddie. God, I've missed you guys." She hugged me and we left. Outside, we got into an old brown Chevrolet.

"Whose is this?"

"Belongs to one of the maids. She loaned it to me for the trip. I want to find a way to take my truck back with me so I'll have my own wheels. Cole says I can use any of the cars in the stable. He calls it that, the stable. But they're all Jaguars and Porsches and Benzes and such. It would make me too nervous to touch them, much less drive them."

"I'll follow you back in the truck, if you want. That way you'll have it there."

"Would you? That'd be nice."

"I won't stay, though."

"I don't blame you." She didn't say anything else.

We got to the Corner Room just after closing. Stan was still there, fixing some sandwiches for himself and a friend. He said that Eddie had taken off about half an hour earlier. We chatted a little then R.E. and I stepped back into the office. She dialed the first of the phone numbers Eddie had given her and sat tapping the fingers of her right hand on her knee. No answer. Then she tried the second. Same thing. Finally, she dialed the last one on the list. After enough time for four rings, she looked at me and started to shake her head no when she said, "Uh, yeah. Is Eddie there? Can I speak to him, please? This is Rachel." I smiled to myself at her change in self-naming. Her expression changed from neutral waiting to surprise then she grimaced at me and mimed pulling a trigger at her temple. "Jeez, I'm sorry, I'll just--no, really, I'm sorry. I didn't--yeah, I know, you said it would be okay." She paused and listened, eyes squeezed shut. Then she nodded and started again, "Okay, I'll let you go. I'll be at the Palace the rest of tonight and all day tomorrow. No, no, you don't have to." Then she giggled and blushed, covering her eyes with her free hand and peeking at me between the slats of fingers. "Yes, you have embarrassed me." She listened intently, the serious cloud returning to her face. "I'll see you when you get there. Thanks. Bye." She hung up and covered her face, "Oh, man! He was in bed with some woman."

"Was she pissed off?"

"I don't think so. She just said, 'Oh, he's right here.' And then she handed him the phone. I could hear them rustling around in the sheets. He said to her, 'That's the friend I said might call' and she said 'Talk. I'll get us some beer.' God, I couldn't even remember what I wanted to ask him. He knew I was embarrassed. He said 'The sound of one woman blushing.' That's when I lost it. I don't believe I actually giggled."

"You were blushing."

"I know. I was burning up." She laughed. "Ah, damn, he's a nice guy. And she must be cool, too. Neither of them sounded pissed off. That I could tell, anyway. And he did remind me he'd told me I could call anytime and ask for him."

"That's true. So, when is he coming? As it were."

She gave me her level stare then said, "At first he sounded like he was going to get out of bed right then. Finally, he just said later. So now, I guess we go back and wait." We said a quick goodbye to Stan and left. As we were driving back to the Palace, she almost ran a light, shook herself and said, "Damn. Wake up, R.E."

I glanced in her direction and finally caught her eye. She shrugged and said, "That call really rattled me."

"How?"

"Well, hell, he was in bed with someone."

"And that embarrassed you? Why?" I grinned, "Oh, all naked and all that. What's the big deal? You've seen everyone at the Palace in the buff."

"Yeah, I know, but that's so brother and sister. I don't know why it should have rattled my bars so much with Eddie. Maybe it was because I felt like I'd intruded."

"I think it's because you wouldn't have minded being there yourself and you can't stand to admit it."

She didn't say anything to that.

I pressed on. "So you felt something. Why is it so hard for you to cop to it?"

She turned to me when we stopped at the next light and said, "I don't know what I'm feeling anymore about anyone. But I just told you how crazy Coleman has gotten. If he even suspects for a second that, well, you know. I have to be careful."

Of course. I remembered that brief moment of sharing minds and how he could read colors. I reached out and patted her knee.

"So when are you going to try to get away?"

We were back at the Palace by then. The yard had filled up with the cars and trucks and motorcycles of people coming to the party. She switched the engine off and we sat in silence for a moment, listening to the band. "I have no idea," she finally answered.

We went in the back door. Amanda was at the table. They sat down and started talking, so I went into the big room to give them their privacy.

It was an hour or so later when Eddie showed up. His hair was wet like he'd just gotten out of the shower and it was combed into its James Dean wave. He was wearing an old leather jacket that looked like it had seen some miles on the open road. He came up to the front porch and we walked back through the house to the kitchen. R.E. and Amanda were still deep in their conversation. Amanda looked up and saw him over R.E.'s shoulder. She turned and smiled at him, the slightest trace of a blush spreading over her cheeks.

He said, "Evenin', ladies."

Amanda said, "Nice of you to come, Eddie."

R.E. laughed nervously. Eddie grinned, his eyes shining with devilment. Amanda looked confused. Raz came in and whispered something to Amanda. They walked out and I followed.

Jesse and Vance were jamming with a new combination of players. Vance was in the groove and laid down a funky bluesy lead, peeling off a hot and nasty lick. Jesse turned back to him, smiling and shaking his head, and answered with the line, his own variation on what Vance had just played. Not to be outdone, Vance took off on it, daring the bass player to stay with him. He did. Dex was a skinny young guy with long straight blond hair, a lefty. He was promising, could even get away from playing bottom sometimes and wander around the melody line himself. They had recently acquired a drummer, too, another skinny blond guy named Charlie. He could rock steady, rarely intruded, never stole a lead, and hadn't the slightest interest in extended solos. It was the best and most functional incarnation of Texas Weather yet. Raz and Amanda went upstairs after a few words. I was wondering about them and how they were going to handle the pregnancy when my body-wandering happened again. The next thing I knew "I" was watching myself from above and then "I" was in the kitchen, listening to Eddie and R.E.

She stood at the table beside the chair where she'd been sitting, rooted and uncertain. Finally Eddie walked over to her. He took his hands out of his pockets and broke the spell of no-contact between them by simply taking her shoulders and drawing her into a friend-hug: non-threatening, calming, reassuring. She relaxed against him for a brief moment then pulled away. He let her go and they sat down.

He said, "You look tired."

She nodded. "I don't know where to start."

He took her hand and held it, keeping his eyes on hers. "God, you're uptight. Just breathe. Relax. You can start anywhere you want to, Rachel."

"I've been afraid to call because he tapes everything now. There's going to be an internecine battle over the will."

"I thought he inherited the biggest part of it."

"He did. But some of the cousins and the old man's other wives are threatening to contest it unless he pays them off. Cole's been deciding on his strategy. And, goddamn, there's so much more." She was shaking.

"What?"

"Someone tried to kill him the other night."

Eddie started to say something but kept quiet so she could continue.

"We were in the old man's study. Cole likes to sit in there at this huge desk, sometimes all night. He said it was his old man's power place. Anyway, a guy, a half-brother I think, kicked the door open and shot right at Cole but he missed. Cole pulled a handgun out of one of the desk drawers. The other guy got off a couple more wild shots then Cole chased him out of the house. He's been carrying the gun with him ever since. I'm really scared, Eddie. I said I'd stay until things were settled, but now I don't have any idea how long that's going to take."

"Rachel, it sounds like it'll never really be settled. And that Cole will never be finished using you. Not until he's used you up."

She nodded. "I know that. I want to get away from him but I don't know exactly when or how I can do it. He'll come after me. If I come back here right away, he'd just make trouble for the family to get back at me. I need a place where I can hide out for a while. Can you help me?"

"There's a place near Bastrop you could use. It's way back off the main roads and deep in the woods. How soon you want to leave?"

"Cole's got a lot of business deals lined up. As soon as he gets everything settled with the families, he'll start wheeling and dealing on those. He'll be distracted. I just don't want anyone to get hurt. Especially not you, Eddie. If Coleman knew you were the one who helped me..."

His eyes narrowed and the light in them went way back into some memory recess. "I'm not scared of Coleman. Seen worse and dealt with them."

"I thought I could handle this without anyone else having to get involved. But that place, that family. I didn't know just how crazy he was until it was too late. And now I'm in way over my head. There're all these family secrets. Another half-brother in a mental hospital, suicide, all these mysteries. I gossip with the maids and they tell me things. Cole will start to talk about it and then he stops. If he talks too much, he has nightmares. Wakes up screaming and throwing punches. He says it makes him lose his edge, remembering too much. He took a lot of abuse."

"How do you mean? Physical? Sexual?"

"Not sexual." She thought a moment. "Actually, I don't know. Maybe. It would explain some things about him, but of course, he wouldn't talk about that. He's so macho it's hard enough for him to admit that he was beaten up by an old man. His father used to kick him and hit him. A lot."

"Blows to the head?"

She nodded.

Eddie grimaced and blew a low, slow whistle. "Then you really can't fix him, Rachel. Has he been violent with you?"

"No," she said, a little too quickly.

Eddie waited.

"Not exactly."

"If he has…"

"He hasn't. But sometimes, I have the feeling that he's holding back, like he'd like to hurt me, like he's fighting some really crazy urge."

"Like the time he was banging you in the study when the guy tried to shoot him? You didn't say, but that's what was happening, wasn't it?"

She nodded, frowning.

He had leaned back by now and was surveying her coolly. His voice came out flat and unmarked by any warmth. "You must like it rough or you wouldn't be staying."

She narrowed her eyes and flinched. "Now wait just a damned minute. Why are you pissed off at me? That's not fair. I'm here because I want to get out but I'm scared that he'll kill me and everyone I love. I'm asking for help, not judgment. You don't know what it's like to be a woman in this kind of situation, Eddie. I'm too scared of him to say no to anything."

He turned away and nodded. "Okay, look, I'll get the place cleaned up for you. Let me know when you want to split and I'll give you directions." Then he got up and walked out the back door without another word. R.E. followed him, arms around herself, keeping her heart cards close. His jaw was clenched and his hands were back in his pockets, shoulders hunched and tense. When they reached his car, he spun around and asked her, "Do you know how hard it is to hear you talk about--damn it, R.E. Look, just because I'm an old man doesn't mean--ah, fuck it."

"You're not an old man, Eddie."

"Sure."

"Where is all this coming from? Why are you so mad at me? What did I do?"

"Tell me all the damn details about being with that bastard, that's what. Thanks a hell of a lot for sharing those mental snapshots." He started to open the car door but she took his arm.

"Look, I'm sorry, Eddie. I wouldn't hurt you for the world. But you asked me what was going on and I trust you enough to tell you the truth. I never thought I'd have to edit myself around you." She kept trying to make eye contact with him, keeping hold of his arm, the pain and confusion of being attacked clouding her eyes.

He stood with his eyes shut, concentrating on something. Then he said, "I guess I brought it on myself. I shouldn't ask about what I don't want to know. Sorry. You've got enough on your mind now without me adding to it." She let go of his arm. He sighed and leaned his head back, studying the night sky. "Rachel, you don't have to go back. I can hide you out tonight. Right now."

"He'd know it was you. Or he'd think it was someone from here and he'd be down on this place like a bat out of hell. I don't want anyone to get hurt because of me."

"I've already told you I can handle him." He hadn't looked at her directly during this exchange. Then he raised his eyes to hers and asked, "Or don't you believe me? Don't you think an old man like me..." The anger was back; he glared at her, his stance full frontal confrontation, both hands out of his pockets now.

"Enough with this old man shit! You're not that much older than we are." She was angry, too, now, hands on her hips, eyes locked onto his.

"It does make a difference, though, doesn't it?"

"Not to me. Not to the people in that house." She ran her hands back through her hair to push it away from her face. "Look. You can talk to me, too, you know. Why are you so angry?"

"Right. I'm supposed to talk now. Be the one to lay the cards on the table first so you'll know my hand. Then you can say very gently and understandingly how yes, we're friends and all but I'm too damned old for you and that you'd rather make it with a guy your own age even if he is a homicidal nut job!" He suddenly clenched his fists, closed his eyes, and stood shivering with anger.

"Oh, I get it now. You don't think I--ah, man." She stepped up, unafraid, and leaned into him, resting her hands lightly on his waist. "Look at me."

He kept his eyes tightly shut for a moment, his whole posture stiff with rage then he slowly relaxed and opened his eyes. They were wet.

"You want me to go first?" she asked. "Okay. I will. When I called you earlier and realized you were in bed with that woman, I lost it. Troy was trying to get me to talk about it the whole way over here. I got this flash of seeing you in bed, thinking about you naked and making love and I felt the heat all over me just speaking to you on the phone. I've had to be so careful around you because I didn't want Coleman to know how much you turn me on, how much you always have."

She didn't get much further than that because Eddie started kissing her. All his restraint reversed into wordless physical expression of sexual hunger. He picked her up and she wrapped her legs around him. He held her like that for a long time, bracing himself back against the car, kissing her again and again, their breathing loud and gasping when they paused. Then he put her back on her feet and she leaned against the car, pulling him towards her, gripping his jacket. They had their hands on each others' belt buckles when a smooth diesel purr on the far main road was suddenly audible as the blues roaring out of the house paused between numbers. She froze, huddled against Eddie, hiding. The car whined and vanished slowly: not him. Not Coleman.

He held her until she relaxed.

"Where were we?" she smiled.

"About to go over the edge, apparently. Look, I'm sorry I was acting like a bastard. You've already got one of those in your life. You don't need another one."

"I didn't mean to hurt your feelings."

"No, that was my problem. I came over here to listen to you and to help you out, not to blame you for what's going on. I guess I've just kept things buried so deep for so long that they came out backwards."

"That happens."

He sighed and ran his hand lightly along her waist, the thumb riding the edge between sweater and belt, not entering. "Rachel, I'd like nothing better than to take you to bed right now. But the timing's wrong. You'd be listening to every car that passed and so would I. I'm selfish enough to want it to be right when it happens."

"At least promise me you won't start with that oldie bullshit ever again."

"I don't make promises with the words ever or never. Not any more. But okay. You'll know what I mean one day, young lady," he teased, his voice creaking.

She grabbed his waist and shook him lightly. "I just hope I don't give you a heart attack when I finally get the chance to go down on you."

He bit his lip and said, "Play fair. I'm trying to be a gent about all this." He held her for a moment then stood back. "Do you want the directions to the place now?"

"No, he might find them. When the time comes, I'll call you from a pay phone somewhere. I got all your phone numbers memorized."

"If you get even the slightest hint that he's going to hurt you, get out of there right away."

"Okay."

He kissed her forehead and said, "Watch your back." Then he got in the Buick and drove away. She waved until the taillights disappeared. Then she turned and walked slowly back towards the house.

I slipped back into myself just as she came in the door. She was flushed and her hair was loose and she was radiating heat from the close call with Eddie as she walked past the band and smiled hello at them. Jesse was waiting for Vance to tune his newly acquired Strat for the next set, doodling around on the keyboard. His eyes followed her until she disappeared into the crowd milling around the big room. Jesse couldn't think about R.E. and jam at the same time, so he turned back to the other players and waited for Vance to start the next tune. R.E. walked up to me and leaned against the wall. "Claire coming back over later?"

"She can't. Her host family's getting stricter about her hours."

"Too bad."

"Yeah. We did have some time together today, though. Got to take it when you can get it."

She nodded, still flushed. "Yeah. That you do. Let's go up to the roof room and smoke another one."

She flopped down on her old mattress with a heavy sigh and pulled a number out of a leather stash in her bag. Lighting up, she said, "Things got pretty warm between me and Eddie just now."

"Really?" The innocent.

"Very warm."

"Great! I've been thinking for some time that you'd be better off with him than with Coleman."

"I think so, too, but hell, I'd be better off with the Devil than with Cole. When that guy tried to shoot him the other night, it came pretty close to unhinging him."

"More than he already is? Why?"

"Because he'd been feeling invulnerable in that house, that room. And then that guy broke in. Now he prowls around to different rooms every night."

"Where are you going when you leave?" I wasn't asking if anymore.

"Eddie said he's got a place I can hide out in down in the Hill Country. Exactly when, I don't know." She groaned. "And now, just when the last thing I need in my life is another complication, it's all out of the bag, how Eddie and I feel about each other. You were right earlier. When I was talking to him while he was in bed with that woman, man, I was burning up, but it wasn't just with blushing. I haven't felt a rush like that in a long time. He was acting strange tonight, too. He got really pissed at me."

I raised my eyebrows, although I already knew why.

"I guess because he's always had these feelings, too, and he thought that because he's older than me I wouldn't and, ah, I don't know. Things are so confusing. What if Cole can sense that I feel something for Eddie when I go back?"

"You'll be back in control of your vibes by then. Listen, the answer seems pretty simple to me. You want out. We want you to come home. Why don't I just drive back with you, you drop off the maid's car and split. Come on back with me. You don't have to hide out first."

She smiled at me. "It sounds so easy when you say it, but it isn't and you know it. I just have to wait for the right time to do this so no one gets hurt."

We smoked in silence for a few minutes then she added, "And one other thing. When I'm on my own again, I'm not going to be exclusive with anyone for a while." She grinned and for just a moment, the old irreverent R.E. was back. "I guess you could say I'm gun-shy."

Amanda knocked on the frame of the open door and in her simple, direct way said, "Thanks for coming all the way up to talk, but I think I'd already decided what to do. I want to go through with it. I feel like it's the right thing to do. I've been eating lots more veggies lately, craving the green stuff, and I haven't been smoking dope or drinking at all. I thought it was because of the flu but it was really because my body was telling me not to." She was standing there with her hands on her belly, glowing like some Renaissance mama, wrapped in her own world, oblivious to R.E. and what might be going on with her. But to be fair, Amanda had been kept pretty much in the dark about the details with Cole and what had been going on with him and R.E. I suppose we were all trying in our own ways to keep what was going on in her belly safe from Cole's influence. Still, I wasn't through talking to R.E. and I felt that her being there was an intrusion.

R.E. nodded but her smile was a little pale. She asked, "So is Raz equally happy about this?"

Then it was Amanda's turn to dim the lights a little as she shook her head no. It was time for me to go. I could feel serious baby talk coming on and I wanted no part of it. I hugged them both one at a time and then went back downstairs.

The party went on until daylight. I was sitting in my favorite living room window to soak up the gray sky turning pink in the east when I spotted Jesse and R.E. out on the lawn. They were locked in a moment, a wordless exchange. She was holding her arms tightly around herself. He was standing still, his eyes searching for something in hers. Then she turned abruptly and walked away. He threw an angry punch at the air and spun around to stalk off in the opposite direction. No one else was stirring so I went upstairs to crash into dreamless sleep.

I was up again about 11 and was apparently the last one back on my feet. R.E. and Raz were out on the front porch steps, drinking coffee. I settled down in the old porch swing with my own steaming mug. He was rolling a morning number. It was a pleasure to watch. First, the sheer ungummed paper on a wooden rolling tray he'd made himself. Then the carefully manicured weed in a straight line just above the long edge and finally, the two-hand flick that pushed the construction along in a smooth roll: he licked it lightly, just enough to hold it together and put it aside to dry. The carpenter and the planner of the household, he paid his own his way through life and balanced his world. He hated it when things were out of kilter, and now his whole life was in disorder and couldn't be righted as easily as a line out of plumb.

R.E. waited for him to start. They were friends but had never been so close as to talk about things of this magnitude easily. She let him get around to the topic in his own way. "So," he said finally, having all his word tools gathered up around him, "you talked to Amanda."

"Yes."

"She told me this morning she wants to keep it."

"Ah."

"You already knew that."

She nodded and asked, "So, how do you feel about it?"

"I don't want to be a daddy."

"Well, if she keeps it, you will be. De facto."

"De juris, if her folks find out it was me. De shotgunnus."

She threw her head back and laughed. I suddenly realized how much I'd missed the sound.

"Oh, real funny," he frowned. "This is serious."

"Sorry, but that was a good one. Look, you know her. She's got her mind made up about this. I talked to her twice last night for a long time both times. She has thought about this from every angle and she's convinced that it was meant to be. She'll have the kid regardless of what you decide."

"I know she'll be a great mom." He sighed and pulled at his thin black beard with his long slim fingers. He was wearing the Russian style shirt that she'd made for him and loose baggy black pants: a troubled Orthodox St. Daddioso. "There's more. She really wants to get married, too. But I don't have a model for that in my life. Neither my parents nor either set of grandparents ever made it official. Big Sur folk don't do that. Never thought I'd be the first in the family to tie the knot and settle down into middle class life."

She said, "Maybe there's a middle way that's not middle class."

"Maybe. But, I'm not going to put her in a position where she'll have to raise it on her own. I'm not that hard-hearted. But I'm just not sure about getting married." He carefully put all the makings away in the stash box before he lit the joint. He glanced back at me but I waved a thank-you-no to him so he passed it to R.E. I'd already had my breakfast taste and needed coffee.

"Then don't."

"It's not that easy. Unlike my family, her folks are real straight. She talks about them like she doesn't really care what they think but I believe deep down she does. She's about two and a half months now. We figure it happened when we went camping to avoid the family scene Thanksgiving. She'll have to tell them sooner or later, but at least we have a little breathing space before it gets real obvious. One thing about her build is that they won't be able to tell right away."

"I thought you liked her build."

"I do," he smiled but only briefly. "Oh, man, I should have known not to trust dumb luck. She's never been able to take the pill. See, even if she did decide not to have this one, we'd have to face the same situation eventually. I hate using rubbers and her diaphragm slips. Anyway, thanks for listening, R.E. So, on to other topics. How are you? When are you going to come back home?"

"As soon as I can."

"How's Coleman? Still crazy?"

"Oh, yeah, Raz. He's still crazy."

Jesse walked out onto the porch and past us without so much as a nod. I got up to follow him and asked, "What's with you?"

He glared at me. "None of your fuckin' business."

"Hey! I'm just asking."

He growled then shrugged, "Got in an argument. With R.E."

"About?"

"Coleman. She's going back there tonight."

"Look, she's afraid that he'll kill her if she tries to leave. But she's planning on splitting anyway. Eddie knows a place she can hide out in Bastrop."

He stared at me. "Why can't she just come back home?"

"Because Cole will have this place busted to get back at her and all of us if she does. You know he would."

After a few seconds he said, "Really? She didn't say anything about that." He frowned. "Not that I gave her much chance. I wish--ah, hell. It was my fault. I'm no damned good with words when I'm not singing. Besides, it was more than Coleman, anyway. I came on to her. It was real late. Real early. She said no. I just thought--well, shit. Real smooth, Jesse."

"Look, you know R.E. Talk to her before she leaves. She's only trying to do the best thing for everyone and still get out alive."

He nodded and walked back towards the now empty porch. I sighed and stayed in the yard. So much to talk about, so many things to say, so many that couldn't be said or were getting said the wrong way.

About an hour later, I saw R.E. and Jesse through the kitchen window. They were out in the well house. She was doing most of the talking. Jesse didn't look at her directly until she was finished. Then he took her hand and pulled her into his arms for a long kiss. From all appearances, she kissed him back.

Later that day, I followed R.E. back to Cole's in her truck. It was late when we got there, well after sundown. She drove past the big garage and pulled into a smaller one full of older cars. I parked her truck in the space closest to the door then walked to the back where she was getting out of the maid's car.

"I really wish you'd stay. At least for the night."

"I'd just as soon he didn't know I was here."

"Little late for that." I turned and saw a silhouette appear in the rectangle of light behind us: Coleman. R.E. had her mask on tight. He walked closer, his eyes glittering like icy rocks as he noticed her truck then they locked onto me.

"Well, well. Troy. How are you?" He whispered, "Oh, my brother."

"Not bad." I took his offered hand and we shook. His dry, smooth skin was so warm, like he had a fever.

"Why don't you want to stay? Come on up for dinner, at least," he asked.

"I can't. Got a date."

"Oh, right. Your French chick. At least let me have Ev arrange for someone to drive you back."

"No, that's okay. No need."

"You shouldn't hitch this late. Too dangerous."

"He's right, Troy. Why don't you stay?" R.E.'s tone was just right, solicitous and friendly. I remembered the feel of her hand on my knee the night Coleman came back to the Palace.

"Well, okay. Claire's got a curfew and I probably couldn't make it back in time to see her tonight anyway."

"Curfew?"

"Host family. They're worried about her seeing us hippies."

He nodded and held his arm out for R.E. "I can understand that."

She took the elbow and they walked ahead of me, back into the mansion.

We ate downstairs in a formal dining room. It would have seated about 50 people, but there were only three plates set that night. He'd had a fire built and I hovered around its warm edge. R.E. went upstairs to change out of her road clothes. Cole watched her back the whole way then he walked over to stand near me. "So, why did she really go to Denton?"

"To see Amanda. I thought you knew that. She's pregnant and she needed to talk to R.E."

"She's going to have an abortion." It was a statement.

"No, she wants to keep it."

"Does Raz?"

"Not really."

"Simple. He makes her have one."

"He's not like that."

"Then he's a bigger fool than I thought he was. Ah, the glamour of kiddies, the miracle of birth, the furtherance of the species. Just what the world needs. More bastards," he said, each word clear and sharp as glass.

"Look, Cole, it's their business."

He looked past me at the flames. "It's everyone's business."

Before I could say anything, a couple of maids brought in the soup. Cole nodded to them and we sat down. R.E. joined us a few minutes later, wearing a long skirt and sweater. It was a pretty meal and probably tasted good, but every time I looked at Cole, I lost my appetite. There wasn't much small talk since we had so little in common anymore. I ate as fast as I could, trying to finish so I could get out of there.

R.E. went upstairs about midnight. Cole watched her again and said after she was gone, "Something's different about her. She didn't sleep with anyone. But something else happened. I can't blame the two of them, coming on to her. But I can blame..." He paused then he asked me, "So why didn't you want me to know you were here?"

I had no answer but the truth. "I don't care to hang around the person you've become. You're different, Cole. You've changed."

"I am the product of my history, Troy. So. I take it I'm no longer welcome at that flophouse."

"I didn't say that."

"But it's true."

"I don't speak for the house. All I'm saying is that this place gives me the creeps and so do you."

"This is my home, Troy. I live here. Anyway, I won't be going back to the Palace from now on. Different circles."

"It doesn't have to be like that."

"Oh, but it does. I don't do anything halfway." He shut his eyes and craned his head around like his neck was stiff. I could hear his joints crack in the quiet. "Well, it's neither here nor there whether you want to see me or whether they want to see me or whether I want to be seen by anyone. I've got to tend to R.E. now. That's the last time she'll be going up there."

I didn't want to give anything away so I just said, "Good night, Cole."

"Goodbye, Troy." He nodded to me and left the room, gliding away as silently as a shadow.

Everett was waiting in the silent, dark driveway as I left the place. "Miss Rachel insisted that I drive you back to Denton." I shrugged and we got into his car, a small but elegant old Benz.

We didn't speak much at first. Then about half way home, I asked, "When R.E. and I first met you, it seemed for a second that you recognized her."

"She looks a great deal like her father."

"So, you know him?"

He nodded, not showing any cards. Before I could ask anything else he closed the topic by saying, "These are stories which are not mine to tell." We didn't say anything else until we said goodnight.

I got in a couple of hours of sleep then went straight to work the next morning. When I caught a break, I called Claire, but she wasn't in. At least her host mother said she wasn't. She sounded more than a little pissed off. Something about her tone left a cold rock in the pit of my stomach. Eddie came in and asked, "So, did R.E. take off yet?"

"Yeah, last night. I followed her back in her truck so she'd have her own wheels."

"Good. Listen, if you talk to her before I do, tell her the house is ready whenever she wants. Couldn't sleep last night so I drove down and checked it out, got it set up. Bought some clothes and blankets and stuff for her, too. Figured she'd have to make a fast break for it when she does make her run." Friend shorthand: his lack of explanation meant that he knew R.E. and I would have already talked about it.

"Okay. Say, has Claire called or left a message?"

"No, why?"

"Just a little worried. Her host mother sounded crisp when I called." We went back to work but there was no call. Something was up. The more time passed, the more certain I was that I would lose her.

Sure enough, Claire came running into the Palace late that night, in tears. One of her host family's daughters, a very straight young thing, had gone to a recent Cloud Shadow gig on a dare. She saw Claire drumming and singing and worse, saw us kissing after the set. That did it. The whole family laid into her as soon as she came back, called her family in France and after a lot of yelling in English, French and Arabic, her fate was sealed; she was to be sent back home. She'd had to sneak out of the house for a goodbye. We held each other for what seemed like only seconds and then she said she had to go so she could slip back into the house without them noticing she'd been away. We ran into Duncan on the stairs. She threw her arms around him and explained everything so quickly mixing French and English so much that most of the message was unintelligible. But he got the gist of it. We stood on the porch, crying. Then she walked away quickly, hugging herself. Duncan came out and stood on the porch with me in silence for a while before going back in to leave me to my grief.

I went back up to my room and crashed onto the mattress with a thud that could be heard all over the house. All our losses sank in on me at once and I started to cry, sobbing so deeply it left me gasping for air. Much later, I fell asleep, passed out from emotion.

***

A day or so later, I was heading over to Stan and Moe's house when Mariah, Eddie's Buick, blasted past me on the street. I loped in to see Eddie on the phone. Moe was standing near him and Stan was just coming out of the bedroom, pulling his pants on, asking with his expressive eyebrows and shoulders what was going on. Moe nodded towards Eddie who was listening intently and giving instructions. "Got that? Good. Then you go about two miles more and you'll see a white iron gate off to your right. You'll have to look carefully. It's almost hidden. Watch for a small grove of chinaberries. Push it open. It's not locked. Then drive on in. The house is about sixty yards down that path. There's a small garage behind it. The key's in a Folgers can beside the back door." He paused and nodded, listening. "Good idea. Okay." He smiled and nodded then the smile disappeared. "You are okay, aren't you? Sure? Okay, just stay at the house. I'll be down as soon as I'm sure we're not being watched. I don't want to lead him to you. Okay, good luck, Rachel." He hung up and sat with his head in his hands. Then he turned to us. "She's at a service station, wouldn't say where exactly. She called me at the Corner Room, said she'd call me back here."

"What happened?" Stan asked, his arm around Moe's shoulders. Moe was paler than ever and shaking.

"Cole went around the bend last night. She said he came upstairs, said that he'd been thinking about what happened when she was up here, and that he was going to kill her."

"Oh, my God!" Moe was pacing back and forth now. "Not that sweet little girl! How could he do even think something like that?"

"He said he knew she'd been intimate with both me and Jesse, that she'd crossed the line and that he couldn't use her anymore." He stopped and put his head in his hands for a moment. "Whatever the hell that means. Jesus, I knew I shouldn't have let her go back. Anyway, she said he started screaming at her, calling her every name in the book, and pulled a gun. Then, he got calm all of a sudden. He stopped screaming and he smiled. For some reason he said 'Right tool for the right job.'

Then he left the room and locked it behind him. She waited until he was downstairs. Then she jumped out a window and into a nearest tree, and climbed down. He must have heard the truck because he took off after her before she got to the highway."

Stan had maneuvered Moe into a chair by now. "I'll get coffee going. Keep talking, Eddie. I can hear you from the kitchen."

"She said she finally lost him but it took almost an hour to be sure. She's been hiding out all day, waiting to call me." He sighed and shook a little tension loose. "So now we wait and find out if she got to the safe house alright. She said she'd call as soon as she got there."

We settled in. I paced and fidgeted. Eddie sat zazen on the couch, his back straight, breathing in and out in a slow, regular rhythm. Moe chatted nervously and Stan kept him occupied with small chores. It was about three hours before we heard from her. Eddie motioned for silence, mostly at Moe, and then listened. After a couple of minutes, Eddie relaxed and said, "She made it okay." The three of us went to the kitchen to let him talk to her privately.

"So, how is she?" Stan asked when Eddie joined us a few minutes later.

"Fine." He shook his head. "I'm going to wait a couple of days at least before I go see her. I'll let Jesse know where the place is, too. He's in Austin more often than I am, anyway, and Bastrop's so close he can check on her. We'll all have to be careful not to tip Cole off about where she is. He'll probably be watching us all for a while. Speaking of which, you should tell the folks at the Palace about this. Might not be a bad idea to stash the stash deep in case Cole or the cops come looking for her."

"Damn, we should've already thought about that."

Everyone was up and the band was back from Austin so I convened a house emergency meeting in the big room. It didn't take long to tell the tale and we all split up to gather incriminating evidence. As I was sweeping my room, the sickening realization came to me that if Coleman wanted us busted, he could easily arrange to have us planted. We jarred all the goodies in a gallon jug and screwed the lid on tight. Then Jesse and I slipped it into a sack and went way behind the house to no-mans'-land and buried it. The only thing we kept in the house was what could be flushed in seconds. As we were walking back, he asked, "Did she sound like she was okay?"

"I didn't talk to her. Eddie said she was, and that he hadn't hurt her. She was scared, was all."

"I swear I'll kill that son of a bitch if I ever see him again."

"I don't think we ever will."

"I'm not so sure about that." We walked softly, guarding each other's backs, jumping with every sound and every car noise. Jesse said, "Even though it's come to this, I'm glad she's away from him. How long is she going to hole up down there?"

"I don't know. Eddie said we should all avoid going there for a while. Don't want to lead him to her."

"Eddie misses her, too, yeah?"

"Yeah."

He sighed. "She told me she likes both of us and that she doesn't want to be exclusive with anyone." We walked along quietly. "I'm not sure I can handle that. But if that's what she wants, I'll have to try."

We walked silently, watching everything that moved until we were back in the house. We all milled around aimlessly for a bit and then crashed in our separate rooms, trying to deal with the psychic threats in our own ways.

"It has been related that dogs drink at the river Nile
running along, that they may not be seized
by the crocodiles."

Phaedrus, *The Dog and the Crocodile*

IV.

The Deep, Dark Woods

The next evening as we were closing up the Corner Room, I asked Eddie, "If you don't mind my asking, how come you have a house down in Bastrop?"

"You feel like a drive?" He flexed his shoulders. "Long story."

"Yeah. I'm too keyed up to sleep for hours yet." We went out to the Buick, he turned on the radio, and we drove away into the night, both silent, replaying the events of the last couple of days and nights, trying to let it all fall into some sort of mental order.

After a while, I asked him again, "So, about that house."

"It belonged to a woman I lived with for a while. Thea. Beautiful, smart, blond, rich. Too rich for my blood, eventually. We lived together off and on for some years, even lived as a threesome with another lover of hers for a short time. Very short. After she came into the family money and left the state, she left me the house as a goodbye gift. I just hung onto it for nostalgia's sake I suppose. Anyway, glad it was there for R.E."

"Do you still love her? Thea, I mean?"

"Yeah. With her, the love will always be there. See, we were friends before we became intimate. That stays with you." Then he added, "Friendship and love take all kinds of forms." He glanced straight at me and then away again.

I nodded.

"Stan and Moe are cool around you, but they asked me to ask you not to mention to just anyone that they're a couple."

It didn't really hit me at first. Then it sank in. "Say what?"

"Well, surely you know they're gay."

I rewound my mental tapes and reviewed everything.

"Why is that so surprising?" he asked, smiling.

"Uh--well--I don't know. It's just--as far as I know, I'd never been friends with anyone who was gay. Maybe I've been sheltered, but that's a fact. "

"Given the probabilities in any population, I'm sure some of the people you've always known probably are, but they just keep it quiet here in Texas."

I nodded and pondered that. I knew that Austin in particular was home to a growing community that was becoming more and more vocal, especially since the Stonewall riots in New York, so the odds were good. "Well, I'm just surprised,"

"Because they both seem so manly?" he teased, obviously enjoying my naiveté. "You're not uncomfortable about this, are you?"

"No, I mean, it's not like I wouldn't be friends with them anymore. Man, I bet it's difficult for them in Texas, home of the macho man."

"Well, they've always been discrete around people who weren't open-minded."

"Well, sure, man. I won't say anything."

"And they won't kiss you or anything," he grinned, his eyes shining.

I laughed and said, "Okay, okay. Troy gets his bars rattled."

We drove for a while; Eddie's smile fading gradually as we both started thinking about R.E. again. I said, "Speaking of lovers and friends and all, I don't know if R.E. had the time or the chance to tell you, but when she was at the Palace, we talked about a lot of things. She said she doesn't want to be exclusive with anyone when she does get away from Coleman for good."

He turned and looked at me.

I shrugged, "Just thought you ought to know."

"She shouldn't be. That's the last thing she should do after an experience like she's had. Fine looking child like her, she ought to be seeing whoever she wants to."

"And that's okay with you?"

"Sure. Why not? Why you asking? I thought you guys were the free love advocates. Besides, I just told you, it isn't the first time I've been in a three-way thing." He grinned wickedly, having a grand time playing fuck-mind with me. "I've done more than three-way scenes, too. It was de rigueur in the Village. We called them group gropes. Makes folks at the Palace look straight."

"Hmm."

"Yeah. Hell, I remember more than once... No, at this point in my life and for lots of reasons, even if she wanted to be exclusive, I wouldn't want to." He smiled as he caught me studying him. "Don't you believe me?"

"Oh, yeah. It's just that, it seems really hard to handle, the politics, I guess you'd call it."

"Well, the ground rules have to be clear to everyone involved. No, for me, no problem. I think Jesse will have more trouble with it than anyone else."

"Probably. But he said that if this is what R.E. wants, he'll go along with it."

"Hell, he's a musician. He's really in love with his music and he's inspired by R.E. She's his Muse. So being part-time with her is probably enough for him, even if he won't admit that."

"Muse. That's a pretty lofty term for old lady."

"It fits. We all have them."

"Women artists, too?"

"I suppose. Probably take different forms. Why don't you ask one?"

"Like who?"

"Like Claire. Write to her about it."

"If I had an address, I would."

"She'll write you eventually."

I fell silent, not wanting to jinx the desire I felt by giving it voice. We continued to cruise around back roads for another couple of hours, smoking, listening to music, talking just a little until we were both wound down enough to sleep. He dropped me off at the Palace and drove away. I stood in the dark yard, looking up at the stars, thinking about all the goodbyes I'd had to say lately and wondering when the hellos would come around again.

***

We held our breath at the Palace and the Corner Room for long days and longer nights. But there were no knocks on the door in the middle of the night, Coleman didn't burst into our lives in a blaze of gunfire, and no one seemed to be watching us as we came and went. At least, not that we were aware of. We grew accustomed to the constant scanning of faces and cars that people who have good reason to expect trouble find themselves doing. Life went on and the pattern became regular, although it was not one that any of us would have chosen. The rest of February finally passed, taking a long time for such a short month. Then one afternoon, I saw a sleek diesel job parked on a back road near the Palace when I was out walking around, on a wander like the one when Claire first came into my life. There wasn't anyone in the car and it was locked. I followed the footprints that led away from it into the woods towards the house but they were so light I soon lost them. When I returned, the car was gone. If it was him, he didn't come directly to the Palace or the Corner Room. Even so, I felt like the Wolf-Boy had circled us and decided not to blow the door down just yet.

Slowly, we began to relax a little. I had been reading the local papers in order to follow Cole's life, hoping to get a clue about his next move as well as to keep up with the news. The Chicago Seven had gone on trial the 18th of February and that circus and its fallout were still being dissected, especially whether or not Judge Hoffman should have had Bobby Seale bound and gagged. But there wasn't much on Cole and it struck closer to home to keep an eye on him than Chicago at that point in my life. Then, the first week of March, I read a notice in the *Dallas Times Herald*: "Mr. and Mrs. Buddy Justin of Dallas are proud to announce the engagement of their daughter, Miss Cynthia Justin to Mr. Coleman van der Veer of Fort Worth. The couple will be joined in holy matrimony at First Dallas Baptist Church on April 5th, 1970. After a lengthy honeymoon in Europe, the couple will reside at the van der Veer estate outside of Fort Worth." There was a picture. It wasn't the same blond, but another one. She wasn't very pretty. She smiled widely, her head tilted towards his in a studio pose; he had his arms around her shoulders, the fingers loosely knotted near her throat. Although his mouth was turned in what could be taken for a smile, his pale eyes seemed to shimmer with darker light, like well water far away in the earth. I felt sorry for that silly looking girl and wondered how she would deal with the ghostly house Coleman called home, and with the shape-shifter she would marry.

***

    Later that month, I went down to Austin to welcome the equinox and to get out of town for a change of scene. It was spring break at N.T.S.U. and business was slack so Eddie gave me some time off, a bus ticket, and some pocket money. He knew I was still getting over Claire and that the tension of being paranoid was wearing on us all. But once the Greyhound passed the Hungry Hobo restaurant and the Roman Inn on I-35, I began to feel the heart magic. Then the sight that always made me smile, the "Austin City Limits" sign, came into view.

    It was our San Francisco and L.A. all rolled into one. Denton, our home and scene, was smaller, the choice of people who were not ready for the wider, wilder cultural waters of River City or who simply chose not to swim in them. For me, it was a tolerant place where the Snake usually didn't seem to freak people out too much so I was able to drop in from time to time and sample everything it had to offer. I knew where I'd stay. Jesse and Vance had so many regular gigs in town by then that they shared rent on an old house in the Deep Eddy neighborhood. The sharing was done with seven, sometimes eight lithe Travis County ladies, sweeties that ran around in cutoffs and T-shirts and little else, spending daddy's money on dope. They also paid tuition to UT so they had an excuse for living in Austin-taceous, but they rarely went to classes. They were huge fans of Texas Weather's music and of Jesse especially. Vance didn't have as many groupies because the boy was truly ugly but there were those who were drawn to the music he made when he played and his growly blues voice. The guys weren't home but the girls were, so they let me in, fed, and doped me. Given my palsy, and the fact that I wasn't actually in the band, they didn't give me anything else, but that was okay. I walked around the Drag that evening and crossed over onto the campus. Sure enough, there was that sugary smell I loved so much: mountain laurel. I relaxed near a bush of it next to the French department building, listened through a window to a late class going on: the vowels, the words, thinking of Claire. It didn't make me sad, though. In fact, I was suddenly hopeful. I knew that she would write when she could. She was probably lying low, too, like R.E. After a bit I went back to the band's house. No one was home but it was unlocked so I went in and sat in the dark. Then, it happened again. "I" slid out of my body slowly, saw myself being very still, and glided up and east.

***

R.E. was on the porch of a little field-stone house, a classic Texas "dog run" with an open space between the two smallish main sections joined by a wooden roof. She was on a bench, her feet up on the porch rail, smoking one in the evening breeze. A car stopped at the gate. She froze, the joint still in her fingers, listening. Then she smiled, put it down in the tin can ashtray and raced towards the sound of the Buick driving slowly and carefully down the path. Eddie had the window down and he stopped as she flew down towards him. Reaching in the window as he stopped, she hugged and kissed him over and over.

"Man, I would have come earlier if I'd known I'd get this reception. Hey, hey, now. Let me park this thing and get out and then you're free to do that some more when I'm not operating machinery."

She laughed and walked along beside him as he drove. They shifted the car and truck until both were squeezed into the garage. Once outside, he picked her up by the waist and swung her around. "So, how the hell are you, Rachel? God, it's been weeks."

"I'm fine, I'm so goddamned fine I can't stand myself most days. But I've been living on lambs quarter and wild onions so you may not be able to stand me."

He put her down and they kissed. "Not bad. Very vegetable. Onions." He kissed her again. "Garlic, too. I take it you weren't expecting company."

"A little baking soda will fix that."

He held her at arms length, teasing, but studying her at the same time. "No spies?"

"Pretty sure none. I don't think Cole would just sit on the info if he knew where I was. I don't go into town. Thanks again so much for all the stuff and the stash you left here. I've been frugal and it's lasted just fine."

"I brought a lot of things with me and some fresh food."

"Oh, joy! No cans!"

They hauled everything inside and put it away. There were a few pitiful greens in the mostly empty fridge. "Man, I'm sorry it took so long to get down here. We were worried that Coleman was watching us and we didn't want to lead him to you. I was nervous about the phones, too."

"How long should I stay, do you think?"

"Well, it's March now. You've been out of there over a month. And the papers say Cole's marrying some society blond from Dallas April 5th. Then they're taking off to Europe. It seems best for you to stay at least until they're out of the country. But it's up to you. You can stay here as long as you want. No one knows better than you how nuts he is. He could easily sit back for months and then whack you anytime after you come out."

"I can't hide from him forever. Sooner or later I've got to get on with my life."

"Well, I'd feel better if you stayed until he's on his honeymoon trip."

She shuddered and he asked, "What?"

"Nothing. Just a flashback. God, I feel sorry for her, whoever she is."

"From the picture, she doesn't look all that bright."

"Even worse. Well, enough of that. I've got company tonight and the makings for a great dinner. I'll decide later about when I'll leave and what I'll do next."

"Let's cook. What would you like first?"

"God, you brought so much. Why don't we sit on the porch and have some wine and the rest of the number I started and just talk and talk and talk about everything else in the world besides Coleman. I've started rapping to myself lately. Interesting, as far as it goes, but not very fulfilling."

They opened a bottle of red, R.E. took two glasses out of the cabinet, and they went back outside. There was enough of a breeze to keep any early mosquitoes at bay. Evening woods sounds: they sat and sipped and Eddie ran down all the news from town, including Claire's departure.

"Oh, no, no, no. Not that. Damn! She and Troy were so happy. Of all the narrow-minded--I hate those people. How could they?"

"They're just ignorant. I have the feeling that's it's not over between those two."

"I hope so. Well, any other news? How's Amanda?"

"Getting bigger all the time. She came down with me to see her folks in Rosebud. I drove her as far as Austin. She said she was going to take a bus on out from there."

"Do they know?"

"She wrote them and broke the news. But she's not sure what kind of reception she'll get because they haven't written back or returned her calls."

"Well, if they're that pissed, maybe they'll disown her instead of going after Raz with a shotgun and making them do something they're not ready to do."

"We'll see. I told her I'd be around for the weekend and that I could meet her in town if she needs a ride back."

She reached towards him with her glass and they touched rims. "To friends."

"Yes. So, lady. What'll we have? I don't know whether it's the smoke or seeing you again, but I'm starving."

"How about that chicken? It wouldn't take long to roast. We could put some rosemary and thyme on it. Whoever was here before had an herb garden at one point. I've been tending it and it's coming back strong."

He smiled. "Okay, you pick the herbs and I'll get the hen ready. Veggies to go along and a salad and some French bread?"

"Oh, yes! And no garlic. I've eaten enough lately."

"Come here."

She got up and he pulled her down into his lap for a long kiss. "Yep, garlic, alright," he sighed when they came up for air.

They fixed dinner and ate by candlelight in the small kitchen, talking and drinking the rest of the bottle, smoking one after dinner. R.E. excused herself for a bit, showered, and changed clothes. She made a little coffee and they drank it while they stood by the back door and watched the moon glide through the trees. She asked, "So how did you know about this house in the first place?"

"It belonged to a woman I was involved with. We were together, on and off for some years. We lived here the fourth and last time we were together. She left me the deed when she got married."

She studied him. "Was that okay?"

"Yeah, fine. She asked me before she accepted if I wanted to marry her, but I declined. Besides, she had to get on with her college life, not hole up here in the woods."

"Does it feel strange to be here again?"

"Oh, it's fine. I come down here now and then, sweep out the cobwebs, make sure the place isn't full of rats and that the pipes haven't burst. I ought to have done something with it before now. But the way things turned out, I'm glad it was available for you."

"It's a great place to think in, to dream in. I've done a lot of reflecting and sorting out, trying to understand what happened. Being with Coleman was like living in creepy fairy tale. The more I tried to help him, the stronger his bad side became until it seemed like it took him over completely. By then, I was afraid to leave him. I knew I had to and that I would, but I wasn't sure how I could do it so no one got hurt. I've thought over and over about that last night you and I were together at the Palace. I didn't want to go back to Cole, but I was scared of what would happen if I didn't, scared of what he'd do to me and to you and to Jesse and everyone else. I guess I shouldn't have gone back, but I didn't know what else to do. There wasn't any good, simple, clear answer."

"I've felt so goddamned guilty about letting you walk away that night."

"You don't have to feel guilty. And I don't either. That's something I've realized in these weeks being here. I made a mistake with Cole. I learned from it. So I don't have to beat myself up about it mentally anymore." She took their empty cups and put them in the sink. Then she turned back towards him. "Why don't we take up where we left off last time?"

He kissed her. It was a tender, friendly kiss at first. Then she ran her hands up his back and leaned into him, ankle to thigh to neck embrace. All the switches kicked over into the erotic: kissing, touching, deeper kissing.

Sighing, he leaned back and looked at her, stroking her hair. "Rachel, I've wanted to take you to bed for a long time. I just couldn't believe that you felt the same way. I couldn't let myself believe a gorgeous kid like you--now, before you say anything, that's just a fact. I'm fifteen years older than you and I've been through a lot of situations and I know people change." He kissed her again. "Troy told me you said you wanted no restrictions on yourself, you wanted to be free to choose who you were with. Okay, tonight it's me. But if you want to be with Jesse or anyone else, all I ask is that you tell me and that you be straight with me, always. No disappearances. You don't have to go behind my back ever, but especially not now, not with Coleman still hanging around. I don't want to lose sleep wondering whether he's snatched you. If you're with someone else, that's no problem with me. I want you to understand that. You need and deserve some space. You dig me?"

"Dig. Te comprendo. Je te comprends. Got it."

"You're very lingual, you know that?"

"You'll find out just how lingual," she smiled as she ran her hands lightly over his crotch.

He groaned a little in pleasure. Then smiled, "God, I hope so. But first things first. All that coffee and wine is going straight through me."

She laughed her laugh and said, "I'm so glad you said that. I have to pee so bad and I didn't want to ruin the moment or anything."

"Ladies first."

When she came out of the bathroom, she was naked. She smiled and walked back to the bedroom as he slid into the bathroom past her, patting her rear on his way.

She was lying on the bed when he came in naked. There was a puckered mass of scar tissue on his shoulder. Tossing his clothes down by the bed he said, "It's not fair for you to look so good."

She stood up, rubbing herself against his legs as she did. He picked her up and held her high as she wrapped her legs around his waist. They stayed like that for few minutes, kissing and looking into each other's eyes. Then he set her down beside the bed. She lay down and held her arms out. He stretched out beside her and slowly ran his hands over her, from her ankles to her neck. "Okay, lady, okay," he said softly, "I've held back long enough," and he went down on her. When she got her breath back, she did the same for him. After a while, he went back to the kitchen and returned with a second bottle of wine and another number. They sipped and toked until they were in the mood again.

He asked, "Are you taking the pill?"

"No. I can't. Not anymore. And I had to leave my diaphragm there when I left. I didn't have time to look for it and the truck keys both. But that doesn't mean we can't make each other feel real good like we just did."

"Well," he said as he reached for his jacket and pulled a condom out of one of the pockets, "being the 50s kind of guy I am, I came prepared. So I could cum prepared. I was hoping you were ready for some lovemaking." She helped him put one on. It wasn't the only condom they used that night. At one point she was stroking his back and found a second scar, this one bigger than the one in front.

He rolled over and looked up at her, reading the question in her eyes about how it happened. "Another time. I'll tell you another time. Right now I just want to make love to you again."

She nodded and smiled, "Please do."

She fell asleep in his arms about two in the morning. He moved quietly away from her and sat on the floor beside the bed with his back braced against the wall, finishing the wine and the number as he watched her sleeping.

"I" came back into my body gently. The house was empty and dark. I shook the numbness out and walked around a little to get the vehicle and the mind used to each other again. Jesse and Vance and crew came in about half an hour later. I asked, "How was the gig?"

"Had its moments. Your evening?"

"Sweet. Very sweet. Spring in Austin. Just wandered around."

He smiled. "Yeah, I love it down here this time of year."

After a couple more days, I headed back to Denton. On the way out of town, I took one last stroll down the Drag. "I Scream, You Scream", our favorite ice cream shop, wasn't open for business yet, but I heard faint voices and walked up the long, dark staircase that led to the tiny front door. As I peeked in through the window, I saw two girls, one wearing a big top hat, Mad Hatter style, complete with two playing cards tucked into the hatband. They were sharing a pipe of hash and waved me in with smiles. I didn't know them, but I wasn't questioning the generosity. One left and then it was only the top hat girl, the pipe, and me. We talked and flirted and talked some more. She didn't seem to mind about the Snake. To make a short story shorter, I got laid behind the counter and we had sundaes afterwards. I love Austin in the spring.

***

On the way back to Denton, I started to feel hopeful for the first time in months. And sure enough, when I walked into the kitchen, there was a letter and a big manila envelope on the table. With my name on them. The stamps were French. I didn't want to open them right away so I fetched a bottle of red, chatted with folks, then headed upstairs. I opened the wine, rolled a ceremonial number at my desk, and then opened the letter. It was written on very thin airmail stationery, light blue. I sniffed it. Yes, there was a little patchouli and something else, that naughty girl. I toked a little. It was the first letter I'd ever gotten from a woman and I was going to savor this slowly.

She said hello and then she started talking about bread, about how the flour and the sugar are a place for the yeast to live and how the bakers nourish the mix and how they grow and how baking kills them so we should honor the dead. She said it was a family tradition to mix a few crumbs from the previous loaves into the dough of the new ones so each following loaf contained the soul of all the preceding loaves. She was deeply into yeasty reincarnation, working at her uncle's bakery in Aix-en-Provence, up to her elbows every day in bread dough and reading comparative mythology at night. She'd taken a little vacation with local friends, a run to the ocean for a few days. She said she missed me and that she hadn't been with anyone else yet. I felt a little guilty about the top hat girl at that point. She said that her father had been the one who was so angry about her hanging out with hippies and with me especially, but that her mother was more sympathetic since she was a musician. She said to be patient, that she was working on a plan to return "some day." She ended by saying that she dreamed about me often. The letter ended with "Je t'embrasse, Claire."

More wine, a little more smoke. Then I opened the packet that had been in the envelope with the letter. Pictures: the first one had been taken in front of a bakery. Her hair was a little longer than it had been the last time I had seen her. She was wearing an apron, a long blue skirt, and a white blouse, wiping her hands on the end of the apron and smiling at the camera. The wall behind her was faded stucco, with patches of different colors showing through. There were shelves of bread in the window. The second one took my breath: Claire at the beach. She was still as skinny as ever and the bathing suit was little more than a couple of strips of cloth. I had seen her naked plenty of times but this was especially erotic, having a photo of her wearing so little. The third and last picture: she was on a hill. It was covered with small plants and blooming purple flowers I'd never seen before. She was wearing the same long blue skirt and a different white blouse, her dark face a contrast to the light clothes. She was in mid-stride, coming from the woods in the background, carrying a little basket and looking carefully at the ground beneath her like she was searching for something. As I looked in the photo packet again, going back for every trace of correspondence, I came across a couple of pressed flowers and herbs. They looked like the ones in the photo and still carried a woodsy scent about them.

I propped the pictures up on my desk and read the letter again, sniffing the flowers. I drank the rest of the bottle while looking at the pictures before I opened the large manila envelope. Inside was a tissue wrapped package and a card. It said only 'I hold my work out to you as a mirror.' I took one more toke and opened it. Inside were two sketches in watercolor and pen. She must have been hanging out in a church or reading the Bible because they were both of a male angel. He had long blond hair, blue eyes, and a divinely peaceful, handsome face. He was naked in one, lying on a bed, with faint wing like shadows behind him. His body was lean and tan, the muscles smooth and well defined. In the second, he was clothed in jeans and a T-shirt, standing inside a latticed well house. My heart started pounding. She was playing some kind of mean trick here. At the bottom right of both pictures was my name, worked carefully into the scheme of the picture. Rage and confusion rippled through me, freezing me into place. I wanted to tear them into tiny pieces but I couldn't. What the hell was she trying to do? Break my heart? I didn't look like that.

Or did I? It dawned on me slowly just how long it had been since I had really studied my own reflection. There had been an ugly scene when I was in junior high school. Those days, no one was cute, we were all gangly and covered with pimples and our faces and bodies were all out of proportion. I couldn't hold still for the seventh grade yearbook photo and the guy wouldn't take another and they put it in anyway: Troy the Blur. Since that day I had allowed no one to take my picture if I could help it and I had perfected the art of never looking too closely in the mirror while I was combing my hair or brushing my teeth or later, shaving, concentrating only on the part I was working on, not the totality of something I hated: my physical self.

I took a deep breath and marched downstairs to the bathroom. The old mirror was a cracked, half-silvered Medusa that someone had inherited and we had never replaced. I stood in front of it then flipped on the overhead light. The angel guy in her drawings stared back at me. Even the Snake was surprised and held still for a second. I studied my jaw line and my cheekbones and my forehead. They were perfect. I was tall, blue-eyed with long blond hair, deeply tanned and muscled up from years of isometric battles with palsy and I had this perfect face. I twitched but it didn't seem so bad suddenly. Maybe that was why the top hat girl invited me to stay that morning. Maybe that was why Claire picked me. The Snake was just part of my body. I flicked the light off and watched the afterimage grow: dark angel emerging. Someone needing the facilities knocked on the door and I wandered back up to my room. I put the photos and the drawings away carefully, read the letter once more, and slipped it into my wallet. I started writing back to Claire, actually quite a long letter. But I never mailed it. I was too afraid of someone other than her reading it. I finally folded it and put it in with hers.

That night, I went up to the roof of the Palace, emotionally high and hopeful, more than I'd ever been. The night sky was clear, almost glistening. The waxing moon was past its zenith and the stars were glittery and gorgeous. I was just a speck in all of this. A vague notion of getting Claire back by offering to marry her started to form in my mind, but the reality around all that sank me like a stone under a wave of sudden blues. Sure: the powers that be were not about to believe someone as fine as her would come back to marry me. They'd smell a green card scam. And if by some chance we did marry, my government disability check would be cut off and I'd be out in the world trying to wrestle the Snake at the same time I was hunting a job. By now I had done a complete 180 of the heart, so I sat and cried, feeling royally sorry for myself. I looked up just in time to see a shooting star. It blazed along for what seemed like a full minute before it disappeared. Like red tail hawks and dreams, they'd always been good omens for me. Finally, I began to feel calm: not up, not down, just balanced somewhere in the middle. I stayed there on the roof for a long time, trying to imagine what the sky might look like from a hillside in France.

***

March blew through like the windy month it can be: prairie springtime tornado roulette. Every time the clouds turned that peculiar, ominous shade of green we watched the skies, holding onto our stuff, ready to jump in the ditch and cover our asses until it blew over. One had touched down the year before, but our little patch of Texas had been spared so far. It was the last week of that unsettled month when things started moving again. Amanda had returned from Rosebud the month before feeling very depressed. Her family had made a real scene about her pregnancy and lack of a ring. Then they completely freaked out when they saw a photo of Raz. A great deal of hell was raised and Amanda had decamped in tears.

In the days since, Raz had called his family in California to explain about Amanda and the baby. They were overjoyed. But they couldn't afford to come to Texas to meet her since they were as freewheeling with their finances as Raz was careful. The next morning, he walked up to Amanda in the big room, in front of us all, and said to her, "Well, it's obvious what we need to do. Let's just get married and get everyone off our backs about it." Never much on words, she answered just as simply, "Okay." And that was that. They hugged and kissed to cheers and whistles, tut-tutting us and blushing. But honestly, I hadn't seen either of them as content and happy in a long time as they were at that moment.

As time rolled on, concrete plans for the wedding were tossed around and around and finally abandoned to their own fate, with only the bare bones of an outline left for events to fill in according to whim. Raz and Amanda would pay for the food and drinks and other recreational items; Eddie and I would do the cooking and cleaning and table duty. Both bands would provide the music. Our happy couple had finally decided that they would go into town and do the legal stuff at the Justice of the Peace's office by themselves on April 22nd. That was going to be Earth Day. Everyone was talking about it being a global celebration of nature and caring enough to do something about saving it, so they chose it for the first part of the wedding ritual. The house party celebration, the heart part of the event remained set for May 1. All we had to do was wait until Coleman was gone and then everything could get back to normal and R.E. could come out of hiding, at least for a few months.

Finally, Coleman's day arrived: April 5th. We followed both the Dallas and Fort Worth papers as they covered the wedding. The church in Dallas was packed with the old guard who knew they were powerful as well as the newer ones who liked to think they were. The ceremony took almost two hours, with lots of songs and a long, long service, the official entrance and exit, and of course, lots of posing for pictures. You could have fed a family of four or five for a year on what the bride's dress alone cost, and she was wearing another unbelievably expensive looking necklace, probably from the same vault that Coleman had taken the emerald one the day of the funeral. This one was diamonds and star sapphires "as big as a grown man's thumb", according to the article. She and all her dozen bridesmaids were arrayed in tiers in the pictures like so many Barbie dolls. Coleman had no one standing with him, no best man, no attendants, only Everett who hovered near him, always in the background. Mazie was not in any of the pictures, but the blond from the funeral was. She was one of the bridesmaids, smiling at Cole from the end of the line while the bride was busy being congratulated, Cole half-smiling back. The reception was at the mansion in that same big downstairs room where the funeral had been. The article mentioned their itinerary for the honeymoon: St. Moritz, the Riviera, Cannes, Monaco, Rome, Paris, and Geneva. The last one was probably a bank pit stop. With his amphetamine jaws and snaky grace, Coleman now looked like the '67 version of Jim Morrison in a ruffled shirt and Edwardian black suit, the dark L.A. death angel all dressed up with plenty of places to go. In one shot he was looking directly into the camera, his searching, heat-seeking look. I sighed as I tossed the paper aside. If it came to it, could I hurt or even kill him to protect R.E.? I had no idea if I had it in me, and I was hoping that I never had to find out.

R.E. came out of hiding about a week later. She spent her first night out of the woods in Austin with Jesse. She went with him to the club where the band was playing and danced until sunup. When she got back to Denton, she stopped by the Palace and visited with all of us until it was closing time at the Corner Room. Then Eddie came over. He walked into the big room and swept her up in his arms while we all laughed and clapped. They kissed and the energy charge of that reunion ignited the mood of everyone looking on. Duncan and crew set up and started a new set of experimental sounds. As the music filled the house, I went out onto the porch for a smoke. Time wandered and I began to let the guardian vibes shake loose one by one. Maybe now we could all just get back to our lives for a while. Eddie and R.E. walked past, heading for his car. She turned and waved, blew me a kiss. I returned it and watched them drive away. I toked and watched the smoke float away from me in lazy blue-white art nouveau swirls. It was the first moment in a long time when I felt like everything was going to be all right after all.

***

R.E. stayed in her old roof room for a day or so. Then she found an apartment in a little four-plex about halfway between Eddie's house and the Palace. We were all worried about that idea at first, but she said that if anything went down with Coleman, she didn't want anyone else getting caught in the crossfire. And she said she wanted a place that was hers, her ground for those times when she wanted to be alone. Still, one or more of us was usually there and sometimes she stayed over at the Palace with Jesse, or at Eddie's place with him, so she was always guarded. We were trying to settle down and to get back to real life as best we could, knowing that Coleman would be back in town by August. But we had those few months of reprieve. And the momentum for the wedding was building, taking our minds off the paranoia we'd labored under for what seemed like ages. It was the calm after a long gut wrenching stretch of white water rapid running and sharp stone dodging when you could lean back and let the current carry you for a while, let your arms and back rest, and let your attention wander.

Part of that floating was the space to think about little things. One day as I was leaving R.E.'s place, I saw her trunk open in the middle of the floor. I wasn't snooping but her letters and photos were right there on top of everything else. As I walked home slowly, I thought about how few I had of my own past, three or four maybe. But now I had a few of Claire. And once back inside the Palace, I glanced at the walls. Jesse had recently taken up photography as a hobby and had started plastering his efforts on whatever space was available. They were mostly black and white, a few in color, snapshots really, but a few were soulful compositions: Raz making a cradle for the kid, Amanda and her huge belly preening in the sun, R.E. dancing at the club the night she came out of hiding, me turning my back, Eddie and R.E. in the kitchen at the Corner Room, Moe and Stan mugging wildly. Someone must have borrowed the camera at one point because there were some shots of the band with R.E. dancing in the foreground. Three or four artier compositions of R.E.'s knees and ankles in close-up against a wooden wall were grouped in the middle with one portrait of her naked from the waist up, holding her hair over one breast, smiling into the camera. There was also a couple of Jesse that R.E. had taken. One was a shot of him in the Palace, practicing at the old piano there in the big room, early in the morning. His hair was wet and he was barefoot and shirtless, wearing his oldest jeans. Another picture was one of him in full non-verbal live communication with Vance on stage at the Vulcan Gas Company.

All these images suddenly became very dear to me. They weren't mine; they were communal property. But I had the urge to catalog them somehow. I took them down one by one and wrote the names, the year, and the place in which they had been taken on the back, then pinned them back up again. If they ever got loose from us and were floating around the world somehow, at least the finder would know who these people were. The space on the back was too small for much more history, but at least there would be names.

Momentum began to build as the wedding approached. People started coming in from all over, but no matter. The Palace was big enough to house all the guests, and it was easy enough to sleep outdoors since the weather was getting so warm. Two days before the party, Eddie and R.E. came over to the Palace to stay for a day or so and handle the food preparations. Moe and Stan and I were in charge of the Corner Room for the duration. Amanda had been ordered by all concerned to take it easy, but she ignored everyone in her quiet smiling way and worked as hard as anyone else. Both bands spent an entire afternoon just getting all the equipment set up so they could both play without a lot of inter-set changeovers. We'd recently acquired a second refrigerator when Eddie got a new one so there was plenty of room for the food that was beginning to pile up: breads, cookies, cakes, pies, roast meats, salads, chips, snacks. Eddie guarded it all with a damp towel he flicked at finger-dippers. Coolers were too small for the number of bottles to be iced down, so we scoured the town for tubs and barrels.

The morning of the party, a team prepared the cake and brought it into the center room about noon to the oohs and aahs of everyone present. It was five layers: chocolate and pecans and cherries with "Raz and Amanda" spelled out in thick chocolate letters on top. And all around it there were chocolate angels doing all sorts of things you wouldn't think angels either had the tools to do or knew anything about. It was, as Eddie called it, a Gregorian Kama Sutra cake. And of course, there was punch: three kinds. One was champagne, one was just juice, and one was marked with signs decorated with nuclear explosions and instructions about needing to stay at least 16 hours after imbibing. The barrels and tubs were iced down and filled with beer and wine and anything else in bottles that came around, with the exception of the tequila and the mescal. They were set up on another table with salt and limes and little ceramic skull cups that Jesse had bought in Mexico. On the same table was a rolling tray, a sizeable stash, papers, clips, lighters and an ashtray, and another platter of acid and mescaline, all neatly lined up. About sundown, we started the bonfire. We were far enough from the city limits proper to do this without interference and we had warned the few neighbors within screaming distance about the party.

The food was officially released to the tables, and joints were rolled and passed. Cloud Shadow was winding down the first set, and Jesse was still wandering around snapping pictures. I kept nibbling at the mushroom pate. It wasn't just your run of the mill mushrooms, of course, but rather a mixture of regular ones and the kind from East Texas that gave you a new way of looking at life. It tasted good, so I kept munching away and soon I was tripping my ears off. I wandered upstairs, through the roof room window and settled down with my legs dangling over the edge, enjoying the bacchanalia going on below and the profusion of shooters in the sky. They may have been trails from looking up too fast, but whatever they were, they were pretty. Several people had doffed their duds and were dancing nude around the fire. Texas Weather was heating up; Jesse and Vance were in some sort of horse race over who could do the most hair-raising solos. It seemed neck and neck so far. After a good 20 minutes of their own version of Quicksilver's *Edward the Mad Shirt Grinder*, they paused and the crowd roared their approval.

Then, Raz and Amanda came out and stood near the fire. Everyone gathered and quieted down. You could hear the wood popping and sizzling in the silence. He was wearing his best Orthodox finery and she was in a blue Arthurian style dress with sleeves that trailed the ground. They both had flower wreathes on their heads and Amanda was carrying an armload of irises, purple irises. I just stared at them, tears in my eyes.

"Friends, family," Raz began, his voice rich and full and shivering with the moment, "welcome." He reached out and took Amanda's hands and they turned to face each other. "Amanda, my wife, in the name of everything that we care for, friends, this family we have gathered, peace and love, I promise you that I will help you raise the child we have made. I love you now and I hope to love you always. Whether or not that remains, I will always be your friend and respect and care for you."

"Raz, Morgan, my husband and friend and father to my child, I promise to help you achieve your dreams and visions and to raise our child in hopes that it will be a world in which it can grow into adulthood in harmony with all the world, with all the life in the world, and that it can know friends and family such as we have." With that they turned to us and Amanda threw the irises one by one to the crowd and Raz took handfuls of flower petals from the deep pockets in his robes and tossed them at everyone. Once their hands and pockets were empty, they turned to each other again and said in unison, "Blessed be and be merry!" Then they kissed. The crowd surrounded and embraced them and everyone began laughing and crying and singing at once. The music started up again and I surveyed the crowd. Eddie was sitting down, his face covered with his hands, his shoulders heaving. He looked up and our eyes met and he smiled, tears flashing on his face. I didn't see R.E. at first. Then I spotted her in the middle of the crowd, hugging Amanda. Stan and Moe had closed the Corner Room early; I could see them at the edge of the crowd, holding hands and smiling at each other. They were both crying and laughing. There was a hand on my shoulder and the whiff of patchouli. Heart thudding against my ribs, I almost fell off the roof spinning around. No one. Actually, that's not correct. No one physical. She was with me in spirit. I knew at that moment that we were linked up and that she was on her way back. I didn't know for sure when she'd arrive, but that she was in transit. The second nibble of mushrooms began to come on about then. I tried to count up: there were at least two more steaming down the track behind that one. Hmm: I crawled back through the roof room window intending to make it to my own room but instead wound up sprawled across R.E.'s old mattress. That was fine. 'Shrooms and I were good friends and I was in safe hands.

The next few hours defy description.

Things began to look more day-to-day after sunup. Once I could stay on my feet, I wandered downstairs. People were still partying. Eddie was in the kitchen working on coffee and toast and regular breakfast food. With all the folks in the state they were, I guess he figured there had to be alternatives to cake for breakfast so we wouldn't all turn into sick puppies by noon. We hugged silently for a good while and he offered me a cup. I sipped at it and ate some of the bread I'd picked up from one of the tables. Jesse came in.

Eddie looked at him and at me and asked, "Where's R.E.?"

Jesse said, "I thought she was with you."

"No. Troy?"

"I haven't seen her for years, I mean, hours. I ate a lot of 'shrooms last night and crashed in her old room. She wasn't there, as far as I know, all night."

Jesse shrugged and frowned, his I-don't-care look, "Maybe she split with someone else and didn't tell anyone."

"No, if she was going to leave like that, she would've told me." He headed into the big room and Jesse poured himself a large cup. We looked at each other, a cold feeling of sudden dread hanging in the warm air like autumn fog.

Eddie came back in after about fifteen minutes. "She's not in the house. No one's seen her for almost an hour. Let's go find her." Once outside, we split up. I headed for the back road where I'd seen that gray car parked a few weeks earlier, those footprints that led to the house. Hurrying now, I hustled to the spot and as I rounded the bend I saw Cole's old black Mustang parked exactly where the other car had been: clear sign. He was back and he didn't care who knew it. Maybe he even wanted us to know. I stood still and shut my eyes, trying to tune into the world around me, asking all the deities for a clue. At first, all I could hear was my own rising blood pressure thudding against my ears.

Then, at a distance, there it was, a faint leafy thrashing sound about midway between that hidden car and the Palace. I started walking softly then trotting and finally running full tilt through the woods, honing in on what I had heard, leaping over fallen trees and old tires. There was another sound, one that lives with me still, like a thick branch being broken inside a rolled up wet towel. It was followed by a loud groan of pain, and a heavy thud, like someone had been thrown to the ground. I slowed, gasping, trying to muffle the sound of my approach. Then I saw them. R.E. was trying to get up, pushing with her right arm. The left one hung at her side at an unnatural angle. Her right eye was swollen shut and there was a bad cut over it that was bleeding, gushing thick ooze over her bruised face. Her clothes were torn and there were other bruises around her neck and wrists. And yes, it was Coleman, dressed in black jeans and boots and a black sweater and leather jacket: a man on a mission. He was so gone in delusional rage that he didn't see me and I was so shocked at first that I couldn't move or speak. That angelic smile: he contemplated her like she was a work of art he wasn't quite finished with, deciding on the final touches. "Maybe the nose," he said then he lashed out in a vicious blur of motion. She turned just as he lunged but he landed most of the blow anyway, knocking her flat on her back. "We'll see how many of them still want you when I'm done with you, you cunt." All of this had taken maybe fifteen seconds. That last punch brought me into the clearing.

"Eddie! Jesse! Over here!" I yelled as loudly as I could, still panting as I staggered out of the brush to stand between them.

Coleman froze and snarled at me, "Back off. This is between me and her." He pulled a pistol out of an inside jacket pocket. I hadn't really counted on that, though looking back, I should have.

"Drop it, man. Everyone in the house is out looking for her." I was hoping for a bluff, but then I remembered that Coleman could read colors.

He just smiled and said, "Everyone? They're still celebrating the marriage. Wasn't it everything you goddamn hippies love? All that peace and love bullshit. Yeah, I saw it. I was around all night. I watched it all, especially this one. Dancing with them, kissing them, fucking who knows how many of them. Whore," he whispered. He turned back to me, ignoring R.E. for a few seconds. I glanced at her. She was trying to focus, stay conscious, staring at him closely.

Distract him, I thought. "Why did you do this?"

"Because I can," he smiled at me. "She belongs to me, whether I'm in the country or not. Whether I want her or not. And because I can get away with anything. I'm a rich 'un. I'm a rich boy." For a few horrific seconds, James Dean's Jett Rink was talking to me. How did he do that, switch shapes so fast? Then it was Cole again as he heard the footsteps rushing towards us from two directions. He smiled. "Ah, company's coming. Good. I can get all four of you at once and be done with this goddamn place."

"And maybe not," R.E. said. She had gotten to her knees.

"Shut up, you slut," he whispered, raising his chin and narrowing his eyes, but as he turned back to her, a rock flew from her good hand straight to his unguarded throat. He instinctively reached for it with both hands, dropping the pistol. I jumped and pushed him backwards, kicking the thing away from him. We could hear Eddie and Jesse yelling then. I fell to the ground and grabbed the pistol before he could. Pointing it at him, I hollered, "Over here! We're over here! Be careful!"

"I know you can't shoot me," he said, spitting and glaring as he bounded to his feet.

"Don't bet on it." But I wasn't sure, and to shoot a person you have to be. I hesitated.

He started towards R.E. again then froze as they locked eyes for long seconds. He began to shiver. Then from deep down, he raised his bone-chilling scream before whispering, "At least I've made you ugly."

She whispered back, "And I can make you crazy. Shatter the frame. Let the black water flow. No control." She banged her right fist on the ground, staring at him.

He staggered like she'd hit him, the color draining away from his already pale features. I kept the gun on him but it didn't matter. He wasn't looking at me anymore. Then he was gone, so fast it was as though he'd vanished. R.E. slumped further to the ground, the rush of defense-adrenalin seeping away. Eddie crashed through the brush with Jesse close behind him. I dropped the pistol and they stood there stunned as R.E. turned her bloody face to them.

"Oh, Jesus God," Jesse said. In the silence we could hear mockingbirds and jays screaming and the sound of the Mustang rev and race away, the faint echo of a high, thin, human scream over it all. R.E. said, "I feel so stupid." Then she lowered herself to the ground and passed out.

Jesse stayed with R.E. while Eddie and I ran back to the Palace to recruit the sober for a rescue team. He told Amanda to find R.E.'s truck keys and where to meet us on the road. Then he gathered up some things: a couple of blankets, some old sheets. He broke the business ends off three mops and busted one of them into shorter pieces. I just stood there and watched him. He thrust some of the things into my hands and we raced back to the clearing in silence as Amanda and Raz took off in the truck. When we got there, Jesse was gently pulling the loose hair around R.E.'s face out of the congealing blood, tears rolling down his cheeks as he held the compress Eddie had made from his shirt on the cut over her eye. "God, look what he did to her," he whispered as Eddie began to work.

"Yeah. Let's see how much of it we can fix while we still can." He directed the rest of us calmly. We rolled one edge of a blanket up in a mop handle, carefully placed her on the blanket and rolled the other long handle into the other long edge. Eddie used the short pieces of the third handle to make a temporary splint for her arm. I excused myself to throw up when he set it, as did Raz. Then he covered her with the other blanket and six of us lifted the makeshift sling and carried her slowly and carefully up to the road where the soberest one of us all, Amanda, was waiting in the driver's seat of R.E.'s truck. We loaded her into the flatbed and piled in. Eddie sat beside her, monitoring her all the way. Raz and Amanda and I were in front, Jesse and the others in the back. It was one of the longest drives of my life. Since she had no ID on her and no insurance, we had no choice except the closest emergency room. Eddie leaped out when we arrived and came back in seconds with a doctor. They seemed to know each other because they were using first names.

A couple of people in hospital whites came out with a gurney. They put her on it and wheeled her inside. Eddie and the doctor followed. The rest of us sat there in the truck. No one said a word. Finally Eddie came back out and said that she was going to be all right. She was in shock and she was hurt, but she would live. Then he went back in, saying he'd call as soon as he could.

I turned to Raz. "Now what?"

"I guess we wait," he said, patting Amanda's hand. She hadn't said a word during the entire scene, but it was clear she was really upset. It was time to get her away from the hospital and back home.

We all nodded to each other and split up to take care of the aftermath. Amanda and Raz drove the rescue team back to the Palace and Jesse and I went over to the Corner Room to let Stan and Moe in on what had happened and to let them know Eddie would be tied up for a while. Eddie must have already called them because they let us in with solemn faces and gave us both coffee. We took it back to the office and tried to drink it. Jesse started to cry again and I did, too. We sat there in silence for some time, trying to let it all sink in.

A couple of hours later, Eddie called with the report: broken arm, broken nose, a dozen stitches to close the cut over her eye. But the good news was she had no concussion or internal injuries.

"Hard head," Jesse said softly.

"Good thing, this time," I nodded.

"Goddamn, I feel so guilty for letting her out of my sight."

"Who knew he would be back? I guess he split from the honeymoon and came back early because he knew we wouldn't expect him."

"I guess so."

I shuddered. "Damn him."

"I'm going to find him and kill him," Jesse said, getting to his feet.

"He's probably not even in the country anymore. He knows he's a dead man if any of us ever see him again." I sighed. "What do we do now?"

"We help her get over this," Jesse said, slumping back into the chair.

We nodded and silently got on with the day.

***

R.E. slept for the better part of the next day. Then she checked out. She couldn't afford to stay in the hospital any longer than that since it was all coming out of her pocket. She didn't want anyone who hadn't already seen the damage to get a look at her, so that precluded her going back to the Palace. And since her arm was in a cast, she'd need someone to look after her for a while. Eddie seemed to know more about taking care of someone during an emergency than any of us, so we all decided she should stay with him at his place on I.O.O.F. Street.

Over the next few days, she told Eddie the whole story. He was pale as he relayed it to me on a break at work. She said she felt so stupid for letting him sneak up on her as easily as he had. There was one moment at the wedding when she'd been overcome by it all. She was heading for the well house for a ceremonial bucketful of water when she felt the gun in her ribs. He forced her to go with him to the clearing behind the house.

"Why didn't she yell for help?" I asked.

"Oh, you know her. She had to protect us all. And it's true, if anyone had wandered into that, Cole would have shot them. Anyone. Even Amanda. And with the music and all, no one would have heard her call for help, anyway." Eddie sat with his face half turned away. "He didn't say anything while they were walking. He made her kneel down with her hands under her knees when they got there and then he started rambling, saying over and over again that all of our left wing bullshit was wrong headed and would amount to nothing, that the far right would rule and we ought to see that and get on their side while we still could. Then she said he smiled at her like he'd just gotten an idea and said that it would be better not to kill her, but to mark her and leave her alive as a reminder of what he could do. She knew what was coming but her hands and arms were numb from the position he'd made her sit in so she was slow getting to her feet." He stopped for breath, eyes shut. "He pistol-whipped her across the face but she kept trying to fight back. Sounds like he was playing with her, letting her get a few feet away then dragging her back. He put the pistol away so he could use both hands. He kept hitting her and kicking her and cursing her and us and everyone at the Palace, me and Jesse especially." He paused before he went on. "She said he seemed oblivious, almost ecstatic."

"Yeah, I saw that smile."

"Bastard." Eddie groaned and asked, "Could you do one more day here? I've got to get some sleep. My head is killing me."

"Sure, no problem."

I went back to work, grateful for every task I could lay my hands on so I wouldn't have to think about what Eddie had told me. The next morning when I went to see her, she was so matter of fact about everything. I could barely look at her. One eye was still swollen shut. It looked like there was a baseball behind it, pushing the lid out. A railroad of stitches closed the cut over it. The other eye was open but the white was completely red. Her cheekbones were bruised and so was her mouth and you could see clearly exactly where his hands had been around her neck from the dark spots. Her hair was braided to keep it away from her face. You could see more dark spots around her wrists and along her arms. Small talk has never been my strong suite, so I didn't say anything at first.

"I understand if you can't look at me. He said he wanted to make me ugly. Did a damn good job of it."

"You're not ugly."

"Well, I have looked better."

For some reason, I laughed. She did, too, and sighed, "Well, damn him. I'm alive. We'll see if I can live well. Best revenge, you know."

"Was that one of Fitzgerald's lines?"

"It's the title of a book about him, Zelda, and their friends."

"Why does Jesse call you that sometimes?"

"One of the first real conversations we ever had, we were talking about artists and their muses and I said that with the exception of Cassady, most muses go pretty much unknown except for the characters and the songs and such they inspire. I said that didn't seem fair and that they should be remembered for their own lives. That was when he started using the nickname."

I nodded and we listened to the neighbors mowing the lawn for a while.

Then she said, "Private language. I guess I do a lot of that with people. I started to tell you once about the healing that I tried to do with Coleman. It's called Tantric meditation. I'd look into his mind, see what he was seeing, and try to visualize it being calmer. The pictures I saw every time, though, just got further out of whack and it got harder and harder to put them in any kind of order."

"So, that was why you said something about the frame?"

She nodded. "It was one mental image he always had, or some variation of it. Probably that big window in that damned house. He was too guarded at first for me to get to him. When you showed up, it gave me a chance to do it. When you grabbed the gun, I put all my energy into visualizing it completely, exactly as I saw it that last time we did it. That's why he screamed when he turned around. He knew I had him and that I was going to bust it all to hell."

I had no idea what she talking about really, but I had seen Cole's reaction. She did stagger him. Whatever it was they used to do, whether anyone else believed in it or understood it, had been one of the reasons he'd been with R.E. from the start and at the last, the only one. When she took her psychic support away, it had been the one blow she could deliver and she had hurled it as straight and true as the rock she'd thrown.

"Are you going to press charges?" I asked, getting back to the material plane.

She did her best to give me her old level stare. I looked away. She went on, "There's no way in hell he would be found guilty and you and I both know that. I'm not going to go through getting beat up again in the courts. I know how the system works. And there's a lot of family history that would get dragged out again. No, I'm very patient. I can wait. There'll be another day."

I nodded in understanding, one marginal person to another. Then I changed the subject. "Listen, what do you want to do about your apartment?"

"Oh, yeah. Well, no need to stay, I guess. Besides, I just remembered. I never paid the rent for this month. I'll bet the landlord will try to keep my stuff. I don't really want any of the furniture, but my trunk is there. Could you talk to him, see if you can get that back? It's just personal things he'd throw away anyway, but I don't want him handling them."

"Of course."

"Troy," she said, "I am going to be okay." She smiled. It was a pretty ghastly sight.

There was a knock on the front door. I answered it and saw it was the doctor.

"Hi. Is Rachel awake?" he asked. "My name's John Watts. I'm the doctor who admitted her to the emergency room. Thought I'd drop in and see how she's doing since she had to check out so quickly."

"Yeah, I remember you. Come on in."

We shook hands, I introduced myself and he said, "I'm an old friend of Eddie's. Just started working here about a month ago."

"I was wondering why you guys seemed to know each other."

"We go way back. I was up in Albany. Hated it. Eddie's been writing me about Texas so I thought I try it out for a while. Flow Memorial's okay. So how is she?"

"Okay, I guess. We were just talking."

"About what happened?"

"Yeah."

"That's a good sign. Man, I've never seen anyone beaten that badly spring back as fast as she has." We walked back to the bedroom. "How's the patient today?" he smiled.

"Gorgeous, as always," she said.

"Actually, I can already see some improvement." He set his doctor bag down on the bed. It wasn't the usual black leather one. Instead it was khaki and had some letters and numbers on it. He saw us looking at it and said, "Korea. I was there. That's where I met Eddie."

"Really?" R.E. asked.

"He hasn't talked about it, has he." It wasn't a question.

"No, never."

"Well, don't tell him I mentioned it. He'll talk when he's ready."

We nodded in agreement then I kissed her gingerly on the one unbruised place I could find on her face and left: more mysteries. Well, all in good time.

Eddie and I mopped and scrubbed up R.E.'s old place, paid the rent for the few days of May she'd technically lived there, but even then the landlord wasn't going to hand over the deposit or release her trunk. Eddie lost it. He picked the guy up by his shirtfront with one hand and held him against the wall with his feet dangling off the floor by several inches and in a low harsh whisper suggested that he be more reasonable. Considering that the guy was not much smaller than Eddie, this was a formidable enough display to help him change his mind. Within a few minutes, the landlord was going for his checkbook and we got her trunk and the entire deposit back, as well as the dribble of rent.

She stayed at Eddie's for a few weeks. R.E. went very non-verbal during that period of time, going deep down into her own well. Then one evening late in May when I went to visit, she and Eddie were in the kitchen. They were smoking one and drinking wine. Her face looked almost normal now and the cast was finally off her arm. "Troy," she asked, "is my old room at the Palace still open?"

"Of course."

"It's time to go back to work and get on with my life."

Eddie poured us all a round and we touched rims: mismatched Mason jars full of Greek red. There never was a finer toast.

"Je m'enracine ici."

Icarian colonist, Texas, winter of 1849, after
most settlers abandoned their site
and returned to New Orleans

V.

Racines

It was summer again. Eddie was working extra hours to give the rest of the crew some time off, Raz toiled away in Dallas on a construction job, piling up overtime and money, and Amanda was getting bigger. They had taken Coleman's old room since it was the largest and needed the most spiritual fumigation. It did seem to help, having her calm pregnant self there, but I worried that the kid, an internal sponge floating inside her, might soak up a few of Cole's traits. No one else thought out loud about it, so I didn't give voice to my concerns in hopes that nothing would come of them.

R.E., in the process of reemerging as her pre-Coleman self, moved out of the roof room into what had been Raz and Amanda's, painted it lilac and white, and plastered the walls with Jesse's photos and anti-war posters. She also started reading the paper aloud to us, getting us talking about what was going on more often than we had been lately. She didn't push it, though. She wasn't strident. But when she pointed out the events of the world around us, it became clear to me that we had been living a rather isolated life in so many ways in Denton. Our little family-to-be was so intent on their private life that the world around them didn't seem to matter much, and the musicians were so unskilled verbally, we all wished they hadn't started talking seriously on the rare occasions they did. But whenever Eddie or John were around, the politics were heavier. R.E. told me once that she preferred talking to them about what was happening in the world rather to most of the people in the house. "Present company excepted, of course," she said.

I smiled. "Not that I'm so well-versed."

"Well, you do read the papers now and then. But all we've got is only our generation's experience between us. Eddie and John have been through so much more. They've got more perspective on things." Then she went quiet suddenly and I knew that the conversation had ended. She was still dealing with everything that had happened to her. At her insistence, Jesse had taken another nude shot of her: the same pose except her hair covered the opposite breast. She framed it and the previous one side by side: "Before" and "After" were written in Amanda's best calligraphy above them. I'd see her now and then looking at them and absently rubbing the scar on her eyebrow, her unreadable poker face hiding her thoughts. Neither Jesse nor Eddie pressed her when she was like that, and of course, neither did I. But they were being careful with her for their own reasons.

Jesse was working hard on the relationship, trying not to be possessive of R.E. or jealous of Eddie. Eddie, true to his word, seemed much cooler with the arrangements; besides, he saw other women now and then, as did Jesse. That was fine with RE. She told me once that she wasn't sure if she could ever trust anyone enough to be in an exclusive relationship again.

"Ever?"

"Well, okay, maybe in thirty or forty years."

I laughed. "Sure."

"No, really. I am so content these days to be with Eddie or with Jesse when they're not with someone else, or just on my own. It's just right. I'm not interested in adding any more guys to the equation, though. I don't know anyone else I trust enough to go to bed with." She passed me a number.

We were out on the porch at the Palace. I suddenly realized it was the Solstice, more than a quarter year since I'd seen Claire. "I'm glad you're happy."

She turned to me. "You will be, too, when Claire gets back."

"You know something I don't know?"

She smiled. "I've believed all along that she'll find a way to come back."

And about two days later, she walked into my room.

Sometimes when you write down the way things happened, exactly as they happened, events seem contrived or too convenient to have been real, but if you were to transcribe anyone's life, you would find those nexuses everywhere: the chance corner turned, the old friend encountered. That's the way it was that morning. I knew she was back before she even got to the door. I could smell the patchouli, the particular way it always smelled on her dark skin. She set her bags down with a thump. Her hair was longer, down to her shoulders, and she was really dark. She was wearing jeans, sandals and a T-shirt that said "Bernie's Deli - Brooklyn."

"Well," she smiled, "no kiss?"

There were a few.

When we had caught up on the initial wordless lovemaking, I opened a bottle of red I'd been saving from the wedding. We drank out of the bottle and kissed some more. Then I asked her, "So, how did you manage it?"

"I came on a student visa before, so I just got it renewed. English Lit majors are an easy way to come in to just about any university. The authorities were actually nice about it since it wasn't my idea to go back to France. I'll take some classes at N.T.S.U. again." She fished out her cigarettes and lit one: the tarry smell of Gauloise. I hadn't realized how much I had missed it. Of all of us, only Jesse and the other musicians smoked tobacco, but nothing as strong as hers.

"Your English is still great. Better than ever."

"I tutored for a short time while I was working at the bakery. Then one day I got into a fight with my father. He said he was going to arrange for me to be married and to settle down. I didn't oppose him directly, I just let him think I would obey. I talked with my mother that night." She exhaled and I paused the story for some more kissing. She sat up, leaning against the wall as she continued. "Mamére said her family had done the same to her. She told me that, in her way she loves my father now, but that she didn't want me to have to go through what she had. She couldn't give me much money. He never let her have any that she didn't have to account for but she had ways of putting little bits aside. I left that night."

"When was that?"

"Not long ago. I went to Marseilles first to make some money and arrange for my passage and visa. After I got to New York, I started hitchhiking. I didn't want to stop to call or write. I just wanted to get here as soon as I could. Tell me," she said as she turned serious, "what happened to R.E.? I couldn't ask. Was it an accident?"

I gave her a condensed version of the story and her dark eyes got darker. She got up and paced, naked and angry. I was too taken with the sight to share her mood.

"That bastard! And no one knows where he is?"

"No. But it's done now. He's had what he thinks was his revenge and she's moving on with her life. Come here. I know you've just heard about it, but we're all trying to put it behind us, and this is our reunion."

She smiled and returned to bed, where we stayed for some time.

A couple of nights later Eddie, R.E., and I were back at our normal late night shift. It was almost closing time and she was in the office checking the market list. Eddie was starting the grill cleanup and I was wiping tables. An older man came in and sat at one of the booths. Something about him seemed vaguely familiar. He was tall and spare with the rough hands of someone who's done a lot of work outside. He took his Stetson off and hung it carefully on the post of the seat. He didn't have that farmer forehead, the one so pale in contrast to the rest of the sunburned face. Instead, he was tanned and leathery from hairline to neck. Although he was mostly gray now, it was clear he'd once been redheaded. His clear brown eyes took me and Eddie and the room in with a couple of sweeps. I went over and asked, "Would you like something?"

"Coffee, if there's any left. Looks like you're closing up."

Eddie turned and said, "Just made a fresh pot."

"Black, please."

I was heading over to the counter to pick it up when R.E. walked out. She was about to say something to Eddie when she stopped in her tracks and stared at the stranger.

"Evenin', Rachel," he said, his face composed and neutral.

She stood there for a few more seconds then picked up the cup without taking her eyes off the guy. "Evenin', Dado." She spaced the two syllables evenly, consonant and vowel, consonant and vowel, making it sound sweetly childlike and somehow foreign at the same time.

Eddie and I looked at the two of them then at each other. Of course: when R.E. went over and put the cup down on the table, it was obvious. She sat down in the booth across from him and he reached out and took her hands, studying her face, assessing the damage. She didn't flinch. She just sat there, the story written plainly in stitches and bone rearrangement.

"Well, it doesn't look as bad as I'd imagined it would."

"Better all the time."

"Who did the sewing?"

"Guy named John, friend of Eddie's. He works at Flow Memorial."

"He did a good job. Your nose looks okay, too. I was afraid when you said it was out of kilter that you were down-playing the damage."

"No, wouldn't do any good. I knew you'd see it eventually."

"Why didn't you come up home to tell me?"

"I wasn't sure how you'd react to..."

"Your being with a fucking van der Veer," he said, his eyes narrowing, his mouth setting in a straight line. I found myself hoping suddenly that he was never pissed off at me.

"Like I told you, I was already involved when I found out."

"And too proud to admit you'd made a mistake. And you'd already given your word and..."

"Yeah, well," she interrupted. "I paid."

Turning now to Eddie, he asked, "Did he?"

"No, I'm afraid we missed him. The first priority was to get her to the hospital. By the time we had a chance to check out his whereabouts, he was gone again."

"Well, we just have to wait until he comes back," he said, turning back to RE. "And he will. They never stray from their territory for long. He'll get careless one these days and one of us will get him." It was said so softly, so matter of factly, yet it was a promise that either he or someone he knew would take revenge on Cole, likely lethal revenge. I looked at Eddie. He was smiling.

The man stood up then and so did R.E. They hugged and it looked like she was crying a little. But she wiped her eyes and turned back to us. "Sorry for the courtesy lapse. Guys, this is my dad, Sam Flanagan."

We walked over and shook hands.

"Eddie Nichols."

"Troy Jacobson." Sam's shake was firm. He used it as an opportunity to study eyes, holding the other person's grip a scant second longer than a normal North Texas shake required. I realized as he released my hand that was the first time I'd ever heard Eddie use his last name, and it was the first time I'd said my own in a long time.

He looked at me closely. "I knew some Jacobsons in Little Creek. Audrey Jacobson and her sister Pearl."

"Audrey was my mom."

His eyes went kind. "She had a damned hard life but she was always a decent woman in spite of it."

It was nice of him to say that. Few people would have been as kind about her having been the town whore. That's what she had been called after I came along, and then she had to be to feed us. But that's history.

Eddie got us all a coffee, flipped the OPEN sign over, and we sat at the booth, R.E. and her dad on one side, me and Eddie on the other. Sam seemed curious about both of us, asking questions and then listening as we answered, assessing us in the same calm way he had R.E.'s facial wounds.

"How'd you come to know the fellow who stitched Rachel up?"

"Korea."

R.E. and I glanced at each other.

Sam nodded. "So you did your turn in the bucket. Never had the honor myself," he said, his tone flat, just a touch of sarcasm on the word "honor", enough to let us know he didn't mean that seriously.

"I was a medic."

"One of those hospitals in tents?"

"No, closer to the front. Evac. I loaded them on the choppers."

He nodded. "Did you join up?"

"No, I was drafted. I filed as a C.O. when I was 18. Raised by Quakers up in Pennsylvania. Thought that would be enough to prove it. But they needed people and refused the deferment. The guy who was in charge of assignments thought it would be real funny to make me a medic."

"Those red crosses make pretty clear targets."

"That they do," he said quietly.

Sam nodded again: 'nough said.

R.E. was looking at Eddie now. They crossed glances and he shook his head in a subtle "no." Sam watched this exchange as closely as he had everything else so far. I jerked around suddenly, a real shuddery one. "Excuse me," I said as I got up to leave. I was on my feet to make my getaway when Sam asked, "Could you get me another cup, as long as you're heading that way?"

Tricky way to get me to sit down again. I managed to refill for him without getting it all over us both then I took the pot back and started the counter cleanup. He let me be and turned back to talk a little more with Eddie and R.E. while the Snake worked me over. It hadn't been that pronounced in a while. Maybe it was thinking about Little Creek and my mom again, those bad old days. I was only six when she died and my aunt took me to live with her in White Settlement. I barely remembered my mother. After fifteen minutes or so, Sam drained the cup and stood. "Rachel, you ought to come up and visit when you can. Your grandma's not as strong as she used to be, though she'd be the last to admit it. That spell of bronchitis last winter almost carried her off."

"I will. Soon as I get some time, I promise."

"How much for the java?"

"On the house."

He nodded then started for the door. Looking at me and back at Eddie, he said to RE, "Bring your friends. We don't get much company and you know how we all love a party."

"Is she still making that god-awful Mustang grape wine?"

"Every summer," he smiled. Nodding at me and Eddie, he said, "Nice to meet you boys." Then he put his hat on carefully and left. Somewhere in time, a saloon door creaked.

"Man," Eddie grinned. "Why in hell have you kept this guy a secret for so long! I mean," he smiled, "he's like everything I ever thought the West would be about when I was a kid growing up back East. Man of few words. That face. That voice! Even the walk! It was like--man, I'm speechless. Knocked out!"

RE smiled. "I'm glad you like him. He liked you guys, too."

"How do you know?"

"Well, he talked to you. If he didn't like you, he would have had his say to me and then left."

I was still shaking. R.E. came over and put her arms around me.

"I don't know why it's so bad tonight," I muttered.

She smiled, "Funny we're from the same part of the country."

I shrugged and she moved away, saying, "I'll take care of the cleanup."

For some reason that irritated me, "I can handle it. I'm not a cripple, you know."

"I know. Easy." R.E. leveled with me as she always had, cutting me no pity-slack. "It's just worse sometimes than others and this is one of them. But don't snap at us about it. We're family."

"Okay, okay." The mood passed. "Sorry. I just don't like to be reminded about my mom and that fucking little town. I hate that place." And I hated to think about my aunt, too.

"Well, I wasn't so fond of the town I grew up in either," she said.

Eddie ran his hand back through his hair. "Do any of us have that so-called normal family you used to see on TV?"

R.E. said, "Well, Raz does, but they're all out in California. TV-normal, though, no. They're second-generation Big Sur free thinkers. He doesn't see them much, but as far as I know they're all okay with each other." We sat and ran silently through the list in a collective pause, eyes glancing at each other or away when we pondered people not in the room at the moment: Jesse (no - we weren't sure about details, but he'd always called himself an orphan), Amanda and Claire (yes, both had parents and siblings, but they were temporarily estranged), Stan and Moe (at one time yes, but not after they came out), Coleman (definite no.) The musicians, well, who knows? They rarely discussed anything other than music, dope, the ladies, and living only in the fabled "now."

"I wonder if there is such a thing," R.E. said. "What about you, Eddie?"

"Well, I was raised by Quakers, like I told Sam. Unofficially adopted. My folks were killed in a car wreck when I was about four. They were Oakies, driving around from state to state, trying to find jobs. I was thrown clear of the crash and lucky for me, knocked out so

I didn't see it burn up. They had just started working on the Harmon's farm." He smiled. "They were good people. They said it was not only their duty, but their pleasure to have me to raise since they couldn't have kids of their own. They did try to contact my folks' families but couldn't because there was nothing left after the car burned. All they knew were their names and mine."

"I'm sorry about your folks," R.E. said.

"Oh, it was a long time ago. I guess you could say I never really knew them. And I figured I was lucky that they raised me. Better them than the orphanage route. They both died, one about a month after the other, while I was in Korea. I think my not getting the deferment hurt them both. They'd always believed that if you played by the rules, the establishment would too. When I didn't get the C.O. status and got drafted, they couldn't believe it. The whole thing just took the wind out of them."

We finished the cleanup quietly, each of us feeling the circles of our lives extending, touching, overlapping the ones that had gone before.

"If you want some time off to visit your dad, just say when," Eddie said.

"I really want you two to come along. Claire, too. You should get to know my family and their friends."

Eddie smiled. "Wouldn't miss it for the world."

"Okay. Troy?"

"I don't know. Like I said, I really hate that part of the country."

She nodded and looked out the window. "Well, think about it."

I shrugged. The Scaly One had started to let me go a little. As I was walking away from the cafe, I turned back to see if R.E. was staying or going. I couldn't see either her or Eddie because the lights were out so I headed back to the Palace slowly, hoping the Snake would ease up before I got home. Yeah. Home. Where the heart is. Where Claire is. Where I lived. Who knew how long it would last and where we would all wind up, but at that moment, the Palace was the only home I had ever known. And that was all right. I smiled and tilted my head back towards the starry sky just in time to see two shooters blaze across in a long streaky show. Okay: if R.E. needed a backup for her journey return to that little town, I'd go along. It was rare that R.E. asked for anything that required any kind of psychic work on my part. I thought about her face, the damage that Coleman had done. No, it would never look the same. Her nose was flatter across the bridge and a little out of line and the scar on her forehead was still an angry gash with tiny railroad marks across it. None of us knew anything in those days about plastic surgery and couldn't have afforded it if we did. Still, it hadn't decreased the intangible combination of elements that make a woman attractive, as Cole had intended to do. Instead, in some quirk of cosmic justice, she had become more intriguing than before. There was something about her now, a mystery. Bar fight in Tangier? Running guns in Mexico? Standing against the cops for some worthy cause? Good love gone bad? She sensed people who didn't know her watching her, trying to guess how the damage had happened. Greeting the stares with an oblique enigmatic smile and faraway eyes, tilting her head back and to the side so they could get a good look, she'd stare directly at them until they turned away or asked. And if they did ask, she would give them a different story every time or say nothing at all.

I was back in the yard by then, under my tree, my favorite contemplation spot. I could see Amanda and Claire in the kitchen window, a warm yellow vignette of hippie domesticity, talking and laughing with Raz, dishing up plates of something, probably red beans and rice from the smell. If this was all that family was to be for me, then I was content. Some people never even have that much, and Cole had nothing now. He was alone wherever he was with his mousey wife and his shattered frame and all that cold, cold money. There was some justice in that.

***

And so it was, about ten days later, on a scorching, clear day, we were on the road to Honey Springs, the little town where R.E. had grown up. She and Claire were in her truck and Eddie and I followed in his car. Jesse had been invited but had turned it down. A promising gig at the Vulcan Gas Company in Austin had come up. That was a high visibility club and the band was cooking those days with Vance and the new guy TyRonne both on guitar. Ty, as we called him, was a crazy Creole guitar wizard from LaFayette who had recently blown into town. Jesse had had some reservations about him becoming a fixture with

Texas Weather, but the fragile chemistry had worked so far and it had gotten them twice as many gigs as they'd been getting, so he was going along with it. Ty was almost too much, sometimes, with his theatrical ways and his tendency to steal any loose leads. Jesse mumbled about "personnel problems" off and on: too much talent too close together. So, as much as he wanted to come along and as left out as he felt, he had a lot on his hands trying to keep Texas Weather from blowing clean out to sea. And, he confided to me as he was helping load the drum kit, he hated family scenes because he'd never had one and he had no idea how to act around other people's. "I can fake a tune," he said, "but not a conversation."

Once we were in Fort Worth we turned out into the flat dry part of the world where, as it says in the Fort Worth city motto, the west begins. The towns grew smaller and further apart. Eddie and I drove in silence mostly, studying the two lane blacktop, the tar paper roofs on the small clapboard houses, the last gasp of summer truck farms picked almost clean, rusted cars on blocks beside porches, kids in underwear playing in plastic pools or old tractor tires full of sand in the yards. Black kids on the small side of town, white kids on the other.

Honey Springs was the kind of place you would pass by without stopping unless you were visiting someone or you needed gas and a pit stop. We turned off the highway and worked our way through small tree-lined streets to the center of town. There was an old two-story red brick courthouse on a grassy main square with stores around it on all four sides: grocery, laundry, feed store, drug store, diner, post office, and a garage. That last one was where R.E. headed and parked. I noticed that both she and Claire had thrown on men's work shirts and tied them in front. It didn't downgrade their gorgeousness but it did cover up a little more of it since they had been wearing nothing but tank tops and cutoffs for the road trip because of the heat. Eddie and I parked beside them and followed them inside. It took a few seconds for my eyes to adjust from the outside glare. Sam was under a car that was up on the rack, tugging at something, his hands and forearms covered with grime. He turned when R.E. said, "Dado?" and smiled, "Well, hello, Rachel. You made good time."

She smirked.

"You didn't speed?" he grinned.

"Only when the cops weren't around."

There were a couple of younger men who were working on another car. Eyeing R.E. and Claire cautiously, casting sideways glances, they mumbled hello. Sam finally got the part loose that he'd been trying to pull, set it down on his workbench, and wiped his hands. R.E. walked over and kissed a clean patch on his cheek. Sam nodded us and turned to Claire.

I said, "Oh, this is my friend, Claire."

She smiled and said, "'allo."

The two guys looked at each other again then back at the engine, sighing.

Sam said, "I planned to be done by now, but this job is taking longer than I thought it would. Damn bolt was rusted solid."

"Need some help?" Eddie asked.

"Know much about cars?"

"Some. How'd that oil pan get busted?"

"Rough roads. Happens a lot out here."

"Well, if it won't screw up your insurance..."

Sam snorted at that and said to R.E., "Well, you can watch him get greasy or go on out to the house. Mom's been talking about nothing else since you called and said you were coming."

She smiled and left with Claire. I was stuck in one of those male ritual situations. I had never been the least bit interested in automotive science yet I didn't want to look like I wasn't. But my ignorance was bone-deep. It was suffocatingly hot in there and I could feel sweat pouring down my back and into the waistband of my jeans, plastering my T-shirt to my body. I'd pulled my hair back into a loose tail earlier but it was stuck to my neck. Sam nodded to an old fridge in the corner and said, "Help yourself to a pop drink."

I opened the door and finally chose a Coke, not my favorite, but the only drinkable one there amid the Dr. Pepper, Orange Crush, Chocolate Soldier, and Big Red. That last one was a nasty Texas favorite that tasted something like what the liquid in hummingbird feeders must be like. Someone in the shop clearly had a sweet tooth.

They set to work and had the job done in about half an hour, working together. Just as they were finishing, a spatter of grease hit Eddie squarely on the chest.

Sam asked, "You want to change? I got a clean work shirt in the office."

He thought about it for a second but Sam had already gone to bring it in. When he came back, Eddie looked at the ground then pulled his T-shirt off. Sam, the two helpers and I saw the wound clearly, the entrance scar on his belly and the larger exit wound by his right shoulder blade. Sam didn't ask about it but one of the helpers wasn't as prairie polite. "What the hell happened to you? You get shot or somethin'?"

Sam admonished him with a glance. "Ought not to ask a man about his scars. He might not want to say."

"No, it's alright. Happened about ten years ago, up in North Dakota, just outside of reservation territory," Eddie said quietly to the other guy as he turned to wash his hands in a basin on a side table. Sam handed him a cake of gritty gray soap and a faded towel. "Thanks. Short story, really. Drunk guy tried to kill me. I got the gun away from him, shot him. Judge agreed it was self defense." He wiped the back of his neck and his chest off with the towel then put the shirt on. "I was in the hospital for a couple of days then I left town before anyone could change their minds."

Sam nodded and smiled. He washed up, too, and paid his helpers. Then we walked outside and he locked up. He whistled as he saw Eddie's car.

"Very sweet. You keep her running yourself?"

"Don't trust her to anyone else."

They walked around Mariah, sharing a little more car talk, opening the hood so Sam could admire the engine. I felt a distinct pang of jealousy: the left-out little brother, no bullet wound, no mechanics chops, no cool car of my own. Then Eddie closed the hood, Sam headed for his truck and we followed him through town out onto the blacktop.

"Was it true about how you got that scar?"

"Yeah, it's true. Funny, huh. Go all the way through Korea and the worst thing that happened to me, physically anyway, was dysentery." He suddenly had his thoughtful face on, remembering something. Or someone. "Get back to the States and damn near get killed in a bar."

"How did you get in the fight?"

"Some other time."

I nodded. Interesting how he was opening up to Sam more than to any of us about both Korea and his wound. But at least he was starting to talk. John had said that was a good sign.

After about fifteen miles on the blacktop, we turned onto a gravel road that led to a packed dirt trail. We followed that for about fifty yards or so then came to the house. It was an old place, two- story clapboard, with a wide front porch, a barn and garage, a well out back with a cover like the one at the Palace and trees all around. As we walked onto the porch, a hot breeze knocked some dry chinaberries loose and they clattered down its tin roof. June bugs buzzed and chickens peered around the corner of the porch, gossiping in chicken-speak about the strangers. Sam opened the screen door and held it for us. Old country houses, smells and sounds: in the living room, I was greeted by the scent of thick gummy varnish on dark wood furniture, the buildup of years of waxing and polishing in alternating humidity and drought. Next, the smell of quilts aired in the strong sun after being stored in cedar or mothballs for the summer: they'd been brought out to be folded and serve as pallets for overnight guests or cranky kids who needed naps. Wallpaper paste drying between paper and wall, worn linoleum flooring in the kitchen that had been recently mopped with Pine-Sol, polished wooden floorboards that give a little independently of each other with characteristic creaks in different places in each room, fresh brewed iced tea, biscuits baking, a radio set to the local country station. Then we came into the kitchen. R.E. and Claire were there with some other women, and there were about a dozen people in the yard. Eddie and I glanced at each other and Sam asked, "Would ya'll like to freshen up before supper?"

"Yeah."

"Rachel, why don't you take your things up to the bedrooms."

"Okay, Dado."

As the four of us headed upstairs, I asked her, "Who are all these people?"

"Friends of dad's and my grandmother's. They're cool."

"Really?"

"Yeah. Old Lefties. You'll see."

We took advantage of the moment to smoke a quick one and to change, going into the small bathroom two by two and washing the road dust off, changing into clean clothes. R.E. put on another one of her long loose skirts, a dark green one and one of her Mexican blouses. It was still sultry hot, so she wound her braid into a coil on the back of her head, securing it with long black old-fashioned pins from the dresser drawer. Claire also chose a long skirt, a black one that fit closely without being impossible to move in and a striped black and white blouse: very French. Eddie and I weren't as finely decked out of course: clean jeans and T-shirts were all we needed. His said, "No more Dicks in the White House." Mine was from Oat Willie's, the finest head shop in Austin: "Onward through the fog." We had brought them along for the road, but since R.E. had said the folks downstairs were cool, well, why not fly our freak flags?

R.E. introduced us to the people in the kitchen. They looked like any bunch of folks you'd see in any farming community: plain clothes, plain faces, ordinary names. So you would expect the inside to be as straight as the outside, but when they saw Eddie's T-shirt, there were lots of smiles.

"Where'd you git that?" one guy asked.

"Denton."

"I'd kindly like to have one o' those. Sure would put some noses outta joint around the courthouse, wouldn't it, Sam?"

"It would. You kids like a beer or something?"

He sniffed suspiciously and grinned, "Smells like they've already had the somethin'."

I held my breath for a second and avoided everyone's eyes but R.E. smiled and said, "Yeah, and we didn't bring enough for everyone. Especially not enough for you, Rafe." She walked over and hugged him. "There ain't enough weed in the world for that."

He laughed and kissed her cheek, "Rachel, it's good to see you, girl. You sure have grown. I swear you're as tall as Sam."

"But better looking'," she said.

Sam set some bottles and glasses down on the table and wagged a finger at her. "No bragging."

Then we heard a thin clear voice from the back porch. "Rachel Evangeline, you come out here and visit with me."

"Evangeline?" Eddie grinned, his eyes shining.

She shut her eyes tightly then glared at the three of us. "Never, ever tell anyone at the Palace that name or I swear..."

"Rachel Evangeline Flanagan, you get yourself out here."

"That's the full name, Rach. You'd better git," Rafe said. She sighed, ducked her head in mock obedience, and went out the back door.

Rafe turned to us and to then back to Sam. All the play went out of his expression. Maybe he was one of the people Sam had alluded to at the Corner Room that night. "You're right. It doesn't look as bad as I imagined it might when you first told me about it. She seems not to have lost her spunk, though. That's good."

Sam smiled thoughtfully, "She's like her mother in that way. Doesn't know how to be a victim."

There were nods and beers were opened and motioned upwards in a silent toast. Eddie was having one, but neither Claire nor I did. We motioned along, anyway.

Sam asked the two of us, "Would you like a beer or a whiskey? Or, if you are made of sterner stuff than I, you could sample some of my mother's homemade wine."

Rafe shuddered, "That nasty stuff. I don't see why you let her keep making it."

"Let her?"

"Well, you know what I mean. She's almost 90 now and she ought not to be drinkin' it anymore."

"Could be that wine that keeps her going.'"

Claire and I wandered out for a sample and to meet the woman who made it. Eddie stayed back in the kitchen, talking to the folks there about possible Democratic candidates, other than Humphrey.

R.E. was sitting in a porch swing beside a very old woman, her arm around the frail shoulders. The body seemed to be the only frail thing about her. She had blazing clear blue eyes and silver white hair coiled in a way very similar to R.E.'s. Her cheekbones were prominent and the fine skin stretched over them was spackled with hundreds of tiny lines. Her voice was steady and solid but definitely in the treble range. She smiled at us and R.E. introduced us.

"Troy, Claire, this is my grandmother, Gwendolyn Millet-Flanagan. And these are two of my best friends in the world, Troy Jacobson and Claire St. Aubin."

"Please call me Gwen," she said as we all shook hands.

Gwen's eyes lit up when Claire said hello and within minutes they fell into speaking French with R.E. I wandered off to the side of the porch where there was a small table loaded with cakes and pies and several unlabeled bottles of red wine. One of them was open. I poured a glass and sipped. It had a character all its own, a character you would run from if you met its human equivalent in a dark alley: rough, crude, and raw. It was probably the youngest wine I'd ever tasted but it would do. I poured a smaller amount for Claire and carried it over to her.

"I see you like my wine," Gwen said to me.

"It's unique."

She laughed and said, "How polite."

Claire crossed her eyes when she took the first swig but gamely hung in there. "It is very, "she gasped, "dry."

Sour was more like it, but after the first glass it seemed to get better.

A few more people arrived then we all went inside to the room with the most tables and chairs. Sam got everyone's attention when all the dishes and plates and bowls had been uncovered and set out. I thought for a second he was going to say grace, and in a way, he did.

"Okay, okay, settle down for just a moment, if you please." His brogue had grown a little more pronounced with each beer. He raised his bottle and lifting it three times said, "One is for Maggie, one is for Rachel, and one is for all those who went before. This land is your land." Eddie and I glanced at each other and smiled at the last line; we knew what it was from but he seemed as surprised as I was to hear it as a kind of benediction. Everyone raised their bottles or glasses high and clinked the rims and we settled in to eating: fried chicken, baked ham, fresh black-eyed peas, biscuits, cornbread and homemade yeast rolls, bowls of potato salad, plates of freshly sliced tomatoes, tons of summer vegetables, jars of chow-chow and relish and pickles. I didn't realize how hungry I was until we started. Every time my plate was empty someone would come around and load more onto it and I obligingly tucked into it each time. The talk ceased because the eats were so tasty, but by the time we were all ready for dessert and coffee, it had started up again.

"You know what Sam was talkin' about earlier, this land is your land?" Rafe asked me as we headed out onto the porch, carrying empty plates and bowls on the way. We dropped them off in the kitchen where a group of women were cleaning up and putting away. Three kids were unloading homemade peach ice cream from an old-fashioned hand crank ice cream maker in the yard, and several people were bringing the rest of the desserts to the outside tables from the fridge. The smell of perked coffee drifted out to me and I scanned the array of pies, cakes, cookies, and cobblers.

"I know the song it was from, but I guess the choice of words just surprised me. Never heard it used like that, in a toast."

"Well, you'd have to understand about the history of farm labor unions to really understand the feelin' behind it."

"That's the problem with the young, these days. Don't know their history," another man said.

"Now, Mack."

"I bet you don't even know who wrote that song."

"Woody Guthrie." Sensing the next question, I continued, "Woody was short for Woodrow, as in Woodrow Wilson."

Mack grumbled a little more but seemed mollified for the moment. Sam came out and patted him on the shoulder, "You badgering the young-uns again, Mack?"

I smiled and Rafe said, "No more'n usual, Sam. See, Troy, that's why we call him Mack. The Knife. He's always jabbin' at someone about somethin'."

"Because it needs to be done!" Mack protested.

"We could always count on you to raise hell when it needed to be raised," Sam smiled.

"And even when it didn't," Rafe teased.

Eddie had joined us by then and he asked Rafe, "So was the Populist movement as strong here as it was in the Midwest?"

We settled down on the porch. It was time for stories and histories, tall tales and jokes and family secrets. These sessions began after supper and lasted well into the night, part of the oral tradition of the South. I propped myself against a banister and got comfortable. I had only heard about it from friends; my own family had consisted only of myself and Pearl and I had never experienced this part of the culture personally.

"In some counties," Rafe answered. "But most of us didn't go along with all their ideas. They were for the workingman, alright, but only if he wasn't a Negro, a Catholic or a Jew. But they were for the farmer. And so were we. Back in the 20s, Sam here was part of the movement to get a farm labor union started here in this part of Texas."

"I haven't heard much about it being strong here."

"That's because it went the way of most of them," Sam said. "Popular for a while then it got lost in other movements. See, there were never enough of us to get anything done independently, so we had to go the coalition route. Just got subsumed. Leaders got co-opted."

"Or sent to jail," Gwen said softly from the swing, tuning into our conversation briefly before going back to French.

"Or that," Sam nodded.

A woman passed by and offered us all plates of sweets and cups of coffee. Mack kept looking at us then he asked Eddie, "So what do you do for a livin'?"

"Run a cafe in Denton. He works for me. So does Rachel."

He nodded. "Small businessman. How much you pay the kids?"

"Mack, that's enough," Sam cautioned.

"I'm just askin'. He doesn't have to answer."

Eddie grinned at the old bulldog and said, "More than minimum wage, if that's what you mean. They set their own schedules. I been lookin' into getting some kind of group health insurance but we don't seem to fit into any kind of category that any company will work with so far."

"Why you doin' that?"

Eddie motioned with his shoulder at R.E., who was still on the porch talking with her grandmother and Claire.

He nodded and ducked his head. Eddie had out-righteoused him on that count. Rafe grinned, his eyes shining.

Mack wasn't quiet for long, though. "You been in any o' those marches against the war?"

"No, but John and I got a lot of letters written, phone calls made. I couldn't take off then. There was a lot going on at the cafe and all." He glanced again at R.E., just enough to let Mack know that she had been the focus for our energies at that time.

I guess Sam had let this go on as long as it had to see how we would hold up with his old pals. I had stayed quiet, since it seemed to be between Mack and Eddie mostly. But he didn't let me off for long. He had let the desserts pass in favor of sips from a bottle of whiskey and was getting more aggressive with each swig. "So you just sling hash and write a letter now and then? That's it?" This was aimed at me.

I turned back to him, a little surprised. "I vote. I'm careful how I spend what money I have. I read."

"And that's all?"

"What else should I be doing?"

"Raisin' hell!" He was on his feet by then. A woman in the crowd was watching him closely. She had the concerned look of someone who'd seen him do this speech before. "That's what young people should be doin'! Marchin' on Washington! Demandin' an end to the war! Makin' some goddamned changes in this lop-sided, rich man's society!"

The same woman who had been watching him closely said, "Mack, that's their business. They'll storm the barricades if and when that's what they decide to do. You can't go telling them which fights to choose. They have to decide that for themselves."

Mack growled but finally smiled at her and she smiled back and shook her head: a long-standing love telegraphed in a few gestures. I felt my second pang of envy that day and glanced up at Claire who had been watching the exchange. She smiled and winked.

Mack went on as he sat back down, "It's just so frustratin' to see so many kids who could do so much just sittin' around, havin' a wild time with drugs and music and not takin' on the powers that be. I've heard all the talk about your U-topia," he said, stretching the word deliberately, "and your Haight-Ashbury and Summer of Love, but it's just talk."

R.E. smiled. "Not all of it. There's been a lot going on politically. And you know damn well we don't claim to be full-fledged Utopianists. Okay, most of us don't. We've been down this road before, Mack. Just because I lent you that book by Buckminster Fuller, you've fixated on that and you think that's all we're up to."

He grumbled, "Sounded pretty Utopic to me, though I do kinda like them dome houses of his, and that car that can park sideways. But I don't believe in the whole idea of U-topia. I don't want no part of any group that claims to be the be-all and end-all for every goddamn person. They all say they got all the answers and that just ain't possible. Don't trust no U-topians. No way. And I still think you and your whole generation haven't taken it to the line yet, politically speaking."

Sam said quietly, "Personally, I hope they don't. I wouldn't want them coming up against machine gun fire like those people did in Mexico City in '68. The Democratic Convention was rough enough. Kent and Jackson State, too." He got up to get another beer and went out of his way to pat R.E. on the shoulder. "I'd hate to see this one hurt. Or see her go to jail."

Mack fell quiet for a bit and Eddie stepped in. "From what I've read about Utopias, they may have been heaven for the men that dreamed them up, and they were men, for the most part, but the accounts that exist about life inside, well, they sound more like hell for everyone else."

"You ought to ask my mother about Utopias," Sam said.

Gwen got up from the swing and Sam fetched a rocking chair for her so that she could sit closer to the middle of the group. R.E. went over to sit next to her on the porch and Claire joined me on the steps. "Réunion." She gave it the French pronunciation. "That is another part of our American history that you ought to know but probably don't."

"I've never heard of it," I said.

"I'm not surprised. Its story and the histories of other such communities have been ignored for many years."

"Suppressed, is more like it," Mack said.

Gwen ignored him and said, "The Fouriéristes. The Cabetistes. They were all dreamers."

"Ah, yes. Fourier, the mathematician." Claire said. "I have read a little about him. Some people became curious about his ideas again in 1968. Because of Paris."

"What was it he wrote about, exactly?" I asked.

Gwen said, "Utopia. They were all attempting, in different ways, to experiment with ideas that had begun in Europe, to transplant them here in what they thought might be more fertile, and affordable, soil." She smiled at some private memory. "S'enraciner. They wanted to put down new roots, grow a new and more perfect society. You see, after the Industrial Revolution, there were a great many artisans and middle class shop owners whose crafts or businesses were replaced by machinery. So, if they had enough money to emigrate, they followed Victor Considérant or Étienne Cabet or Charles Fourier and came to America. My grandparents were among them. They came with a group that planned to build a community in North Texas in 1852."

Eddie smiled. "Huh. 1852. Goes to show you. I had no idea the history of communes went back that far."

"Further than that. But they aren't like the way you kids live these days, a lot of people sharing houses and rent and chores. They were a lot more structured," Sam said. "There were many, many rules and regulations. And Fourier's people never got around to actually building the, what was it, Mother?"

"Le Phalanx. It was like a grand mansion, the building laid out according to the ideals of his plan." She paused and then went on, "I would have come to America at that time," Gwen said, "but I don't believe I would have followed Fourier or his disciple, Considérant. You are exactly right about the rules. No, that was a dream for my grandmother."

"What happened to Réunion? Did it succeed?" Claire asked.

"No, they never really began. Land fraud, other difficulties. My grandmother Vivienne, wanted to be a part of the new life, the new way of living. She was the one who talked my grandfather into coming. But they didn't get far with their plans. After La Réunion was dissolved, some others went on to communities further north. But my grandparents didn't have enough money. So they stayed in North Texas and tried to farm. My mother was born in 1856 on the very spot where La Réunion had stood." She smiled. "All that remains is the place in Dallas that is now called Reunion Plaza." She gave the word the Texan twang this time.

"You mentioned the Cabetistes," Eddie said. "That rings a bell. They set up a little commune in Nauvoo Illinois where the Mormons had been, right?"

Sam nodded, "They did pretty well at first, made and sold goods in town, distributed the profits fairly equally amongst themselves."

"What happened with them?" I asked.

Gwen continued the story. "Eaten by their young, in a way. You see, the original Icariens were really just farmers who wanted a new start, nothing more. They were not very stringent politically. That can be dangerous," she smiled as she gestured towards Mack with her slender left foot. He grinned back at her and swigged quietly. Then she continued. "The Young Icariens came later. They'd been on the barricades of the Commune in Paris. Thus, they saw themselves as the only true Communards. When they arrived in Illinois, everywhere they looked they found evidence of the great demon, personal property." She was suitably dramatic and gestured to R.E. to refill her glass. Obeying, R.E. hopped up then returned with a fresh bottle and a glass of her own. "This happened just after the original Icariens had tried to extend their businesses in town. The young people decided they were too pure to co-exist with the old, so they split the community. Literally. They put their cabins on skids, hooked them to ox carts, and moved some miles away."

I laughed at that.

Gwen smiled at me, "It must have been a rather ridiculous sight. Well, the community collapsed from within in that case. Later, some of them decided to move to California. They established Espéranza, the last of the Icarien outposts, even imported snails from back home in France for one of their projects. They say they still live there."

"The people?" Claire asked.

"No," Gwen smiled, "les escargots."

I asked Sam, "You said there were other places earlier than 1852. What were they?"

"Robert Owen began New Harmony in the early 1800s. Every generation or so, sometimes it skips one, a group of idealists decide to withdraw from society and make a more perfect union." He paused to sip his beer and savor that irony. "1820s, 40s, 70s. They followed the depressions and the panics of the national economy. Usually didn't work. This is a capitalist society and you got to have it to get along. Otherwise, one or more of the people in the new and perfect society have to work harder than the others or contribute more of what they brought along with them, there are hard feelings, and the thing collapses from pressures within or pressures without."

Gwen said, "Some do make a mark. The Amana Colonies are still there, but in much different form than the original."

"Amana," Claire asked, "Like the appliances?"

She nodded, "The names are connected but that did not take place until much later. And you children believe you are so radical with your free love. But John Noyes started the Oneida community over a hundred years ago. He had the grand notion of the complex marriage in which you were married to the group, not to a single partner. Didn't take long to fail, of course. People are people," she shrugged.

The stories continued for a long time, Sam and Gwen and Mack and his wife Grace, and Rafe and his wife Maddy taking turns. Now and then our group would pitch in when we remembered something, but mostly we listened. If I could have recorded it, the transcription of the evening's talk would have made a text taken entirely from the margins of the American experience: Sam Fielden and the Haymarket Riots of 1886, Sam Gompers and the American Federation of Labor, the trials of the Scottsboro men and Sacco and Vanzetti, the death of Joe Hill and how all that compared to the trial of the Chicago Seven and the murders of the Black Panthers, the emerging women's and gay rights movements, the various unions and the one big union, the Industrial Workers of the World, the writings and work of John Reed, Louise Bryant, and others, on and on and on.

After three hours or so, I suddenly remembered how much I had eaten and drunk at supper. I excused myself to find the bathroom and as I walked through the dark house, I realized how quiet it was out there. I began to notice a ringing in my ears: the residual buzz of life in town, music, the din of cars and people. I never heard it when I was around urban noise. I went upstairs and settled down for a long meditative movement while I pondered the physics of country plumbing. Sam must have put in a septic tank and dug a well and hooked up a generator because they were too far out in the country for city services. Having indoor plumbing and running water was one of the finest improvements any farm family could make; carrying water for every little chore is backbreaking work. I remembered that much from the time we'd let the Palace water bill slide and it got cut off for a few days before we got hooked up again.

I came out of the bathroom to see Eddie rolling one in the dark. We sat down and smoked in silence. There was a knock and Rafe poked his head in at Eddie's "Yes." R.E. and Claire followed him in and we shared the number.

He grinned at Eddie and said, "Surprised that an old man like me smokes?"

Eddie and R.E. shared a glance; at least in this crowd, Eddie was one of the "young-uns", too.

"I guess I always knew somehow that we weren't the first people in the world to smoke marijuana. I know jazzers do."

"But not farmers. Who do you think grows it for the jazzers?"

I laughed at that. "Yeah, that makes sense."

R.E. smiled, "Rafe was the guy who taught me how to roll one. I was about, what, 16?"

"Sweet 16," he said. "Boy, I thought Sam was going to kick my ass all around the county for that."

"He doesn't smoke?" I asked.

"No, not at all. Says it dulls the senses. That's what he thinks, anyway. But he doesn't judge those who do. He was just bein' extra protective of Rachel. You should have seen her when she was a kid. Bones, bones, and more bones. Then one summer, she just filled out." He gave her a cartoonish wolf whistle and she grinned. "Sam was so worried about the men around here he practically followed her everywhere she went. He was afraid she'd fall in love with some farmer and wind up not gettin' an education, seein' the world, stayin' put right here."

"It was just after Rafe turned me on to smoking that Dado decided I should go to high school in Dallas, live with his sister, get out of Honey Springs." She turned to Rafe and they did their Sam imitation in unison, "Pretty lean pickin's 'round here for a young girl."

Sam coughed softly at the door, his hand blocking what was surely a smile. We all jerked around, swallowing smoke, fanning it away. "I suppose I did say that several times." Rafe got up and followed Sam out to the hall. He said, "Just don't leave any hods around, or whatever it is you kids call the butts these days." He smiled before he closed the door, "It's good to see you happy, Rachel."

Eddie shook his head and said, "Man, I envy you your dad. Say, why did they name you Rachel? Was it after some famous communist?"

"No. My great-grandmother named me."

"Vivienne? Wow, the women in your family live a long time."

"Yeah. And the family has always been careful with names, with their meaning. Vivienne means 'life.' Her mother's name, Espérance means 'hope.' My mother wanted to name me Rachel after her mom. Just that, no middle name. But it means 'ewe.'"

"Like the sheep."

"Right. The follower. The breeder. My mother was set on it, and she didn't care about the etymology. So, Vivienne insisted on the middle name."

"Why don't you like it?"

"You know why. That stupid ass poem everyone had to read in grade school."

He grinned.

"Ah, I hate it. I was teased about it that whole year. But its meaning isn't too bad. It means 'the bringer of good tidings.' The evangel."

We finished the smoke. It sounded like the party was starting to break up downstairs. I asked as we walked downstairs and back towards the porch, "So who is Rafe and how does he fit into the picture?"

"He and Mack and Dado are all old friends. Rafe and his wife live here, take care of the place and my grandmother while Dado works in town at the garage. He's the jokester, Dado's the serious one, and Mack, as you know, is the firebrand."

"No shit," Eddie smiled. "I haven't been grilled like that for a long time."

"There was so much I didn't know," I said.

RE nodded. "Well, this was how I grew up. Hearing all these stories."

"I've never heard of any of it," Claire said. She'd been quiet most of the evening, listening to it all. Now she was looking out at the yard where a young woman carrying a sleepy little girl with one arm and leading a little boy with the other hand was walking with her husband to their pickup. Claire sighed and I felt a shiver of sight work its way up my spine and into my brainpan. I kissed her neck lightly. She turned to me to say something then stopped.

Mack and his wife were talking to Sam when we walked outside. They said their goodbyes and she got into the driver seat of their old Chevy truck. Mack leaned out the window as they were driving away and yelled, "Long live the Left!"

Claire surprised us by singing loudly and clearly enough for Mack to hear, "So come brothers and sisters, for the struggle carries on. The Internationale unites the world in song. So comrades come rally, for this is the time and place, the international ideal, unites the human race." We could hear him laughing all the way to the gravel road.

Gwen was still up and ready for some more talk now that the crowd had thinned down to family. Maddy was sweeping up the kitchen when we walked back to the porch and we all pitched in to get the rest of the chores done. With so many hands, it didn't take long. Then we settled back onto the porch. Gwen walked across to the table where the wine bottles and glasses still were. She poured herself a drink and turned back to Sam, a don't-preach-to-me look on her face. Then she very regally strolled back to her seat. R.E. had her hand up over her mouth, trying not to laugh.

Sam caught that and said, "You enjoying the reunion?"

She nodded. Rafe and Maddy joined us, Rafe carrying a fiddle case. He opened it, tuned, and began to play: "Bonaparte's Retreat." Sam stood up, held out his hand to R.E. She stood, bowed, and they began to waltz around the porch. When the song ended, we all clapped. Rafe broke into something rowdier. Sam and R.E. did a wild dance that I somehow knew was Irish. When it was done, they sat down, sweating and gasping for breath. Rafe continued playing songs for an hour or so, taking requests, naming them as he started up so we'd know what they were: Kerry slides, double jigs, reels, more waltzes, some Cajun tunes. Different pairs danced now and then. At one point Gwen did an elegant waltz across the bare dirt front yard with Sam. It was one of those tunes that define the term "haunting", very Celtic, a minor key that yanked tears straight from your heart to your eyes. R.E. leaned over and explained to us while they were dancing that her grandfather was named Sean Flanagan. He had been born in what the world calls Londonderry but what most Irish call Derry. He immigrated to New York in 1900 through the Ellis Island route. From there, he went west, and joined a threshing crew, winding up on Gwen's family's farm in north Texas early in 1901.

"That was a group of people who worked the grain harvest from Canada all the way down south, following the seasons. People hired them to cut and thresh their grain and they fed them and put them up while they were working. Sean finished out his contract then came back to marry Gwen." The song ended about then. "That was the tune they danced to on their wedding night."

"Oh, that is so romantic," Claire sighed.

"Yeah, well, you mix French and Irish in Texas at that time, yeah, it's pretty romantic alright."

Claire was sighing again. Something was going on with her.

It was about midnight when Gwen stood up and said, "Well, it's late. I should go to sleep soon. Strange. As I get older, I sleep less and less. I just nap." She held out her arm and Sam went over and took it. They walked into the house. Rafe and Maddy were both yawning. He put his fiddle away.

"Thanks for the tunes," R.E. smiled.

"Anytime." They nodded goodnight and went inside. Sam came back out after a few minutes.

"I can't tell you how much it means to her to see you again, Rachel."

"I miss you both so much sometimes."

"But I understand why you don't like to come back." He turned to us. "It was tough on her, growing up here. We lived closer to town then, but many folks wouldn't let their children come over and play. My politics. My--record."

R.E. nodded.

Maddy called from the inside of the house, "Rach, honey, could you help me put these chairs back?"

"Coming." She smiled at Sam and asked, "Dado, would you tell them how it happened?"

"I guess, if they want to hear it."

We nodded.

"I robbed one of the Dutchman's banks back in '33. Told everyone working there to leave and then I burned it down. It was a rash act, pretty dramatic stunt that cost me. Cost me a lot."

We dropped jaws in amazement. This was going to be good.

He paused and narrowed his eyes, looking out into the dark field, remembering. "He and I go way back. I worked for him back in the late 20s, foreman on one of their big farms. He and I were both young. He wasn't head of the family yet and was about as wild as I was in those days. Me, I was a dyed-in-the-wool Red. He just flirted with it to aggravate his own father. A couple of years after he hired me he came into the fortune and the name. I'd been trying to make some changes in the way he was running things, make life more livable for the Mexicans and Negroes and poor whites he hired. We had a real doozy of an argument one day, mixed it up pretty good. I got fired. Worse than that, I made one of the first real enemies of my life."

"How?"

"I called him crazy to his face. In front of people."

We all glanced at each other.

"It must run in the blood," Sam said softly, looking back to see if R.E. was still in the house. "Sounds like the youngest one has got it, too."

I nodded. "He does."

Claire asked, "Why did you rob his bank?"

"Because he crippled my wife."

Eddie whistled. "Why would he do that?"

He leaned back and watched the sky for a moment, his eyes moving from one constellation to another. Finally, he sighed. "After I was fired by the van der Veers, I got other jobs pretty quick, even though times were tough. I had a name as a troublemaker, but I was also known to be a hard worker. Maggie and I kept trying to organize the farm workers, and we did manage to get a small, troublesome group together. Rafe. Mack and Grace. Maddy later on." He smiled then it faded as he continued. "We'd made plans to organize a strike against the Dutchman and some of the other big owners. They found out about it, rode down on the meeting, scattered us. Maggie and I got separated. I yelled at her to run, but she didn't run fast enough. One of them swung at her with a club, hit her across the back, broke her spine. She ended up in a wheelchair. I know he was there. I remember his laugh. It was very distinct. I couldn't tell for sure if he was the one who actually did it, but just his presence was enough. And I knew he was the only one with the clout to order such a raid. But, it could never be proved. We couldn't take it to court because what we were doing was considered pretty close to illegal, anyway."

Eddie looked over at him. "I'd say robbing and burning a bank was the least you could do."

Sam smiled at that. "I thought so. But it backfired pretty quickly. I hadn't bothered to cover my face like he'd done. It wasn't well planned. One afternoon I was sitting in our kitchen, looking at Maggie in that damn cheap used wheelchair. I took my pistol and some kerosene and drove to the bank just as they were closing. When it was done, I went back to the house and left some of the cash with Gwen and Maggie. Said goodbye. Maggie said she was proud of me. I didn't feel so proud just then, looking at her so thin, that old shabby dress, that old shack. But there was nothing else to do except go on the lam and go fast. I buried the money under the footstone of my father's grave. Figured it was a safe place to leave the swag so my mother could get a little out every time she went to the cemetery. Then I went up to the Indian Territory. Hid out with some of Maggie's cousins. She was part Cherokee and a few of the family still lived there on the reservation. I wasn't very good at being a criminal or a fugitive and they caught me in about six months. I went to Huntsville." He paused. "I was in there almost seven years. All that time, my mother took care of Maggie. She still had the use of her arms and hands and was still making trouble, writing, sending letters. I eventually got out. I'd behaved myself in stir and I had shown the decency to empty the building before I burned it down, so the parole board became convinced I was a good risk."

Claire said, "I believe that R.E. is very much like her mother."

"That she is. Looks like her, too, except she's got my mother's hair. All our side of the family's red o' the head. She had it pretty hard, growing up here. Only child. The doctors said Maggie shouldn't even have had her, but it wasn't that difficult, really. The difficulty was her being teased constantly about having a mother in a wheelchair and a jailbird for a dad. They all said we were Communists, too, and in those days, the late 40s, early 50s with old Tailgunner Joe and H.U.A.C. making everyone's life so miserable, it was hard for me to find steady work. Then I started that garage about ten years ago. At first, no one would come around, but gradually I made it a business. Maggie just kept writing and talking to people and speaking in public now and then. She even started writing a book."

"About what?"

"A re-write of American history, no less, from an outsider's point of view. Then, when Rachel was almost five, some men from town came around one afternoon. I was mending fences on the far side of the property we were renting then. Maybe the Dutchman sent them, maybe not. I had plenty of enemies by then. I guess they thought the house was empty. I believe they only intended to burn us out, make us leave. Maggie was home sick with a fever. Gwen and Maddy were keeping Rachel with them out in the field that day. The men threw a couple of cans of kerosene onto the porch and lit it. The house burned down before she could get out. I could see it from the other side of the field where I was working but I couldn't get there fast enough. Just an old frame building. It was gone in minutes."

Eddie asked quietly, "So, you all raised her? R.E.?"

He smiled. "It took the whole team. Gwen was getting too old to be asked to do that all alone. She'd taken care of Maggie for years and Rachel was a handful of a child. Ran around and played all day like a wild Indian. We all moved in here with Rafe and Maddy since everything we had was gone. They could never have kids so it seemed like the logical thing to do for everyone. Between the four of us we managed." He was smiling now and she had rejoined us. "You were a devil child, you know that?"

"You remember when Rafe decided to teach me to fight with my fists?"

He leaned back and laughed. "He will never live that down."

Claire asked, "What happened?"

"She knocked him out. Little stick figure thing. I guess you were about, what, 14? She'd been taking a lot of teasing and had come home so mad one day she was crying. Well, Rafe decided he was going to teach her to use her fists. They were out in the yard and he was holding his hands up and telling her how to throw punches."

R.E. took it from there. "It was absolutely exhilarating. I got carried away and asked him to really fight me. He just batted at me at first but I kept hitting him harder and harder and hurt him at one point. That pissed him off so to make me quit, he really punched me, which made me madder, so I caught him with a combination and knocked him out. I was terrified, Mack and Dado were laughing so hard that Mack split his pants when he fell down, Maddy was cussing me. I was crying. What a mess!"

Sam and R.E. put their arms around each other and held each other for a while but it wasn't sorrowful. They seemed peaceful, at ease with what had happened and why. Then he smiled, nodded and stood up. "Well, that's enough storytelling for one night. I'm glad all of you came up. Plenty of quilts in the living room to make pallets. You can sleep there or in the upstairs bedroom. Just don't make too much noise." He smiled at us, kissed R.E. goodnight, and went inside.

We sat on the porch, free now to smoke one openly. No one said anything. The clear night sky was an explosion of stars and the fields around chirped and creaked and rustled with nocturnal life. So many ghosts in the yard: I couldn't stop thinking about all those lives that had gone before, all those others who had tried to make something more perfect, something closer to the heart's desire. There were so many questions I wanted to ask R.E. about Sam and the Dutchman and their feud, about the labor unions, about the Réunion stories Gwen must have told her when she was growing up. And about Maggie Flanagan. So much history, so little of it known. I glanced over at Eddie. He was sitting a couple of steps above R.E. on the porch, his arms around her shoulders. He asked quietly, "Let me take your hair down, Rachel."

"Please. I'm tired of being the good little me."

He smiled and slowly took out the long hair pins, freeing the braid of the coil. Then he untied the ribbon at the end of the braid and began unplaiting it strand by strand. When it was undone, he shook it loose around her shoulders, gathering handfuls now and then and rubbing it thoughtfully against his cheek or her neck. The breeze had picked up some and it was pleasantly cool there in the moonless dark. He asked, "When he said take any room you like but don't make any noise, did he mean he doesn't mind if I sleep with you tonight?"

"He doesn't mind. But Gwen is a light sleeper and the floors are old and creaky. He just doesn't want us to disturb her."

He looked at the field. "Then let's take an old quilt out there before we crash."

She leaned back between his legs, her head resting against his crotch and he ran his hands down over her breasts and back up along her arms. Caressing her throat, he leaned over her and kissed her. Claire and I were transfixed by their open sensuality. R.E. stood up after a while and went to the door. Then she turned back to us and said, "I'll bring you guys some quilts, too."

"Please."

We went different directions: me and Claire to the barn and them towards the fields. Claire said she'd always wanted a roll in the hay. Her blood was up. Maybe it was the French or the wine or all the talk of revolution. She stripped slowly for me, teasing me as I lay naked and waiting for her on the quilts. We'd found the least animal scented section of the upper loft and scouted it for critters before we bedded down. I was horny as usual. All my years of longing finally having a regular venue for expression only fueled my new found sexuality. I had the near constant urge to make love with Claire every chance we had and as many times as possible. We were lucky because she was able to take the Pill so birth control mechanics were not a problem. At one point she was astride me, riding her orgasm to the ground when I half split from myself: two places at once--under Clair--and--under a tree midfield.

Eddie was kneeling over R.E., loving her with his right hand and himself with his left. She gripped his knees, bracing herself, eyes shut, breathing long shallow gasps as he made her come. She opened her eyes, sweating, smiling and took his hand, kissing his fingers. "I like the way I taste on you," she said as they both fondled him.

He let her continue while he ran his hands over her belly. "Are you doing okay with the Pill?"

"Yeah. It's a different kind from before. Less estrogen. No problems."

"You didn't have to go back on it."

"I wanted to."

"I'm glad you did. I like the feeling of being inside you, skin to skin. Oh, Rachel," he whispered as he fell on her, in her, rising and falling faster and faster, pounding against her unrestrained as he came, soaking them both even further, sweaty Texas summer sex. He rolled away quickly, patted her sides, "God, are you okay? I just got carried away."

"I'm fine, I'm fine. All healed now. I'm glad you could finally, really let go. Oh, that was good."

They lay side by side and held each other as the wind rustled the leaves above them. He whispered her name again, "Rachel." Then he took a handful of hair and tickled her with it. She shivered from the sudden breeze and the intimate torture. He whispered, "Evangel. Angel. It's a beautiful name, Rachel. It suits you."

I was back. Claire was slowing down, still rubbing back and forth on top of me. I could feel another hard-on coming just looking at her, her bad-little-girl body. Then she said, "I think I want your baby."

That scared me so much I almost lost the urge. Not quite, but it did take something out of the moment.

"What?"

"Your baby. Bébé. You know, enfant?"

"I--I--I heard you."

"You do not seem very enthusiastic. About the baby, anyway," she smiled.

My mind had indeed stopped cold at the mention of the word 'baby'. My body had its own ideas though and was still quite willing to at least go through the motions of making one. "I don't know, what about, you know this problem I have that makes me shake."

"It doesn't bother me."

"I know that."

"Maybe it can't be inherited." She was merciless. Claire had a way of running her hands over her body, pretending she was all alone and playing with herself. It made me her abject slave. And she was doing that now.

It was almost four in the morning before she allowed me some rest. We gathered our clothes, wrapped the quilts around ourselves and made as discrete a dash as possible up the stairs. Eddie and R.E. were asleep on the bed so we crashed on the rug.

When I woke up late the next morning, I had a horrific hangover from the wine and the severe dehydration brought on by the French Inquisition. I was alone in the room. I felt like I'd been kicked in the head. Maybe that was why they call them Mustang grapes, I thought as I literally crawled into the bathroom and into the tub to let the water run over the back of my head and around into my mouth.

"Be careful you don't drown," R.E. smiled.

I didn't even care if she saw me naked. I groaned and asked, "Is there any coffee? Aspirin? Morphine?"

She laughed, "That's a yes to the first two. On the night stand in the bedroom. Oh, and I brought you some toast."

I waved the thought of food away with one feeble hand.

"You should try. It'll make the aspirin easier to keep down."

I think I said thank you but I can't swear to it.

About an hour later, I felt more human. It was lunchtime. Amazingly enough, the smell of the food didn't turn my stomach. In fact, I was a little hungry. Rafe and Maddy were there, as were Claire, R.E., and Gwen. Rafe grinned wickedly, "You look like ten miles o' bad road, son."

"I feel like I've been dragged for twenty."

"Behind a team o' mustangs!" he laughed.

"Face down," R.E. said, throwing her head back in an uncontrollable fit of tickled laughter, the kind that strikes without warning, leaving you unable to breathe or to stop laughing. That set Rafe off and soon they were all laughing and begging R.E. to stop. It took everyone several minutes to quit completely. In Texas, we called it "gettin' the simples."

I, however, remained unmoved.

Gwen smiled sweetly. "It takes some practice to be able to drink as much as you did. Two bottles, I think."

I winced. Everyone smiled at their plates or at each other surreptitiously and we finished lunch without any further comedy.

"Where's Eddie?" I asked as I helped R.E. wash up.

"He went back early. Said he wanted to take care of the lunch shift." She was smiling through the window, watching Claire and Gwen and Maddy working in the vegetable garden. Rafe had gone to the far side of the property to work on the fences and Sam was in town at the garage. "You know, sometimes I think I could move back here. Go back to the land. So many folks are trying that without knowing what hard work it is. But I already know that. It's just so peaceful. Sometimes it seems very attractive."

"Yeah. But you know you'd be bored stiff within a few weeks, if not days."

"True." She smiled at me. "There's a lot to be done before I retire to the bean patch. I've been thinking about Mack, what all he said last night. He's right. I should be more active."

"But only if you want to be. You shouldn't be just because he was trying to make you feel guilty."

"Well, he does. I admit that. There's a family heritage of the Left that I haven't even begun to live up to yet."

We hugged and I thought about that word she'd chosen: heritage. And about Claire's remark about having a baby. My baby. That was truly a scary thought. I knew at that moment how Raz must have felt when Amanda told him she was pregnant. R.E. and I both had a lot to think about.

Claire didn't mention the "enfant terrible" topic again, but once we were back home at the Palace, I could see her looking at Amanda with a distinct hunger in her eyes, rubbing her own flat little belly absently. I knew what I had to do next. It was time for my own journey return.

"It is the exception that probes the rule by
testing and exploring its consequences
in altered situations."

Stephen Jay Gould, *The Panda's Thumb:
More Reflections In Natural History*

VI.

Backwards Through The Light

Once we were home, Claire didn't let up on the hints and then the open requests and finally the demands that I start a family with her. She stared at Amanda's growing belly with dreamy eyes that turned to lighting launchers when she looked at me. I kept insisting I'd need to check out my own family history first, but I also found one excuse after another to put that off. Finally, there was the first really big fight: swearing in three languages, oceans of tears, a shivery lipped reconciliation, make-up sex, and a desperately guilty promise on my part to take the big step. My only brief reprieve was that I had to square things with Eddie first.

"Then, you should go to his house," she sniffed. "Now."

I went to I.O.O.F. Street that same Sunday morning. I knew Eddie would be off. It was mid-morning, early enough to catch him at home and late enough not to wake him. I knocked on the back screen door and he let me into the kitchen. John was at the table, drinking coffee and chain-smoking cigarettes. Eddie poured me a cup and we all sat down. After a few minutes, a sleepy R.E. wandered out of the bedroom wearing one of Eddie's old shirts. She smiled at us, dreams and drowsiness still fogging her eyes, and headed for the bathroom. Eddie asked me, "So what gets you up and about so early?"

"Just wanted to touch base with you about taking a few days off."

"You know you can. Just get your shift covered."

"Already done. Claire said she could." I paced and frowned.

He raised his eyebrows over the lip of his cup. The non-verbal question hung in the air.

"See, she wants to have a baby. With me. I guess that's okay, but this twitch that I have, I don't know if it's something that can be inherited or not. And if it can, I don't want to have one. She agreed to that. So I need to find out." I was sitting there with an ex-medic and a doctor, but they were off-duty and I extended them the courtesy of not having to say no to someone asking for free advice.

But John offered, "I could check you out, if you'd like."

"Thanks. But wouldn't you need my records and all that?"

"It would help."

"What would you need to know?"

"Mostly the conditions under which you were delivered and the medical state your mother was in while she was pregnant with you."

Since Pearl was the keeper of that information, I had grown up without a clue. I asked, "Would you need to know anything about my father?"

"Yeah, whatever you know about him would be helpful, too."

"I don't even know who he was. All I know is they weren't married."

"Ah." He sipped thoughtfully. "Well, whatever you can find out."

Eddie said, "You want to borrow Mariah for the trip?"

"Your car?"

"I hate to think of you trying to hitch in unfriendly territory and she's a dependable beast. I can always borrow wheels if I need them. You can drive, can't you?"

"Yeah, sure." I didn't say how I'd learned. Coleman taught me and loaned me his Mustang for the driving test so I could get a license for an I.D.

"Okay. When do you want to go and for how long?"

I remembered Claire's teary-eyed, pouting face. "As soon as I can."

"Just let me know. Don't wait too long, though. When classes start up again, we'll be pretty busy."

R.E. came back out of the bathroom, her hair brushed, wearing cutoffs and a white T-shirt, barefoot. She poured herself a cup and joined us.

John said, "Say, total change of subject, but I've been meaning to ask since I got into town. What the hell does I.O.O.F. stand for?"

R.E. laughed, "International Order of Odd Fellows, some kind of lodge thing, you know, like the Lions or the Mooses."

"Ah, okay. Odd indeed. Only two blocks long and next to, of course, the I.O.O.F. Cemetery,"

Eddie nodded. "One of the reasons I took the place. Very quiet."

John smiled. "It's as good as Normal Street. That's where I'm looking to get a place so I can say I live on Normal Street. It's strange enough that I work on Scripture Street."

It was already hot in the room, early as it was, so Eddie reduced the meal chores to whipping up some quesadillas on the stove top while R.E. cut up some fruit. John rooted around and found guacamole makings, using up the several ripe avocados that had been on the windowsill. With all that and some salsa, we had a lazy Tex-Mex feed on the table in only a few minutes. We were in a quiet mood, not talking much, listening to the radio news, a commentary about New York's new liberal abortion law that had been passed on July 1st. Discussion was still running pretty hot about the topic and the announcer's bias was slanted more than a little against the idea of choice. Then, without any kind of transition, he went on to the next story. It was about a woman in Dallas who had been beaten up by her husband and left for dead. No one said anything. It was R.E. who acknowledged the moment. "I've been thinking about taking some kind of self-defense course. Or getting a gun. I don't ever want to go through what happened to me again."

"Do you know how to shoot a gun?" John asked.

"Yeah. My dad taught me when I was about ten or so."

"What kind of gun?"

"All kinds, really. We used to go quail hunting every fall with the bird guns. And deer hunting, too, with rifles. And he showed me how to use the pistol. Said it was better I knew how to use it and never needed to than the other way around. He was always afraid that another bunch of people would come out to the house to try to burn us out again or something worse."

"There are problems with using them for self-defense," Eddie said quietly as he put the dishes in the sink and started washing up. R.E.

remained at the table. It was something I'd noticed about house rules. When Eddie cooked at his place, he washed up and no one helped him. Whenever anyone tried, he's steer them away saying it was part of his routine. When he was the one who put things away, he always knew where they'd be when he wanted them the next time.

"What kind of problems?" I asked.

"Well, it's easy for someone to get it away from you and use it on you." He stood with his back to us, washing the last water glass slowly, rinsing it carefully, drying it. Then he filled it to the brim and took a long ceremonial drink before he turned back to us. "That's how I got shot." He went to the stove and poured the last of the coffee, started making another pot. We all waited. If he was going to continue, he would. Someone in the neighborhood was mowing their lawn and the scent of freshly cut grass drifted in to us. R.E. had taken a joint out of her pocket but was waiting for him to join us before she lit up. When the second pot was on the way, he sat down, hands cradling the cup, not looking at anyone. It was John's eyes he met first when he did look up. John smiled and nodded at him. Eddie sighed and looked past all of us, the thousand yard stare. "John said a long time ago that I would eventually need to get all this off my chest by talking about it. I have, a little, in pieces, now and then. And it's only because it's apropos to what you were saying, Rachel, that it seems time to talk about it now." We nodded. He looked at the joint and then at R.E. She lit it and passed it around. John put down his preferred smokes for a moment, passing more than toking, in it just for the ritual.

Eddie began. "You know that I went to Korea as a draftee, a C.O., a medic. It's not something that I like to remember or to talk about. Sometimes you hear people telling war stories or saying that they're vets." He snorted. "They probably weren't there or they weren't in much action. The ones who saw things usually don't talk about it, especially with people who weren't there. There's no frame of reference, too much to be defined or explained. No situational shorthand that makes it easier."

He sighed and drank most of the cup, got up, and slowly went about refilling it. The mowing continued. He turned off the radio before he sat down and continued. "John and I were in a front line unit, the kind that did the immediate patch-up work on soldiers before they were airlifted to M.A.S.H. units. It was gruesome. A person who has been shot or blown up or burned doesn't look like a person anymore. They look like bags of sticks and goo, mostly. I threw up for what seemed like weeks before I got used to it."

John nodded. "We all did."

Eddie went on. "It's crazy, living like you do in war, one second to the next, concentrating on what you're doing, not giving in to screaming, wanting out, wanting to be somewhere safe and clean and dry. The lull times, they were the worst. That's when you had too much time to think."

The mowing had stopped by now. Someone in another house put on some music, some jazz. I couldn't be sure who was playing. At least it wasn't Led Zeppelin; that would have been distracting.

"It was one of those lull times when I met Maja. Maja Kim. One of the thousands of Kims in the world. She was a bar girl at one of those inevitable dives that spring up around military installations. Spoke pretty good English. It was months after we'd met that she trusted me enough to tell me anything about herself, to let me take her to dinner, to call her Maja instead of Kim, to act like a person with me instead of..." He paused.

I shifted slightly and opened my mouth to ask a question. Eddie didn't see me and I never asked because John raised one finger and shook it gently, not taking his eyes off of Eddie. I nodded imperceptibly and sat back. Eddie didn't see this exchange. His eyes were fixed on the surface of the coffee in the cup. It was vibrating from the tension in his hands.

"Why I fell for her, I don't know. Maybe it was all that death. I wasn't the only guy there who thought being in love with a Korean woman would stop them from going crazy. Who knows why we feel the things we do. Underneath all her toughness and street smarts, there was a lonely young woman from a once well-to-do family, educated, capable of speaking more than one language very well. I found myself wondering one evening, watching her work a customer in the bar, what she would have been like if the war hadn't happened, how she would be if she had a shot at a different life somewhere else. It wasn't easy getting close to her. She hated men, soldiers especially, Korean and American equally. Very democratic. Since I wasn't a solider per se, she didn't know what category to put me in at first. She was a pro, went to bed with anyone who could pay her price, which wasn't just anyone, because her price was high. She had a well deserved reputation for skill."

He paused for a minute or so and we all sat in silence, waiting for him to go on. Then he continued. "The way I got to know her was professional at first. I had started out being the unofficial medic for the guy who ran the bar, checking the girls, making sure they didn't have clap or anything else, giving them black market penicillin when they did, taking care of other things eventually. It was several weeks before I became one of her customers, too. Not long before my hitch was over, when I was giving her her regular checkup, I found out she was pregnant. She made no pretensions of knowing whose it was. She didn't. It could have been mine. I told her that if she wanted to, we'd get married when my tour was up, and I'd take her and the kid back to the States. She didn't believe me at first. But when I started going through the unbelievable amount of paperwork and hassle, she started to realize I meant it. Since she was well known, I had to do a lot of talking and interviewing to convince the powers-that-were that we were on the level. Finally, a guy high up in the Korean army who had known her family before the war convinced the clerks I was dealing with that she deserved a second chance." His eyes darkened and the light retreated even further. He got up and tossed the rest of the coffee in the sink, poured us all a fresh round, and returned to the table. "As Maja watched me going through this, she began to change. At least, I thought she was changing. She softened towards me, started really smiling now and then, letting what might have been her real self come through. The chaplain for our unit married us on the fourth of July, 1952." He shut his eyes, and then continued with an edge to his voice. "She thought it would be very American. We shipped out the next day, and were in San Francisco a week later. She loved it there. At first, all she wanted to do was go to the grocery store. Not so much to buy, but just to look. I had forgotten, too, about the abundance, the choices, the full shelves. And the dress shops. She would try on everything in her size, the smallest women's size in the store, and then buy the cheapest thing they had. Funny, but the owners usually didn't mind. She looked great in anything so it was like having a model working for them for free. I bought a house on the G.I. Bill, started working days and weekends, getting ready for the kid. I read the papers like a starving man. The *Chronicle*, The *Times* from both L.A. and New York, everything I could get my hands on. Both political conventions were going on that July and I'd been away from up-front politics for what seemed like a lifetime. Talk in the City was big and bold and unlimited by army policy, so we hung out in the coffee houses and soaked it all up. She was amazed that you could say anything you wanted to, anytime. Granted, the Red scare was in full swing and H.U.A.C. had a lot of people on the run, but compared to Korea, it was a free speech fest, as far as we were both concerned." He squinted. "That was the best time of my life. Being a husband. Being a dad. I loved that little girl. She was born in November. November 26th. We named her Elizabeth after Maja's favorite actress, Elizabeth Taylor. Maja didn't work. She was a housewife and a mom, very 1950s. I was working for the railroad then, working in the yards, driving into San Jose every day and back again. I didn't mind it. Hell, I loved driving. And we had the City. After Elizabeth was born, we'd stroll around the cheap side of Russian Hill where we lived, showing her off. She was a beautiful child. And she did look enough like me to make it reasonable..." He winced. "It didn't last long. She'd applied for her green card as soon as the ink was dry on our marriage papers. I remember the day it arrived. Easy to remember. It was on Lizzy's second birthday. She met me at the door, so excited. We went out to our favorite Italian restaurant, just the two of us, got the neighbors to baby-sit. It was so incredibly romantic. That night we made love like we couldn't get enough. The next morning, she packed my lunch, just like always. But when I got home, she and Elizabeth were gone. No note, no nothing. Just gone. I knew it before I opened the door."

He got up and paced around for a bit before he could continue. "She had emptied the savings account before she left. I was still working, so I could make the house payments and the monthly bills. They were low enough. I kept everything that she had left, which wasn't much, in the house, in case she changed her mind and came back. It never occurred to me to go to the police. I knew deep down she'd simply split. About a month later, I got a letter, no return address, postmarked from San Diego. She said not to follow her. She had written her old boyfriend back in Korea, the army officer who had convinced everyone to let her go. He was going to join her there. There wasn't much in the way of an explanation. She said that it would be easier for Lizzy if both her parents were Korean. And she said that she owed the officer. That was all, just that she owed him. At the end of it, she said it would be better if

I could just forget her. Right. I tried. I sold the house, bought a Harley, hit the road, and started drinking. I don't remember much about some of that time. Eventually, I wound up on the East Coast, spent some time in the Village. I fell into the Beat scene head first, traveled a lot. I was back and forth between the coasts so many times, I lost count. And I drank. A lot. You think I can hold my liquor now, back then--well. It was a little like those old Celtic tales of someone walking through the woods and running across a King and Queen and hanging around drinking fairy beer for what they think was a weekend, only when they get back to town, decades have passed. They called it sleeping in the arms of the Grey Lord. There were some blackouts, not just gray times, some periods of time I can't account for. Other times, I was straighter, like when I was with Thea." He glanced at me then explained briefly to RE. "She's the woman I was with who owned that house you hid out in."

He stood at the window, arms around himself, his back to us. "This brings me, long way around, to what you were saying earlier, Rachel, about using a pistol for self-defense. They aren't real useful in one on one fights. I know." He ran his hands back through his hair then went on. "At one point about two years after I'd hit the road, I was working in North Dakota, just outside the Rosebud reservation. It was a bar. They had a grill, needed someone to run it. Rough joint. Lots of fights. That was back before the Civil Rights Act, of course, so it was for whites only. No Indians allowed. Rednecks and cowboys and truckers, they'd all duke each other out on a regular basis. I had long since abandoned the nonviolence I'd been brought up with. When things got too far out of hand, I'd wade in with a baseball bat or just my fists and mix it up. So the owner made me the bouncer as well as the cook. One body, two jobs, same pay."

R.E.'s eyes darkened. Eddie wasn't thinking about the Now, only about the bleak Then he was remembering. She knew that, but I saw John pat her hand gently. She nodded.

"I loved to fight, even when I lost. It was as though the pain made me feel alive, made me feel something, like I was really in my body and not floating somewhere just outside of it. The owner of the joint kept a gun under the counter by the register, one in his office, and one in his truck. It was that kind of place. Guys who came to the bar came packing most of the time. He never shook them down. He showed me how to shoot the damn things so I could cover for him now and then. It's easy, as you probably know, to shoot a pistol at a target. Not so easy to shoot a person who's looking straight at you, if you never have before."

I glanced at John. He was watching Eddie closely. R.E. was looking out the screen door, listening, her face sad and thoughtful.

"One night, this couple came in the door. They were obviously lost. Middle class, white, well dressed. Tourists looking for the Badlands. They found them, all right. They had a little girl with them. A little Korean girl. Must have been one of those couples who had adopted an orphan after the war. There were enough TV shows and movies about the subject to make it a brief fad." He frowned. "I'd been drinking all day but the desired effect hadn't set in so I was clear. Really clear. At first, no one said anything. The woman started back for the door, but the guy was determined he was going to act like nothing was wrong, like nothing was happening. Funny how middle class people can do that, pretend that the rest of the world abides by their rules, that there is no insanity, no madness, no potential for sudden, irrational violence, nothing out of order in the universe. He was heading towards me, maybe to ask directions, maybe to ask to use the toilets, I don't know. The hassling set in so fast they couldn't get back outside. The owner had stepped out for a break, so it was just me in charge. The little girl didn't cry. She just stood there. And for some reason, she looked at me, right straight at me, asking with her eyes if I was going to help, going to join the hassling, or just going to watch it all happen. It started getting bad. They had separated the man from the woman and were trying to separate her from the kid. I pulled the gun out and fired into the ceiling. Everyone froze. The woman grabbed the kid and ran out and the guy, after standing there like a fool for almost too long, ran after them. I held the pistol on the crowd until I could hear the family's car drive away, and then I came around the counter. The guy who had started it all came out of the middle of the room, walking towards me, swaggering all the way, pushing everyone aside, calling me a gook lover and worse. He was the town bully, the baddest ass of them all and the biggest one. The rest backed off. Then he rushed me. I'd only intended to scare them all, not to kill anyone, so I didn't shoot him when I still had the chance. Before I knew it, he was on me. We struggled and he got the pistol away from me. And he shot me. I remember his laughter more than anything else. He said he was going after the family and blow them all away. I still don't know how I did it, adrenalin probably. I slid down the floor behind him when he turned around and tripped him. He wasn't expecting it and wasn't braced so it gave me a couple of second's advantage when he hit the floor. I jumped up, kicked him in the head, kicked the pistol out of his hand and grabbed it. No one in the place was taking his side or helping me, they were just standing in a big circle around us waiting to see what was going to happen. He stood up and started for me. I shot him. Three times. Then he finally fell down. The owner was back by then. He saw the last shot. I don't remember much after that. I woke up in the hospital. The judge didn't even consider the case. Seems most everyone in town was breathing a sigh of relief that someone had finally killed that asshole. But just in case anyone changed their mind, I left town as soon as I was able to." He sighed and turned back to us. "Rachel, will you roll us another one, please."

"Sure." She stood up and hesitated for a second. Then she walked over and hugged him. He resisted for a moment before relaxing and hugging her back. They didn't say anything. None of us did. Eddie looked tired, like the telling had taken everything out of him. John nodded and Eddie nodded back. I just sat there quietly: witness. When R.E. came back with the number, Eddie smiled at her. "So. Long story. Told. Thanks for hearing all that. I just meant to tell you about the shooting, but it wouldn't make any sense unless you knew the rest. And, I guess it was time to talk."

She smiled back. "Thank you for trusting us enough to tell it."

"So you see my point? Even if you know how to use a gun, they're not much good in close quarters. And that was one man against another man, both drunk, both full of crazy energy, and I was fighting for my life. It would be another story if a man wanted to get a pistol away from a woman. Smaller wrists have less leverage, that's just a fact of physics. Pistols are more useful for short distance defense, when you can see someone coming and you know they're going to hurt you."

"So, what's good for up close stuff?" I asked.

John said, "It's getting fashionable to use karate, but that only works if you're really good at it. If you kick at someone and they catch your ankle, pow! Down you go."

"Well, there must be something," R.E. said.

We talked about it a little more, but none of us had any answers. All that we knew for sure was that it was a problem with no easy solution. Soon, it was time for me and R.E. to go to work. She hugged Eddie again before she left and we walked over to the Corner Room. He stayed at his place with John, taking a well-deserved day off. It was a silent walk. After such a confession, small talk would have been comforting but inappropriate and we knew that. We worked a shift, both playing the mental movie of Eddie's story over and over again in our minds, talking to each other and to customers only when we needed to. Then we headed home once work was done, still quiet. I asked, "You going to see him tonight?"

"I have a feeling I won't." She turned to me. "After all that, he may want to have some time to himself to brood."

"I'm sure. Man, what a story."

"Yeah. You know, he didn't say whether or not he ever got divorced from Maja."

"I have the feeling he didn't." I thought about the conversation we'd had while we were driving around, just after R.E. had gone into hiding, about how he didn't want to be exclusive with anyone. I was beginning to understand why. We came in the back way and headed up to our rooms. Eddie was there, waiting on the stairs.

"Hope you don't mind my dropping by."

"How are you?"

He held out his arms and she went over to him. Eddie hugged her for a long silent time then stood back. "I need to be alone tonight. Maybe for a few weeks of nights. I don't know how long, maybe not that long. It's the dreams. I don't want you to hear them."

She nodded but said, "Dreams don't scare me."

"Nerves of steel," he smiled. "No, they probably wouldn't. But they scare me. They come back when I even talk about one little bit of what I said today. I've never told anyone the whole thing, from front to back like that. John said he was real proud of me. He stayed for hours. We talked some more, about things that happened there, things I couldn't tell you. Things you didn't need to hear. So, I expect to be haunted for a while." He turned to me and pitched me the car keys. "The papers and all are in the glove box. I left a note in it with my phone number saying I let you borrow it, in case you get stopped or hassled. There's a little magnetic holder under the right front fender with an extra key inside in case you lock yourself out. I know I have. Also, if you look carefully, you'll see that the back of the glove box is false. Push it just a little at the top left corner and it'll come loose. Stash place." He smiled at me then kissed R.E. "I just need some time, okay?"

"Of course. You ought to know without asking."

"Yeah, but you know what a polite guy I am." He kissed her again, hugged me and left.

"I should have given him a ride," she mused.

"No. It was fine like it was."

***

And so, a couple of days later, shift covered and promises made, I found myself sitting in Mariah's driver's seat, under an overpass, waiting out a blinding thunderstorm, on my way to Little Creek, the small town where I had lived with my mother until she died. I was six when it happened and all I had of her were vague memories that were more somatic than intellectual and muttered half-stories Pearl had told me. I had been dreaming heavily, vividly, ever since I'd decided to go back. All those faded images had been coming into my head so strongly that I could almost remember some things about her. About the town. About the ghostly men who had come to my mother's bed. All I knew for a fact about her was that she was beautiful. Pearl had one picture of her in the house. It had been taken when my mother was about fourteen. She had blue eyes and long blond hair and an ethereal, far-away look. Of course, the photo was from the era when she was still pure and going to church every time the doors were open. I knew from Claire's artwork that I looked a lot like her, especially around the eyes. Small wonder Pearl hated me so much.

Pearl moved from Little Creek to White Settlement just after I was born, after my mother had refused to give me up for adoption. It was only after she died and when Child Custody was threatening to take me that Pearl returned to Little Creek, claimed me, and took me to live with her in White Settlement. She made it plain from Day One that I owed her. She was wildly, blindly religious, a Hard-Shell Baptist, the most aptly named branch of the Protestant tree, and my mother had committed the most blatant transgression a woman of those times could commit: getting pregnant without the benefit of marriage. To compound it, she wasn't repentant. She was almost proud of it, Pearl said once, like it was some wonderful, secret thing she'd done. The little knowledge

I had about my mother I'd gained from Pearl when she was whipping me for one petty child crime or another. She would alternate between beating me with something, rarely with her hands because she didn't like to touch me, and growling in a low voice about how my mother had betrayed her, how ungrateful she had been, how she'd only done it to spite her, how she was burning in hell for it and for being a whore afterwards, and how I was as wicked as she had been and was hell-bound just like her.

As I sat there in Mariah, thinking back on it, I wondered why she had taken it so hard. Surely it was more than just religion. Maybe she felt my mother had been unfaithful to her, not just to Jesus. After all, it had been only the two of them for so long. She had raised my mother all alone after their parents had died in a car wreck when Pearl was fifteen and my mother was eight. So she never married. She worked one low paying job after another, dropped out of high school, spent what little free time she had doing church stuff. She never had a boyfriend, she told me, because Jesus didn't want her to have one. Even as a kid, I had to wonder why Jesus, who was as far as I could tell from stories I heard in church a very busy deity, would take such a personal interest in my dried-up, bitter old aunt. I'm still not sure why she didn't let the authorities take me to an orphanage. Maybe she needed another thorn in her side after my mom died. She loved to suffer. Pearl was bone-deep mean, hating the sister and the child she had chosen to raise and loving us, the crosses she bore, at the same time since it gave her an excuse for being like she was.

She ran a little sewing business out of her house in White Settlement, altering people's clothes, making quilts, making bright, pretty, new things from material and patterns other people brought to her. Our own clothes were all from the Salvation Army, though. She wore gray or black most of the time and the things she always got for me never fit or matched in any way. This along with the Snake and the fact that our house was one of the smallest and dreariest in the neighborhood made it hell for me at school, of course. My classmates had a wide variety of taunts they could throw at me. She did have one dress that was the closest thing to being called nice, and I had one good shirt and pair of pants with a jacket for cold weather. These were worn on Sunday mornings, Sunday evenings, Wednesday evenings, or any other time there was anything at all going on at church: same outfit for her for years, until it went from gray to a kind of shiny green and the same one for me, until it became ludicrously short, in which case it was replaced by a duplicate which was just as ludicrously long so I could grow into it. Her dresses were also replaced by duplicates that slowly went green as their predecessors had done. She made me go to services with her all the time. I colored the little Marys and Jesuses in Sunday School with the other kids and sang along with the dreary Baptist tunes that were required both before and after the unbearably long sermons but mostly I daydreamed while I was there, marking time until I was old enough to leave her and the church far behind. People would ask Pearl what was wrong with me while I was standing right there, as if I were deaf, mute, or just stupid. I hated them. I hated her. I hated myself.

Going out in public didn't happen at all when she first took me in. She kept me inside the dark, shuttered house all the time and I missed what would have been my first year of school. I was a small kid, frequently sick. Maybe she was hoping I would just die. She would make me hide when other people came around. Then one day I accidentally wandered into the living room when another woman was there. She looked at me and asked who I was. Pearl said I was her sister's child. Then she stared at me with the strangest expression on her face, one I'd never seen before and never saw again, a poor white epiphany limited by her narrow personality and lack of education. She said, "Looks like I'll have to raise another one." When fall came around again, she enrolled me in school, saying that I was six. All she had to show the registrar to prove it was a Bible. She had written my name and a birthday and a fake name for my father alongside my mother's name in the "Family Records" part in the middle, saying that his name had been Jacobson, too. I guess no one asked for further proof. So, even though I was really seven, I started elementary school in 1955 with a class of six year olds about the same size as I was.

I loved it. Even though everyone at school was as bad as the people at church about the Snake and my general appearance, for at least a few hours during the day, I was away from Pearl's scorn and the ever present threat of being hit with something, and I had books, lovely books, as many as I could read. I didn't know at that time how I learned, whether I'd taught myself or somehow absorbed the skill by osmosis from the world around me. All I know is that as far back as I can remember I have always understood the mysteries of script.

I escaped into the worlds inside those books. Not one of my teachers ever believed I was really reading. They thought I was just looking at the pictures. They rarely asked me any questions in class and even when they did and I knew the right answers, I gave them nonsense. They thought I was retarded as well as spastic, and as long as they did, they left me alone most of the time and that was fine with me. So I slid through school being socially promoted every year. No teacher ever wanted to deal with me more than once.

Things changed a little when Coleman came along; I had a pal and a champion. I never really understood why he decided to be friends with me. Maybe it was because he had sight even as a child and knew I was harmless. Maybe it was because I had told him about Pearl, about not having a real family. We were the only kids in our grade without at least one real parent. We would escape together, cutting classes on those days when parents were supposed to come. None of the teachers ever gave us any trouble about it. I had always thought that they just didn't care, but now, remembering Cole's story, I suppose it was because they didn't want to get into any trouble with the van der Veers. Even though he was living with that other family and was enrolled under the name of Jackson, given the tale he'd told me, I'm sure that the long reach of the Dutchman extended to that little White Settlement grammar school. And why no hassle for me? I guess it was partly because I was with Cole when he skipped and thus included in the van der Veer net and partly because I was considered a nuisance and a burden by all my teachers so they didn't bother to call Pearl. At any rate, Cole and I were friends and he became my defender. Anyone who teased me ran the risk of a sudden, brutal attack from my dark brother. Ex-brother. I sighed and thought how I had only too recently held a gun on him in a vain attempt to stop him from hurting R.E. Now he was wandering Cain-like somewhere in the world and I was in a newer brother's car, waiting out a storm, trying to find out who my blood family was and what they were like so I could start a family of my own.

Half an hour later it was still raining and showing no sign of letting up, a late summer gully washer. I rolled the windows down and decided to investigate the secret stash. As Eddie had said it would, the back of the glove box popped loose and there was a silver cigarette case behind it. I opened it and smiled at the carefully rolled numbers, different sizes, looking like surgical instruments all laid out in order.

Selecting a small one, knowing Eddie's taste for strong weed, I lit up and toked twice. Yep, rich and fragrant: I let it go out and since the glove box was open, poked around curiously. Beside where the stash had been was an envelope with some photos in it. I took them out and examined them one by one, keeping them in the same order as I had found them. There was one of R.E. pre-Incident, probably one of Jesse's shots. She was in the well house at the Palace, in the dappled light, wearing a long skirt and a Mexican blouse, her hair loose. There were others: some of the wedding, some at the Corner Room, a mix of people from his life now. And there were a few older pictures. A young Asian woman and a baby in a stroller: on the back it said "Maja and Lizzy, Russian Hill." The woman was dressed in a close fitting suit, gloves, a little cap of a hat, and chunky high heels, standing in front of one of those fine old row houses, smiling at the camera, the shadow of the person who was taking the picture angling off to the side. There was another one of a younger, thinner Eddie and the same woman in some cafe. She really was beautiful. He had a Beatnik beard in those days and the wave of his hair was even more pronounced. They were talking and leaning close to each other, espresso cups on the table, street scene visible through the window. A third old photo was a shot of him and another guy in work uniforms: overalls and caps and work shirts and heavy shoes. It was taken in a railroad yard. There were tracks and boxcars in the background. You couldn't see the other guy's face very well, because he was bent forward slightly and the bill of his cap covered about a third of it. The shot had captured some motion he was doing with his right arm. I couldn't tell what he had been holding because that was a blur. It looked like a long pinwheel turning in front of him. Eddie was laughing. I turned it over and read, "On the back of the real. Railroad yard in San Jose. N.C. and me, the daily day heroes, him the sure handed hammer flipper and word slinger, me the ham handed would-be poet." Interesting. So Eddie wanted to be a poet back then. I took one more light toke, wondering who N.C. was, probably another one of his old friends. Then I looked through the rest of the pictures. There were a couple of a beautiful blond woman sitting on a Harley, wearing a pair of tight jeans, motorcycle boots and nothing else. She was leaning back, teasing the camera with her smile and her gorgeous naked breasts. It must have been Thea. That was just a guess because there was nothing written on the back of either shot. She was a knockout. Eddie sure had been lucky. I restashed the stash, put the pictures back, and shut the glove box. Sitting in that car, looking at those faces, I felt like Alice falling through the rabbit hole of someone else's memories. The storm was passing so I started the car, and headed towards my own very important date.

Locating Little Creek was no problem, but finding the doctor and his office was going to be another matter. I pulled off the road just after I saw the city limits sign and sat there for a moment, the engine idling. The town was so small. I could see all of it laid out in little squares on the great flat nothing around it. Okay. Let's do it, I muttered to myself as I put my hair into a tail and tucked it under a camouflage Texaco cap I'd picked up in Denton when I gassed up before leaving. Having the Snake mark me was bad enough, but I didn't need shoulder length hair, too. Then a panic hit me. Who was I going to ask? How was I going to find the doctor? Was there more than one? Was the one who'd delivered me still there, still alive? I gripped the steering wheel, heart thudding against my ribs and turning my guts to water, and stared at my white knuckled hands. But a promise is a promise. I spotted a service station and crossed the border into old bad dreams. I wondered if all those crippled hero types back in all those folk stories had felt the same way when they crossed over dark rivers and went into creepy caves to locate some rare nugget of truth.

At the station, an old Black man was sitting in a chair, propped back against the wall of the station, pitching pennies against the side of an oil drum. He was thin, gaunt almost, with a tight cap of gray curls, dressed in overalls, a blue work shirt, and cracked, worn black shoes. I stopped well back of the pumps, got out, and walked over.

"Morning," he said. He seemed to be the only one around.

I nodded. "Got a phone book? I'm looking for some kin."

"Sure do. Right inside, son, by the register," he said, pointing with his chin towards the office. I went in quickly and found it. It was about the thickness of a D.C. comic, so it didn't take long to look through the Yellow Pages. There was only one doctor listed. I went back out and asked the man where Bois d'Arc Street was.

He laughed and said, "You don't already know where it is, you're not from around here."

"I was born here. Lived here about six years."

He looked at me more closely. I'd been keeping my head low. Then he said, "You look a little like one of the Jacobsons."

"I'm Troy." I paused. Then added, "Audrey's boy."

"I recollect you now. You were just a little tow-headed thing when your aunt came and took you away. So, who you looking for now? Ain't no Jacobsons here any more."

"I'm just--looking to find out some things. Looking for the doctor's office."

"You mean Doc Thompson?"

"I guess. He the doctor here?"

"Only one we got. He's on Bois d'Arc Street, all right. It's back behind the square a ways. Little place like this, you won't have any trouble finding it."

"Okay. Thanks."

He nodded. "You take care now, young man."

"I will. You, too."

"I do. I do. That's how I lived to be so old," he smiled: co-conspirator, one marginal person to another.

I got in the car and drove slowly away, glancing in the rear-view mirror. He had gone back to pitching pennies.

I was downtown, as it were, in a couple of minutes. After figuring out that Bois d'Arc street wasn't one of the four that bordered the square, I started circling outwards one at a time until I came across it. From there, it was a matter of following the numbers until I spotted the clinic. I'd already drawn a little attention as strange cars and drivers do in small towns, but not so much that I felt any threat. So far, so good. I parked, breathed deep, and went in.

There were a couple of people in the waiting room. I asked the woman behind the reception desk, "I'd like to talk to someone about my medical records. And my mother's. I'm trying to get a medical history done and I need to see them." The Snake was working me over something fierce by then and I could barely get the words out. Eyes were crawling all over me, too.

She made a church of her hands, peered at me over the steeple, and asked, "What's your name and when were you born?"

I told her and stood there waiting, trying to pretend I was cool, fiddling with the stack of appointment slips while she went into a back room, feeling like she could see the long hair right through the cap: X-ray attitude-o-meter. She came back in a few minutes with another woman, one I could see from the doorway wasn't going to help me. This second one glared at me coldly and said, "Those records are confidential." 50ish, heavy, cigarette dangling from her red lipstick coated mouth, dressed in a white uniform and huge square white shoes: with the exception of the cigarette and the lipstick and the white clothing, she reminded me so much of Pearl that I began to feel small and guilty for no reason and scared that she was going to swat me with her clipboard.

"But they're my records. I need to see them. At least, get copies of them."

She took another long pull from her cigarette and blew the smoke my way. I held my breath and let it go around me. "I told you already, no. The only doctor here in 1948 was Dr. Wilson and he passed away five years ago. He's the only one who could give you permission to see those records."

I knew that wasn't true. But she sat like the hell hound at the gate and there was no way I was going to get any further just then.

"Okay, okay." That was enough. I could feel the blush of anger and embarrassment eating into my skin so I turned quickly and left, feeling whipped and low. Once outside, I was pondering my next move and walking slowly back to Mariah, when I heard, "Sst." I turned and saw another nurse about the same age as the hateful one.

"Over here," she whispered.

I walked over and asked, "Yes?"

"You're Audrey Jacobson's boy, aren't you?"

"Yeah."

"I thought so. You are the spitting image of her. Poor little thing. Look, I can't talk now. You come back here about nine this evening and I'll let you see those records. There are some things you ought to know about."

I nodded. "Okay. Thanks."

"Nine. Right here." She shut the door.

So. That was interesting. Who the hell was she and why did she decide to help me? I felt distinctly uncomfortable in Little Creek since I hadn't seen anyone else with long hair in the vicinity. To add to the situation, I was really hungry but I didn't feel like daring the local diner alone. I had gotten in Mariah and started driving when I realized that Honey Springs wasn't very far away.

***

"Hand me that wrench," Sam said.

"Which one?"

"The one by my feet," he said patiently.

"Oh. Right. Here you go." I had been drafted to help him finish working on a car since his helpers were on their lunch break. He twiddled and twisted and tapped then pronounced the job complete. I had no idea what he had done but if he said it was fixed, I believed him. I'd been telling him about why I was there and what I had found out so far: one old woman in the clinic seemed to hate me on sight and another one said she would help me out. He knew them both.

"So," he said as he washed up, "Florence Watson's still around. She always was a bitch."

I figured he was talking about the mean one. "How do you know her?"

"Small towns like these, everybody knows everybody else. And their business, too. She and your Aunt Pearl were distant cousins. She'd visit her brother here in town. Too often. They lived for gossip and making life as miserable as possible for folks like your mother. And for me and mine." He turned and spit into the dust. "Damned old hen. If I'd had the chance..." Then he shrugged.

"So you knew Pearl, too?"

"I knew of her and that was enough."

I asked, "So who is the other one, the one who said she would help me?"

"Her name is RaeAnn Dennehy." He started to go on, but the two guys who worked for him came back so we dropped the subject.

"How about something to eat?" he asked. "There's a little place on the other side of the square."

At the diner, I was as much an object of curiosity as I had been earlier in the day at the clinic. I'd removed the cap when we sat down to eat, because I was copying Sam's actions, and down tumbled the telltale tail. But I was with him so there was no direct hassle at first, twitch and long hair or not. Mack was also there. He had already finished eating but he joined us for a coffee. Sam asked for a sandwich but I ordered the chicken fried steak with fries and salad and pie on the side. When it arrived I attacked the plate with the ferocity of a starving dog. Mack and Sam grinned at me. The Snake yanked me around as it always did when I was nervous and folks in the cafe either blatantly stared or watched me more covertly from the corners of their eyes. During one of those silences that open up unexpectedly in a room full of overlapping conversations, I heard a guy in the back say, "Some kind of freak, I guess."

I looked down at the plates. They were empty and that was good because I suddenly lost my appetite. It was just like old times again. I had been spoiled by the insulation of the Palace.

Mack was the one who spoke first. "Who you calling a freak, Lucas?"

The guy stood up but didn't wander any closer. "That hippie or whatever it is that you're sittin' with, that's who. He jus' fall off a circus wagon or what?" That started a round of hoots from the crowd. Must be the town wit, I thought to myself as I fished a few bills out of my wallet for the meal and tip.

Mack stood up and smiled at him. "Anyone whose second cousin could pass for his twin brother ought not to be callin' anyone else a freak, you know what I mean?"

The guy blushed and the fickle crowd laughed at him that time. Sam left a couple of bills for his sandwich and got up. "Come on, Mack. Let's leave it at one for one."

Mack nodded. The local comedian fumed but remained silent and we left. The diner conversation started up again before the screen door had shut.

Sam was as politic as ever. "Rafe and Maddy are bringing in the last of the truck garden today. If you don't have anything you need to do before you go back to Little Creek, maybe you could lend them a hand."

And stay out of sight, I thought to myself, but I was grateful for the shelter so I said yes. Before I walked away to the car I turned back and said, "Thanks, Mack. I didn't know what to say."

He shrugged. "Glad to do it. That goddamned inbred idiot thinks he's so goddamned funny." Mack was still grumbling as he and Sam headed in separate directions. As I started the car, I mentally thanked Eddie again for the loan of Mariah, imagining what it would have been like to try to accomplish this by hitchhiking around this part of the country by myself.

***

"Why do you call these truck gardens?" I asked as I stood up and stretched. I had never done any kind of fieldwork and even though I was only 22, I was already aching after a few hours of stoop labor.

Maddy smiled and wiped her forehead and cheeks with her chapped hands, leaving little smudges of black dirt behind like war paint. "I don't know. We got kitchen gardens and flower gardens but anything bigger than that is called a truck garden. Rafe honey, you know why we call them truck gardens?" She wiped her chin, noticed her hands, and then cleaned them and her face with the edge of her work apron. Sweat ran down her neck, sticking her bangs to her forehead, soaking the edge of her sunbonnet.

He squatted on his heels, his long legs bent double like a six foot tall grasshopper and fanned himself with his cap. "No, I don't either. Funny how you just call a thing by a name all your life without ever stoppin' to ask why."

We pondered that one for a minute, taking it as an excuse to breathe. The plot of land had been covered with rows of late summer vegetables when we started and now they were almost picked clean, just a row or two left. We had filled bushel baskets one by one and loaded them on the back of the flat bed truck. It was late afternoon now and we were almost finished.

"Well," Maddy sighed then we went back to work. I picked the rest of the black-eyed peas while Rafe cut the okra and she picked the tomatoes. I snapped them off carefully as they had said to do, leaving the older and drier ones on the vines for fertilizer. Rafe told me he was going to let everything wilt then plow it under in a few days. The storm earlier in the day had blown past Honey Springs before dumping its load: typical capricious Texas weather, drown one part and parch the other. A blue jay screamed in the live oaks that bordered the garden. Rafe and Maddy were already far down the rows, working steadily. A cloud shadow passed over, surprising me with the perceptible shift in temperature it caused. I paused for a second and looked down the long rows at the shimmering visions made by the rising heat and suddenly realized how apt Duncan's band's name was. I thought about Claire and R.E., Jesse and Texas Weather, Eddie and the Corner Room, and everyone else. I wanted to be home in my room at the Palace with Claire. Little Creek was not my home: never had been, never would be. Neither was White Settlement. And as much as I already loved everyone in Honey Springs, that wasn't home either. I dove into the work, loaded the last bushel, and set it on the flatbed. Time to get this finished and go home. If I found out nothing else, at least I knew where I belonged. Filling a blue enamel cup with ice water from a jug in the cab of the truck two or three times, I drank slowly so the sudden cold wouldn't make my teeth hurt. Rafe and Maddy were finished too by now and I walked towards them, took Maddy's load, and carried it the rest of the way. We were all quiet but content as we headed back to the house to wash up and have supper.

I helped Sam fix the meal. Gwen wasn't feeling well and Rafe and Maddy had other chores to finish before we ate. It was late and everyone was tired, so Sam and I made it as quick and simple as country suppers get. We cut and breaded okra in cornmeal and fried it, opened some jars of home canned black eyed peas and heated them up with bacon drippings, sliced tomatoes and cleaned some green onions, peeled some potatoes, cut them into chunks and boiled them, breaded and fried some pork chops, and mixed up a batch of cornbread to bake in a big cast iron skillet. While everything was cooking, I made two pitchers of iced tea, one with lots of sugar and one without any. Maddy set the table when they came in and Rafe opened up some jars of pickles and chow-chow. I set out the plates and silverware and got the butter dish out of the fridge. Gwen joined us but just picked at her food. She was at the end of the table with the setting sun directly behind her and at the moment it went down, for just a second or two, it seemed that the light came directly through her. I glanced discretely around the room but everyone else was talking. When I looked up again, she smiled at me and nodded very slightly.

After we had eaten and talked and relaxed somewhat, I volunteered to do the cleanup. Maddy left to help Gwen get ready for bed. Rafe and Sam went out to do their nightly security check of the perimeter: an old habit and an understandable one. I rinsed the dishes and wiped them dry, taking care of everything but the nearly full coffee pot. It didn't take long to put everything away so by the time they came back, I was sitting on the porch. Rafe asked, "You want some of that coffee 'fore you take off?"

"Yeah, thanks, that would be nice." He went in, asking Sam as he opened the door, "You, too?"

"No, I believe I'll turn in early. Getting too old to stay up all night like I used to." He rubbed the back of his neck and craned his head around.

I waited a minute or so. Then asked, "Sam, did you know my mother? Anything about her?"

He leaned back and studied the night sky for a few minutes then said quietly, "What say you talk to RaeAnn tonight and come on back here. I'll set up a pallet in the living room for you. If you got time to stay another day, I can talk with you tomorrow night about what little I know."

"Eddie said I could take four or five days if need be."

"Good. A man needs time to do what you're trying to do, track down his past."

I felt a sweet thrill run my spine. Sam had called me a man.

He nodded and stood up. "I'm not trying to dodge talking to you about her for any reason. I'm just tired and you have to leave pretty soon. And a person's story deserves a little time and attention if it's to be told right. Besides, RaeAnn and JaeDeen were closer to her than I was. They can probably tell you more about her."

"Who's JaeDeen?"

He paused. Then said, "A friend of RaeAnn's. She was pretty close to your mother, too." He stood up and turned to go inside, saying, "Well, take it low and slow. You holding dope? The local coppers haven't caught any people your age up here with any yet. Don't be the first."

"Thanks."

Rafe brought me out a cup. "I'd be all too glad to keep an eye on your smokes for you," he smiled.

"Sure, why not. Hell, I already counted them."

They both laughed at that and Sam patted me on the back. I felt a flush of pride at his touch and the inclusion. Being around grown men I admired was something I had never experienced when I was a kid.

And both times I'd been around Sam, I'd begun to notice how deep the father hunger was in me. Rafe and I walked to the car and I removed the stash. "This is mostly Eddie's stuff and it's real strong. I don't know what you're used to smoking, so take it slow. I know it sneaks up on me sometimes."

"Oh, I didn't mean you should..."

"No, no problem. Have some if you want."

He nodded and smiled and went on inside the house. Sam had already gone in. I sat on the porch by myself for a while, drinking the coffee, pouring two more cups. Before I left I washed the cup and cleaned the pot, and made a quick trip to the bathroom. Then it was time to go, time to find out who this RaeAnn Dennehy was and what she had to tell me.

***

I drove the last block or so towards the clinic very slowly and parked well away from the doctor's office. After sitting inside the car for a few moments and seeing that no one was out on the street, I got out, locked the car, and walked quickly to the back entrance. All the lights were out and it was very quiet inside. I looked around and then knocked lightly. No answer. Strange, but the whole day had been strange. I waited a moment then knocked a little louder. Still nothing. I could hear a car coming and felt a sudden panic. How was I going to explain loitering around the back? There was no place to hide either. I crossed over to the other side of the street quickly but the headlights of the approaching car caught me full on. As casually as I could, I started strolling down the street heading for Mariah and a fast getaway, feeling glad that I hadn't smoked anything that evening. The car slowed and the driver rolled down the window. I kept walking then I heard a woman's voice, "Hey, Troy. It's me."

"God, you scared me. I thought I was supposed to meet you in the clinic."

"Not in it, exactly, just at it." She glanced around and stuck her hand out the window. "I'm RaeAnn Dennehy."

"Troy. Jacobson," I said, adding the last name after a second for the sake of formality.

"You got a car?"

"Yeah."

"Which one?"

"That black one over there."

"Okay. Jump in and follow me. Not too close. Just don't lose me. We're going out of town a ways."

I did as she said, staying back a couple of blocks. There were only a few other cars on the road in town and no one seemed to pay any attention to us. It was cloudy and had started raining off and on, the storm gathering again and paying its attention to this part of Texas now. I thought to myself that it was a good thing Rafe and Maddy had decided to bring the garden in today. RaeAnn drove into the black, dark, empty countryside for several miles with me following her then we turned onto a smaller dirt and gravel road that led to a small house. When we pulled up, I could see that there was an old Chevy parked outside and that the lights were on. She pulled into the driveway and I stopped behind the Chevy and got out. The rain was heavier by now so we hurried in.

There was another woman there. She was younger than RaeAnn but older than me, about what would have been my mother's age if she were still alive. She was dressed in a black waitress uniform and was wearing black nylons and pink fuzzy house shoes. She wore her blond hair piled up high in a lacquered bouffant beehive, unlike RaeAnn whose gray hair was cut in a neat, short style. Glancing up at us, she smiled and said, "So you found him okay."

"Yeah. Troy honey, this is JaeDeen Walker."

"Hi," I nodded.

"Troy, you are the spitting image of your mother. Ain't he, RaeAnn?"

"That's how I knew. When you walked into the clinic today honey, I swear I almost fell out. You should have seen Flo's face, JaeDeen. She didn't know whether to shit or wind her watch. It was like a ghost had come back."

"Well, you just sit down honey. You want something to eat? We both just got off work and hadn't had nothing yet."

"No, I ate already. Been staying in Honey Springs with Sam Flanagan and his family."

They exchanged surprised smiles. "You know Sam?"

"I live with his daughter." At the jawdrop, I went on, "And a bunch of other people in Denton. We share a house."

"Oh. Well, I tell you what. They broke the mold when they made Sam. There ain't another man like him," JaeDeen said. "Ain't that right, RaeAnn?"

"I always thought he hung the moon."

I sat down and smiled at them. "Can I help you get dinner ready?"

"No, you just set and visit with us while we fix something. JaeDeen, how are your feet doing, honey?"

"Hurt like hell. I swear those people at the diner couldn't make up their damned minds about anything. Kept me running from pillar to post all day long." She stood up and padded around in the house shoes. It didn't take the two of them long to make their meal: leftover meatloaf, some canned corn and peas from their shelf, cold mashed potatoes fried up in little cakes in bacon drippings and refrigerator biscuits. But instead of iced tea, they were both having beer. They poured me one in a tall frosted glass: Pabst Blue Ribbon.

I observed the country etiquette of letting people eat before talking business and we chatted about the rain, the drive time, how Sam and Gwen were doing, what I thought about Rafe and Mack, what hippie life in Denton was really like. After they'd finished I offered to wash up but that was as politely declined as the offer to help with the preparation had been. Then it was time to talk.

We went into the front room and they closed the curtains and locked the front door. Then RaeAnn pulled a stack of files from her bag. "These are your records and your mother's. You won't be able to make much sense of them because they're all in Dr. Wilson's hand and it's all doctor talk anyhow. Doc Wilson, he was the doctor here when you were born."

"You won't get in any trouble for taking them out, will you?" I asked.

"No, honey, not at all. I get in long before Flo does and I work later than her, too. She'll never know. Besides, she doesn't even know I knew your mother, so she won't suspect I would take these or try to help you."

We opened the first file: my mother's. Born March 15, 1931. The Ides of March. She was 17 when I was born. No high school graduation for her. There were no pictures or anything, just those little hand and footprints they used to make and include in files. RaeAnn was right. Even if I'd been able to see the files, I couldn't have learned much from them. She sat beside me and read off the facts as she flipped through the pages. "She was about as normal as they come. Slight, though. She was 5'4" and only weighed ninety pounds or so soaking wet. Never had any of the childhood diseases, I suppose because Pearl would never let any of the other kids come over to play. She was always dragging Audrey down to the church house every damn time the doors were open, though. Not that Audrey complained. She just went along as sweet as could be. Your mother was one of the quietest people I have ever known."

"Some people used to say she was simple but she wasn't. She was just real quiet, like RaeAnn said, real thoughtful," JaeDeen added. "Ya'll want another beer?" We both nodded.

RaeAnn went on. "She never ate much, just picked at her food like a little bird. I think that may have been one of the problems when she was pregnant with you. She didn't gain enough weight and I don't think she was eating right. Not enough of the things she should have been eating. I believe Pearl was trying to make her, you know, lose you. I know she only brought her in to see the doctor twice. Once to find out for sure she was pregnant and once more the night you were born. That's how I know she was underweight. It says here she'd only gained about 15 pounds between those visits."

I nodded. "I wouldn't be surprised." It came out more bitter than I had intended and she patted my knee.

"Both of you had a harder row to hoe than you should have, I know that for a fact."

JaeDeen came back with the beers and RaeAnn continued. "See, it says here you were about three weeks early, too. And you were light yourself, only about six pounds and something, I can't read how many ounces exactly." She smiled at me and added, "But you sure have grown up nice and tall."

"Weren't you there when I was born?"

"No, I wasn't. I wasn't a nurse then. I started nursing school in '59 and I've only worked for Doc Thompson for a few years. I started just a year before old Doc Wilson died." She took a long drink of the fresh beer and said, "The reason I know about what happened the night you were born is this. One evening, Doc Wilson and I were going through old records, moving them from one cabinet to another and he was drinking, like always. We came across your momma's file and yours and he started crying and talking. He told me something then that he said he'd never told anyone else before."

"What?"

"See honey, he was drunk when he delivered you. It was real late when Pearl brought your momma in to the clinic. His nurse had already gone home and he was sitting in his office, nipping away like usual. Pearl wasn't any use at all. She just sat out in the waiting room crying and praying. You were earlier than he had said you would be, your momma was such a slight thing and he was nervous. He should have used his hands but he used the forceps and he used them wrong. It didn't mash your head out of shape or nothing, but it may have cut the blood flow for a minute. That may be why you have what you have." She picked up my folder and opened it. Born April 1, 1948. That's right--the April Fool. That's the reason I had never told anyone my birthday. When Pearl registered me at school, she had changed the year to 1949 and the day to the 2nd. However, she never let me forget what the real day was. In my file in an old person's scrawl was written "athetoid cerebral palsy due to complications."

"What does that mean?"

"It means that if your mother had been treated right and fed right when she was carrying you and if you hadn't been delivered by force by an old drunk, honey, chances are you wouldn't have what you have."

I let that sink in. "You mean---if I had a baby with someone, the baby wouldn't have this?"

"Not if it was a normal pregnancy and delivery, no. This is one of those things that happen because people are so damned stupid. It's not something that can be passed on."

"There's something else," JaeDeen said. "Pearl dropped you once. Hard. I truly believe it was on purpose. It was the day Audrey brought you home. It could have come from that. I was there when it happened. I saw Pearl do it. She was standing there in the kitchen and your momma and I were in the hall and she just let you drop. Your poor little head swelled up and was so black and blue, I thought she'd done you in. Audrey grabbed you and stood up and slapped Pearl and said that if she touched you again, she'd kill her. That was the one time in her life that Audrey ever stood up to Pearl. I don't know who was more surprised. It was a few days later Pearl left and moved to White Settlement."

"How did you know my mom?"

"We were best friends in high school. In fact, I was just about the only friend she had. We were opposites. I was wild and loud and fast and she was sweet and quiet and so good. Pearl didn't like me so we couldn't visit or play at her house and she wasn't allowed to play at other kids' houses, but she could go to the picture show sometimes when there was a kid's picture on, nothing grown up, of course. Pearl would drop her off and we would meet there. We'd sit in the crying room and talk. And we'd skip study hall sometimes and talk at school. I tried to teach her how to smoke and to use makeup, but she didn't want to. Afraid Pearl would find out and yell at her."

"What's a crying room?" I asked.

"Oh, they probably don't even have them anymore. It was a little room with a glass front and an inside speaker where mommas could take their crying babies and still watch the picture without bothering everyone else."

"Good idea. Wish they still had them," I said absently. We were all quiet for a few minutes. I was still reeling from the information. So, the Scaly One had been visited upon me by circumstances, not genetics. In an altered situation, I would have been completely normal. And handsome. A lady-killer, no doubt. But I was a freak instead. I had always hated Pearl but now I began to seethe. "Damn her," I said, standing up and pacing around, wishing to God I had a joint. Or a gun. Or both. "Damn her. Why did she treat my mom so bad?"

They watched me, letting me work it out some. Then RaeAnn said, "I don't rightly know. Pearl was always just a mean old woman. Even when she was young, it was like she was already old. And Audrey got all the looks in the family, too. Pearl was always, well, plain."

"Plain, my ass," JaeDeen said. "She looked just like an old warthog. She was jealous of Audrey so she tried to drag her down, make her look as ugly as she was, but she couldn't. Even in those old feed sack dresses and with no makeup and her hair pulled back tight, she was as pretty as the day is long and there wasn't nothing Pearl could do to change that."

I turned back to them and said, "So this is something that happened because my mom didn't take care of herself or wasn't taken care of or because I was born too early or because of the way I was delivered. Or because of Pearl dropping me."

"No one knows very much about the kind of palsy that you have, honey. It could have been any one of those things or all of them. They don't know. For one reason or another, a little part of your brain didn't get enough blood either when you were being carried or when you were being delivered or when you were a newborn. And there was some damage. It's not as bad as it could be though. Lots of people with palsy can't speak or walk at all. You don't seem to have the stammer that some of them have. And it's not as bad as it was when you were a child."

"It's worse when I'm nervous."

"And you don't have it when you're sleeping, do you?"

I remembered that Claire had said she did the drawings of me when I was in bed so I answered, "I don't think I have it at all. No one has said that I move around when I'm sleeping."

RaeAnn put the file folders back in her bag. "Well, at least you know. I always said that if I had the chance to set the record straight on this one, I would. And now I have."

I came back to my senses long enough to realize that she had taken a big risk to smuggle those files out. "Thank you. Thank you very much. I had to know. See, my girlfriend wants to have a baby. But I didn't want to until I found out about this. At least, I can tell her that it can't be passed on." Then the other mystery loomed. "Or, at least it can't be passed from my mother. Do either of you know who my father was, what his name was?"

"She never did tell me his name," JaeDeen said. "All I know is that he was a man who was driving through town one day, not someone from here, not someone from Texas even. He gave her a ride back to her house and she asked him in. That's when it happened. I do know she said she wasn't forced or anything like that. And that he was a real handsome man. I think she wanted to keep how it happened and who it happened with a secret, even from me. Maybe it was because she had so little in her life that was really hers. That day with that man. And you."

"So he was just a drifter," I said.

"Just a man in a car, going someplace else," JaeDeen said. "That's not such a bad thing."

"I wonder why she did it," I said to no one in particular.

"I don't know. Maybe she wrote about it in her private journal."

"She kept one?"

"I went out to see her one day not long after you were born," JaeDeen said. "She was in the kitchen. I walked up to the screen door and knocked. I suppose she hadn't heard me drive up. She was looking at some pictures but she put them back in an envelope and back in this little book and shut it real fast when she saw me. I asked her what it was and she said it was her--how did she say it exactly--oh, yeah. Her private journal. That's what she said. Journal. It was just one of those little plastic diaries that girls our age used to keep. I thought then it was a pretty fancy word for such a little book. I don't know what she ever did with it. I never saw it again. She must have kept it hid somewhere in that house so nobody would find it."

"How did she manage-- I mean, after--after I was born. I know she--I mean, I remember a little about the men. You know, the men who would come." I couldn't say it straight out for some reason.

They looked at each other then RaeAnn said, "There weren't that many, honey. It was just now and then. This is a small town. Not many men could go to see her without someone finding out about it, so not many did, mainly just a few of them, a couple who had never married, and a few others who had bad times at home, and one who was real crippled up from WWI, an old man who'd been gassed. His brother would bring him over."

I flinched at that and sighed.

JaeDeen added quickly, "But it wasn't all that. People from the church who thought she'd been treated wrong would stop by and leave a bag of groceries or some clothes and things for both of you now and then. And we would, too. And Sam helped her out a lot. He made sure that no one tried to hurt her. He put the word out all around that if anyone did, he'd see to it they paid for it quick, up front, and personal."

RaeAnn said, "She was a real proud person, Troy. I believe that if it hadn't been for you, she wouldn't have taken any charity or done the things she did, but she had to think about you. She couldn't work in town or anything, because no one would have given her a job and even if someone would have, there wasn't anything she really knew how to do, anyway, because she never finished high school. And there would have been no one to take care of you while she was working. Anyway, she didn't trust you to anyone else, not after what happened with Pearl dropping you and all. So she made ends meet in her own way. She had a little garden there, and some chickens and a milk cow that Rafe and Maddy gave her. She'd leave eggs and butter at the store and old man Hawkins would sell them for her, see that she got credit for it when I brought her in to buy groceries. She never did get a car."

I stood up and glanced at the clock on the wall. It was almost midnight by now and I felt the sudden urge to be alone, to sort through all of this privately. "I should go now. You both have to get up early. I don't know how to thank you. See, I never knew any of this. Pearl would never tell me anything when I asked." I sighed and said, "I just need to think about everything that you've told me and decide what to do next."

They stood up too and we all hugged. Then I left. As I was driving away I looked at the two of them standing on the porch. They were hugging each other.

I don't remember much about the drive back. Too many memories were flooding in on me, too much information to digest all at once. But I found myself back in the yard. I parked and walked in quietly, remembering that Gwen slept lightly. Sam had made the pallet for me and Rafe had left the stash on the pillow with a note: "You were right. One little one was fine for me. Thanks, Rafe." I took one for myself and went back outside to the porch and sat still in the swing so it wouldn't creak, smoking and thinking. I was physically tired but mentally and emotionally wound too tightly to even consider sleeping for hours, maybe not all night. So. The Scaly One was mine all mine and couldn't be passed on. I still didn't have a clue as to who my father was, but at least it seemed he wasn't one of her customers. Someone I might have passed on the street when I was a child. Someone who flinched every time he saw us. Saw me.

I even started to make peace with Pearl's ghost that evening. I knew that she had passed on to some sort of next-life situation a couple of years earlier. The only positive thing she'd ever done was to get me on government disability. It was for, as she had so kindly reminded me, "imbeciles and cripples who'd never be able to work". But it had actually given me a little financial shelter since I was eighteen. On that last birthday, she handed over the paperwork and the first check and wordlessly pointed to my already packed paper sack. I nodded and walked out the door without looking back. So. Enough. What she had done, she had done, and she'd be the one to pay for it, not me. I did a little meditation trick R.E. had been trying to teach me. Letting all the negativity I was feeling build up like a dirty cloud inside my chest, I held it tighter and tighter until I thought I was going to burst. Then I released it into the air in a great, slow exhalation. For a second, I thought I could actually see it, like a hit floating away in lacy curlicues. It didn't get all of it, but at that moment, I felt more at peace about who I was and where I'd come from than I ever had before. The rain had let up while I was driving but now it started again so I listened to it roar in the darkness. For hours I sat in silence, smoking a little and thinking a lot. The sky to the east was just beginning to turn color when Sam and Rafe came out to start their morning chores. They nodded to me and I nodded back.

"Find out what you needed to know?" Sam asked.

"A lot of it. Still okay if I stay here today and we talk tonight?"

"Sure is."

I nodded, went in the house, and slipped my jeans and shirt off under the top quilt of the pallet, sinking into dark dreamless sleep the moment I shut my eyes.

It was close to noon when I woke up. What was different--oh, yeah. All the information came pouring back into my mind. I reached for my shirt and jeans and, looking around quickly, stood up and slipped them on. Gwen was in the kitchen when I wandered in, following the coffee aroma trail. It was almost ready. There were jars and jars of freshly canned peas on the shelves.

"I heard you mumbling in your sleep and figured you were about ready to wake up, so I started a fresh pot. Hungry?"

I nodded. "I can't believe I slept so long and didn't hear you all doing all this work."

She smiled and said, "You were dead to the world. And we tried not to make too much noise since you'd been up all night."

"I should have helped out."

"Well, Maddy's just taking a little rest now. You can help with the rest of it this afternoon, if you want to."

"I'd like to."

She started to get some things together to make lunch but I suddenly snapped out of my self-involved haze and said, "You don't have to do that. I can whip something up for both of us, if you'd like."

She smiled and sat down. "That would be very nice. It's good to see such a young man who knows how to cook."

"Well, it's nothing fancy, for sure. You want an omelet or some grilled cheese sandwiches maybe?"

"Do you know how to make egg salad?"

"Tell me and I'll make it to your specifications."

She smiled and directed me through the routine. Boiling the eggs was easy but everyone had their own way of dressing and spicing it. I toasted the bread and made the mix as she directed then we sat on the porch eating our sandwiches and drinking iced tea.

"So. You talked to RaeAnn," she said.

"I did. She told me just about everything that there is to know. How I got what I got, what she knew about my father."

She looked surprised. "She knew who he was?"

"Not much. He was a guy who was just passing through town. He gave her a ride. They went back to her house and..." I paused, wondering how to say it.

"She seduced him," she finished for me.

"JaeDeen didn't say. I guess that's how it happened. She told me my mother told her she wasn't forced or anything."

"She was an incredibly beautiful young woman who had been under virtual house arrest all of her life, so of course she seduced him. It was probably the one opportunity she ever had to do something illicit and daring. There was a great deal of suppressed passion in her. You could tell that much when you heard her sing."

"She could sing?"

"She could raise the hair on your neck, the purity of her voice, her range, the subtle intensity of her projection. I heard her once at a Christmas pageant in Honey Springs. It was one of those that several churches put on together, get their best singers to stand around the town square at night and do their best songs. We all went, mainly because there was so little else to do then. 'Oh, Holy Night' was the high point of the program. When she got to the 'fall on your knees' solo, people all around me burst into tears. She was so angelic, so delicate, about fifteen years old, dressed in blue and white and gold choir robes with that long blond hair down on her shoulders and those clear, sky blue eyes. Almost made me a Christian."

I laughed. "That good, huh?"

"That good."

"What else did you know about her?"

"Not much that you don't already know, I'm afraid. I never really knew her, just spoke to her in town a couple of times when I saw her. We all thought Pearl had done a terrible thing, leaving her to fend for herself like that, so we did what little we could in the way of food and clothes. Not too much or too often. She was very proud and I could tell it hurt her to be so dependent. And Sam looked after her in his way."

"That's what they said last night."

It was still and hot, the steam rising from the soaked ground as the sun hit it. We went back into the kitchen and I cleaned up. A breeze lifted the curtains on one side of the room and undulated through, sighing past us. Raising the curtains on the other side, it floated on out to the yard. For several seconds, I almost floated out with it. Something was pulling me towards the field but it stopped when Gwen said softly, "That happens with you frequently, doesn't it." It wasn't a question. I wasn't completely sure that she meant my as yet unnamed phenomena, so I turned to face her without comment.

"Rachel was chosen for the task, too."

"What do you mean?"

"Sight." She smirked. "Some artistically call it 'the gift'". She mimed a fortune-teller and made me laugh. Then going serious again, she said, "And she has another. Healing. It's stronger in her than it was in me, though she's just beginning to know she has it and it will take her years to know how and when to use it. I'm sure that is why she got in over her head trying to help that van der Veer boy. Young girl, Rachel. Too young to be taking on a task like him. And she was lovers with him. Dilutes the power. She was always headstrong. Even when she was little there wasn't a thing you could tell her she didn't already know. But she paid a heavy price for being so proud. And she learned." She looked directly at me in that same focused way that R.E. did the day we met, right through me. And she said, "How long have you had it?"

"I've been aware of it since R.E. moved into the house."

"Tell me about what happens."

"I go out of my body sometimes. And I see things and remember them." That was all I wanted to say about it. It was a relief to finally be able to talk about it with someone who seemed to understand, but I was hesitant to put too much of it into words. She seemed to understand.

"Not always pretty, is it?"

"No, most times I'd rather not have known."

"Better to know than not."

Maddy came down the back stairs, her face rippled slightly from sleeping on the chenille bed spread. "Oh, you're up, Troy. You sleep enough, honey?"

I nodded. "Sure did. Can I help you with the rest of the vegetables?"

"Please. There's some more bushel baskets out on the porch if you want to get started with the shelling."

I went to the screen door and turned back. For just a second, it seemed that Gwen's spirit moved out of her body and floated in front of her then settled back in. It was so fast I would have missed it if I'd blinked. She wasn't looking at me but out the window at the trees.

Everyone turned in early that night, tired from the hot and sweaty work of canning. Everyone except Sam and me: we were sitting on the porch, waiting for things to quiet down so we could talk. I started, "So where do you know RaeAnn from?"

"She and I go way back. You see, when my wife first got pregnant, we weren't sure whether or not to go through with it, what with her being in a wheelchair and all. We wanted to, don't misunderstand. It was just that we didn't know of any other woman in Maggie's situation who'd had a baby. There was only one doctor in town at that time so his information was all we had to go by, but he was an old drunk. God knows where he got his training. He just came to town one day, hung up his shingle, and started patching people up. Wasn't much more than a snake oil artist, really. He told us a paralyzed woman couldn't deliver a baby the regular way, so he'd have to operate to take the baby out when her time came. Not that I would have let him." He snorted. "Damn dirty-handed quack. But we didn't have much choice as to doctors, so Maggie and I talked at first about getting the situation taken care of."

"You mean an abortion?" Just the thought of there being no R.E. in the world chilled me.

He smiled to himself and leaned back to look up at the night sky. "But we didn't. Goes without saying, we were both awful glad."

"Such small towns here. Who were you going to go to?"

"RaeAnn. She used to work for a woman doctor in Wichita Falls who knew how to use quinine to do it. No cutting. She helped out quite a few young women back in those days. At the time, she was working at the drug store here in town, so it was easy for her to get the things she needed. I believe the man who ran the store must have been in on it with her because he never let on. We talked to her but then we decided to go ahead and have Rachel. And that doctor was wrong, by the way. Maggie had Rachel at the house. Gwen and RaeAnn delivered her. No problems. She just popped out. I was there, too." He turned to me. "You ever seen one come out?"

"No."

"They turn when they do, like they're squirming past all the corners inside. When her head came out, she opened her eyes and looked straight at me." He looked away. "Now, I know she couldn't really see anything, but I'll never forget the way I felt."

"I'm glad you both decided to have her."

He nodded. "There were other young women in town who didn't go through with it, though, and a damn good thing, too. Weren't ready to be mothers, or weren't in the right situation to be. Audrey's friend JaeDeen, she got into trouble twice and RaeAnn helped her out both times. So when you were on the way, JaeDeen said your mother ought to go see RaeAnn, but she wouldn't have anything to do with the idea. They got into the only real fight they ever had when the subject was brought up. She was dead set on having you."

I smiled. That was nice to hear. Then I remembered something about the way the two women seemed to share so many secrets and said, "That would explain some of the knowing looks last night."

He started to say something then paused.

I went on, "They said you protected my mom."

"I let it be known I would take it personal if anything happened to her. Having been in prison carries a little weight for the good sometimes. And I used to take her a bottle of whiskey once in a while."

"Really? Did she drink a lot?" That was a new dimension to the picture.

"No, not much at all. And it was always late at night when I went by her place. She didn't want anyone to know that she drank."

"You wouldn't think it would have made any difference."

"It did to her. She had her own rules."

"I wonder why I didn't remember you when we first met."

"Oh, you were just a baby back when I used to come around."

I nodded. Then I asked, "How did she die?"

"Pearl never even told you that?"

"No. And I was so blown away by everything else last night that I forgot to ask."

"Pneumonia. It must have happened real fast. Doc said she probably caught a summer cold, caught a chill on top of it. Easy to do. That little place where you two lived wasn't much more than tarpaper and pine boards. JaeDeen went out to see her and she was almost gone. She said that Audrey kept trying to tell her something but that she just didn't have enough breath and then she just gave a big sigh and that was it."

"Where was I?"

"You were playing outside."

"I don't remember anything about that. I just remember Pearl showing up in my life all of a sudden and I remember the funeral, that they made me kiss her. Pearl took me back to our place right after the burial and told me to put everything that I wanted to take with me in a paper sack. One paper sack. That was all. I kept looking out the back window at the house while we were driving off, feeling real sick. I guess I knew what was coming." I paused for several moments and we sat in the dark, listening to the June bugs roaring, the sweeps of sound that would start in one tree, wash over to the next and on down the line, other waves following from other trees. "I wonder if the place is still there. I don't even remember where it was exactly."

"It's out south of the city limits about a mile. You take the road towards Blue Devil Thicket and you'll pass it on the left. It's pretty near falling down now, but there are two old chinaberries, one on either side of the front porch, so it'd be easy to spot. No one has lived there for years, not since your mother died. The old man who owns it lives in Dallas now and he never bothered to rent it out again, tear it down, or build anything else. I believe he may have forgotten it's there. At any rate, it's empty. Kids go there sometimes to party, but not too often."

There was so much more to ask and so much more that he could say, but something in me made me want to put the questions away for another time, like jars of summer vegetables on a shelf: other visits with Sam that I could take down and open one by one in years to come. So he left me alone on the porch to sit up and ponder. I didn't stay up all night again, though. The tiredness had begun to seep into my bones. And it was time to go back home in the morning: home.

***

When I woke up, everyone was gone, even Gwen. At least, I didn't see her in the house. I didn't have any breakfast, just warmed up the coffee that was in the pot. Then I sat at the table and wrote a note to everyone, thanking them and asking them to thank RaeAnn and JaeDeen for me. After cleaning the pot and my cup, I walked out and sat on the porch for a few minutes then got in Mariah and drove off. But I didn't leave town right away. I wanted to see the old place once more and try to find the journal, if it was still there. It never crossed my mind to find the cemetery and her grave. What there was of her wasn't there. What remained were the stories and memories that had been shared with me.

The house was easy to find. And as I spotted it, a tape from the muddy river bottom of my memory began to play in reverse and I could see again the day that Pearl took me away, except I was going back down the road towards the house and not away from it, looking out the front window, not the back. I pulled into the yard, and then drove around back to park in front of the garage. It was very quiet. An early morning breeze picked up and made the high wires whine a little. The garage was leaning dangerously to the south, about to tumble down with the next big storm like the outhouse and the little barn already had. No one came to the back screen door. I sat in the car for several minutes, just looking at it, trying to remember: her, myself, those first six years of my life. No cars were coming, so I got out and went up to the door. It opened with a shove and I walked into what had been the kitchen. So small, had we actually lived there? A red and white checked Formica and aluminum table remained along with a couple of chairs that once matched. Rats or mice had gnawed away the remains of the cotton batting inside the seats and back pads. Dark stains on the cracked and faded yellow linoleum floor marked where the stove and refrigerator had once been. A 1954 feed store calendar hung on the wall, the little square for December still stuck on its cardboard backing. On it, a faded picture of a couple of barefoot farm kids in overalls and straw hats, heading towards that mythic fishing hole, poles over their shoulders and bait buckets and lunch pails in hand: they grinned back over their shoulders at the onlooker, their smiles and freckles and blond health still beaming after all these years. My mother had died in August of that year, August 14th according to her file. A little more than 16 years ago, I had lived there with her, had taken meals with her in this room at that table. And now, nothing: I picked up nothing from the musty air, the empty spaces, the silence.

The only other rooms were the bedroom and a small front room. I visited the bedroom first. The old gray iron bed frame and what was left of the tattered, stained mattress were still there. There had been no closet, only an old chiffarobe and a chest of drawers that Pearl had taken back to White Settlement with her a few weeks after she'd claimed me. So this was where they had come, those lonely men. I had always slept with her since there was only that one bed. But of course when one of them came, she would put me down on a pallet in the front and shut the door. I remembered their dark forms, like solid shadows, moving quietly from the front porch to that room, my mother whispering to me to be good, to go to sleep. I turned away and went into the other room.

Wisps of what had been curtains at one time still dangled from the rusty curtain rods and some yellowed magazines on the floor rustled in the breeze. I heard a faint scratching, scuffling sound under the floorboards. It was probably a skunk or possum that had taken up residence under the house. The sun spattered me with light as I looked up through the holes in the roof. It was so tiny, that house. I felt like Alice again, only large this time. I suppose it's always that way when adults visit locales of their past, but the shack was actually that small, maybe 600 square feet. I couldn't pick up anything more in those sad spaces, no more memories, no more flashes of her, of me, nothing, and no journal, either, not even a place where it could be hidden, except the mattress, and I couldn't bring myself to look under it or cut it open. I didn't want to touch it. I didn't go out onto the front porch because I didn't want any passerby to spot me and intrude on the reverie at best or run me off at worst. I looked out the windows at the cotton fields beyond, some already defoliated and brown, a few others still green and ready for harvest, their load of white fluff ready for the chemical and mechanical stripping or the field hand labor, which ever system the owner would use. It was hot and I was starting to sweat.

I went outside and into the garage. The old doors had long ago rusted in the open position. There was little to see there, either: some empty beer cans and bottles, a few whiskey bottles, a couple of cardboard boxes full of things wrapped in newspapers. As I toed them lightly, a nest of field mice ran out. I jumped then laughed at myself. But I didn't bother looking through it: probably old dishes or Mason jars, anyway, from the paper-wrapped rattle. A book would have been nested in or eaten or rotted away by the weather long ago. The walls were patched with rusty license plates and flattened tin cans. The roof was in worse shape than the one on the house. In fact, you couldn't really call it a roof anymore. It was more like a network of beams that was blotched here and there with a rash of rotten wood. Streaks of yellow light beat down in crazy angles that flashed off and on as the wind drove clouds past the sun. I glanced around again and was about to leave when the light bounced off something shiny, something half buried between the back left corner posts. The roof above was the most damaged section and the rains had poured down the sluice of the long edges of the posts for years, wearing away the packed dirt floor. I walked over and kicked the object.

It was an old cracker tin, sealed around the top with duct tape. Kneeling down, I tugged at it and when it didn't budge, I dug it loose with my fingers. I shook it and heard something clunk around inside. Someone had taken a lot of trouble to seal it. It was rusted but still intact. I went back to the car and sat with the door open, examining the find. I tried to pull the tape off. It had been wrapped around the top so many times that at first, I couldn't get it loose. But it finally gave way and I looked inside to find a piece of tarp, also taped all the way around. Opening that required the use of my pocketknife. Inside, more wrapping: this time it was a bundle of cellophane that was taped. I was hurrying now. I pressed the last layer of plastic tight against the contents. It was a little book, one of those old fashioned girl's private journals. At one time, it must have been pink. Now, it was faded but not so much I couldn't read the name-plate: "Private Journal of Audrey Jacobson, Summer, 1947." This was written in a girl's hand, neat and precise, round letters carefully scribed atop some kind of straight edge line. Her journal, her voice, preserved like some kind of rare fruit after all these years and I had found it. Then I heard a truck grinding down the road. It slowed. I held my breath for long minutes until it passed and the sound faded away. Heart pounding, I tossed the wrapped journal in the glove box, fired Mariah up and got back on the road. I didn't look back. I just drove and drove and drove, the legal limit, taking no chances, going home. I had answers and I had her journal. Mission accomplished. I could leave the underworld and return to the light.

Once home, though, as I parked Mariah safe and sound in Eddie's garage, I couldn't bring myself to open the little plastic Pandora's box. What if I found out who my father was? What if he was someone wonderful, like Sam? What if he was some demon, like Jake? Or some sad nobody. Like me. I knew I'd have to read it some day, but not today. I'd already found out that I could make a kid. That was enough for a few days.

"It seems to me that evolution adds greatly
to the wonder of life, because it takes it out of
the realm of the arbitrary, the exceptional, and links
it to the sequence of natural causation."

John Borroughs, *Time and Change*

VII.

Plate Tectonics

I went straight over to the Corner Room the next morning, but I knew things weren't right just as soon as I walked in. Eddie, for some reason, was handling the A.M. shift alone, so I put my things away in the office and pitched in. His face looked a little thinner and there were dark circles under his eyes. When we stood close at the grill or behind the counter, I could smell alcohol sweat on him, and it looked like he had slept in his clothes the night before.

R.E. came in for the afternoon shift, checked the work board and asked, "Was it just you this morning, Eddie?"

He shrugged.

"You should have let me know."

He shrugged again and walked out of the room.

I raised my eyebrows and motioned towards him with my right shoulder. She answered with both hands up, elbows at her side, a concerned frown. Eddie came back out in a few minutes, a bottle of vodka bulging out of his back pocket and asked me, "You got the keys on you?"

I nodded and handed them over. He took them and turned to walk away. But he paused without turning back to face me before he left and said, "Hope you found out what you needed."

"Most of it. Thanks. Oh, here's ten for gas. I didn't have a chance..."

"No need. Another time. See you. Take care, Rachel," he said softly, making eye contact with her for a moment.

She nodded. "You, too."

He nodded, keeping his back to us. Then he left. The screen door sighed to a close and we saw him walk slowly away.

I sighed, "Wow. Really bad, huh?"

"Yeah. He's been that way since you left. At least, he's a little more verbal now. Man, I thought Jesse could be silent. So," she smiled at me, "you had a fruitful trip?"

"Oh, yeah. Man, I found out so much. I stayed with your dad and Gwen."

"Really? That's great. How are they?"

"Fine, they send their love. And I found out that the--what I have can't be inherited. It was a birth accident. A kind of palsy."

She went thoughtful, rubbing her chin with one hand, the other cradling her elbow. "And so you and Claire are going to make a baby?"

"If she still wants to."

"God, does she. That's all she and Amanda ever talk about anymore. Baby this and baby that. They're driving me crazy."

A few people walked in and ordered burgers and shakes, so we got to work. Then it seemed that the entire place filled up and stayed that way until closing. Stan showed up later but Eddie stayed gone all night. We were up to our ears in food and dirty tables and dishes until past midnight. After Stan left, we did the last of the closing chores. R.E. sat at one of the tables to write Eddie a note. We locked up and sat outside in the dark under the live oak by the storage shed smoking one in the hot, still, dark night. There wasn't a breath of air and the sweat ran down our arms and legs and backs, plastering our jeans and T-shirts to our bodies. R.E. turned to me. "Things got so crazy today I didn't get a chance to ask you about how the rest of your trip went. What else did you find out? Did you talk to anyone who knew your mother?"

"Yeah. A woman who was her best friend. And I did find out some things." I started to mention the journal, but I couldn't. I still hadn't even peeked at the thing. The same "What Ifs" that had stopped me when I found it continued to ride my neck and shoulders like proverbial monkeys, tugging at my hair and skin. But I had it. There would be answers one day, one way or the other, so I just smiled. Tired, she returned it. There really wasn't anything else I wanted to say, and she was distracted by her worries about Eddie. We finished the number and went home.

Later that night, after Claire had heard that the Snake was mine and mine alone, she made a ceremony of throwing her birth control pills out the window and then she had her way with me. Several times. Until I begged for mercy. She finally let me go to crawl out to the well house for water close to the edge of sunup. I hauled up a bucket and sat there, back braced against the cool stone, splashing myself and sipping slowly. Then, wham, the fastest and most powerful episode of sight I'd gone through in months yanked me up and out of myself. "I" was somewhere on the road, hovering above a two lane blacktop.

Eddie was at a filling station out west of town with most of his things jammed into Mariah's floorboards and back seat in a tumble of boxes. The sun was just peeking over the low curve of earth now. He was studying the sky, looking back behind him where he'd come from. Then he turned to face the highway that led away from Texas into the flat, open western desert. The kid who worked at the station said, "That'll be $7.50. Oil and water are fine. Tires, too."

Eddie handed him a ten and said, "You never saw me today, okay?"

The kid shrugged and said, "Saw who?"

Eddie nodded and got in. He sat still for a second then pulled slowly and carefully out and away. He didn't look back again. In the seat beside him, amid the detritus of maps and other road trash, was a photo of a young Eurasian woman who seemed to be in her late teens or early twenties. It was a recent shot. She was wearing a 60s bouffant hairdo, pale lipstick and Modrian-print mini-dress, standing in front of a little stucco house with a low hedge around it and an orange tree in the front yard. Eddie's mouth was set in a straight, tight line and his eyes were red and slightly damp. He faded slowly into the distance until he dropped over the western rim of the world and disappeared.

Then I was back at the well house, slammed into my body so quickly I couldn't tell at first if I was still seeing things or if I was really back. Someone in the house was moaning. I shook myself and dumped the rest of the bucketful of well water over my head, trying to get back in the vehicle. Must not have been too long: the water was still cold enough to give me goose bumps. There it was again, louder now, sharper. I ran back in and loped up the stairs. It was coming from Raz and Amanda's room. As I stepped up to the door to ask what was going on, I was nearly bowled over by Claire as she dashed out. "There you are. We have to get dressed. Amanda's in labor. Come on." She zipped past me to our room and I stood rooted, looking inside.

R.E. and Jesse were helping Amanda to her feet. She was as naked as the rest of us. Her thighs were covered with some kind of bloody mess and she was in pain, terrible pain. Raz was zooming around in circles, looking for something and not finding it, going faster and faster until he looked like a roadrunner cartoon. I laughed and got a glare from Amanda who said between clenched teeth, "Funny, this ain't."

"Sorry. Can I help?"

"Yes. Get dressed. It's time and someone has to help me get cleaned up, get something on, find my bag, and get me to the--Ah! Hospital. And tell them drugs will be okay if they think it's necessary," Amanda managed to say between moans.

R.E. shook herself and said, "Okay. Troy, come help hold her up."

Claire was back already, dressed and carrying some wet towels. She wiped Amanda's legs off as R.E. found a loose fitting dress and slipped it over Amanda's head. Raz was circling smaller and smaller now.

"Is this what you mean, your bag?" Jesse asked, picking up a little suitcase.

Amanda nodded. "Now all we need are keys and a driver. Not Raz," she said.

"I'll drive," R.E. volunteered.

"Then let's go. This kid's coming out. Real soon. Unless any of you know how to cut a cord, we need to get on the road."

We all managed to throw some duds on, get her downstairs and into the back seat of Raz's car. Claire settled down in the floorboard beside her. Raz, babbling away in what he thought was a supportive manner, knelt in the front passenger seat, leaning over and holding her hand. R.E. smiled at Jesse and me and said, "Well, you guys coming?"

We looked at each other in panic.

She grinned, "Kidding. Only kidding. See you later." Then she backed out and drove away carefully down the rutted driveway, picking up speed when she hit the blacktop.

"Oh, that was disgusting," Jesse shivered, sticking out his tongue. "All that blood and goo. Oh, man." He brushed his hands over his bare chest, "I feel like I need a shower."

"Makes you think, though. That's the same way we all came out."

"I thank the gods every day I ain't no woman." He threw up his hands in mock benediction and headed back inside. I watched until I couldn't see the car anymore then I went back onto the porch. I could smell coffee, Jesse's strong brew cooking away. Then I remembered it was September 1st. Labor Day. In the U.S., anyway.

Melany Alexandra Cooper, who would be called Mel by everyone in the house, was born about an hour later after what John called one of the fastest and easiest labors he had ever attended. Amanda, apparently a natural breeder, had needed no drugs at all. There were no complications and the little dark-haired girl had been happily nursing away when R.E. left to come home and tell us the news.

"John told us she just popped out, slipped right into his hands like she was greased," R.E. said, accepting a cup of coffee from Jesse and leaning back against the wall of the house, her long legs stretched out in front of her across the porch. I was in the swing and Jesse settled down again on the steps.

"Melany Alexandra. What a straight name," he sighed.

"Means 'dark defender'," R.E. said.

Jesse laughed and leaned back, stretching. "What? They setting her up to be a professional wrestler or something?"

"Who knows?" she smiled. "Well, better see who's on first at the Corner Room. Don't know why, but I feel like I ought to get over there." She was so tired she was drawling, something rare for her.

Then I remembered that episode of sight and was anxious to get there, too.

When we arrived, we were greeted by a jittery Moe and a much calmer Stan. "Well, he's gone," they began.

"Who?" I asked, hoping hard that my sight was, for once, off that day.

"Eddie."

R.E. stood stunned for several seconds. Then she shook herself and blew past them into the office. It was a shambles. Boxes overturned, things pulled off shelves, a pile of clothes in the middle of the floor. No note, no letter, nothing.

"What the hell is going on?"

"Eddie's taken off again," Stan continued, as though he were announcing something as mundane as the work schedule.

"And left a real mess, thank you very much," Moe muttered, looking for a way to start the cleanup.

"You act like it's a normal thing! What do you mean, taken off?" R.E. was shivering now, a running river of anger, concern, and the load of one more damned thing to deal with that day.

"He's done it before. Nothing new."

"I need a little more in the way of explanation," she growled between clenched teeth as she glared at the two friends. They saw she meant business and that no cop-out or briefing on Beatnik 101 was going to calm her down. Stan went to fetch coffee and something for us to eat while Moe started, "Look. Just sit down. It's a pattern that we've seen more than once." He sighed. "See, Eddie gets flashbacks sometimes. From Korea. And the breakup of his family. And the shooting. When he let it all out the other day to you and John, it got his emotions all stirred up. He hasn't slept well in days. When I was leaving his place last night, he was already going through his stuff."

Stan came back in and set full plates and cups in front of us. "I can hear him now," then he and Moe chanted in unison, "Precious. Semi-Precious. Worthless."

R.E. only sipped at her coffee but I tanked up for what was sure to be a long afternoon and an even longer night.

Moe went on, "He calls it the life triage. Always does it before he hits the road."

"Why does he just leave like that? So suddenly?" R.E. asked, almost in a whisper.

"There are two schools of thought about why he does it." Moe rolled his eyes in a rare feminine gesture as he glanced at Stan. "I believe that our Eddie has a deep-seated guilt he carries around with him, from what, who knows. The death of his parents may have started it. Survivor guilt. Why them, not me? He seems to believe he doesn't deserve a real partnership and so he usually gets into client-caretaker relationships. You, R.E., are most definitely not one of those. You represent a chance for something real. That happened before a couple of times and both times, he flipped out and split rather than reward himself with something he thinks he doesn't deserve."

"Why do you think he does this?" she asked Stan.

"Well, I think Eddie has some more dharma to do before he can settle down. He made a contract with Maja to raise her child and even though she disappeared, he's still bound by that. He won't truly be at peace until he knows that Lizzy is okay. And Maja, too."

"But at any rate, he…" She started to cry and clenched the cup so hard it shattered in her hands. Wordless with rage, she wheeled out, slamming the door behind her.

"That went well, "Stan said quietly as he sipped his coffee.

I followed her at a distance until she cooled down. Then caught up to her side. She seemed a little calmer but was still red in the face. We walked a few blocks in silence before she turned and said, "Surely, nothing else can go down today."

"I wouldn't be saying that if I were you."

She laughed suddenly, the sound shaky and harsh but genuine. "Point taken. I can almost see a Robert Crumb God in a cloud behind my head, finger all cocked and ready, saying 'Oh, I wouldn't be so sure, babe!' She wiped her face. "Okay, back to work. But I'll tell you what, I'm about half tempted to get Dado's .38 and take it out in the country later, murder some beer bottles." We returned to the Corner Room to help clean up and sort out the mess that remained. R.E. never did get around to the glass slaughter but she was a fiend towards the piles of "worthless" category that Eddie had left.

***

It took R.E. and the rest of the Association, as we'd started to call ourselves, a few days to look over the bookkeeping and to hammer out a plan that would keep the Corner Room up and running. It wouldn't leave much in the way of salaries for a while, but at least we'd all be employed. And that way, if Eddie had indeed only taken off for a short while, things would still be there when he got back. "And if not," R.E.

said one evening, "we'll have some sort of continuity until we decide what to do next."

"Continuity. What the hell does that mean?"

"Beats me. Used to think I knew."

Part of my dharma-duty had been to go over to Eddie's I.O.O.F. Street house and sort through things there. R.E. couldn't bring herself to deal with it. It wasn't easy for me, either. He had taken some books and records, a set of things from the kitchen, a few of his clothes, and all of the photos he'd pinned or nailed to the walls. Every one. But then I remembered from seeing the ones in Mariah's glove box that pictures were special for him, so of course he wouldn't leave any behind. I almost overlooked the two hardbacks that had been set apart from everything else on the old kitchen table, under a pile of clothes. One was a signed first edition of On the Road. There was a piece of paper wrapped around it. On it was written "Troy." That was all. Just my name. The other was a blank book, one of those hard bound personal journals. I glanced through it. It was all poems and drawings. I didn't delve into them too deeply because the piece of paper on that one said "Rachel." No goodbyes, no explanations. Just two books. I smiled and sighed as I sat down, keeping my hands on them, drawing power from their pages like true believers used to do from their radios back in the days of airwave preaching. A little closure. I put the two precious items aside carefully and then went about starting the job of putting the house into some kind of order.

The God-Finger that R.E. had joked about held back for a couple of weeks and when we had almost forgotten about it, it thumped us good. The one and only thing left standing in my life was yanked out from under my heels just as quickly as everything else had been. It all started with the mail. Amanda got a letter one morning, read it, and then burst into tears as she dropped it on the floor.

Raz picked it up and started to read, his face changing colors and moods as fast as Amanda's had. "Those sons of bitches!"

R.E. asked, "What in the world?" Amanda couldn't speak, so Raz answered, "Her family. They're saying that if we don't quote straighten up and fly right unquote they're going to see if they can take Mel away from us and raise her there with them."

"Can they do that? I mean, you guys are married. She was born afterwards. You have a job. You're a family."

"But we live where people smoke dope all the time!" Amanda said suddenly. "And where other people aren't married. And where there are anti-war posters all over the place. And--and..."

We stared at her as though she were an alien dropped in our midst. "And your point is?" Jesse growled from the doorway. He'd just woken up and was in no mood such strangeness. "Any coffee yet?"

R.E. aimed her shoulder towards the full pot on the stove, eyes focused on Amanda. Jesse could wait on himself. He shrugged and went to tank up. "So," she asked, "Is there? A problem?"

Amanda was still struggling with postpartum blues and hormonal tides, so it took her a while to get her breath and speak. "Of course not. You know that. But to the court there would be. I know my parents. They love me and Mel."

"But not me," allowed Raz.

"Well, they would if they took the trouble to get to know you. Anyway, they think that they're doing the right thing."

"Right. In so many ways," Jesse added, sitting down with his giant mug filled to the brim. He knew better than to inquire about breakfast for a while and was making do with a piece of leftover chicken from the fridge. "Do you think they're serious? Or they just trying to throw a scare into you?"

"Well, if it's a scare, it's working," Raz said. He and Amanda exchanged a glance that seemed to have meaning for both of them. She nodded and he strode out of the room. We could hear him on the telephone.

Amanda said, "We've been half way expecting some kind of problem. Nothing this drastic, of course." Sniffing again, she went on, "See, my folks were hinting around that I should leave him and move in with them the last time I saw them, when I took Mel down for them to meet her. So, Raz and I got to talking when I got back, you know, 'what if' situations. All his family is in California. They've been asking him for some time to move back out there. But we didn't want--I mean, you guys..." She had to stop talking again as she looked around the room at all of us, and tears marched to the edges of her eyelids. R.E. put her arm around Amanda's shoulders and nodded.

Raz came back in. "I called them." Turning to us, he explained, "We can stay with Mom and Dad until we can find a place to rent."

We were all shocked by this sudden turn of events, no one more than me. "Why that far? I mean..." Now, I couldn't go on for my own impending throat-lump.

Raz explained, "If we're in California, her family can't do anything. The courts are really different there. After all, we haven't done anything illegal. But a Texas jury could be swayed by the way we look and the way we live and award custody to her folks. And besides, they know nothing at all about me or mine, so it would take a long time to find us anyway. That is, if we move quickly enough."

In spite of the heat, cold sweat jumped up all over my body, pooled, then started running down my back. "You mean, move? Like, for good?" I just couldn't get my mind around it.

"Yeah, why not? Pacific Grove is a sweet little place, real hippie heaven. It's literally cool. Foggy and cloudy all summer. In fact, real sweater weather, almost year round."

Amanda nodded and smiled, wiping a little sweat from her brow. "I like the sound of it already." It was going to be another early fall hot day, no cold fronts in sight for weeks yet.

Raz went on, "I could work for my uncle. He's in construction in Salinas. And I want Amanda and Mel to get to know my family. They're good people. I can't afford to go there to visit them much. Same for them coming here. They were a little confused about me and Amanda getting married since they aren't, but they're over the moon about Mel. So, as much as we don't want to leave you guys, we really don't have much choice."

R.E. nodded. "Well, damn. I can see where you two are coming from, but you know we don't want you to go." She bit her lower lip and sighed. Then, always practical, she asked the rest of us, "Where does that leave the rest of us fixed for the hole in the rent budget?"

We looked around the table at each other. Jesse said, "Well, I'm not sure the band could take up that much slack. Fraternity gigs are killing us. Almost literally. Ty got into a fistfight with one bunch last week. And Vance is getting restless, wanting to play bigger clubs. But, you know, California. I wonder if they would be interested." He trailed off and left the room. I could hear him walking around upstairs.

R.E. also went quiet. I could see the calculations adding up in her mind. She was trying to find a way to keep the Palace going on her salary and the bits and pieces from the rest of us, juggling the books the same way she was at the Corner Room. But business had been slow since fall classes weren't in session yet. She went out to the porch in silence, her arms wrapped tightly around herself. Amanda stood up and started walking Mel, who was becoming fussy amid all the unsettled vibes. "We really don't have any choice. I don't want to leave, but I know my mom and dad."

"We all understand," I said out of reflex, but I sure as hell didn't deep down. I knew she was focused solely on the kid and keeping her family together. Of course. But it left me potentially out in the cold, and I didn't appreciate it one little bit. In the space of a few minutes, everyone that I loved was dropped down on separate ice floes, racing away from me and each other at an alarming pace. I went to the well, as I always did when I needed strength from the source. Claire came out and sat with me. She'd been the silent observer through all the conversations, her huge brown eyes taking it all in. She wasn't going to say anything, but I knew that wherever that baby went, she went. And thus, so did I. How do you deal with times like these? You would give anything to wake up the day before when everything had been okay, regular, the same old daily day. But you can't. Like it or not, you have to figure out a way to hang on to the precious and the semi-precious while leaping from one chunk of ice to the next.

***

It didn't take long for the family to make their final decisions. For Raz and Amanda, it was cut and dried. His family was overjoyed that they had finally decided to come back to the coast. Raz had just been in North Texas for Amanda, and now Amanda had no reason to stay and lots more reasons to go. Claire was already talking about transferring to Monterey Peninsula College.

Jesse talked to the band about moving and they were all but packing before he finished the sales pitch. Pacific Grove would be a good jumping off place for them to start working the San Francisco clubs and for most of them just the thought of playing so close to the birthplace of our counter culture was reason enough to decamp.

Stan and Moe could easily run the Corner Room for a few months. The always gregarious Moe had made lots of friends in town so new help would be easy to hire. They'd already decided that if Eddie didn't return or get in touch before winter, they'd sell the place and move back East. Eddie had made that simple by becoming full partners with all of us regulars after R.E. had been hurt so badly. "It's much easier to be us there," Stan told me one evening as we were cleaning up. "I hate having to be so closeted, always having to think twice before I even hold hands with him in public."

Claire had her things gathered up in the room, ready to leave at a moment's notice. She knew that I would go with her wherever she went, but it irritated me that she would take me so for granted. It also got on my nerves that she seemed to be in love with that baby more than she was with me. Those facts burrowed themselves into my psyche like ringworms, making me peevish and petty. Claire punished me by staying away and hanging out with Amanda until I snapped out of it. They spent many an hour in the kitchen, debating over which pot or pan to take, which to send to Goodwill. For people who prided themselves on not having many things, we certainly seemed to have accumulated quite a few.

R.E. was the last to decide. We ran into each other one afternoon, passing through the big open room downstairs. Without a word, she came up and hugged me. "So you two are going."

"I don't want to, but I seem to be the Ruth in this story."

She nodded. "I have to go up and square things with Dado and Gwen first. But it seems like the thing to do. I will not stay here with a house full of ghosts and I don't want to fill it up with strangers just to pay the rent. And Jesse's been selling the idea like crazy. He's got the California bug and he wants me to go with him so bad we've even had a couple of fights about it. He can't understand why it's harder for me to pull up roots and move."

"When are you going to see your Dad?"

"Soon."

"Let me know when you do. I want to see everyone again, too."

"Deal." We hugged again and I went upstairs, suddenly drowsy. I fell asleep face down on the old mattress in the roof room. Later, as I was waking, I could feel a presence in the room. Rolling over on my back, I saw him. Coleman was standing over me: long wavy black hair, slim wiry body, pale skin, glistening winter blue eyes, dressed in jeans and boots and his white shirt, just like the day he found out his dad had died. He was holding a pistol pointed at my heart. His slow smile bared his teeth just enough to let me know I was a dead man. "Thought I was gone, huh?" he hissed in his silky voice. "Big time mistake, oh my brother. You forgot about me, didn't you? Well, I never forgot about any of you. Especially her. I'm back now. And I want what's mine." Then he pulled the trigger.

I shouted "No!" and sat up so fast I almost passed out. I was alone in the roof room, really awake now, and I had pissed all over myself. Relieved that it was just a bad dream and embarrassed by doing something I hadn't done since I was a baby, I laughed nervously. I looked around and listened. Still alone. Well, at least no one uses this room anymore, I thought as I quickly stripped off my soaked cut-offs. After flipping the mattress over to cover the rest of the evidence, I sneaked out and got a quick shower, rinsing my shorts at the same time. As I washed the piss and the dream away, I wondered to myself what that had all been about. Then I remembered. His honeymoon was over and he was probably back in town. Maybe it was time to leave, after all.

R.E. decided that evening to move all of Eddie's discarded books and records up to Honey Springs for safekeeping, since she couldn't bear to throw them out or give them away and because there was no where else permanent to take them at that time. She called her father and told him she was thinking about going to California but she was still a little uncertain about the permanence of the move. "I don't want to haul all this stuff all that way and then decide I don't like it." After she hung up, she said "Ouch! He doesn't play that guilt card very often but he plays it well when he does."

"What did he say?"

She mimicked him perfectly as she replayed the conversation. "Girl, you know you owe us a visit first."

"Man, I even felt that sting. He is good."

"Yeah," she smiled sadly, "he is."

It took a couple more days of heavy cleaning and sorting to go through the rest of Eddie's I.O.O.F. Street house and Corner Room things, as well as R.E.'s at the Palace. We were back and forth between the three places so many times I lost track of what was where, but R.E. managed to keep things organized. As we were loading the last of it into the back of her truck, I noticed that her trunk was part of the load. She'd never been far from it since it held all of her precious things.

She noticed the direction of my glance and shrugged. "I'm just taking the essentials to the coast for now, one suitcase. I'm not sure about this move at all. If it turns out to be a permanent thing, Dado will send it to me. Hell, he might even drive it out himself. He said he's always wanted to see the ocean. But until then, I want to know that all my real stuff's in safe hands."

Then we were finally on the road, using the time on the blacktop as a break from all the hard physical and emotional work. She had said it would be a sweet little vacation before the long drive out west. We both knew by then that it was a done deal, moving to California and we'd even started to look forward to it. Mostly, we had hoped for a special time with her family, a hiatus from all the upset and changes. It was special, all right, but hardly in the way that we had wanted it to be. It was a time set apart from all others in the way that passages are separate and distinct in our memories.

***

When we pulled into the yard that night, R.E. sighed and switched off the lights and the engine. The country silence whooshed around us and I could hear the city noise ringing in my ears again. It was especially quiet around the house. The inside lamps and the porch lights were on, but both Sam's and Rafe's trucks were gone. R.E. got out and stretched. "Must be a dance or something else going on." I got out too and then I could see headlights coming, barreling down the road behind us.

"Ah, that's Dado's truck," she smiled. I'm going on in." She waved as the truck, racing now, turned in the gate and caught us in the lights, the driver leaning out and shouting something we couldn't hear, honking. She walked on in and I stood waving back at the oncoming vehicle that screeched to a stop beside me about the same time R.E.

walked in the door. It was Sam. He jumped out and said, "Oh, Jesus. Was that Rachel? Did she go inside?"

Then I heard her scream.

Sam shook his head, grabbed my arm and dragged me alongside him as he ran towards the house. "I've been driving all over Texas trying to catch up with her and tell her." The screaming went on. "It happened a couple of days ago. Kept trying to call but couldn't get anyone on any phone." We were at the door then. I froze as he opened it and walked in quickly to take R.E.'s shoulders and turn her away from the coffin that was set up in the front room. Gwen was in it, all laid out in a pale violet dress with her hair free and loose around her on the violet satin inside. R.E. was still screaming as Sam held her and then picked her up and carried her back out onto the porch. He rocked her like a long-legged baby until she calmed down enough to just cry.

"I'm sorry, honey," he kept saying, "I'm sorry you had to find out like that. I tried to find you so I could tell you to your face, but I kept missing you everywhere. I saw your truck a few miles back but I couldn't catch up with you in time. There, there. Calm down. She went real peaceful. She just died of old age. Just passed on in her sleep. It's okay. There, there, Rachel," he soothed.

"No! It's not okay," she gasped. "It's not. Damn it, damn it, damn it. That's the second one, the second one that didn't bother to say goodbye to me."

Sam nodded and continued to hold her. I got up and walked away, back down the dirt road into the moonless dark of the country night, listening to the crickets pray for rain. I don't know how far or how long I walked or even where. It must have been in circles because I kept seeing the house off on my left. The lights stayed on until just before sunup. That was when they went off and I went back up to the porch. The screen door was unlocked and there was a note on it, held there with a rusty bobby pin. "Troy, clean sheets on the bed in the upstairs bedroom." It was unsigned but it wasn't R.E.'s writing. Must have been Sam's. I hurried in past the now closed burial box and went up to lay me down to sleep, wondering what else was going to happen to us. I fell into a deep dark trance and remained there until Rafe woke me up about noon the next day.

He was dressed in a clean blue shirt and slacks, his sunburned face shaved and solemn. "Troy, why don't you wake up now, son. I brought you some coffee and breakfast. People are starting to get here."

I sat up and shook my head, trying to clear it then all the pictures from the day before sank in. "How's R.E.?"

"Well, it was a hell of a way to find out, but she seems to be taking it alright. She's as tough a little gal as her momma was."

"Yeah. Man, she's been through hell lately." I told him about Eddie and the decision to move to California and all of the other changes, large and small, that had taken place since I'd seen him last. He nodded and listened as I drank the coffee and nibbled at the food.

"When it rains, it pours," he sighed. "Poor kid. She sure was close to her grandma. To have to see her like that, not knowing about it before. Man, oh man. Well, look here. The funeral's this afternoon. Folks are coming over here first. We're going to bury her out in the little cemetery where Maggie is. Won't be no church service, of course. Sam's just going to say a few words. Gwen always said she didn't want no fussing." He motioned over to the side of the room where a pair of pants and a shirt about my size were on the dresser. "Maddy asked around and borrowed these for you. Now, if you don't want to go, you don't have to. But you're welcome to."

"Of course I'll go."

He nodded and walked out. "Poor little Rachel. She sure has had some troubles come down on her of late."

"Maybe it's the last of it."

"Let's hope."

I sat there for a while, listening to the voices downstairs and to the cars and trucks pulling up slowly and parking. The smells of ham, potato salad, pies and cakes drifted up to me: country custom. You never go to a funeral without bringing a dish for the family. It was assumed that they wouldn't feel like cooking, so other people did that for them. I always wondered why. If you didn't want to cook, then you probably didn't want to eat. But maybe the food wasn't just for the surviving family. It was a way of affirming that life goes on. The living are hungry. And suddenly, I was ravenous.

R.E. was surrounded by well meaning people most of the day so I didn't get a chance to talk to her. When I wasn't sneaking a piece of meat or a scoop of vegetables from one dish or another, I stayed as close to her as possible. She was distracted, gone down deep inside herself in the internal reverie I had witnessed before, trying to sort out the chaos within so that she could deal with the ritual functions going on around her. Every time I tried to tap into her attention, she was pulled aside to be greeted or comforted by someone. I was introduced and reintroduced several times by the same distracted people to more distracted people but I went along with it on each occasion, saying yes I was Audrey Jacobson's boy and yes it was a shame about the way people treated my mother and so on all afternoon.

In spite of all their political savvy, the folks that gathered there that day were having trouble coming to terms with the final passage of their oldest friend. They didn't know what to say, so they made the dreaded small talk. More than one person said that Gwen looked like she was asleep. A few commented on how natural she looked, what a good job they'd done at the funeral parlor, and how fast too, given the short notice. They talked about the weather and the crops, gas mileage and recipes, anecdotes, and a little politics. No one directly addressed the fact that there was a dead woman in a box in the room. But that was customary. Death is not a topic any of us are comfortable with talking about directly so we dance around the edges, saying inane things sometimes: avoidance as ritual.

About four that afternoon, a big black shiny hearse pulled up and a couple of men walked in. Sam nodded to them and then said to the room, "Well, we'll go ahead with them. Ya'll come on over to the graveyard in an hour or so and I'll say a few words like she asked me to. Just wait here, if you like, until we can put her to rest in the ground. You're all welcome to come on back here after for a late supper." With that, people began to file by the coffin for a last look, a touch or kiss. I flinched as I watched that part. Then it was time for the family to say their goodbyes. The two men waited by the door, their arms folded in front of them, eyes averted. Rafe and Maddy went first, crying now, talking softly to the body. Mack and his wife Grace were after them. I lost it when I saw Mack crying, the tears rolling down the ruts in his old bulldog face, his chest heaving. I looked at R.E. who was sobbing, too. Sam took her hand and then turned to include me. We walked over together. All of my losses seemed to be getting mourned at once. Sam patted the folded waxy hands and said something in French. R.E. held them too for a moment then turned away abruptly, saying that she preferred to remember her in life. I looked up at Sam and then back down at Gwen's remains, speechless. He nodded and ushered us away, saying to the men, "You can go ahead now." We all waited outside while they did whatever it is that they do to seal a coffin and then we watched them carry it out and put it in the hearse. They waited for the immediate family to get in our trucks and follow them. There was no limo for the family. Again, this was the country. You didn't need such affectations as that for a simple service.

And it was. The men, with the swift assurance of professionals, went about the business of lowering the coffin into the freshly dug hole and covering it up with earth. Then they unloaded a few round wreathes of flowers with their swatches of ribbon-messages: "Rest in Peace," "In Memoriam", "In Fond Memory Of Gwen." One we knew was from Mack and Grace: "Shoulder To Shoulder." We helped the men set them around the head of the grave. After a while, the cars and trucks of family friends began to arrive. Once again, I found myself among a group of people gathered around a graveside. But it was late afternoon this time and although the purpose was the same, it was all so very different. R.E. stood by Sam. She was dressed in a long print thing that she had borrowed from Maddy who was about her size but not exactly, being a little shorter in stature and wider through the hips. R.E.'s red hair was braided and in a coil, like Gwen had always worn it, a few loose wisps shimmering in the breeze that had come up. She was as pale as I'd ever seen her and seemed thin, her cheeks almost gaunt, a color version of some '30s Depression photo in that ill-fitting dress and borrowed flats, no jewelry. Sam was in a pair of suit pants and a white shirt, his lean brown arms and face in sharp contrast, his gray hair neatly combed. He was calm and strong and rooted there on the land, balanced with his hands in front of him, as I had seen Coleman stand that day, but again different in that he was blessing each one of us with his gaze, not blasting us. I suddenly felt calm, too, like his inner peace was somehow working its way through the ground under my feet and up through them into my backbone, filling me with a strange kind of light. I looked over at R.E. and smiled. She returned it after a moment's uncertain pause, straightened up, and filled her chest with a deep breath before releasing it calmly.

Sam began. "Well, she passed on peacefully. I found her in bed. Looked like she was sleeping. But I knew when I walked in, that she'd gone on ahead. To what, none of us know. She always said that it would be to something. She wasn't sure of what, either. Gwen wasn't the kind of person to say she knew what would happen if she didn't. She didn't completely like the Christians' story or that of any other religion. None of them seemed to make complete sense to her, though she kind of liked parts of their talk. She never bought into anything 100 percent. Always said that people who were 100 percent sure of something were selling snake oil."

There was a round of relieved smiles and Rafe snickered a little. Maddy nudged him so sharply he moaned and Sam smiled. "No, that's alright, Maddy. Gwen would have wanted a little laughter today. You know her. Or knew her. It's going to be hard at first to talk about her as part of the past. But she lived a long, long life. And she did just about everything that she ever wanted to do. And right up until the end, she was as healthy as any old woman had the right to be. No, we are all going to miss her. That's a certainty. But we ought not to grieve too much. Some grief is natural." He turned to R.E. at that point and the tears welled up again in her red eyes. She batted them away with the back of her hand and wiped her face, struggling for composure. He looked away, letting her settle down then he said, "And I know that none of us got to say goodbye like we would have wanted to. But let's not think about ourselves too much here. This is her moment and we all know how she hated saying goodbye. You all remember that. Even when you came to visit, she would just slip off to the barn when it was time for everyone to go. And that's what she did. She just slipped off, by herself, to whatever will be next for her. So, let's all join hands and be thankful for the times with her that we had." I stepped up and took Rafe's hand on one side and some little girl's on the other. We all stood there for a moment, linked in a circle, looking at the fresh scar in the earth, the flowers around it, the wooden marker that would be replaced eventually by a more permanent one: "Gwen" was all it said for now. After a few moments, Sam said, "Well, come on, then. Let's all go back to the house, why don't we?" R.E. turned to him and he held her while she cried a little more. Then she looked up at him and said, "That was perfect, Dado. Just perfect."

He smiled. She returned it with a silent nod. They walked back to his truck with their arms around each other and I followed a short distance behind, leaving them to their thoughts.

Later that night, after all the food had been tasted and all the last stories had been shared, after Rafe had played a mournful tune that had everyone in tears and then several lively ones to buoy us up again, everyone left, car by truck, until it was just us again. R.E. sat up with her father and family until they turned in one by one and then it was just us two, sitting on the empty porch, smoking one in silence. "Well, what else do you think is going to happen?" she asked as she passed the number to me.

"I have no idea. I just hope we can get out of town before anything else does."

She exhaled, "a hearty amen to that. I almost lost it for good when I walked in and saw her in that casket. Jeez Louise. What a shock."

"Sam still feels bad about that. He asked me earlier if you were okay."

"What did you tell him?"

"As far as I could tell, you were dealing with it."

"You're right. I am. With all of it. But you know, if things were going to change that fast--Eddie leaving, Mel being born, everyone going to the coast, Gwen--dying--I'm kind of glad it all happened at once. Kind of a package deal. Maybe that's better than one thing happening. You get over that. And then something else. And then you get over that. And so on. You know?"

"I guess. So, how long you want to stay before we go?"

"I'd like to leave tomorrow, but we both should take at least a day to rest up before we start driving. Dado's leaving soon, too, you know."

"Really?"

"Yeah. That old man is moving to South Texas."

"You're kidding. Why?"

"Well, a friend of his, one of the old organizers, has been trying for some time to get Dado involved with the Mexican farm labor situation in the valley. You know, as a kind of unofficial advisor, given his age. Dado said he felt like he had one good fight left in him, but that he didn't want to leave Gwen. And now, with her gone and my leaving the state, for a while, anyway, he said he felt like there was nothing keeping him here."

"That's great that he would go down there. Man, I love your father. I wish--I wish he'd been mine."

She nodded. "I got real lucky on that count."

"So, are you going to leave all the stuff here anyway?"

"Yeah, Rafe and Maddy will look after the trunk and Mack is thrilled to have all the books and records. Said he had a lot of catching up to do."

"You don't think Sam would mind if we took off so fast?"

"No. Not at all. None of us like long, drawn out farewells."

We slept in the next morning, all of us, getting up about noon. When we came downstairs, Rafe had breakfast going and we all sat around the table, eating and drinking coffee and talking. Maddy was sleeping in. I was surprised at how good I felt. It was like the crying and the grieving had cleansed me somehow. R.E. looked better, too: a little more color in her face, her eyes clear and more gold and brown than green. Sam at smiled her and asked, "So, how are you, honey? You ready for the road?"

"We'll take off tomorrow, if that's okay with you."

"You know it is. I think you'll like Californ-i-a," he said, deliberately mispronouncing it. "Oh, and I got out the old .38 this morning and cleaned it. You still remember how to shoot it?"

"I think so. But why?"

"I want you to take it with you." His face had gone serious.

"You think I'll need it." It was a statement.

"Better to have it and not need it than the other way around. I hear tell the van der Veer boy is back from Europe and they got a long reach. I don't want you to face him empty handed like you did last time. Come on outside. I got some bottles set up behind the barn. Let's see if you're still the little eagle eye you used to be."

Sam took the handgun and a box of bullets from the cabinet and we all four walked out to where they had dumped and burned their trash for what looked like years. There were dozens of brown glass bottles, tin cans, and other castoffs set up in rows at different distances. He loaded the gun and took a few practice shots, hitting all but one of the six. "Sight's a little off," he smiled. R.E. and Rafe returned it as though it were an old joke. He reloaded and then six out of six exploded into glass powder. "Your turn," Sam said as he handed it to her. R.E. took it and raised it to eye level. She smiled and all six bottles she aimed at fell. She reloaded and dropped six more in rapid succession. One more reload and another six went one after the other.

"Annie goddamned Oakley," Rafe hollered. "Go, baby, go!"

"Not bad," Sam smiled, "for a girl."

She grinned, "Shouldn't tease an armed woman like that."

I just stood there with my mouth open. "Man, I had no idea you could do that."

"She could drop quail with every shot when she just a little thing. Never wasted a pellet," Sam said, beaming. "A real natural shot."

"Had a good teacher," she smiled as she hugged him.

"Troy," Sam said to me, "your turn."

"Whoa! I've never held a gun in my life. I wouldn't know what..." But he had already loaded it and was handing it to me. Caught once again in a male ritual, I was torn between a lifelong aversion to weapons and their uses and desperately wanting Sam's approval. Approval won out, especially when he said, "If you are going to be traveling with my Rachel, I want to know that you can defend her, if need be." I remembered my inept hesitancy that day in the woods when Cole had seen through me so clearly and knew that one, I wouldn't shoot him and two, I had no idea how.

"Okay, but I've never done this before."

"We all lose our cherries some time, son," Rafe said solemnly.

Sam named each part of the thing and described the functions clearly. It was a simple matter, really. Pull the trigger, it slaps the firing pin which smacks the blaster on the back of the bullet which makes an explosion and forces a projectile down the spiraled insides of the barrel and the load sails out and plows into whatever it is what you're shooting at. He took the bullets out and had me handle it for a while empty. Then he showed me how to load it and had me finish that job. Standing behind me, he patted me on the shoulders then lifted my arms up level saying, "Now, the most important thing to remember when you're firing one of these at close range in self-defense is, you have about one second to get a clean shot off. Chances are, the person you're aiming at has already made their decision and drawn a bead on you. So, don't hesitate. Just aim and squeeze the trigger."

This was not making me relax. In fact, my arm began to shake.

"Son," he said softly, "if that van der Veer bastard gets within range of my girl, he will kill her this time. Make no mistake about it. Don't let me down."

That steadied me. And Sam had said "son." Once again, his strength filled me. I shut my eyes and squeezed off a shot. I heard it zing away in the distance.

"Another thing. Never shut your eyes. You aim better with at least one of 'em open," Rafe laughed.

I did, too, relaxing a little. "Okay." That time I tried again, focusing hard on a bottle, which remained jeeringly unshattered after I'd shot at it twice. Sam held out his hand and I gave him the gun. "Sorry," I muttered, completely humiliated. I wanted his approval so transparently that he gave me some.

"You're doing just fine. Getting closer every shot. See, Troy, when you aim, don't think so much about it," he said, stressing the word 'think'. "Aim like you're pointing at someone. This close of a range, you don't have to think about curves or any fancy physics, like you do with a bow. If someone is moving, shoot just a little in front, so they move into the shot." He raised his arm and casually blew away another bottle, but not the one I'd been trying to blast. Then he handed it back to me.

I took it and raised my arm just like he had and then I saw Cole's sneering face the day he'd battered R.E. so badly. I pointed straight at him and the bottle exploded into powder. It was like I had struck him. I could feel the contact: Zen and the amateur marksman.

Sam patted my back and smiled, "That's my boy."

In all my years before, I had had few flushes of pride. That was the first one in a long time. We practiced some more. I missed more often than not, but I was beginning to get a feel for it by the end of the session. As we were walking back to the truck, R.E. put her arm around my waist and smiled, "Thanks for doing that. I know you hate guns, but Dado's a little worried about Cole."

"More than a little, and with reason."

"You sound just like him now."

"Thank you," I smiled. Any comparison to Sam was fine by me.

I didn't have much chance to talk to Sam by myself, and I knew that R.E. needed the time more than I did. Those days I had wanted to save up to share with him weren't possible anymore. That was a lesson learned which I have never forgotten. If there's something you want to say to someone, say it. You never know if you'll get that chance again. We did go out to the old stock tank and have a cold picnic dinner under the pecan trees, just the three of us, that last evening. It had been one of Gwen's favorite places.

R.E. asked, "It seemed like it all happened so fast. I mean, she died, and you guys had the casket and all the arrangements done the next day."

"Well," Sam said, picking a bit of fried chicken from between his teeth, "that's not so unusual, really. She had it all planned for some time now. Back when she got sick last winter, she took me aside after she got well and showed me this box in her chiffarobe. She had that violet dress, a new set of underwear, shoes, everything in there. She said she wanted to be buried in it and to be sure that they put the shoes on her. She didn't want to go on ahead barefoot."

R.E. laughed. "She hated that, didn't she."

"It was a sign of poverty, not having decent shoes. And you know how proud she was."

"And vain."

"Well, she was just about the prettiest woman in these parts when she was young. Yes. She was proud. And independent. She had the plot chosen and paid for, she'd talked to the undertaker and chosen that old style wood casket and paid for it too and for everything else. She showed me all the receipts. Said to be sure they didn't try to make me pay twice. No, she said she'd gone all her life without a single debt and that she didn't want to go on ahead with any, so she saved up and got it all taken care of. She even told me that she wanted me to say a few words over here at the cemetery but not to let people go on for too long. She hated a lot of fussing."

We sat in silence for a while, listening to the frogs. Sam picked up a stone and chunked it at nothing in particular.

R.E. asked him. "You sure about this South Texas thing?"

"'Bout as sure as you are about this California thing," he smiled.

She nodded. "That's fair enough, I guess."

"Troy, you promise me you'll look after her. She's a headstrong gal, my Rachel. She's gotten into the deep end of things more than once."

"I promise."

"And who'll look after you?" she asked, a little wistfully.

"Well, you don't have to, Rachel. You never really did, though you tried, after your mother was killed." He frowned. "We still owe those bastards, you know."

She nodded and said, "Yeah," before going thoughtful and silent. Then she got up. "I'm going walk around for a while. We'll be sitting on our butts for days, so I feel like a stretch."

We watched her without speaking until she was out of earshot. Then Sam said, "She has always felt this sense of guilt. Or duty. I suppose it was because of me. Of the way she came up. This damn little town. She's always trying to prove something, prove that she's better than folks expected she would be. Smarter. Tougher. Completely independent. And that makes me feel guilty."

"You couldn't help what people would think. You did what you did."

"I was supposed to be the one to pay society back for it. Not my wife. Not my daughter." He sighed. "I suppose that's why she always took up with boys that needing fixing in some way. That little van der Veer bastard wasn't the first. It's like she feels somehow that she doesn't deserve a regular partner, like she always has to be patching someone up."

I nodded. I was, in some ways, one of those strays.

Sam must have felt that. "Now, you know I ain't including you in that. You are a true friend to my girl. That's why I showed you how to use the .38. I'm expecting you to take care of her," he said, stressing you and her, trying to make it clear to me he didn't consider me part of her caseload.

I nodded.

We shook hands. There wasn't anything else to say, so we both picked up the stones within reach and took turns skipping them across the pond or chunking them at whatever poked its head up. R.E. came back not long after and I took off on my own walk. After a mile or so, I looked back. They were still there under the trees.

We left late the next afternoon. R.E. hid the handgun and a box of bullets in a little place she and Sam constructed under the dashboard and Maddy loaded us down with a full picnic cooler and two thermoses of iced tea and coffee. True to their natures, neither Sam nor R.E. went through a long goodbye. They hugged and then we got in the truck.

"Write when you get work," he smiled.

"You, too."

"Por supuesto," he smiled. "Cuidate, querida. Y siempre vaya con dinero y pistolas."

She laughed and we backed out and drove away.

***

It didn't take long back at the Palace to get everyone else sorted out. Raz and Jesse would take turns driving the van Raz had acquired in order to haul all of our things. Amanda and Claire would go with Mel in Raz's old car. R.E. and I would bring up the rear later and be responsible for closing up the Palace and settling matters at The Corner Room. Amanda had put her family off the scent briefly by pretending to bow to their demands but insisting that she and Raz needed a couple of weeks to settle their affairs in Denton. She even swore that he was going to cut his hair and "straighten up." They bought the story, but she wanted to put as many miles between them and her baby as possible before they got wise. The rest of the band had already set out caravan style to play gigs on the way and raise a little cash for getting set up on the coast. Duncan had all but moved to Austin on a permanent basis anyway since Cloud Shadow could get work there more easily. He had stayed in River City rather than face a long drawn out goodbye, but he had left stash and letters for everyone as parting gifts. He had also made a small, quiet ceremony of presenting R.E. with his cartridge box before he took off the last time. "I can always get a new one. But you might need a little bank you can access anytime."

We were doing the last cleanup when our old landlord came by. We'd called him to let him know we were moving out. He was a straight guy, only about fifteen years older than us, Eddie's age, it suddenly hit me when I saw him, but he looked like he was fifty: overweight, with the pale skin of an office worker. He was wearing a polyester shirt with no undershirt and too-short brown pants that bared his sheer nylon socks when he walked up on the porch. His shoes were brown, too, so every time he turned his back, Jesse mouthed "Brown Shoes Don't Make It." He'd turn back to face one of us and we'd deadpan it until he turned around again then we'd clamp our eyes shut and stretch our mouths out wide, trying not to laugh.

But he sobered us up quickly when he said, "Good timing, you kids giving notice when you did. I'm selling the place anyway. Meant to get around to telling you but I kept forgetting. Church of Christ has been interested in this lot for years now but they could never get the money together until this month. Some construction company decided to back 'em and they finally gave me a Christian offer for it. Deal ought to close in about 30 days so I was gonna have to give ya'll notice this week anyhow." He giggled at his own little joke as he walked around the porch, peeked briefly into the windows. "Christian offer. I kill myself sometimes. Well, good luck, boys. You're been damn good tenants. Never missed the rent once. People told me I was crazy to rent to a bunch of hippies but I thought well, hell, might as well give you kids a chance. I was kind of wild myself when I was a young 'un." He winked and elbowed Jesse then he walked away and got into his car, a pale green and white Buick Electra. Honking, he backed out then drove off.

"Church of Christ?" I said. "I don't believe it. That bastard was going to sell the place to the Church of Christ and he didn't even tell us."

"Man," Jesse said, equally amazed. "He could have just waltzed out here any day and told us to get out. That son of a bitch. Sell this place to a goddamned church."

R.E. was stunned, too, and speechless. That was rare enough. She threw up her hands and walked back inside.

Closing up the Palace was done even more quickly at that point. I stayed busy beating myself up because when matters dictated that I be away from Claire for the duration of the trip, the first thing that washed over me was relief. It was taking turns with guilt for feeling relieved, and the tumble between those two stones was grinding me to a pulp.

We spent the last evening of the last day with everyone together, walking through the empty, echoing rooms either in pairs or alone, smoking, and drinking red wine straight from the bottles, except

Amanda and Claire who were guzzling herbal tea. Claire had sworn off all stimulants, including her beloved Gauloise, in her effort to further her desires. But stimulated she was. She followed me from room to room, talking incessantly about the past and the future, one tense tumbling into another, stroking my back and arms, reluctant to leave any physical or verbal space between us. Jesse also clung to R.E.'s side like a shadow that last evening. She kept her eyes down and her smile tight but didn't push him away. None of us wanted to crash but Raz insisted since they were taking off early the next morning. We had decided to leave the mattresses in a circle in the big downstairs room, laughing about what kind of stories the church people would tell about us. It took some time for everyone to quit talking and then we tossed and turned in silence before one by one, we drifted into restless sleep.

The next morning, with a great deal of ado on Jesse's, Claire's, and Amanda's parts, we loaded everyone's things into the van and the car. Raz just rolled his eyes at the uproar and gave both me and R.E. a big, silent hug. Then, finally, the little caravan set off, one gent driving and one gent along with the two ladies hanging out the windows, crying, throwing kisses, hollering at us until they drove past the last stand of trees that blocked them from our sight. We stood and waved back until our arms went bloodless from holding them up in the air. "I am so damn glad that's over," R.E. sighed.

"Oh, man! I know what you mean."

"Don't you hate scenes like that?"

"You are your grandmother's child."

She nodded. "Well, let's go to work and then get on the road."

That had been the plan, anyway. We did our last shift for the Beat lovers, said goodbye, and left without a great deal of ceremony that last evening. After all, they would have liked a big deal drawn-out farewell about as much as we would have, which was not at all. So it was just a "Happy Trails", with our hands wafting through the air, trailing imaginary acid streamers of color and that was that. We had already loaded our road bags into her truck, intending to leave straight from work, but she said, "You know, I can't go without one last look around the old place."

"Oh, man, I'm so glad you said that! I was already wondering how I could talk you into it."

"One more ride on the nostalgia-go-round. Then we leave." But of course there was one more seismic shaker before we were able to, one more thump of the God-Finger. As we were pulling back into the yard, we saw that someone had been to the Palace since we'd been at work. It was boarded up and there were two signs in front. We walked up on the porch and looked around carefully. One sign said, "No Trespassing. Property of the Denton Church of Christ." The other said a bunch of stuff about a construction company that was going to do the building, and on the very last line were the words, "van der Veer Inc." We hissed and turned to each other, "That bastard," she snarled. "He was behind this. He bought the Palace and sold it out from under us to a damned church. I knew something was funny about that deal. I've been thinking about it since the landlord was out here. Cole was planning to just waltz out here one day and evict us. Or get us busted. Or both. Well, he is not going to get the pleasure of seeing this place torn down." R.E. had on a face that I'd never seen before. "You drive down to the pay phone by where the old store used to be and call the fire department."

"What? What are you talking about?"

"I'm going to burn it down. Go on. Call, and then drive back here for me. I'll wait a few minutes before I start. That'll give them time to get here before the woods go, too." She tossed me the keys and then said, "Hurry. I'm going to do it, I swear."

Yanking the signs off the front door, she kicked it in. I stood there for a second, watching her. "Go! Do it!" she yelled and I woke up. Legs wobbling like cold noodles, I hopped in the truck and careened down the road to the phone booth. Keeping the engine running, I threw it into park and stumbled out. Somehow I managed to fish a dime out of my pocket and with trembling hands, get it in the slot. When the operator answered, I babbled that there was a fire and said I was a neighbor and gave directions to the Palace. Then I hung up. I jerked my T-shirt off and hastily wiped the phone and the door clean of any prints before I remembered I'd already touched the dime. Then I leapt in the truck and peeled off back to the Palace. I saw the first red-orange tongue lick through the roof. After a few more moments, R.E. came pounding towards me, gasping for breath, laughing in her most maniacal way.

"Have you gone completely over the edge?" I asked.

"Nope. Just a little frontier justice, pardner," she grinned, goofing on the Westerns we'd grown up with. We could already hear sirens a few miles away. "Good. They'll make it in time to save most of the trees. Well, our work here is done. Time to git outta Dodge. Move over. I'll drive."

"You bet you will." I put my T-shirt back after I slid over, trembling like I had the flu. "And quit talking like a bad Saturday matinee. This is serious! You just committed arson! I can't believe you did that."

"It'll be just fine, she said as we jumped in and drove away.

"R.E., they'll know it was us. He'll know it was us."

"I want him to know."

"You do?"

"Yeah. He wanted everyone to know he damn near killed me. And he put the sign on the door that said van der Veer so if any of us came around we'd know he'd bought our home. Bet he was crushed that we were already gone. Why shouldn't he know I burned it down before he could wreck it?"

"He'll try to get even. Maybe even follow us."

"He might anyway. But I'll tell you what, he wasn't expecting this. I got the drop on him. I just know it."

"How did you get it started?" I finally asked.

"Wasn't hard. It's amazing we didn't do it before now by accident, what with all the candles and the smoking and cooking we did there. It was so dry, all that old wood. All I did was catch the curtains in the roof room on fire. I kind of hate that the trees closest to it are going to go, but they would when the bulldozers came, anyway."

"Why did you do it?"

She turned back to me. "Because it was ours. Our land. Not their land. I didn't want them to be the ones to knock it down. And," she paused, "it's a tradition between our families. We burn their stuff down when they piss us off." She seemed almost serene. Strangely enough, at that moment, I began to feel her calm as well. And so we drove away into the west, leaving Texas as outlaws, fleeing a burning building, disappearing down a long dark road that led into the night, into the unknown.

"I set out running, but I take my time,
A friend of the Devil is a friend of mine.
If I get home before daylight,
I just might get some sleep tonight."

Robert Hunter / Jerry Garcia / John Dawson,
Friend of the Devil

VIII.

Neither Here Nor There

It was the first long road trip I'd ever made. We drove the rest of the night, R.E. staying just under the speed limit, careful not to attract any undue uniformed attention. And it wasn't just our rate of travel that was deliberately low key and conventional. I had noticed the night we left Honey Springs the last time that the truck, once a mobile billboard of stickers and statements, was now carefully neutral from without, politically speaking. When I asked her if she'd thrown them away, she said she had, but she added she'd bought new peace flag and Oat Willie "Onward Through The Fog" bumper stickers. They were in the glove box along with the maps and the road stash. Once we were safe in hippie territory again on the coast, she planned to attach them and to redecorate the truck with new coastal slogans. But in the meantime, she had said, "I don't know if the cops between here and there are as prone to stopping hippies as they can be in Texas. No need to invite trouble." We traveled in the late afternoon and at night, to avoid the heat. As the hours and the miles passed, I relaxed into the monotony of the drive. It was a sweet reprieve from the river rafting of recent events, just mile after mile of desert and blacktop rolling by in the long yellow late daylight and the evening dark. And what a joy to find that R.E. was a dream road companion: no dreaded, mindless small talk to fill the void of silence. We'd roll for hours at a time without a word, both of us lost in reverie, only short exchanges about location or miles or short comments about something out the window.

For me, it was time to review. I wondered about where Eddie had gone and where we were going and whether or not Cole would find us after we'd found ourselves. Those mysteries of the heart and mind tumbled and rolled into each other: Claire and the baby-to-be, where I would work, and most of all, the growing whispers from the unread journal.

R.E. had chosen to take the southernmost route, planning to stick close to the Mexican border so we could cross over if the need arose during our exodus. We finally stopped in Carlsbad, New Mexico and got a motel room about 10:00 in the morning. R.E. had decided to spring for beds instead of camping along the way so we could really rest up. In order to rent the room, she put her hair up and pulled on her cowboy boots and Rafe's old Stetson he'd given her for luck. Then she sauntered in and took care of the paperwork. The cowgirl costume was a disguise she felt she needed; Carlsbad was well known to be one of the most conservative bergs in the whole Wild West. She told me when she came back out with the room key that she'd signed us up as man and wife, saying that the old brother and sister routine made desk clerks too suspicious. I didn't care. I was so tired I was seeing trails. We took everything in with us and I crashed on one of the twin beds while she showered. I don't remember her coming out and I have no idea what I dreamed, if anything. We had taken turns at the wheel and close to 14 hours had passed since we had burned the Palace to the ground and made our getaway. I fell into the darkness and floated there in numb suspension, welcoming the familiar wordless oblivion of dreamless sleep.

When I woke up late that afternoon, I was as stiff and sore as I had been the day after helping Rafe and Maddy bring in the truck garden. R.E. sat on the other bed, studying the map. She'd gone out for coffee and her coming back in had shaken me back into semi-consciousness.

"Hey," she smiled as she handed me a Styrofoam cup full of precious caffeine.

I sat up and said thank you then I drained it, held it up, and did my best Oliver Twist.

She grinned and refilled for me out of her own, saying, "I've already had plenty at the cafe. It's too damn weak. We'll have to wait 'til we get to closer to the coast for more decent grinds."

"It'll do," I shrugged as I guzzled it down as fast as the heat would allow. "So, trail boss. How far we going today?"

"Well, it's only about three. We could hang around here until dark and then drive again tonight. At least the sun won't be right in our eyes that way. Okay with you? Or you want to sleep some more and drive during the day tomorrow?"

"I don't mind at all driving in the dark." I hadn't said anything to her yet, but I was about as comfortable being in the limelight of stares of strangers as I had been that day in the clinic in Little Creek when I was trying to track down my birth records. The Snake had been working me over fiercely ever since I woke up and the thought of being on the road, in public, around people I didn't know, straight people, just made it worse. As if to announce its agreement with me, the Snake rattled me so hard that I splashed some coffee on the sheets. "Damn."

"Hey, don't worry about it. Maybe it'll make sure they wash them before using them again. Okay. We'll head out after sundown." We read the local newspaper and killed time until it was almost dark. A quick bite at the diner and then it was time to hit the road again. The perceptible sigh of cool desert night air swept towards me as I stood and admired the sweep of stars while R.E. settled the bill.

She was the first driver again that night and she was being as quiet as usual. But I was in the mood for a little more conversation. It was beginning to sink in that we couldn't simply turn around and go back home to the Palace. It was just the two of us at that moment, moving through the dark silently, going to a state neither of us had ever been to before, a fabled place we'd only known through music and movies and myth. And I wanted the comfort of speech.

"R.E., what are we going to do out there?"

She sighed and thought about it for a long while before she spoke. "Well, I've been thinking about it a lot. I still feel real guilty about Dado going down to South Texas all alone."

"He said that you didn't have to take care of him."

"I know that, but it's just that I feel like I'm letting the family down, all of them, all the way back to those first folks who came over here from France to be Utopianists. I haven't done anything, really, like they did."

"But you aren't obligated to."

"Oh, yes I am. Or at least, I feel like I am. I mean, even if there weren't all the burden of history on me, I would feel some guilt. Civil Rights, the war, the women's movement, the American Indian movement, gay rights. There's so much going on right now that should be fought against. Railed against, as Mack would say. All of those people, Dado and his friends, they really put it on the line for what they believed. They suffered."

"And you haven't."

She nodded.

"I don't think there's anything wrong with not wanting to suffer, R.E. Besides, you paid dues of some kind when you were with Cole."

"That's not the same thing. Doing time or being arrested or at least hassled by the cops is a badge of courage in old Lefty circles. How much have you lost for the cause? To tell you the truth, I'm a coward. I don't want to lose a kidney and die like Jack Reed did. I don't want to end up like my mom, crippled like she was. And I really don't want to go to jail."

"You think that just protesting something would land you in the slammer?"

"It's the fear of it that's held me back in lots of ways. Dado talked about jail once when he and Rafe got real drunk one night. It was about the only time I remember him getting close to out of control when he was drinking. He started telling Rafe some stories about prison, about the brutality, prisoners and guards alike. He'd forgotten I was in the room, I guess, because the tales were pretty graphic. Then he turned around and saw me and remembered that I had been listening to it all. But I still remember some of it. The rapes. The beatings. The murders. So, I have always been scared of the police. Really scared of them. And of being locked up. Tortured. No, I definitely do not want to be arrested. Ever."

"Just speaking up or being in a march won't get you put in jail."

She turned to me and the lights of a passing car illuminated her features for a second. It was her serious face. "Think back on our history. Look at what Black people down south went through to get the right to vote. And it's still going on. And women. It took a long time and a lot of hunger strikes in prison to get suffrage. And labor leaders. And war protesters, any war. Folks at Kent State, Jackson State, Chicago. No, if you make enough noise to be heard, someone in a power position will notice you sooner or later and try to smash you to shut you up. That's just a fact."

I nodded. The conversation wasn't granting me the peace of mind I'd been after. "Well, if you are going to get political, it'd probably be easier and safer to do it in California."

"Well, easier than Texas. Safety in numbers." She was quiet again for a few minutes then she said, "But places like Texas need change the most. That's where the fight really is. Sometimes, I feel like being on the Left in California is like preaching to the choir."

I laughed.

"So. What about you? And Claire?" she asked.

It was my turn to be quiet while I marshaled my scattered images. "She really wants to have a kid."

"But you don't." It wasn't a question.

"No," I confessed for the one and only time. "I don't. Please don't tell her that, okay? Or anyone else."

"Of course not."

"But I really don't. It's just that I never thought someone like Claire would ever come into my life in the first place. But she did. I'm not sure how long she can be a student this time since her parents aren't paying for it. She saved up some money working illegally while she was coming back here. There. To Texas. So, if she can't find a way to scare up tuition in California, I don't know what she'll do."

"What if someone married her? You know, one of those paper marriages. You could still get your check."

I stared at her. The thought had never occurred to me. Claire, marry someone else? What if they wanted to take advantage of the situation and play husband with her? I was so quiet that R.E. finally said, "It was just a suggestion. I've heard that people do it all the time. One of the family could do it, someone you trust. I don't mean she should be with someone else. You know that."

I nodded, unconvinced. But the germ of it had entered my brain. I mulled over the pluses and minuses for a few more miles then said, "Well, if it was someone like Vance, I guess it would be okay."

"He'd probably forget that he was married," she laughed. "Oh yeah, married," she mimed her best imitation and slapped her forehead. Then smiling at me she added, "It was just a thought, man. Don't get all worried about her being with someone else. She loves you."

"I know. And that scares me."

"Why?"

"Well, before Claire, I had no future and really, no past. It was because of her that I went up to Little Creek. So, now I have all this baggage that I never had before. No one ever expected anything from me before. Not Pearl. Not the schools. Not even the family at the Palace. I was just Troy. Old shaky Troy. But now, Claire's expecting me to find work. Make a family. Do the daily day. And how I can--ah, hell. I have no idea."

"Why don't you roll us a small one? I drank so much coffee before we left, I'm wired." She rolled up her window.

I did the same. Fetching out the stash kit, I balanced the tray on my lap, cleaning the weed and stretching out the paper as I went on with my worries, working by the light of the tiny glove box bulb. "I guess the strangest thing about Claire wanting to have a kid is the possibility of there being some kind of future plan laid out for me. Working. A house. All that. I never even considered it. I'm one of those day to day people, moment to moment."

She nodded. "That's something that we have always had in common." Then she sighed, "Well, who knows? Maybe we'll find our--what is it Campbell calls it?"

"Our bliss."

"Yeah. Bliss. I like that."

"But I've got absolutely no experience in doing anything but washing dishes." I held up the number after I put the stash away. "And rolling joints. Suppose there's such a thing? Wanted: experienced marijuana cigarette prep man. Maybe I could work for the Dead. Now there's a blissful path."

She laughed. "Well, you never know. I mean, we've all heard so many tales about life out there. Jesse once told me, straight-faced, that the traffic signals said 'Boogie' and 'Don't Boogie'. He seems really happy about the move, though. All of us being together."

"Me, too, in that regard."

Her voice changed a little as she held the hit and continued speaking. "His mom was real young when she had him. Fifteen, I think. And not married." She released the hit in a curl of smoke. "Just before you and I went up to Honey Springs that last time, he filled me in on the details about his life. He said when he asked his mother who his father was, she said she had no idea. Could have been any one of four or five guys." I rolled my window back down a little once it was going well to keep the cab aired out. "And she really drank a lot. He said he never had a Christmas tree or Thanksgiving dinner or anything that the other kids in school did. And that their place was always trashed. And there were guys there all the time. One of them was beating on her once when he was about fourteen. Jesse jumped into it and the guy pounded the shit of him for it. His mom didn't do anything to help. In fact, she got pissed off at Jesse for making the guy mad. So he just left. Started sleeping at the Y. He always looked older than he really was. They thought he was an adult. That was when he got in trouble, stole a car. The judge sent him to the juvenile slammer until he was 18 because his mom was dead by then. When he got out, he was alone until he found us."

"So, I guess it's no surprise he wanted to come along to Oz with everyone else."

"Follow the yellow brick road," R.E. sang in her version of the Munchkin voice.

"And watch out for the flying monkeys," I said.

She nodded. "And everything else evil."

I hesitated for a while then I said, "Do you think Coleman will leave us alone now?"

She frowned and flipped her free hand back past her forehead as though she were swatting away a pest. It took her some miles to formulate her thoughts then she said, "I honestly don't know. Sometimes I think he may have moved on to other concerns, other targets. Other times, I'm not so sure. He did buy the Palace, after all. But I've had the feeling that it was an offshoot of some real estate deal, not a prime concern. He probably just saw it as icing on one of his many cakes." She went quiet for a few more miles then said, "But there were times when I thought I could feel him close to the Palace. I also thought I could sense him close to me on the streets some nights, lurking there in the dark, watching me. I wasn't sure if it was true perception or just paranoia, so I never said anything about it. I didn't want to make him real by verbalizing about him, you know?"

I nodded in agreement, thinking about the day-mare in the roof room. After a moment, I asked something that had been gnawing at me that evening. "I hope you don't mind if I ask, but, why do you think he..." I didn't know how to finish the question more artfully.

"Decided to take up with me? Other than the healing I could do?" She glanced directly at me, eyes searching mine.

I ducked my head. "Well, the more I know about your families, I've just been wondering. I don't know." I was suddenly afraid she was mad at me.

"Hey, relax. We can talk about stuff, you know that. I suppose the answer is, I don't really know. I've been questioning myself about it ever since that day at the Palace when he said what his real name was. At first, we never really exchanged any personal information. It was all flirting. Then, not long after we got involved, he saw my driver's license one time when I was writing a check. I don't know if it hit him then or later, but sometimes I'd catch him just smiling at me for no special reason." She sighed. "I guess I won't ever really know and that's okay. If I could figure it out, it might mean I'm as crazy as he is."

I nodded and left it at that, just one more thing to ponder on the road. About eight the next morning, she checked us into another small motel well off the main highway somewhere in Arizona. We figured we had another couple of nights of driving before we got to the coast, and that we could take it lower and slower now with so much ground already between us and Texas. When we woke up hours later, it was the cusp between late afternoon and early evening and already cooler. We showered then listened to the national news on TV as we ate sandwiches from the diner across the street. The United Auto Workers strike was still going on, with no end in sight. It was the largest in 20 years and was against General Motors of Canada as well as the U.S. I don't remember now how many people were involved but it seemed then like a huge number. There was also the latest Vietnam body count, the grim footage of young men with stunned, smudged, bloody faces. When the local news started, we switched it off and headed out into the wide open unknown once again.

More silence at first, more darkness, the V shape of head-lighted highway flowing ahead of us like a black mythic river, the starry sweep of desert sky: it could have been a lovely evening, but my mood was sour as curdled milk: bad night's sleep, heartburn from the sandwiches and cheap coffee, and most of all, delayed reaction to everything in my life being turned upside down and blown to bits. And there was also that dark star in my private night sky: the journal. It had been on the edges of my attention since I'd found it but so much had been going on around me that I'd had no time to consider it. Now, it was all I could think about. And I wanted silence. But R.E. turned on the radio and kept searching for decent stations. The sounds lurched from static to country to static to preachers to static, on and on. I clenched my teeth, trying not to say anything, but she kept exploring the dial. Finally, I snapped and said, "Damn it, R.E., either find one and stay there or just turn it off!"

"What?"

"Oh, screw it. Never mind."

"What's your problem?"

I sulked and said nothing, my arms folded tightly across my chest. She turned off the radio with a click and stayed quiet, too. The mood kept swelling up in the cab until she finally pulled off the road, shut off the engine, and got out. I sat there, watching her disappear into the moonlit caliche until it started to worry me. I realized she'd taken the keys, so I felt okay locking the doors and following her.

"I'd really rather you leave me alone for a minute," she said when I caught up to her, her voice soft and low. I knew by that tone she was mad.

"Look, I'm sorry. I was being an asshole. I don't know what got into me. I'm just at the end of my rope all of a sudden."

She turned to face me. "And you think I'm not?"

"R.E., your rope doesn't have an end."

She laughed, "Oh, that's what you think, huh? Well, let me tell you something, mister, there's an end to it, and I'm hanging on to it by my fingernails. So I don't need you going peevish on me."

"I know. I know." I sighed and repeated, "I'm sorry. Let's walk back, okay? I feel nervous leaving our wheels alone."

"Okay." We started back and then she asked me, "So, other than having your whole world scattered to the winds and the pressure of a family suddenly being crammed down your throat and being on the run to a place you've never lived in before, what else could possibly be bugging you?"

I started to make a joke of it, but I couldn't. I was close to crying by then. "I don't know where I'm going or even where I'm from." I stopped and she turned to face me. "There's something that's been weighing on me since I was up in Little Creek. There hasn't been a single moment to think about it, much less talk about it. See, I found a journal. It was my mother's."

"Oh, man! Really?" She was beaming. Then she looked more closely at me. "Uh-oh. Did you find out something awful and you just haven't talked about it yet?"

"No. I haven't even read it yet. I've been too scared. I want to know and then I don't want to know. Maybe..."

"You could find out who your father was," she finished for me.

I nodded. "I've been praying, if that's what you could call it, that it would be--you know--Sam. But that would be too wonderful. That kind of wonderful doesn't happen for me. I've also been dreading it could be someone..."

"Like Jake."

"Yeah. Or even worse, some nobody, some zero. Like me."

"Don't start that with me," she warned. "You know how I hate it when you put yourself down."

"Okay, I know. But it's a distinct possibility. For so long, I wanted to know who my father was and now, I might find out." I turned my back to her and then whispered, "R.E.?"

"Yeah?"

"Would you read it for me?"

We pulled completely off the road into a little arroyo, hidden from any potential traffic. R.E. hauled out the map, we figured out where we were, and she marked the spot with an "X". We smoked a small ceremonial one, listened to the silence and determined that not another soul was around, none that we could hear anyway. She turned on the lantern we'd brought along in case of emergencies. I brought out the journal and unwrapped it. Inside there was a small envelope with what felt like photos inside. R.E. asked, "Do you want to see them?"

"No, not yet." I handed it to her.

"Okay." She flipped through the whole thing quickly. "There are only two entries. One is dated September 20, 1947. The other is August 13, 1954."

"The day before she died," I said. "Look, I'm going to turn around and not face you, okay? If you get to something horrible--well, just let me know so I can brace myself."

"As you like. Here goes." She took a deep breath and then said, "The handwriting starts out very neat and orderly, like she'd been using a ruler to line up the sentences. Then as it goes on, she starts writing faster and faster. The words slant a little to the right."

"Like mine, when I'm in a hurry."

She took one more deep breath and then she started. At first, it was R.E. reading and then as she continued, another voice began to creep in so by the time she finished, I swear I was hearing her voice. My mother's. Audrey's.

"My name is Audrey Jacobson and this is my real and true story. I am going to write down everything that happened, just exactly like it happened, and I don't care who knows it, except Pearl, because there isn't anything wrong or bad about it. It was a natural thing to do. That's what Neal said and I believe him. And anyway, it was my own idea. I had it just as soon as I laid eyes on him. But I am going to keep this secret from Pearl so she won't know and secret from everyone else, too, because I want a secret that is all mine. She will never understand what I did and why I did it. I am now about two weeks late for my period and I think I must be pregnant. JaeDeen said that when you don't get your period, it means you are going to have a baby. Wouldn't that be lovely? A real baby of my very own. I hope it looks like me, so nobody will ever guess who the daddy is. Not that it's so bad. He was so handsome and that way he talked, it was like nothing I ever heard before in my life, like a river of words, like he couldn't say them fast enough, not as fast as he was thinking them. The other man with him was a real talker, too. I just listened to both of them with my mouth closed. It was like I had never really heard English before, like some of the poems we had to read in school and some of the other ones that JaeDeen gave me in secret to read, too. Neal was blond and tan and he was so well built, real strong and slim and he had the most beautiful eyes and these long eyelashes, almost like a girl's except that there wasn't anything girly about him. The man with him was the opposite. He was shorter and he had this curly black hair and dark eyes and he was wearing glasses. I met them when I was walking back to the house after Sunday school one day. I didn't want to sing for the church service that day, I just didn't feel like it so I lied to Pearl and said I had a stomach ache so she let me go home. She had to stay because she was teaching the lesson and she couldn't leave so I got to go back alone. I walked real slow because it wasn't very often I got to be alone and I wanted to savor the time. I like that word savor. Neal said it means like when something tastes real good. I was wearing my very best white dress and white shoes and Pearl had let me tie my hair back with a blue ribbon since I was supposed to sing. I felt so good I did start to sing but I waited until I was on the road and clear of town. I didn't want to sing any church songs, so I started singing Cool Water. I was just walking and singing and feeling so nice when this car slowed down and I knew all of a sudden that it was following me. I stopped singing and stood there on the side of the road real scared. It was a Ford and it had Colorado plates on it. The man who was driving, that was Neal, but I didn't know his name just then of course, he leaned out the window and called across the road to me to come over and say hello and he said to the other man say don't she sing pretty and whoo boy was I beautiful. The other man, the dark one his name was Allen I knew that because Neal said hey Allen, he must have been sleeping in the back seat because he sat up and rubbed his eyes and said something I couldn't hear. So Neal called me over and that's when I heard Allen say Neal so I knew that was his name."

She stopped for a moment as the suspicion began to creep up on both of us. "I want to see those pictures," I said as I turned around. She handed me the envelope and I opened it slowly, carefully, hands trembling. There were three. The one on top was my mother and me sitting on the porch of the house. I was just a little boy. I turned it over it and read, "Me and Troy, when he was three. Little Creek, Texas." The second was one of her and JaeDeen. She was holding something wrapped in a blanket. On the back it said, "Me and JaeDeen and Troy, one week after I brought him home. All alone now, just the two of us." Then the last picture, the one that gave me the long desired answer: it was her and a handsome blond man, standing in the back yard of the house beside a Ford. That face, one of the icons of my youth and of so many others: on the back, it said simply, "Me and Neal, August 1947, Little Creek." It was him all right, Neal Cassady, Dean Moriarty, Further's driver. My heart was beating so hard I thought I was going to pass out. I remembered the pictures in Eddie's glove box: the one of him and the man in the railroad yard. That was when the first two lines on the back came to me. They were from the last part of Howl. Eddie must have written them some time after the picture had been taken because the poems came out after the time when Eddie had worked in the yards. "N.C." So he had known him, had worked with him in those fabled times in San Jose.

"Troy?"

"Yeah, uh, I was--later. Go on."

She nodded, the moment too portentous for comment. After a sigh, she continued and that voice, my mother's voice, came back to me again:

"I heard Neal say something like would you look at that vision Allen isn't that something way out here in the middle of all this nothing to see this something. He called me a vision. I had never heard that word before outside of church so I got interested and didn't run off. And Allen said Neal again then he didn't say anything else. He just looked at Neal in a real funny way I didn't understand. But Neal kept talking to me and I wasn't scared anymore. Not really. I just felt excited. There weren't any cars coming so I stood there and listened to him some more. He asked me where I was going and I said home and he said he could give me a ride if I wanted him to. And the next thing I knew, there I was in the car sitting next to him with Allen still in the back being real quiet like his feelings were hurt or something. It wasn't very far to the house. We were there in just a few minutes. I didn't want him to go so I asked him if he would like to come inside. Allen asked where everyone else was and I said it was just me and Pearl who lived there and that she was at church still. I asked Neal again if he would like to come inside for some lemonade or something. But I knew why I was really asking him to come in. It wasn't for any lemonade. We didn't even have any lemons and we had been out of sugar for a couple of days. That wasn't why I wanted him to come in. It was because I wanted to do with him what JaeDeen had said she had been doing with Bobby all summer. She had told me about it in the crying room at the picture show how sweet it was and how it felt so good and how it hurt a little at the same time and how good it made you feel down between your legs. There. I said it. I talked about that place. Pearl always said when you started thinking and talking about that place it meant you were a real bad person. But JaeDeen said it wasn't at all bad, it was just a natural thing to do and lots of fun, too and besides Pearl didn't know anything about it so how could she say for sure. I knew I would never have any chance to do it with any of the boys in town and besides I didn't like any of them very much anyway. But as soon as I looked at Neal I knew I wanted to do it with him. He was sexy. I had heard JaeDeen use that word and I had never understood what it meant until I saw Neal. Then I understood. He knew why we were going inside. So did the other man. He seemed a little mad and said he was going to stay in the car and Neal shouldn't take too long because Pearl might come back soon. I wasn't worried about that. I knew she would be at church at least another couple of hours and that that would be plenty of time. JaeDeen had told me it only took about five minutes when a boy wanted to do it. But when we got inside and I asked him if he wanted to kiss me, he asked if I was a virgin and how old I was. I told him I was a virgin but I lied and said I was 18. I think he knew I was lying about my age but he didn't seem to care. And when he kissed me I felt that funny feeling between my legs like I had felt before when I was washing myself there. I felt it the first time when I was just a little girl but I knew even then I shouldn't tell Pearl about it. I was washing and I was rubbing and all of a sudden it felt like it did that time I was standing in the bar ditch in the water and grabbed that electric fence by mistake. It was like getting a shock but it felt so good at the same time that I just kept rubbing. Then it quit. I was so afraid I'd hurt myself that I didn't say anything. It happened now and then when I was washing and sometimes I even did it at night on the sofa bed when Pearl was already asleep in the other room. I know this is awful but I'm going to write it all down anyway so there. Anyway I had the same feeling again when Neal was kissing me. He asked if I wanted to lie down on the bed with him and go to heaven. That's what he said, to go to heaven with him. He said I was an angel and that he could make me fly like one. I said that the bed was Pearl's but we could lie down on a pallet in the living room if he wanted to. I went out on the porch and got two old quilts from the quilt box and when I came back in, he was sitting on the floor cross-legged and he already had all his clothes off. I just dropped the quilts in a pile and stared at him because I had never seen a man naked before. I don't know how to say this next part without being a little bit dirty but maybe it wasn't really dirty maybe I was just shy but he had this really big thing. I mean I had heard JaeDeen say that boys' things get big and hard when they want to do it but I had no idea they were that big. But it was real interesting and I wasn't really afraid. I was just surprised. So I took my clothes off too and laid them on the chair real careful so they wouldn't get mussed up and give Pearl a chance to get mad at me. Neal looked at me and I swear to God he got tears in his eyes and he called me earth angel and fragrant goddess and a lot of other beautiful things that I can't remember he said so much and he asked me what my name was and I told him and he said it wasn't good enough for me that it ought to something royal or mystical or from a dream. And then he said he was going to call me Aurora and said that was the name of the goddess of the dawn. And I got down on the pallet with him and we did it. Only it wasn't just five minutes like JaeDeen had said. And he did a lot of things to me that JaeDeen had never told me about boys doing to her. I bled some but I had picked the oldest red and brown quilt, the one I'd been using when I had my first period so it already had some bloodstains on it and Pearl would never suspect. And it was my idea to keep on doing it. It did feel good. JaeDeen was right about that part. And the way that man kept talking, I could have listened to him forever. But after a while I heard the kitchen screen door open and the other man's voice and he came in and looked at us saying they should be going or we were likely to get caught. And I looked at the clock and knew he was right. Neal picked up his clothes and walked out with the other man, still buck naked. I cleaned myself up with the edge of the quilt and put my everyday dress on. Then I remembered that I still had a couple of pictures left in my Brownie from the class picnic so I got it and ran back outside. Neal and Allen were talking in front of the car and Neal was finishing buttoning his shirt and his jeans. Neal hugged me and said that I had been an oasis for him and Allen looked at us both like he was a little bit hurt but he understood what Neal had said. Then I asked Allen if he would take a picture or two of me and Neal. He smiled and said that he would so we stood beside the

Ford with our arms around each other and he took two. Then he gave me the camera and said that I had entered into the realm of the mythological along with the most famous ignoo in the world. I had no idea what he meant but then again I hadn't understood much of anything either of them had said anyway but it sounded nice so I smiled and said thank you. They both laughed and Neal hugged me again and they got in the car and drove away. I ran out to the road still holding the Brownie and waved until I couldn't see them anymore. Then I ran back in and cleaned everything up and myself again too and hid the Brownie. I sure do hope those pictures come out good. I'll have to send them away to some place to get them developed so Pearl won't know. I'd have JaeDeen do it but I know she'd peek, so I'll just have to be on my toes and catch the mail soon as it comes. So that's how I met Neal and how I became a woman. I do hope the baby looks like me but it would probably be okay if it looked like him since he wasn't from here."

I was crying softly by now. She gave me a few moments before going on.

"More?" she asked.

I nodded. "Finish it. Read the second part."

She resumed the role of the channel once again. This time, the voice was a little older, sadder, and tired.

"I'm real sick and I'm real afraid. This cold has gone down into my chest and I can't shake it. Today I feel so bad I think I'm going to die. Times like this I wish we had a phone or a car. JaeDeen will be by tomorrow like usual and maybe she can take me to see Doc Wilson then. I'd go see him now but I don't think I can walk into town with Troy so I'll just have to go to bed and hope for the best. I don't know what will become of him if anything does happen to me. He is the only thing in the world that has happened to me that has been pure and natural and good. I don't care if he does have palsy. It doesn't matter. He's a smart little boy and always so good. He never cries or gives me any trouble, not even a little. I always meant to write more in this book so he would have some kind of notion about his childhood but I was always so busy I didn't and now maybe it's too late. I want him to know about who his daddy was but even if I tell him now he won't remember when he grows up and now maybe I won't get a chance to tell him at all. I never told anybody about that day Neal and I made him. I have to smile when I read those first pages. God, I was such a child. So innocent. That first time seemed so magical. All the other times since have not been, although some of them have been sweet or even tender, especially with Mr. Holden. He can't help it that he was gassed like he was and that none of the women in town will have anything to do with him. He always cries when he finishes and I spend most of our time holding him and listening to his stories about the Great War as he calls it. Never sounded that great to me. No war does. I wonder who will comfort him when I am gone. Nobody probably. Nobody in this damn town has any heart. No, I shouldn't say that. There's JaeDeen and RaeAnn and Sam and all the rest who have been so kind to me. I asked Sam if he could take Troy and raise him up alongside his little girl Rachel and he said he would like to but we both know he probably couldn't. Not with Pearl still alive. She would raise hell about Troy going to an ex-con, but Sam is about the only one I would trust him to. Maybe Pearl will take him and maybe she won't and he'll just go to the orphanage. Either way it will be hell for my little boy. I am so glad at least that I could teach him how to read. He has that at least. He's so smart. He already knew all his letters when he was just four. I just hope he finds out someday that I loved him and that I tried to do the best for him. I'm going to bury this in the garage so no one else will find it in case anything happens before JaeDeen comes by tomorrow. I can tell her where it is so she can dig it up and give it to him when he gets to be a man. I'll tell her not to read it but I know she will because she has always wanted to know who his daddy was so I'll tape it up real good first. I guess it doesn't really matter if she reads it or not since Neal wasn't from here, anyway. At least she'll have it so she can give it to Troy when he's old enough to understand. Maybe that way he'll know I tried to find a way to tell him. There's so much more I want to write but I'm feeling so bad and I need to get this wrapped in something so the rain won't get to it and get it buried and see about getting us something to eat before dark. I'm so tired and I can't think of anything else to say right now except I hope that someone takes care of Troy and raises him right so he won't hate me when people in town tell him all the gossip and the bad things I did. I didn't do them because I was bad. I just did them because I didn't have any other choice and because I loved him so much I'd do anything"

After a minute, it was R.E. who spoke again. "The last sentence has no period." I turned to face her. She looked drained and pale, but she was smiling. She handed me the journal and I reverentially put the photos back in the envelope and tucked the envelope in the back of the book. Hugging it to my chest, I sat cross-legged, smiling at her and nodding. There was nothing to say. Only silence. And answers.

***

We passed the rest of the time between Texas and California, driving in the dark, smoking a little to keep ourselves amused, talking about our doubts and dreams but keeping an eye on the road behind us as well as the one ahead, sleeping during the day in cheap motels, reminiscing about Texas, dreaming about California, going back to the journal again and again. And one evening as we got closer to the Golden State, I caught my own reflection in the window. For just a second, I could see mental pictures of both my young mother and N.C. floating above me. Then swinging towards each other, they melded into--me. More Audrey than Neal, but that's the way she had wanted it. I said softly, "R.E.? Can I ask you a huge favor?"

"You know you can."

"Please don't tell anyone about Cassady." I turned to face her.

She glanced at me then looked back towards the road. "Sure, it's your special story. I won't say anything."

I nodded.

"You are okay with it, aren't you?"

"Yeah. It's like my mother said in her journal. It was her secret for so very long. And now it's mine. I mean, ours. I'll let people know about it when I choose to. Or not. I've never had a real secret, not like this one. It does feel kind of special."

She smiled. "I still can't believe it. Neal Cassady. Your father. That is so mythical."

I almost said something about seeing the photo of "N.C. and me" in Eddie's car. But something stopped me. Maybe it was the fear it would make R.E. sad again, thinking about Eddie. Maybe it was part of the special secret I could hold in my heart. Another day. I'd tell her another day.

And then, as all road trips do, that one began to draw to a close when we saw the deep blue dream of the Pacific for the first time. R.E. and I had decided on a daylight drive that last morning. We'd slept in Fresno and had gotten up early, made the wild and wooly ascent over Pacheco Pass, and then we wound down the other side until we sighted her: blue rollers, white capped from the breeze, the rooster tail of rainbow light spraying off behind in an opposing curve to the wave as the sun combed its fingers through the crests. It remained in view for some time until we got close enough to explore. R.E. pulled off the road, parked, and locked up. We got out, shucked our boots and walked onto the sand, felt the surprising coolness of it between our toes, smelled the salt and the kelp, heard the seals barking, saw the gulls crying and circling.

"Man, it feels so cold," she smiled, looking at the goose bumps that rippled up on our bare T-shirted arms when the afternoon breeze hit. We didn't realize how rare it was, a sunny afternoon in the summer, but the place was showing off for us, I guess. And after the desert, it did feel cool, though later we would think of it as warm. We decided against a swim or a wade since neither of us had ever been that close to that much deep water. It was such a moment of epiphany for me, unexpected as those moments always are. I had come home, and I knew it. I don't know what R.E. was feeling. I was too immersed in the unexpected ease of being there, in that place. But after a while, she said, "Well, come on. Let's find Pacific Grove and the house before dark."

It wasn't hard. And when we walked in and everyone hit us at once with hugs and kisses and food and drink, we dropped our road-armor entirely. It didn't seem to matter if Coleman did come for us, at least we were on the familiar ground of family again. It felt just like the Palace, seeing all those sweet faces in the much smaller living room of Raz and Amanda's little house. That night, I walked out in the back yard at one point to be alone for a minute. There was a huge tree, what I would later come to find out was a Monterey Cypress, its limbs swaying in the ocean breeze. I smelled the air and looked up at it and wondered how long it would take before that was as familiar a sight as Texas live oaks.

***

We settled into the new routine in a matter of days. R.E. lived with Jesse and the band in the place he had rented, and I moved into Raz's house with Claire. All I had to do towards the common budget was get the mailing address on my check changed. R.E. cashed it for me through her bank account. I had her deposit most of it there, and I paid my portion of upkeep to Raz and Amanda. Raz got up every morning before the sun, which crept up over the fog shrouded mountains later than it did over the flat edge of the prairie in Texas, throwing off my internal clock for weeks. Amanda and Claire were also early birds at that time, fussing over the baby and Raz equally, Claire feeding and holding Mel while Amanda packed a huge lunch kit for her old man: thermoses of soup and coffee, thick sandwiches on homemade bread filled with different kinds of vegetarian goop, fruit, homemade cookies or cake. Nothing was going to go into Mel or Raz that she hadn't cooked by hand and from organic scratch. After reading the paper while eating a huge breakfast, also vegetarian, Raz left for work in Salinas, and it was just me and the womenfolk. Claire would study English Lit at Monterey Peninsula College for a surprisingly small amount of tuition so she could be square with immigration and she'd already set up with some people majoring in French to tutor them on the complexities of the verb system, all for cash, of course. Amanda had started the groundwork for the garden out back and I escaped into the field-hand role as often as possible. I didn't know if she was going to have any luck since the sun seemed so stingy with its rays there in the fog belt where we were, but I'd help out by digging or planting. When it was naptime for the three ladies, I was free to roam around the new environs.

I was most taken with the fog those first days. Now, I had seen fog in Texas but it was so different there, a lacy veil that always lay low to the ground, seeming to rise more than descend. But on the coast, it was an actual presence, so thick and cool and sudden, creeping over the edges of the mountaintops and drifting down the sides, filling up the valleys and then rolling up the next rise, finally overtaking you and wrapping you in a palpable dream, a shifting cottony condensation in which people or animals or birds would suddenly leap out at you and then disappear again. I would borrow one of family cars or take the bus outside of town, get as high up as I could into the foothills of the Santa Lucia range and then sit on the pine needles and drift and dream and occasionally snooze until sundown, watching the subtle shifts of light and admiring the stillness, listening to the swoosh and sweep of the ocean below, chilled to the bone by the cool. Then it was back to the house with its smells of soup and bread and freshly bathed baby, Raz tired but smiling, rocking the kid on their tiny front porch. We would eat, Claire and I would wash up the dishes, and then it was off to bed early. I would join her for our nightly round of baby making athletics, but my nocturnal habits were resisting major changes, so after watching her doze off, I'd slip out and go over to Jesse's to see what the flip side of the clean life was like.

Jesse was content, more so than I'd ever known him to be during those first weeks. The band was fitting into the groove of the City very quickly, especially Ty, since he was the most theatrical. Maybe it was growing up around Mardi Gras. He'd taken to wearing a black hat bedecked with feathers and to wrapping scarves around his upper arms and thighs when he played, á la Jimi. Vance thought it was pure affectation to dress up so much to play but allowed himself a black vest bedecked with the remains of an old concha belt and black arm garters, like some tintype sheriff. Jesse was just so happy that Vance and Ty were behaving during the sets that he didn't care if they went on stage naked, which probably would have been just fine with the crowds anyway. He still wore jeans and boots and the closest shirt that came to hand before he left for the gig, staying back a little, guiding the band through their numbers and in search of their particular sound, caring more about the music than the show.

Once in a while, R.E. would go along with them on their forays into the scene, but more often she would stay behind in the house, being domestic, trying to figure out her role in the new life. She wasn't as into the details of homemaking as Amanda and Claire were and she had made it plain to all the guys that she wasn't going to be the sole cook, maid, and shrink to everyone just because she was the only woman there. But she did wind up doing most of the cooking, since it gave her some kind of definition. I know that Jesse liked the arrangement. He told me so one evening when we were all over there for dinner.

"You know, it's like it's too good to be true. Playing the City. Being here with all you guys. Being with her." He smiled and passed me one as we stood in the cool foggy darkness behind the house.

I took it and toked. But I stayed silent.

He looked over at me and asked, "You okay with things?"

"I guess."

"What's wrong?"

"Well, hell, it's just that I feel like I'm extra. I mean, Claire is so close to that baby. She'd nurse it if she could come up with some milk."

"Oh, you'll make one of your own soon enough."

"I suppose."

"Oceans o' time, man, oceans o' time." He was smiling, looking back at the kitchen window where he could see R.E. in silhouette. And we did have a little. But not as much as any of us thought we might. Maybe that's always the case.

***

The months passed. Raz and Amanda made several improvements on the house, ordering gadgets and gizmos from the *Whole Earth Catalog*. We were all amazed by the wide world of counter-economy that was being mutually financed and supported. I did begin to believe that maybe I could find my own niche in that growing eco-system. After all, if that many people were running their own little businesses out of their homes and advertising them, why couldn't I? I nursed that proposition as summer turned into fall and then into winter. But I didn't do anything about it, and that was starting to wear on Claire's nerves. As she left the house to meet her tutees in various cafes, she'd always give me a meaningful look. And yet, I couldn't shake the inertia. I was afraid of starting something that might not make it and in the process, losing my government check, the only sure form of income I'd ever known. But if Claire did manage to snag one of my sperm, we'd have to tie the knot and there would go the check anyway. But she didn't, so I drifted and dreamed my way through the seasons.

And soon, our first Christmas on the coast was upon us and so were the winter storms. It had been a little over a year since Coleman's father had died and set all the events of 1970 in motion. And now we were all there in P.G., as we'd come to call it, making homemade presents and cookies, decorations for the live tree that Amanda had insisted on, sitting in amazement in the cozy kitchen whose windows were steamed up from the activity within and the wild, wild wind and rain without as the Pacific systems roared in from Japan and hit us, dumping smooth, steady downpours that would last for days sometimes. I rarely heard thunder or lightning, though, and I missed that a little at first. But coastal winters had their own glories and mysteries that I knew I could spend years unraveling. In many ways, it was one of the most lovely and loving times of my life. But it troubled me that I had no job or nothing particular to be doing during the times when everyone else was busy. And it bothered R.E., too.

She was having the same problems as I was with her own definition. One night, we were at Raz's place, drinking hot rum punch, sitting in the living room and admiring the tree, just the two of us. She got up and fingered one of the decorations, a lacy Victorian angel in tie-dye garments.

"I feel like this thing."

"An angel?"

"No. Not seraphic. Not that. More like an ornament."

"How do you mean that?"

"There was some interview with The Doors not long ago. I caught just a bit of it on TV. They were on tour. I think maybe Europe. Can't remember. The guy doing it asked each of them what they did. And that's what Morrison's old lady said. She said her name was Pamela Morrison and then she said, 'Ornament.' Just like that. And she smiled."

"Well, that's her."

"But it's beginning to be me, too. I'm just Jesse's old lady. That's all I do."

"Is that bad?"

"It's okay. I mean it's wonderful. He's really great. But I just wonder sometimes if that's all there is for me here."

"Look, R.E., you had a hell of a time last year. What's so bad about living in a beautiful place like this with a guy who loves you and wants to take care of you? You don't have to work. You can just figure out what you want to do. Enjoy the space."

She laughed and turned back to me. "Yeah, when you put it like that, I guess I ought to be grateful, right? Lots of people have it a lot worse. I just keep thinking about Dado. Got a letter from him yesterday and some packages for us for Christmas."

"So you got the guilts."

"Heavy."

"Well, don't. Look, if I can be thinking about finding my way out here, you can, too."

Claire and Amanda called us from the kitchen. There were fresh cookies coming out that needed icing. R.E. and I smiled at each other then I hugged her; we went in to the bright room with all the family and another evening passed.

Christmas morning, we all gathered near the tree and opened our presents after a big, late breakfast. Amanda, in the spirit of the day, had relented and made sausages for us carnivores, homemade sausages, though, she insisted. And they were great. We ate slowly, asking for seconds and then thirds of the pancakes and French toast and the lovely cinnamon coffee that Claire had made. Then we went into the living room and Jesse took a bunch of photos with the new camera he'd bought recently. It was supposed to be an old-fashioned holiday and we were inventing new customs that we hoped to carry forward into the future with us. We had decided to give each other one gift only and to draw the names from a hat full of folded paper slips. I had gotten Jesse's.

It had taken me about a week to come up with something. The rule was supposed to be that it had to be something that you made and that the makings of it couldn't cost more than $5. I pondered and wandered and fussed over it, obsessing more than a little about the problem. Then one day, on a walk down the row of old canneries that Steinbeck had made famous, it suddenly came to me. I spotted a nice piece of driftwood stuck between a couple of big rocks below. After easing my way down to it, I managed to dislodge it and drag it back up with me. I decided to use it to make a frame for one of Jesse's photos. Raz lent me some of his tools and I spent the rest of the week cutting and shaving and sealing. When it was done, it was curvy and graceful, with smooth waves and a soft gray finish. When Jesse opened it Christmas morning and showed it to everyone to admire, I knew I had hit pay dirt.

Claire took me aside later than day. She had on her practical face. "You know, cher, that frame was a lovely thing. Do you think you could find more wood like that? Make some to sell?"

"Well, I hadn't thought about it."

"Please think about it. You saw how everyone liked it."

"Yeah, but it's Christmas. And this is family. They were just being polite."

"Well, you could try," she insisted.

I said that I'd consider it. But the dark cloud that passed over her face scared me, so I told her that I'd go looking for driftwood the very next morning and see what I could do about joining the artsy crowd. I couldn't say no to any idea that would further Claire's dreams. But I hated being pressured. Twin emotions of guilt and resentment coalesced around a grain of emotional sand that burrowed into my heart, a gritty growth of black pearl that would begin to crowd out the pleasure and sweetness of the other feelings I had for Claire.

R.E. was quiet, too. Jesse had drawn Amanda's name and Vance had gotten R.E.'s, but Jesse traded him. I noticed that he took her over to one side of the room to open a little box and that R.E. had gone thoughtful afterwards. It was the next morning when I went over to see them on the way to the beach to do my driftwood duty that I saw her out on the porch. She was wearing jeans, sneakers, and a heavy gray Greek-type fisherman's sweater, her hair loose, drinking coffee. I waved and she waved back so I allowed myself a little break before "work." As I sat down, I saw something on her left hand that I'd never noticed before: a ring. That was something about R.E. She rarely wore any jewelry other than her bracelets. But now, there was silver ring on her little finger, decorated with alternating sun and moon faces. It seemed a tad too big, like it was intended for another digit.

"Oh, that's nice. Jesse give you that?"

She nodded as she spun it thoughtfully around with her thumb.

Then it hit me. It wasn't just any old ring.

She knew it had registered and she looked up at me and nodded, sighed.

"Wow. Really? So, what did you say?"

"I said I'd think about it."

"Was that an okay answer for him?"

"I don't think so. But, damn! What was I going to do? Make a scene on Christmas Day? That was no time to corner me like that." She was frowning.

A change of scene was needed. "Come on. I'm going to work. Why don't you help me out?"

"Work? Really? Where?"

I told her about Claire's suggestion that I try to make some money from wood art. She brightened a little and said it was worth a shot, so she left her cup on the porch and came with me. As we strolled away, she glanced back and said, "They're all still asleep. No need to wake him up just to tell him I'm taking a walk. They didn't get in until almost 4." I knew she needed a stretch and a conversation. We were both getting hemmed in suddenly and I wanted to talk to her as much as I thought she might want to talk to me.

Once on the beach, we just walked for a long ways and admired the size of the winter waves. The crash and the roar and the amazingly varied palette of grays absorbed our attention for a long time and then I asked her, "So, are you going to marry him?"

"No. I don't want to marry anybody right now. Everything's fine like it is." She fingered the ring, still spinning it around with her thumb. "I think he asked because things are really so sweet right now, and he wants to make sure they stay that way."

"Won't they? If you get married?"

"I don't think they will. I'm scared of being a shadow in someone else's life. I don't want to marry anyone until I know what I want to do with my own life. I'm afraid if I'll start to resent his success if I don't have some of my own."

I nodded. "Yeah. I have no idea about my own direction either. I'm just doing this frame thing because Claire insisted." I was so mopey and melodramatic that it made me laugh at myself. "Come on. Look at us, man. We're with people who love us, living in a gorgeous place during interesting times. We're both taking all this way too seriously."

She smiled and shook herself like a wet dog. "Get rid of that mood! Hey, there's a nice hunk of wood over there." It was a keeper, but it was too big to carry. So she headed back for her truck while I wrestled it closer to the path up the dune-mountain. Waiting there for her to return, I fished the remains of a number I'd been nursing all day out of my pocket, and toked a couple of times on it. I could have stayed right there on the beach for the rest of my life. But I knew I had to go home and so did R.E. We made a bigger deal out of loading the wood than we needed to and wound up staying gone most of the day, driving around, looking for more material. It was almost dark when we got to Raz's. Jesse was there. He glared at me and took R.E.'s arm a little too quickly as soon as she got out of the truck.

"Where have you been all day?" he asked.

She stood her ground and shook his grasp. "Helping Troy get some stuff together for a project. He's thinking about making more frames like the one he made you. Selling them."

Jesse glanced at the load we had collected. I didn't want to get into it between them, so unloaded the stuff as quickly as I could by myself. Between trips, I could hear them arguing and when I came back after the last load, it was just Jesse. R.E. and the truck were gone. He gave me the X-ray eye.

"Jesse, you know damn well that's all that was going on."

He sighed and ducked his head. "Yeah. I know. Sorry. It's just I was so freaked out when she went missing. I saw her on the porch one minute and then the next, she was gone. She could have come in and told me where she was going at least. I was afraid--you know--him--he'd come back and snatched her."

"She thought you were still asleep. Look, she was just trying to help me get started on this frame thing. You know how R.E. is about helping people. Claire's been after me to make some money one way or the other, and when she saw that frame I made you, she started really pushing me to make some to sell. That's all. I'm sure she didn't mean anything by not telling you where she was. Man, we aren't each other's parents. We don't have to punch clocks, ask permission."

He blinked and mulled that one over. "Yeah. I guess. I know I shouldn't crowd her. She's still skittish after Cole." He kicked a loose rock around. "That bastard. He really did a number on her head."

"She loves you, you ought to know that."

"I know. I know she does. Well, hell." Then he walked away into the foggy, growing darkness and back to his house.

I could see that dinner was in the offing inside. Smelled like more spinach and beans. Claire was sweet and supportive that evening. Even though it was a potential baby-making night according to her calendar, she didn't start anything. And she didn't ask me how long it would take to make frames and sell them. But I noticed that the Whole Earth Catalog, which had somehow landed in our room, was opened to the hand tool section. She was at our desk, studying a French textbook, making notes for her tutees. Every now and then, she would look up and smile at me. I smiled back but it was pretty thin and she must have known it. Why was I so afraid of being in love, married, and a father? Why did I resent her for asking so much of me?

***

A few weeks later, I had a couple of dozen things ready for sale. Not just frames: I had made two little stash boxes, a couple of rolling trays, other little gewgaws like that. They were pretty nice, actually. I had been afraid at first that all of them would seem like some stoned wood shop projects, but they had their own aesthetics and I was even a little proud of a couple of the frames. My problem was where to sell it. There was going to be a Renaissance fair up in the City. Claire kept talking to me about taking my stuff up there to hawk it to strangers. She also kept mentioning the Montgrove Craft Guild there in P.G., saying I should talk to them about showing my work. They had a little storefront on Central Avenue, not far from our place. I hadn't joined, but I had passed by now and then and glanced in the windows at the tie-dyes and such. The Guild just didn't feel right, somehow, but I finally agreed to try the fair. But by then, Claire had stopped talking and started just watching me. I would feel her now and then staring at my back and the expression on her face when I turned around and caught her was thoughtful, distant, and critical. It was time to do something, anything, to show her that I could keep my end of our agreement.

The day I left for the City, Claire helped me pack my little odds and ends, a blanket to sit on, and a cigar box half full of change. But she was quiet and avoided making eye contact. Jesse and the band were playing several gigs around Berkeley over the holiday, and R.E. had said she would go too, to get a feel for what was doing in the way of businesses. Claire said she was staying behind. As we all pulled away in Jesse's van, I watched her grow smaller and smaller and then suddenly disappear as the fog ate her up.

Jesse dropped us off at Golden Gate Park, the site of the event, which was as 16th century as I'd imagined. There were strolling musicians, ladies in long dresses and flowers and paint, street food, the dreaded mimes and jugglers, a troupe of actors who portrayed the Royal Court. R.E. wandered off to explore the scene. I laid out my blanket, arrayed my wares on it and squatted on one edge, keeping my eyes down and begging the Snake to let me off lightly. Of course, he had other plans, pulling my strings and making me dance like a manic puppet.

Time passed, people walked by. Now and then someone would pause to admire the stuff, but I knew they were too scared by my jerking around to ask me anything. It was worse than I thought it would be, hunkering out there in the glare of strangers' curiosity. And yet I couldn't leave, immobilized by guilt but too afraid to pack up and go. It would be hours yet before I was scheduled to be rescued by family, so I just went down deep into my self and tried to pretend I wasn't there. I watched a lot of feet go by in a lot of different shoes and then suddenly, I heard her say, "Need some company?"

"Oh, man, do I ever," I sighed.

R.E. sat down beside me, loosened her hair and spread it around her shoulders and onto her legs in the most attractive arrangement possible. A passing guy stopped to smile at her. She turned his gaze to my bits and pieces for sale. "Genuine, handmade, driftwood art. He takes it from the world for free and turns it into wonderful things for your home." She beamed her most radiant smile and wound up selling him a frame for five times what I would have dared to ask.

"Not bad," I said. "Not bad."

"Say, why don't you take a stroll? Get some chow. Lots of cool food being sold. Try some of the falafel. That's bean meatballs in pita. Good stuff. I'll spell you."

"I'm not hungry. But you can take over. Thanks."

She nodded. I pulled away from the blanket and into the protective covering of a little tent that had been set up for the vendors. I watched R.E. as she worked the crowd, wishing for all the world that I had her nerve with strangers. Within two hours, she had sold everything that I had made. For good money, too: when she came over to me, she had over a hundred dollars in her hands.

"I think we're onto something here. You make the stuff, I sell it."

"And we split 50-50," I nodded.

"Oh, no. Not 50 percent. You take 90."

"You sure?"

"Hell, all I do is talk to people. That's not worth half of your take."

We shook on it and then wandered around the fair. It was distinctly different from Texas gatherings. People weren't the least bit afraid to look strange. Not that we didn't in Texas, but there weren't so many of us and we weren't quite as flamboyant. Go for baroque seemed to be the watchword of the day: paisley swirls and tie-dyes and face and body paint, feathers and beads and tattoos.

"You ever think about getting one?" I asked her as we passed a woman with a delicately inked parrot on her shoulder.

"I've been considering it. Something discrete, of course."

"Of course."

"Why? You thinking about it?" she asked.

"Yeah. I am. This thing I got, I always call it the Snake."

She turned to me as that same Scaly Lord shook me hard, warning me. I'd never said his name out loud. "I want one of those, what are they called? Ouroboros? You know, the snake in a circle? On my back. Only problem is holding still enough for it."

"Maybe they could put you to sleep. You don't move at all when you're sleeping."

"There's an idea."

The woman with the parrot on her shoulder caught up with another woman and kissed her. Really kissed her. I blushed and turned away.

R.E. caught me and nudged my ribs. "Come on. You're seen gay folks kissing before."

"Yeah. In Denton. But not in public."

"Stan and Moe were pretty cool about things. They liked their privacy," she nodded. Then she added, as an aside, "So do RaeAnn and JaeDeen."

Once again, I found myself doing a rapid rewind of a couple of mental tapes and another set of observed but not identified at the time facts fell into place.

She smiled, "Surely you knew."

"Uh, no. I didn't. Then again, I was pretty self-involved when I was there, you know, finding out about my medical history and my mom and Cassady and all that."

"Yeah. And they have to be especially cool, stuck there in that damned little town. I've told them a hundred times to move out here to the coast, but RaeAnn loves that house. JaeDeen would come in a second, though, if RaeAnn would."

A guy walked by with a fabulous serpent inked on his shoulders and before I could reflect on what R.E. had just told me, I said, "Something like that one, only more elaborate. That's how I envision the Snake." Then, to remind me who was in charge and to punish me further for saying his name out loud twice, the Snake shook me so hard I slipped and fell. Several people around us stepped away as though what I had were contagious and a couple of them laughed. R.E. glared and helped me to my feet. I was shaky and nervous and very self-conscious all of a sudden. Agoraphobia swept over me and I had trouble getting my breath. Fear of the marketplace is aptly named. R.E. guided me back to the tent. After a few minutes in its cool, slightly darker interior, I got control of my shaking hands and legs.

"Hey, enough of this circus," she said. "Let's get a coffee and go check out City Lights. You deserve a little treat for making all those beautiful things."

"I don't know about that. If you hadn't sold them for me, they would still be junk out there on the blanket." I rolled it up, pocketed the money, and left the cigar box for another vendor to use. Since we were afoot, it was going to take quite a while to get over to the fabled bookstore but that was okay by me. I needed some distraction and besides, I loved wandering around the City.

Once away from the park, I immediately felt like my old self again. We walked some, trolley-carred a little, bused even more. When we were just a few blocks away from City Lights, she stopped to call the club where Jesse was playing and left a message that we'd be there for a while if he wanted to come pick us up, since the gig wasn't too far away. As she hung up, she wrinkled her nose and shrugged. "Don't want him to get uptight like he did the other day about my being out of pocket."

"He was just worried."

"It was more than that. You know it was. But I think we got it worked out." She looked down at her hand. "He understands that I don't want to get married right now."

"You still got the ring."

"Yeah. But it's a gift from one lover to another. That's all it is."

I got the strangest shiver when she said that word "lover", a prickle of sight that ran all the way from my ass to my scalp, so fast, so cold like icy feathers. I shuddered and blew it off without comment. Just city fog, I told myself. We went inside the fabled bookstore and stood for a moment to soak up the history before going our separate ways, drifting through the aisles. Since I was freshly flush, I went on a little shopping frenzy then thought better of it and went back the way I'd come, carefully replacing the books where I'd found them, though in the end I did treat myself to a used copy of *Cloud-Hidden: Whereabouts Unknown*. I paid for it, tucked it into my blanket roll, and walked out to the street. It was cool and cloudy, a typical City day and I was feeling much better than I had earlier at the fair. Maybe the artsy routine could work after all. I could make the junk and R.E. could hawk it for me. I wouldn't have to expose myself to the public at all next time. I had already decided that 10 percent was too little for what she had done for me.

I was debating how much Claire would let me get away with giving to R.E. when I looked back inside the shop. The memory of what I saw is a little fractured since it all happened so fast that even as it was going down, it seemed like a slide show, one still picture after another, not the flow of normal-time events. Accidents, wrecks, and collisions of the heart are like that, too, much to deal with at once so your brain just parcels it out to you in little dabs.

Eddie was in the shop. R.E. was talking to him. He was standing with a young Eurasian girl I suddenly recognized from the moment of sight the day Eddie left Texas, the girl in the photo. She was glancing back and forth between Eddie and R.E. like she was watching an emotional tennis game. Eddie wasn't making much eye contact with either of them, standing between them and at a sideways angle to R.E., not facing her full on. She reached out to touch his arm. He held his palm up towards her and shook his head, his mouth set in a straight tight line. The girl tried to say something but he turned back to her and said something quickly. She looked puzzled but shook her head yes, turned, and headed out the door. Eddie turned back to R.E. and said something else, also very quickly. I could see the tears roll down her cheeks but she didn't reach out again. She just stared at him. Then Jesse was there, too, over at the side of the store. He spotted the two of them and clenched his jaw, heading for them silently. Eddie pushed past R.E. and out the door behind the girl. From where I was, I could only see them for a second before they disappeared down the street. When I turned back to the window. Jesse was holding R.E.'s shoulders, shaking her. She looked like she wasn't listening to him. Then he slapped her. It wasn't a punch but it was angry enough to leave the clear mark on his hand on her cheek. She suddenly focused on him as though she were looking at him for the first time. He stepped back, dropping his arms, one hand flying to his forehead, the shock of what he'd done dropping his jaw and widening his eyes. R.E. stepped back from him. He reached out but she raised one hand and pointed her index finger at him. I could see her mouth form the word "no." Then she wheeled around and ran out. She didn't see me either and took off down the street in the opposite direction from Eddie and the Amer-Asian girl. I looked back in, caught Jesse's eyes, and nodded yes: witness. His shoulders slumped and he shut his eyes, shaking his head.

I started running down the street after R.E. And then, I felt a cold shiver again, not from the fog, but around my heart. People in Texas used to say that when you felt it, someone was walking on your grave, saying bad things about you. And I knew who it was. The urge to get back home was so strong I impulsively held out my thumb to a van full of fellow hippie travelers stopped at a light. They said they were going down south to L.A. I was a little surprised they weren't put off by the Snake, but I suppose it didn't hurt that I offered to pay for gas.

As soon as I walked in the kitchen and saw Amanda's face, I knew it was true. She was sitting at the kitchen table, her eyes red and puffy. "Oh, Troy," she began.

"She's gone," I nodded.

"How did you know?"

"I just did. What happened? Why--where?" I stopped. She got up and hugged me and I let her. Then she motioned for me to sit down.

"See, I found out today that I'm pregnant again. It's okay. We were planning it this time. But when the doctor called and I told Claire, I didn't stop to think how she would feel. She just went crazy. She started saying all these things about how she was never going to get pregnant, how things weren't working." She started to say something else. Then stopped.

"What else did she say? About me."

She looked up. "She was too upset to make sense. Just blowing off steam. She didn't mean any of it."

"It wasn't just things that weren't working. It was me, wasn't it? What else?"

"I don't need to repeat it."

"Then what?"

"Then she went back to your room and came back out with a suitcase after about an hour. She said she was going back to Texas. I tried to get her to wait, to talk to you, to reason with her. But she can be really stubborn."

"I know that."

"And then she just left." Amanda started crying again. "Damn mood swings," she apologized. "Sorry. Anyway. I don't think she really meant it. She just needs to get it out of her system. She'll be back before dark, I just know it."

I nodded, but I knew I would never see her again. Amanda fell quiet and we listened to the kitchen clock ticking. I went back to our room--the room--and grabbed some pants and shirts, a blanket and other things, absently tossing them into a pile on the floor. When I carried them into the kitchen, Amanda was gone. I could hear her throwing up in the bathroom. I left a note saying I was going south for a time, down to Big Sur. I didn't say anything about Jesse and R.E. That would all be made plain, if they cared to do so, in their own time and in their own way. At that moment, all I wanted to do was to be completely alone. I unrolled the blanket and heaped the clothes and a few things from the kitchen inside, running across the Watts book as I tied the roll up with a belt. I almost left it on the table but threw it in with the rest of the stuff on impulse. Then I left, started walking, and wound up on the highway. This time, the first van that stopped was headed to Pfeiffer State Park. It was a bunch of college kids already on the way to a major drunk. I don't think they even noticed my palsy since they were barely in control of their own bodily functions. I got in and they sped and swayed down Highway One. I didn't care if we all went off the cliffs and into the drink. There were six or seven big jugs of Gallo that they kept passing around, including me every time. I finally Bogarted one and drank so much I vomited when we finally got there. They were still whooping and hollering when I got up and staggered off up a hillside,

dragging my bedroll with me. I walked for hours that night, stumbling, getting up again, hauling myself up and down the trails and through the undergrowth and across streams, falling sometimes, sliding others, until I passed out.

"We believe that according to our desire we are able
to change the things round about us, we believe this
because otherwise we can see no favorable solution.
We forget the solution that generally comes to pass
and is also favorable: we do not succeed in
changing things according to our desire, but
gradually our desire changes."

Marcel Proust, *The Sweet Cheat Gone*

IX.

Ignu, Too

I hid out on Pfeiffer Ridge, clinging to my misery and wallowing in quickly purchased booze, sad howling, and deep depression, thinking about every negative aspect of my life, blaming first everyone else, then only myself, finally alternating between those two rocky sides of my own Scylla and Charybdis. Watt's book did help when I was able to read, but the sadder parts just set me off again. After a span of four days and nights of that self-indulgence, I created an emotional balance sheet that helped me come to terms with Claire's leaving. My fault: I had put off being honest with her for too long because I didn't trust our relationship enough to be myself: "Worthless" had hung over my head like a neon sign. Her fault: she took me for granted to the point that something as big as moving to California and being uprooted from the only home I'd ever had wasn't even discussed, it was just assumed. Shared faults: I was in lust with her and in love with the idea of a relationship more than I was in love with her, or at least the her she'd become. She only wanted a family and perhaps, a green card ticket to a life here. Final tally: I was glad she was gone and I didn't hate myself for it. I had not wanted a family. I just wanted her, the way she used to be. Or at least the way I thought she was. And that, apparently, was never to be. So. With a final gut-busting river of tears, I purged myself and headed back down towards what was left of home for me. Tired, achy and filthy, the pilgrim left the woods and reentered the town.

R.E. opened the door when I knocked. She let me in and reached to hug me but I held up my hands and said, "I'm covered with all kinds of muck and so are my clothes. And I think I've got a poison oak rash."

She glanced at me more closely and asked, "So how long have you been in those duds?"

"Four, going on five days."

"Think it's against the law to burn them in this state?"

I just laughed. It was good to be back. She suggested several cures for the itch; I opted for a hot shower and one of her herbal creams. She had taken what had been Claire's and my room. I knew why and didn't ask. The remains of my things were still in the old dresser I had salvaged from a back alley. Her things were in a jumble in her suitcase on the floor. Once clean and dressed, I joined her in the kitchen. She had been making breakfast and now simply doubled the ingredients, silently pouring me some coffee. We didn't have anything to say at first. There was so much. Finally, after we had eaten and put the things away, she poured us some more coffee and pulled a number out of the pocket of her flannel shirt. I nodded a hungry yes and we took our cups out into the foggy back yard. It was sweet to dive into the green wave again after my short hiatus. Then I asked, "So, I gotta know. What the hell was going on with Eddie?"

"So, you saw all that?" I nodded and she shrugged. "All I can figure is that the girl was Lizzy, the one he and Maja were raising. Either that or he has suddenly developed a taste for real young 'uns."

"I don't think it would be that."

"Well, he sure didn't seem like his old warm self. He was so freaked out when he saw me. And especially when the girl saw me. It was like--I don't know, worlds colliding or something. Anyway, he really didn't want to talk. He wouldn't let me even touch him and he barely made eye contact. He just said that he didn't want to see me or talk to me and that I shouldn't try to contact him."

"Mysterious."

"Yeah, I know."

She wasn't going to talk about Jesse, it seemed. So I scooted around the edge of that topic by observing, "I noticed all your stuff has landed here."

"Amanda said you weren't going to be using the room for a while. And I needed some space to think about what to do next."

"Have you talked to him?"

She sighed. "No. I'm assuming you saw all that went down?"

I nodded.

"After he slapped me, I ran out of the store and down the street. I was so angry and hurt and lost. I didn't know what to do. I couldn't believe he'd raise a hand to me, not after what happened with Coleman. So, I finally found the bus station and came back here. Amanda said that he'd been calling all night. They must have known that something had happened, but they didn't ask and Jesse didn't explain. I got all my stuff and brought it here and that's been how we've all left it for now."

"Has Jesse come over?"

"A couple of times. Once I wasn't here and the other, I slipped out the back and down the alley. I don't want to see him just yet. I'm still really angry."

"Why did he do it?"

"He thought I'd arranged to meet Eddie there, that I'd been seeing him on the side, that that was why I didn't want to get married."

"Oh, no. Couldn't he tell you were upset?"

"He didn't even notice." She shook her head then looked at me. "So, how are you doing?"

"You know," I smiled. "I'm doing okay. At first, I mean, I was like you said, lost. But yesterday, it hit me that I'm going to live over it. And, deep down, I'm glad it happened. I never would have had the nerve to break up, so her leaving took the matter out of my hands."

"Really?"

"Yeah. I feel free of all that pressure and obligation and the baby stuff." I sighed. "I miss her. Of course. Now and then, something crosses my mind and blindsides me and I go all blue, remembering her. But I miss the old her, like it was when we were first together, not the her that she was becoming. Does that make sense?"

She nodded, fetching another small joint from the bottomless pocket. "I feel bound for glory this morning."

"No need to explain to me," I said. "I feel like being nice and loaded, too. I didn't indulge at all while I was in the woods."

"I didn't that much either when I was in that little cabin in Texas, hiding out. Being there, with the trees and all that forest noise, that was enough. I felt stoned all the time anyway."

"Really does help you think, sort things out. I went totally silent. Never did like to talk a lot when I was outside like that."

"Me, neither."

"So, you doing okay here in Babylandia?"

She grimaced and shook her head. "I have to help out. Amanda knows that I'm not into all the details like she is. So she doesn't go into the full frenzy. But I feed and change Mel. I think I'm going to like her as a person, when she starts to be one. You know, one you can talk to. We already seem to have a nice little bond going."

"Looks like we're both stuck."

She turned back to me. "How much is your check?"

"Why?"

"Well, look. If I go out and land some kind of job, waitress or something, you want to share the rent on a cheap place?"

It seemed like the only real alternative we had. "Sure. Why not?"

"Okay. Tomorrow. Good. That's settled. I'll look through the paper and see what I can scare up. See about finding a job and then a place. But today, I just feel like being really loaded and maybe walking on the beach for a while."

"Let's go."

"Pit stop first. Too much coffee," she smiled.

We went back in and I made some sandwiches while she went to the bathroom. Then I could hear her rustling around in the back bedroom, probably rolling some more. That was when I heard the knock on the door. At first, I didn't want to answer it since I was well on the way to a major glow but curiosity won out. It took a few long seconds before the recognition set in but the face and the voice finally registered.

"Can I come in?" Eddie asked.

"Uh, sure. Wow, I'm just so blown away to see you."

"And stoned, too, looks like," he smiled.

"Yeah, that. Been a lot of changes. Just rolling with that fabled flow."

He nodded and stepped in. "Nice little place."

"It's Raz and Amanda's. And their kid's."

"Finally hatched."

R.E. had heard the voices and came out, the surprise as clear on her face as it must have been on mine.

Eddie shrugged. "Sorry about the other day. I panicked."

She nodded, still stunned. Then recovered enough to say, "Well, sure. I was surprised, too. How did you find us?"

"Easy enough. Just called your dad's place. Rafe gave me the address here."

It was both familiar and yet very strange to be standing there with the two of them again. None of us said anything. Finally Eddie turned back to look out the door. "Well, I just wanted to apologize for cutting you cold, Rachel."

"Say," she smiled. "We were just about to head for the beach. You want to come?"

He nodded and returned her smile. "Sure. I'll drive, how 'bout?"

I hung back as they headed out on the porch but R.E. leaned back in and said, "You got those sandwiches?"

I mouthed "Me, too?" and she brushed my reluctance away with a wave of her hand. "Come on."

We decided on one of our favorite haunts. It felt so weird to be in the back seat of Mariah again. The inside was so familiar but the scenes through the window didn't match my memories of being in it. R.E. gave directions and Eddie drove. There wasn't much talk on the way. Once on the white sands, we walked a little apart at first, letting the wind and the waves speak for us. Finally we came to a sheltered place in the rocks and took up our positions, each on the point of a triangle, close enough to hear each other but with enough distance to shelter our hearts. R.E. started to fetch a number from her pocket but Eddie put up a hand then brought one of his own out. "Peace offering," he said as he lit it and passed to her. She toked then passed it on to me. It did seem to smooth the way slightly.

As I handed it back to him, he leaned back, hit once more then said, "You two finish it." We settled in and he looked away from us, out towards the ocean. After a while, he sighed and turning back to us said, "It's a long tale to tell, but you already know the first parts of it. Korea. Maja and Lizzy."

I looked over at R.E. who was watching him. She nodded.

Eddie went on. "That girl you saw me with is her. Lizzy." He smiled. "Liz. I have to call her Liz now. She insists." He got up and paced around a little, kicking at the sand as he went. Then he faced R.E. and started. "Remember that Korean officer I told you about? The one that helped convince the upper echelon to let Maja out of the country?"

She nodded.

"He was the reason she took the baby and split on me. He just showed up one day. Blackmailed her. Said he would spill the beans to immigration about her having been a whore if she didn't go along with him. See, she wasn't the only one he helped with papers." His voice put an edge on the word "helped" that would have sliced a ripe tomato. "He had a whole string of girls he'd known and some others who were fresher, as it were, shipped over. And then he came. He rounded them up and set them to working at their old trade down in San Diego."

"What about Liz?"

"Oh, he let all the girls keep their babies, boys and girls. Seems he had plans to put them to work, too."

"Oh, man, that's awful! What a bastard!" R.E. sympathized. But she remained seated as Eddie paced.

"That's one word. I thought of lots of others."

"So, how did you find her?" I asked.

"I didn't." He ran his hands back through his hair and stretched. "God, The Corner Room seems like a hundred years ago. I got to work that last day there and found the letter. It was from a detective agency I'd hired ten lifetimes ago, at one point when I was sober and had some cash. I'd remember them periodically, check in, give them my address du jour. Not long after starting up the restaurant, I wrote them. And they finally wrote me back. They'd found Maja." He almost smiled. "Some detectives. They only found her because they saw the house being busted on the news. The camera happened to catch her being dragged out first. Anyway, she and all the girls were about to be deported. The agency guys blasted down to the jail, talked to her, said they could put her in contact with me. She gave them a picture of Lizzy to send me and that was that. I tossed all my stuff in Mariah and hit the road. I thought... I don't know what I thought. Maybe that I could help. See, we never got divorced. Or at least, I had never filed anything. I thought maybe if they knew she had an American husband..." He stood with his back to us for a while then turned around again. "I got to talk to her a few times. For about ten minutes a session. Through glass."

"Was Liz--okay? I mean, did--the guy put her to work?" I didn't know how to ask.

"Was she a whore, too? No. Maja gave her to a john when Liz was about three. A guy who was pretty sound, stable. He and his wife were having problems because he was sterile. They set it up so he could spirit her away one night. Maja told him to take good care of Liz or she'd kill him. Guess he took it to heart." He smiled. "Liz is far from abused. Spoiled, is more like it."

"So, what happened to Maja?" R.E. asked.

"For giving Liz away?"

She nodded.

"She cut a devil's deal with her pimp. Helped him recruit other Korean women in exchange for letting Lizzy go. She told me it didn't matter what happened to her since she was already in so deep karmically speaking, just as long as Lizzy got a clean start."

"What happened to her? Did she go to jail?"

"No, she was deported, though I don't know how much better being in Korea will be, given her history. She told me where Liz was. That was part of the deal, that the john and his wife send Maja a picture every year, stay in touch. They did. So, I came up to the City. That's where they live now. Liz is in high school, 17, but she looks like she's 25. Maja's genes. Maja wrote them just before she was sent back to Seoul to tell them to expect me, that I was taking over the watchdog role for her. She said she knew she couldn't square things between me and her completely, but she could at least give me the chance to know the kid a little better. Liz thinks I'm just an old friend of the family. They're going along with me visiting her now and then, I guess because they went along with Maja for so long."

"Are you going to tell her anything?"

"I don't know. Her foster family seems to understand that I just want the contact, so I don't want to push them. Anyway, Lizzy remembers almost nothing about Maja, it was that long ago. She knows she was adopted, that's all." He turned away from the waves and back towards R.E. "I was so flipped out when I saw you in the bookstore, Rachel. I thought for some crazy reason that you would figure out who Lizzy was and say something that would tip her off." He went back over to her and held out his arms. She stood up and they hugged. "I'm sorry. You deserve more faith than that."

I figured that it was time for me to take a long, solitary walk. They didn't stop me.

R.E. took off with Eddie when we got back to the house, so I hung around, waiting on her to show up again. Or not. Raz and Amanda both kept me busy with little chores. I told them about seeing Eddie and all the things he'd told me. I figured it would be okay since they were family, too. But I put off seeing Jesse right away. Raz and Amanda said he was at his place in P.G. and that they had filled him in about Claire for me, so that when I did see him, I wouldn't have to go through pulling that particular band-aid off my heart. He was taking things really hard. He'd even canceled gigs. I finally went over to see him a couple of days after Eddie's return. He let me in with a shrug and a deep sigh. "So, you want to kick my ass, too?"

"No, I figure you've been doing it enough for both of us."

"Man, oh man, what an asshole I made of myself." He looked back at me over his shoulder.

"Well, don't expect me to disagree."

"I know. No sympathy. I don't deserve any." He took another pull off a Camel and a swig from a bottle of whiskey. He always started smoking tobacco again when he had the love blues and then kicked the habit when he was more upbeat.

"Easy, Jesse."

"Why should I?"

"You still got a few friends in town."

"Not after they find out why we split up. She tell anyone?"

"No. But they know you two had a fight. She's been staying over at Raz's place."

"I can't believe I hit her," he moaned. "It just happened. I was so pissed when I saw Eddie. It was like I went crazy. What was going on? Do you know?"

"Well," I said, "Yeah. Do you want to hear it?"

He nodded, so I ran down the story in shorter form. He listened to all of it. Then asked, "She there with him now?"

"I don't know. I just know she hasn't been back to the house."

"Well, I guess I can't blame her if she is or him for getting back with her. Damn!"

"I don't know if that's the case."

"So what are you going to do now?"

"Maybe get a place with R.E. for a while."

He glared at me out of habit then shrugged. "Hell." He finished the bottle with a noisy suck and tossed in on the floor where several others lay in a heap. "Band's been gone, too. Staying up in the City. In the Haight. Playing without me. Vance almost quit when I told him I was taking off for a while. He said I was being unprofessional." I winced with him. That was one of the worst things Vance could have said. "Maybe. But damn. I just needed a while to catch my breath. You think she'll forgive me?"

I sighed and put my hands up in the air.

"Okay, bad question."

"It's just that I don't know. She's got a soft heart and she doesn't stay mad at anyone for long. Give it some time. Go on back and play. She'll do what she does."

His eyes met mine and we nodded. Then he reached out and hugged me: brothers, no matter what. He did go back to the City later that evening, after some sleep, a shower and lots of hot, black coffee. And he called about three to ask if R.E. had shown up, which she hadn't. He didn't say anything else but I asked how the gig had gone before he hung up; he said it had had its moments, which meant to most mortal listeners that it had been great. And if the blues in his heart had come through clearly in his music that night, it would have been one of those sessions that people talk about for years. I just hoped a producer had been in the crowd. Jesse needed for something good to happen to him. We all did.

I sighed and stretched and went back out onto the porch for a smoke. It was quiet and clear, a rare starry night. It was about an hour later that R.E. pulled up in the truck. She parked, got out, and walked over.

"Evenin'," she smiled.

"Back at ya," I nodded.

She glanced around. "Is he here?"

"No. Went back to the City. Playing a gig."

"That's good."

"You okay?"

"Yeah," she said as she joined me on the porch. "I am."

"I know it breaks outlaw tradition, but I'll ask anyway. Where you been?"

"With Eddie."

She seemed so peaceful and content that I left it at that, offered her the stub of a number I'd been working on. She finished it and then said, "It was more of a wrapping up, a saying goodbye than a starting over. I stayed at his place. We went to several of his favorite haunts. He showed me a lot of the City. It was a very, very special time."

"How is he?"

"Still very tender. Hesitant. He doesn't know what he's going to do. About Liz. About me. About anything. We agreed to stay in touch. See what happens."

"I talked to Jesse."

She turned to look at me.

"He feels like the lowest of the low."

She looked out into the yard. "I'm not mad at him anymore. He's my friend and I've already gotten past that. He just over-reacted. That's Jesse." She shrugged. "We'll talk when it's the right time and place, but I don't want to live with him again."

"Still want to get a place?"

"Sure. Looks like the only option we have."

We sat on the porch for a while longer then crashed in separate rooms. So much had been said. So much had been done. We were both tired and out of words, plans, thoughts. It was time for oblivion and rest, time to make camp in our dreams, sit by the internal river for a spell and think things through.

***

We rented a weather-beaten cottage further down the Peninsula on a woodsy lot. The ad said it all: "Carmel Doll House", code for ultra-tiny. We liked it from the moment we saw it: a little fairy tale place, barely visible inside its cocoon of brambles and pines. It was only one small bedroom, a small kitchen, a smaller bathroom, and a little common room that had windows all around. Given my love of light, I really wanted it more than the darker back bedroom so that was how we divvied up the space. We borrowed a few sticks of furniture from the other two houses, gathered our meager possessions, and that was that. We put all rehashing of past events behind us, not so much by any discussion but by mutual avoidance of those topics and people, all the dead horses we were tired of beating. And there was one especially that neither of us wanted to invoke: Coleman. He was always there in the margins of our dreams and attention but with some effort, I at least, was managing to push him even further away. It was time to look forward and to move on.

R.E. picked up work quickly, first at a little beanery and then by way of a chance conversation with two customers, a part-time job at the Pilgrim's Way Bookstore. R.E. continued to cash my checks for me and deposit what we needed in her account so our finances were sufficient for two frugal people. The extra hours between the two gigs gave her lots of time to spend at the lovely old library in Carmel. So much reading led to an urge to write, and she started filling pages of legal pads with notes, sketches, and ideas. I'd noticed how the mound of paper was starting to build up on the kitchen table. She started to clear it and I said, "No problem. Just good to see you enjoying something new."

She smiled and took another drink of one of her herb tea concoctions. "I really do. You know, I think I'm on to something with writing. I've got a couple of things in mind. Articles. They're about half done now. Mentally, anyway."

"How much are typewriters?"

She looked over at me. "I've been thinking about getting one, but I didn't know if the racket would bug you."

"Hardly."

She went out the next day and acquired a used one. When she was on a roll, it made the cabin sound like a machine shop. But I liked the rattle and clank. It made me feel as though we had joined the ranks of the Big Sur scene that started when Jack London's old Telegraph Hill gang came down from the City. Harry Dick Ross and his wife, Lillian Bos Ross, moved to Livermore Ledge in 1939 and became caretakers of both the place and the lifestyle: him with his "whim of iron", her with her novels about the early pioneers. Then Henry Miller added his own brand of outlaw style when he arrived. Now it was us and ours. I tried to imagine what those worlds had felt like, sounded like, smelled like, and there were moments in that little cabin when other decades overlapped, when R.E. seemed like Louise Bryant, Emma Goldman, Voltairine de Cleyre, or some other woman from the margins of history, working away, drinking cup after cup of coffee, eyes glued to the white pages rolling off the machine.

My only minor stab at art was to borrow Jesse's camera. When I had a chance, I snapped a few photos for my tiny but growing scrapbook. R.E. insisted on copies, which she paid for, of course. I even bought a small album to keep them all in. I added the few of Jesse's from the Palace he'd given me, but the three most precious ones stayed with my mother's journal. They weren't for public viewing and this one could be, if I so decided.

I had really fallen in love with our little berg. Carmel had a longer official name: Carmel-by-the-Sea. And since Pacific Grove had originally been a Methodist church camp retreat, it was sometimes called Pacific Grove-by-God. That only left Monterey-by-the-Smell. I'm sure it was worse when the sardine canneries were running full tilt. They say that the beaches below them used to be strewn with guts and heads and an orange-colored industrial steam from the factories that would linger over the area like a fogbank. But there's stink and then there's smell. The sea, the ocean anywhere smells: living and dead marine life, fresh and rotting kelp. But I didn't care. I loved the briny sweetness and the fresh cool saltiness of it when the wind blew and swept away the deeper layers of decay. For someone who had resisted moving to the coast at all, I had been totally won over by life there and now considered myself a "Californiano." The realization that I could move and change so quickly pleased me and made me feel more connected to my own history and to Cassady. I'd even started reading my special copy of On The Road with fresh eyes. I never found out why Eddie had chosen that particular volume from his library to give to me. Maybe he'd seen something in me that reminded him of Cassady. Maybe it was only coincidence.

A scant few weeks later, Sam wrote from South Texas, a long newsy update. He was deeply involved in the politics there, had already been arrested once at a sit-in, and was going to meetings and organizing groups on ranches and farms all over the state. She read it silently then handed it over to me. I could see that the guilt she felt about her own lack of political commitment and involvement was kicking her hard. She just shook her head and left wordlessly for work.

When she came back that evening, she seemed lighter of mood. I asked her as we were cooking dinner, "So, you look like you had a good day."

"I did. I think I'm going to write an article for The Bay Guardian."

"About what?"

"I saw in the Chronicle that there's going to be some kind of event in San Diego next weekend. That's close to May 1st, yeah?" She wiped her hands on a dishtowel before she flipped through the garden shop calendar on the wall. "Yep. Kind of funny, that." She went thoughtful. "Anyway, I thought I'd try to find a way to get in, see what the deal is."

"Why? What?"

"It's the grand opening of this new right wing think tank. Something called the New Dawn Foundation."

"I wonder if those folks know that they're opening their tank on the real Labor Day?"

"I don't know." She finished putting the preliminary prep things away to make room then said, "You know, the editor of the *Pine Cone* is a regular at the café. Maybe he would give me a press badge and let me be a roving reporter from the North. I bet I could talk him into it."

"Oh, no doubt." We laughed and settled down to dinner and a smoke afterwards in our little yard. It was that night that we felt our first temblor. There was a booming sound, and we felt the ground shimmy. It bucked and heaved as though a giant armadillo had started running underground at us and then charged past, lifting us and our little house what felt like several feet off the ground. I know it couldn't have been more than scant inches, if that, but it did get our attention. The initial rocking was followed by a series of little jolts and jerks and then it all settled down as quickly as it had started. The neighbors, Californian folks who had grown up there, came out of their backdoor and hollered over to us, "You kids okay?"

We nodded and walked over, arms tight around our waists, jumpy as cats. "Was that an earthquake?"

"It was indeed. Felt like it was about a 5."

"Closer to a 5.3."

They were evidently used to this nonsense. I suppose our shocked faces seem comical to them, but they were gracious enough not to laugh. "Just a ground shaker," the man said.

"How often do they happen?"

"Nature sets her own schedule. No way to tell really."

We all talked a bit more and then went back to our respective houses. As R.E. and I were walking inside, she smiled, "I hope that wasn't some kind of portent." I started to answer flippantly but something held me back. Just as suddenly, I also hoped that it wasn't. But as soon as those words were out of her mouth, I knew better. And from the suddenly serious look in her eyes, she did, too.

When I woke up the next day, she was still at home. I followed the smell of coffee, poured some, and went out back. She was walking around, one arm tight around her waist, the other balancing her largest cup. I raised my eyebrows. Her habit had been to work in the library on her days off.

"You feel okay?"

"Didn't sleep much at all last night." Her eyes were shot through with green, a sure sign of stress.

"Me neither, not deeply anyway. I dreamed all night." About what, or more exactly whom, I didn't want to say.

She glanced back at me and then nodded. After a couple more sips of coffee, she said, "If something were to happen, earthquake, fire--anything--how would we handle it?" "Depends on what it is. Natural disasters, we'd handle as always. Just pick up what remains and move it to another house."

She gifted me with a deep, real laugh. But after a pause, she looked straight through me.

I knew she didn't want to make anything, or anyone, real by speaking, so I said, "For everything else, we'd have to get out of town, very quickly. I guess we should start keeping our stuff in a centralized place, like the closet. One stop grab and go."

"Might not be a bad idea to keep more cash in the cartridge box, too. Just in case."

Later that day, we did gather our most precious items closer together, hers in the suitcase and mine in the backpack. She stopped by the bank and drew out most of our cash. Snapping the lid back on the box, she smiled as she put it back in the closet. "How nice to have such prescient friends." And that night, she seemed to sleep more, but I couldn't. I kept pacing the perimeter, much as Sam and Rafe had always done.

R.E. did talk her way into getting a press badge. She also started doing some background checking on the think tank, but she wasn't finding much. Apprehension started gnawing on my peace of mind, and she grew more silent as the date approached.

***

It was April 30th when the door slammed on our lives there. I woke up late and found her already gone. She'd left a note on the kitchen table. "Troy, I'm heading down to San Diego today. I found out that Coleman is the money and the idea man behind that think tank. Remember at the van der Veer house the night his dad died, he kept talking about 'a new dawn' for the family? Well, this is it. I'm going to confront him somehow during the opening press conference. It's time to take a stand." All my air went out in one breath and I thumped to the floor. I dragged our things out of the closet and swept around the place, adding to the pile. I triple checked that my mom's diary and my most precious photos were in my backpack. I even took her precaution of binding them in plastic to waterproof them as much as possible. After a long debate about whether or not to take any road stash, I finally adding a few carefully rolled ones, also packing them in plastic. The day and longer night passed slowly. The next day was even worse. Every noise outside, even rustling leaves, transformed into boot falls. I had the worst feeling I'd had about things since R.E. had left The Palace that night to return to Cole's mansion. The last piece of business took care of itself when Raz dropped by late that afternoon. It was Saturday, the 1st. A generous man, he always offered to bring us over for dinner on payday. As soon as he walked in and the door was shut, I blurted everything out in one flowing rap I think Cassady would have been proud of.

He listened and I watched the wheels turning as he took it all in. "You'll need more cash. Here. Amanda will understand." He shoved five twenties towards me. Out of habit, I shook my head no. Then I accepted, more for R.E. than myself. We waited in silence for the most part until R.E.'s truck came wheeling into the yard. She threw it into park, shut off the engine, and ran inside. It took a couple of seconds to recognize her in hose and low heels, a white blouse, a torn black skirt and rumpled black jacket, and her hair hidden somehow behind her and under a black beret. Before either of us could ask, she blurted out, "Coleman is on my tail. He's armed. He said he'd kill me."

I grabbed my backpack and Raz got her suitcase. "Get the cartridge box," we said at the same moment. One last deep, true laugh, and then we were out the door.

"You sure?"

"Sam told me to look after you. That's why I learned to shoot that damned gun in the first place."

She smiled and nodded. Raz asked as he tossed things in the truck bed, "How do you know he'll find you here?"

"Cole got a clear look at my press pass. I needed gas about halfway anyway, so I called the office to tell them not to give any information to strangers. But sure enough, they said someone had just called saying they were long lost family and the friendly folks there spilled all the beans. Gave them this address, phone number, everything."

We all hugged and Raz shoved us away. "Go, go quickly."

We took off, back down the same highway we'd only so recently come in on, hopes so high now dashed.

After we were outside city limits, R.E. told me to drive. We pulled over to switch seats and I asked, "Any reason for this?"

She nodded as I pulled back into traffic. "I'll ride shotgun. Literally."

"Oh."

"Unless you want to."

"No, no. Anyway. How did it all go down?"

"I waited outside their building. Then, I saw him get out of a limo and scan the parking lot before he went inside. He had his top-of-the-world smile on. So many things were going through my mind just then. I knew I had to confront him somehow, get the drop on him, rattle him in front of people, make him lose it in public. Getting inside was the problem. I knew he'd recognize me right off. That's why I wore the beret."

I didn't have to ask where she'd gotten it. I knew it was one of Claire's. R.E. had stopped wearing it some time ago. But now it seemed okay.

"I managed to charm my way to the front. His handlers thought it would be cute to have some little hippie chick ask one of the first questions so they could all have their laugh and then get on with business. I kept my head down and my vibes to myself. I know he didn't recognize me for those first crucial seconds, and by the time he did, I'd already asked, 'Why did your father feel so free to cripple my mother and then have people burn our house down around her? Was he jealous of how much she loved my dad? Was it politics? What? You owe me an explanation.'"

"Oh, man! I'd give anything to have seen his face!"
"I'm not so sure about that. I don't think I've ever seen him go so quickly from having his craziness locked up tight to it being right out there for everyone to see. He went paler than ever, his pupils spread, he started breathing faster and faster. Then he let out that skin-crawler scream. Everyone around him just froze. I was already starting to back up. He jumped over the podium in one move, landed right in front of me, and pulled a gun out of his jacket."

"Of course."

"Yeah, I should have realized he would. I just didn't think he'd go into such a situation armed. Anyway, why I don't know, but a guy next to me shoved me back and got between us. Then all hell broke loose. People woke up, started screaming and running in all directions. Damn heeled shoes! I don't know why women wear them. And the skirt was slowing me down, too. I tore the seam while I was running so I could pick up some speed. I was on the highway before I heard a car rev up, so I think I got a little lead on him. I know he had to take some time to call the *Pine Cone* office to ask where we live. Lived."

"Where do we go now?"

"Back towards where we came. South Texas this time. We'll make a stand there with Dado."

"Sounds good." We drove in silence for some time. Then I said, "He's going to be so proud of you."

She nodded but didn't speak. I knew she was crying, but not from sorrow or fear. She patted my knee and we blasted away into the darkness once more.

***

Moonrise, a waxing moon on a clear night in Arizona: we'd been driving in shifts, only stopping for gas, sandwiches and coffee to go, and pit stops. R.E. had changed clothes the first chance she got. "Easier to run in jeans and boots", she smiled. At one point, R.E. pulled off the road just outside of Yuma, drove over a small dune and onto a hidden stretch of empty flat nothing. Then we both got out for a stretch. "You know," she smiled, "this isn't far from your X."

At first it didn't register, it seemed so long ago, but then I caught on: the place where she'd read my journal for me. I nodded as I walked off to take care of business while she swept away our tracks with a creosote branch. The white sand and caliche looked like snow under the near-quarter moon. It beamed down brightness as it watched me watching it. I could hear the soft rustle of night hunters in the dark. I managed to keep my cuffs dry and watch the road at the same time and then it hit me. The Snake had left me alone for most of this entire day and night. Small victory, to some, a major one to me. I smiled and headed back towards R.E. A couple of times headlights had appeared on the curve of the horizon, zoomed towards us, but they went on past without slowing or stopping.

She was walking towards me, arms around herself, shivering a little.

"Cold?

"No, just nerves. Thinking about Coleman. His face. I've never seen anything like it. Damn, I hope we lost him, but you never know with that guy. He could be closer than we think."

"Really?"

"Really," Coleman said as he walked out from behind a stand of scrub brush. As always, he was armed. He was wearing black dress pants and a white shirt that glowed like the desert dust in the fading moonlight. He gestured with the pistol for R.E. to move closer to me. She did, taking my arm, her eyes fastened on him.

"Don't try that focus routine with me again, R.E. Got my guard up." He laughed softly. "You're both so fuckin' predictable. I figured you'd be running along the border. Saw you at that gas station back in Yuma. All I had to do was follow until you pulled off the road, loop back around, and walk up on you. Just like old times."

R.E. looked him straight in the eye and said, "You never answered me about why your father crippled my mother."

He started shivering. "Shut up about him," he said between clenched teeth.

"Your friends drop you?" she needled.

His shaking was getting worse. "Don't need 'em."

"You need something. You stink like a goat. You always do when you split inside."

He snarled and raised the gun. A heavy bodied night bird sailed silently over him, close and low, almost grazing his head. I lunged for him as he instinctively ducked. Landing on top of him, I grabbed his wrist and banged it against the ground, making him let go of the pistol. Then I fought like I had never fought before: viciously, trying every trick in the book, going for balls, eyes, throat, every soft spot I thought he might have. But it was like R.E. had said. It was like he was impervious. He actually seemed to be enjoying it. Cole punched me in the throat and bounded to his feet as I gurgled and staggered. It was all his show from that point on. He'd get up close to hit me then dance away from my hapless blows, always staying between R.E. and the pistol and me, triangulating perfectly every time so that neither of us could get to it, kicking it back and away with his feet. I figured R.E. must have left hers in the truck since she hadn't pulled it and there was no way now that she could break away to get it. The beating went on for what seemed like forever. I knew I had to keep it up at any cost though, because when I quit, he would kill us both. R.E. kept trying to get into the fight but he would only wag a finger at her and say, "One at a time, wench. I'll deal with you next." Deal with her. I remembered the day in the woods when I knew I couldn't stop him. But this was another day. That gave me my critical second wind and I rushed him, knocking him down. But he bounded up, grabbed me, and tossed me aside like I was weightless.

"Come on, you fuckin' spastic. Try it again," he teased. As I got up, he lashed out with his foot in an unexpected, graceful leap and tapped me just under the diaphragm. I landed in a heap, windless. R.E. ran to me.

He scooped up the pistol and I gasped, using the last of my air, "The Dutchman."

"What about him?" He glanced back over his shoulder, the pistol still trained on us.

I managed to say, "He's inside you. You're too weak to fight him. Now he's controlling you. He won."

For long seconds, he just stood there. Then he began to shudder. Two personalities battled in his slim frame: my old friend and the newer, more vicious Coleman, his father's creature. His features became a quicksilver slideshow of van der Veers who played themselves out on the canvas of his skin. "Never got inside me, no, never inside me. He never got inside me." His hands were shaking and he was breathing hard and raggedly, squinting, trying to aim. At me. R.E. screamed and flew at him.

He clubbed at her viciously with the barrel of the gun. She raised her hands to protect her face but the force of the blow stunned her and she fell heavily to the ground: still, silent, unconscious. Vulnerable.

But Cole was too busy battling his demons to take advantage of either one of us just then. He cursed and swung his arms like he was fighting someone, wobbling on his own shaky axis, getting closer and closer to the highway and away from R.E. I followed him over the little dune and towards the blacktop then I jumped him and wrestled the pistol away. Rolling over on my back, I aimed at him. He was so close that he was practically standing over me as he had been in that waking dream in the roof room of the Palace. I pointed up at him along the barrel like Sam had told me to, squeezed the trigger, and shot him in the shoulder. He staggered back towards the road. I rolled to my feet and followed him, wheezing, in shock from the beating. A red stain grew on his white shirt, round like those little corsages that men wear at weddings, except that this one was ringed in black. He kept trying to brush it off, smearing the blood that was now pumping faster and faster from the hole. His demons quit him for a second and he looked up at me in surprise. "I didn't think you had it in you."

"More than that. Oh, my brother. Don't even think about following us, you bastard." Just as I aimed at his right knee and pulled the trigger again, a car appeared over the horizon and caught us both in its lights, him bleeding and me holding the pistol. It slowed and I caught the driver's face for a second: an older man, mouth agape. Everything was in slow motion for another heartbeat, and then time slipped back in gear. The car wheeled around and sped away in the direction it had come from, tires screeching.

R.E. came out of the night, fighting for clarity, shaking her head, trying to focus. Cole tried to say something, trying to rise on his elbows, but a wheeze came out instead of words. More than anything else, he looked puzzled, as though this circumstance had never occurred to him. The light in his eyes seemed to recede until he looked like a doll that had been shaken too many times, whose eyes had fallen back into the sockets. With a sigh, he fell back to the sand.

"Come on," R.E. whispered. "Let's go." We ran for the truck and got in. We hadn't gone a mile before we blew past what R.E. said was his car, parked on the side of the road. "Damn. How could he have gotten the drop on us like that? Careless, just damn careless," she sighed, banging her forehead lightly with her fist.

"Easy, easy now. No blame." We drove like bandits, the truck shuddering from the speed. Plans whirled around my head like trash in a tornado. Then I knew what I had to do. A few more miles down the road, I said "Pull over."

"What? Why?"

"We can't go together. Not now. A guy in a car that passed saw me. And him. And the gun. But I'm sure they didn't see your truck, not where it was. It was too far off the road. And he didn't see you at all."

"I'm not leaving you here."

"It's the only way, RE. It's too easy for us to be spotted if we're together. You can go back to Texas, back to Sam. I can't." I took a deep breath. "Don't you see? We can't be together. Not now."

"We'll think of something."

"There isn't any time."

"You don't know that."

"We can't take that chance. I'll be okay. I'll cross over to Mexico. If I'm careful, I can cross without getting caught."

"No." She didn't slow down at all and in fact, was driving even faster.

"I swear I'll jump out if you don't stop. I won't put you in danger of being arrested for something I did. You know you don't want to be arrested. Go to jail. You would if they caught you with me." We drove for a long, silent minute as she checked the depth of my conviction and when she realized I meant what I was saying, she whispered, "I don't want to lose you."

"You won't", but I was less than certain about that. After all, I had just shot someone and for all I knew, he was dying back there. "Look, I'll stay in Mexico until this blows over. Then I'll come back." I tried to smile but I couldn't so I just said, "Find out where you are."

I don't know if she fully accepted that I was right but she knew I was determined. She finally said, "At least a little further. Get you away from the scene a little more." I nodded and we drove in silence for a short while. I let her get used to the idea and when I saw she'd digested it I said, "Okay, here. When I think it's safe, I'll send you a postcard. To Rafe's. No writing. Just a card with a picture of the place where I am. That way, you'll know."

She nodded. "Okay. Okay." She slowed, pulled over, and stopped. I grabbed the backpack but she stopped me for a second. Reaching into the glove box, she pulled out our envelope of money and split it between us, shoving half of it into my hands. I tucked it away and grabbed her in a quick, hard hug. Without another word or look, I opened the door and took off into the night, across the desert with the money, my backpack, the map with the X on it, and Coleman's pistol, running for hours like I had never run in my life, alternating between loping and resting. At one breath stop, I buried the gun. Finally, I got to the Gila River. It was an easy cross. Once on the other side, I took a couple of minutes to dab a little water on my face and knuckles and change my shirt, burying the old bloody one. From there, it was all walking until I walked into San Luis, Mexico. I was a little disappointed that there hadn't been some kind of official boundary, even a dotted cartoon line in the sand. Maybe there had been, some signs I'd ignored. For someone who'd been brought up on political maps, the actual crossing of a geographical border came as a surprise, almost a letdown. But suddenly, there I was, in Mexico, just like that, and it was morning.

I headed straight for the bus station, bought a ticket for the farthest point south on the local line's route map, and settled down on a bench to wait. Of course, people stared at me. I was ragged, smelly, bruised, and Snake-ridden. But I didn't care. I just stared back.

Once we were deep into the night, the others fell asleep around me. Sometime before daybreak when the sky was just turning rosy, I dozed off, slipping into a dream about The Palace and the well house. I had just taken a drink from the wooden bucket and was walking towards the back screen door and the echo of voices inside. To my left, there was a slender man with thinning blond hair. He was dressed in jeans, a faded blue denim shirt, and old tennis shoes. In his left hand he held two fishing poles. He motioned with his empty right hand: come with me. I shook my head no, and I glanced towards the house again. When I turned back to the fisherman, he beckoned once more with his empty hand. His shirt unbuttoned by itself, opened in a noiseless breeze to reveal the sky behind him where his chest should have been. I shook my head no once more and glanced back at the house. When I looked for the fisherman again, he was gone.

"This first stage of the mythological journey --
which we have designated the 'call to adventure' --
signifies that destiny has summoned the hero and
transferred his spiritual center of gravity from
within the pale of his society to a zone unknown ..."

Joseph Campbell, *The Hero With A Thousand Faces*

X.

Counting Railroad Ties

I got on one Mexican bus after another and gradually kept heading south. Whenever I saw a town that looked big enough to have some kind of hotel or room to rent, I'd stop, get off, and stay awhile, lost in emotional pain, culture shock, the blur of hearing and trying to speak a foreign language, the infamous travelers' diarrhea, and the constant buzz of drinking and being hung over.

Those first few weeks, I was mostly unaware of anyone around me, but slowly I became more and more self-conscious and realized that I stood out in a crowd for four reasons. I was tall, I was blond, I had the Snake, and I still had very long hair; the latter was the only one of the four I could do something about. So one afternoon, when it was steamy hot and I was sufficiently wasted, I took out my pocketknife and chopped most of it off. It wasn't the most becoming do I've ever had, but they stopped calling me "jipi." They did start calling me "El Reposado": the well-rested one, the one who is still. Typical 180 degree humor. Whenever I'd get to a new town, I'd just say I was from El Norte and that I was El Reposado. This usually brought a round of nervous laughter and then curious questions about how I'd learned so much Spanish.

It did come easy for me. I have a real talent for remembering words and phrases. My dirty Spanish is especially good, and I can remember entire corridos, the ballads that always have the same tune. That always stood me in good stead with the macho types I ran into. Coupled with my ability to absorb large amounts of booze, I was usually able to come into a new place and find a niche in the local cantina society after a couple of days of being looked at and avoided. Being stared at in México affected me in different ways than being stared at in the States. Gringos are always a curiosity anyway, and one with the Snake is just a twitchy foreigner, a variation on a theme. Besides, I wasn't Troy Jacobson who hated other peoples' eyes crawling all over him. I was El Reposado, who just stared back.

Being in México seemed so natural. I certainly wasn't the first Texas outlaw to take it on the lam down México way. I wasn't sure how long I'd have to lay low so I was careful with the little bit of money I had. I usually found work in small cafes. Most of the owners thought it was pretty funny to hire a white illegal. They even trotted me out for everyone's amusement on slow, late nights. And so, for months, I roamed further and further south.

Spring found me in San Juan Chamula, Chiapas. I was sitting on a chair, leaned back against the front wall of the little flophouse where I was staying, watching the street parade of people and animals pass by. It was early morning, I'd just gotten paid, and I was already anticipating a long afternoon of ritual drinking when a woman stopped right in front of me, blocking the sun.

She was in her fifties, short, slim with a slightly rounded belly, gray hair cut in a Dutch bowl-chop, wearing slacks, a sweater, closed toe leather shoes, and a variegated black and white Jaliscan rebozo, not the local Zinacantecan weave. She looked into my eyes, fixing me with a curious stare, like some lean old lizard or bird, setting down the empty woven hampers and bags she had been carrying. She had very blue eyes, like mine. Putting her hands on her hips, making a diamond shape out of herself, she cocked her head to one side and said in English, "Is that all you plan to do with yourself? Drink?"

"That's the plan for today," I shrugged.

"What about tomorrow?"

"I don't think that far in advance."

She turned her head and looked at me with her other eye. Yep, bird, not lizard, I thought to myself. Then she said, "Get up and come along. I need some help carrying things."

I shrugged. Maybe she would give me a few pesos for being a good burro. I followed her to the tianguis. She poked and prodded the vegetables, haggling for a long time until she got the quality, quantity, and price she wanted. Then it was off to a meat stand. Those places will make vegetarians out of the staunchest carnivores. But I was used to them. As it is with the ocean, so it is with foreign meat shops. There's smell and there's stink and this one was all right. I set her bundles down while she asked the owner about the weather, the state of health of the pig that he was raising, his kids and wife. I yawned so loudly the owner laughed, saying she needed a livelier burro. Finally, the deal was done. As she was tucking the basket of pork parts into another hamper I was supposed to carry, she clucked and chided me about minding my manners.

The shopping took the rest of the morning. By the time she was done and we had walked all the way back to her house, me carrying everything, I was about as tired as I had been in recent memory. She carefully unlocked the front door and gestured to the maid who appeared as soon as we walked inside. A flurry of Spanish and Zinacantecan rustled around them like a sudden dust devil on dry flat plains. The maid, Mary Chuy, found the basket of pork and the other more perishable items and hustled off to what I presumed was the kitchen.

It was a big home, an old hacienda with a square courtyard open to the sky just inside the front door. Along two sides of the square to the right and left were rooms, shaded by long narrow roofs that ran the length of the courtyard. The main entrance to the rest of the house was directly across from the street entrance. I smiled as I listened to water splashing in the stone fountain in the middle of the flagstone yard. The whole place was dripping with plants and flowers and there were dozens of birds in cages, all singing different tunes in different pitches, imitating the cacophony of the market. I turned to her and said, "So. Do I get a tip for all of that?"

"Of course not," she said. "Go with Chuy when she comes back and put the rest of these things away. Listen to her. She'll tell you exactly where each item should go."

"Why should I do that?"

"Because you're staying here now and you'll need to know where everything is. I assume you are in possession of more than the clothes on your back?"

I nodded yes.

"Very well. After you help Chuy put all this away, go and get your belongings. Your room will be ready when you return. There will be a light dinner at 8:30 and you'll need a bath before then. Don't be late."

Then she walked briskly away, listing chores for both me and Chuy, who was back now. She seemed used to her boss's crisp manner and took the announcement of my impending presence in the household with the calm of someone who'd seen stranger things happen.

I stood there, blinking.

She turned back at the door and said, "Come along now."

So I did as I was told. I'll take a hacienda over a flophouse any day. I lived there, in my second home, for almost twenty years.

***

Her name was Consuelo Dolores de las Casas-Rourke and she was every bit as strange and colorful as the name suggests, a rare old bird like the ones she bought from vendors and kept safe there at her hacienda so they wouldn't be eaten or blinded to make them sing more sweetly. Her father was a fiery Mexican professor of literature and a writer of fiction; her mother was an equally wild Irish woman from upstate New York who had given up reporting because she said the field was too dominated by men and had taken up writing political diatribes about life on both sides of the Rio Bravo instead. Theirs had been a match made right on earth: passionate, supportive, and built on equal, solid ground. Consuelo had been raised in both countries: winters in the south, summers in the north. Encouraged by both parents, she went as far as she could educationally in México and when it came time for college, she was sent to New York. Although she had inherited not only the hacienda and a lot of land when first her father then her mother died, she worked every day of her life. She was also a writer, and she taught both English and Spanish at local schools. She had been married, but the union hadn't been happy, so after her divorce she took her parents' names back. She had been living there alone for a long time when she noticed me and took me in.

It was years before I had any clue about why she had suddenly decided, on the spot, to include me in her life. She had me installed in one of the upstairs rooms that looked out on the town. It had a beautiful view. I could see the spires of the churches and hear the leaden thudding of the bells, watch the sun go down from my little balcony every night. She didn't stop me from drinking. In fact, she made the well-stocked liquor cabinet available to me. I began developing a taste for the real Reposado: smooth, golden, aged tequila. The days passed in a mellow alcohol soaked light that was as straw-and-honey colored as the cactus brandy I grew to love.

She drank, too: gin, and a lot of it. We slowly developed the habit of checking in on each other at night to see if the other was still breathing. It was a cautious relationship. She was imperious, stubborn, and absolutely in control of every emotion, the very essence of Mexican nobility. And yet, there was the torrential Irish under-layer that she was always trying to subdue, to wrestle to the ground. One evening, as we were sipping the drinks of our choice in the courtyard, she called that side of herself her "dark angel." And I found myself explaining the Snake to her. She nodded. She understood. Then she asked me if I was able to see colors.

I said no, but that I had sometimes gone outside of myself. She gave me her sideways bird-glance and asked me to explain. I gave her a little rundown of a few instances of sight and then it hit me that they had stopped as soon as R.E. and I weren't around each other anymore. That realization knocked a ragged sigh out of me, which she didn't ask to be explained. She was very courteous in that regard. Then she said that she could see colors, she had always been able to. That was why she drank. She couldn't when she was drinking. She said the ability was like a red phone in the closet that she kept for emergencies only. Most of the time sight was such a nuisance, she fussed. Then she turned to me and fixed both eyes on me, and said, "That was why I took you in. You have that ability too, and you don't need to be wandering around the streets unguarded. You needed shelter. There aren't many of us, the ones who can see. We must stick together." That was first explanation she offered as to why she'd taken me in. Not for just one reason, as R.E. had said: there was another, but it did not come for a long time.

***

After that night, she would test me now and then, bring in things and plop them down in front of me, sometimes when I was sober and sometimes when I wasn't. She would say only, "Tell me what you see." Most of the time, I would describe the thing itself to her objectively, the details of its appearance only. She would remain impassive, the Zen-poker face. But sometimes, I would know something about the objects, who had handled them, where they had been found. Once, she gave me a statue and I suddenly "saw" the view that it had had from the mountainside niche where she had found it. I could see it so vividly. She made me hold the image for a long time. It wiped me out, that incident of seeing. They didn't happen often, but they were powerful when they did, leaving me weak and irritable for days afterwards.

And she made me work, too. After I had lived there for almost five years, she woke me roughly one morning and had me come downstairs with her, very early for me. I had become the complete night owl, rising in the late afternoon and staying up all night, sleeping all day. I greeted this turn of events with a sullen stare and some muttered cursing at the breakfast that was shoved in front of me.

"Come on, now. You have to get dressed. We're going to school."

"Why?" I asked, suspiciously.

"Because you need to start work," she said briskly, polishing off her English muffins, lemon curd, fruit, and tea with cream and cubes of sugar. She ate local style food for every other meal, but breakfast was always more European.

"What kind of work?"

"You're going to help me in class."

"Teach?"

"Yes. Why not?"

"I don't know the first thing about it."

"You'll learn."

"And why should I?"

She gave me a level stare so like R.E.'s that I sighed, all the fight and spite knocked clean out of me. "You see, you know why. I have given you time to get over whatever it was that made you run away to this place. I have never asked what it was and I never will. Neither will I use my sight to find out. That is your business. But teaching is my business. The people here do not know how to read or write Spanish. It is not the home language, for most of them. But it is the one that they will need if they are going to be able to protect themselves and to have choices in the future." She dusted the crumbs off of her slim, blue-veined hands; they seemed so much older than the rest of her. "So. Finish up. I'm getting old and I need help."

The schoolroom where she worked was really just an old storeroom behind one of the churches in town. It was dark inside as we entered. The floor was dirt, packed flat and smooth as stone. She had a desk in front, a little bookcase along one wall, and there were a few ratty old tables in rows in the center of the room. Behind the tables, students sat on benches worn smooth by years of rears. After opening the wooden shutters, there was a little more light, but not much. The first students were already standing at the door, timid, unsure about the tall blond stranger. Consuelo nodded towards the back of the room and I obediently headed that way, took a back bench, and leaned against the uneven, worn adobe wall. The first few days, I only watched her, napped a little, and helped out when she motioned for me to do something.

Gradually, as I adjusted to daylight hours, she let me take over a small group. I felt like such a hulking fool, sitting there, the Snake jerking me now and then to the delight of the eight year olds I'd been saddled with. But I made a joke of it, laughing at myself, and then it was mostly down to business. They came and went, those kids. Sometimes they'd be there for only a day or so, sometimes weeks, a few were actually able to finish a school year. It was rare that they could do more than one. I never knew how many I would be working with or exactly when they would arrive. After the first year, Consuelo arranged for me to have a desk and some chairs in the back of the same room where she taught. And slowly, I found my own way of teaching that was at first a little different from her stern European methods and then, greatly different. I started teaching them to write their own stories and then using the stories for reading in class. Even though they had grown up together, there was at least one surprise every day, something they hadn't known about each other. It did seem to give them some small power in a world where they had none at all. It was not an approach that would work in any classroom anywhere, but for where I was and for the people I served, it seemed to motivate them in ways that traditional books did not. Although it wasn't a way Consuelo would have chosen, she never commented or criticized me. In fact, it was like we were in different worlds when we were working. And, they taught me things, too: their own languages, slang, gestures. Sometimes I would be invited to go to their homes for dinner. I rarely accepted. Not because I didn't want to or because I wasn't curious. Consuelo was getting old, but she didn't want to admit it. She was as vain as they come. But increasingly, she had trouble walking long distances without stopping to sit and puff for a while. So I would give polite excuses and walk behind her like a good servant should do, making sure she got home safely every evening.

She looked after me, too. She never inquired about my love life, but she made it easy for me bring women home now and then. She always seemed to know when I was getting close to someone. During those sweet, rare times, she would go to bed earlier than usual and give Chuy the night off. I would meet the women downstairs and we would have drinks and then it was up to my room. There weren't many. But I was a man and a human being and there were a few local women who were curious enough about the blond angel, El Reposado, who lived with the old woman on the hill. Nothing ever came of the romances, of course. Some of the women had been married. Others had never had the opportunity and never would. I had sense enough not to take any virgins to bed, or women who weren't but were still young enough to marry and just hadn't tied the knot yet, or any currently married women. I didn't push my luck. No, the ones who did end up in my bed were as grateful for the loving as I was. We would meet now and then, cure our mutual aches, and then that was that until the next time or until their curiosity was sated.

Mostly, though, it was only Consuelo and me. We lived a life that was on 19th century time. She had had a complete falling out with the U.S. over Vietnam and had vowed that she would never return. She didn't allow U.S. newspapers in the house or even the *México City News*, an English language paper. And on the few occasions when there was company, topics related to the U.S. were dismissed with an imperious glare and a toss of her head. All of the talk was about México, South American, Europe, Asia. I learned a lot about those places, things I had never been taught in school or read about in my days of unlimited reading time. I was mostly in the dark about what was going on in El Norte, enmeshed in the cocoon of that house and her life. Not that I didn't hear things. I did talk to those women I took to bed and there was always market place gossip. But I got little in the way of real news and that was all right. I didn't want to know. I didn't want to run the risk of picking up a paper one day and reading that Coleman had somehow lived and had finally taken his revenge on R.E. or Sam or anyone else I loved. I didn't want to read about his exploits or his successes. I didn't want to know if he had died that night, if the police were hunting me, if R.E. had been arrested in place of me for his murder. I didn't want to read about her going on trial. I had blocked all of that out of mind and memory and the fact that news from that part of the world was prevented from reaching us was greeted with pleasure and a sigh of relief on my part.

Besides, I was deeply in love with México and my home state of Chiapas. There was so much to know. On the days when I wasn't teaching, I explored her on foot or by bus, taking off for days at a time. I got to know Bonampak, Palénque, and Yaxchilan like old friends, sitting for hours in the jungle and studying their silent Mayan mysteries, wondering about what the hieroglyphs would say if I had had the Rosetta stone key to unlock their stories. It wasn't easy to get to any of them and the travel was exhausting sometimes. My fascination with the canyon of the Grijalva River was just as deep and the physical work of getting to know it was just as demanding as my trips to the rain forest. I'm sure that those arduous treks were what kept the weight I should have gained from my drinking off me. Or maybe it was genetics. I'm not sure. But in any case, every time I had to get new clothes, I could count on them being pretty much the same size as the old ones.

***

My life with Consuelo was calm and cordial, marred only by the inevitable bickering that occurs when human beings live in close proximity to each other. But towards the last couple of years together, there was one thing that I did that angered Consuelo so deeply that we got into the one and only real fight we ever had. I got tattooed. It was on a trip I took to Acapulco to pick up a shipment of books for her. I had taken her car, an antique Mercedes she had nursed for decades. She had allowed me to take it out for its weekly spin for years by that time, saying it needed its exercise just like a person. It responded to me beautifully and I adored driving it. I was motoring along, having a grand time, just mildly buzzed from a little sip from the silver flask of tequila she had doled out for me, insisting that it was the only liquor I could have while behind the wheel.

That was when I saw the old man at an excuse for a bus stop on the side of the road. At first, he looked like any other leathery Indian but when he waved with his fine, bony hand for me to stop, I got a better look at him and realized that he was Asian, not Hispanic. He had been waiting for the bus for some time, he explained in Spanish, and asked where I was going. When I said Acapulco, his face flashed the old hitchhiker hopefulness I knew so well; he didn't want to ask flat out for a ride all the way there, but it was blazing hot and he was so ancient and fragile that I had no choice. Besides, how often would I get the chance to talk to such a person?

"I am called Akio Watanabe," he said, extending his hand, speaking English. He said that he was a little rusty but would like to practice. I could tell it had been a while since he'd used it and what he'd learned had been more than a little formal.

I told him my name and we shook hands. After we settled his bags into the trunk and him into the passenger seat, I offered him a sip from the flask. At first he refused. Then he swigged away. I started the engine, it purred to life, and we were on our way. As the miles passed, he relaxed and began to talk about his family. They had lived on the coast for about thirty years. His sons were importers-exporters who dealt with all the paperwork for their small company. His part of the business was to make contacts with small town artisans. He asked about me and I gave him the briefest of outlines. After we had passed the Oaxaca border, he winked at me and asked if I liked my sake a little warmer than it should be. "After all, you were such a gentleman and shared your tequila with me. Surely, you wouldn't mind having a little of my own personal favorite."

"Sure," I grinned. This was getting more interesting all the time.

He made a little magic trick of producing a small ceramic jug from his inside coat pocket. "My family doesn't like for me to drink. They say I am too old. But if I am, what's the harm? What could happen that might not anyway?" The conspiracy between us grew and shortly after we'd gotten close enough to town to hit some traffic, he leaned over and confided in a boozy whisper that he was not a businessman. "My sons are," he said softly. "I was a tattoo artist until I retired and we moved here. I have done work for some of the biggest gangsters in Japan," he said softly. "Ya-ku-za." Then he grinned, "And some of the most beautiful women, too. Such canvases," he smiled. "Skin like cream turned to warm silk. Flawless." He sighed, lost in memory.

In return for the ride, he invited me to stay at his home while I took care of business there in town. He was pretty soused by the time we arrived and his family was both a little pissed off at me and relieved at the same time that the old man had not had to endure Mexican buses all the way.

After a great Japanese dinner and a bath and a soak in their home-style bathing room, I joined the old gent in his garden. It was a little bit of Japan, tucked away on a back street near the ocean. I admired the plants, the old temple bell, the raked rocks. Then he asked me to sit down and he showed me an album of drawings and photos of his work. That was when I knew I had found the person who could do the Snake. I explained what I wanted and he sketched out a design. It was perfect, exactly as I'd always imagined it: a dark red and gold serpent curling around my back down to the base of my ribs and up again. At the knob of the bone between my shoulder blades, the tail flicked towards the mouth, not quite meeting. I told him he would have to put me under so that I couldn't move around. He agreed. "It has been years since I have had the opportunity to practice my art," he smiled. "You shall have the most beautiful serpent I have ever drawn."

It took him three weeks to do the job. I stayed more than a little groggy from being anesthetized by the herbal potion he used. It looked like a botanical specimen: a big bottle of plants and other slightly decayed stuff that had been pickled in booze of some kind. It was like drinking ginseng brandy. The warmth spread from my belly along my limbs and then to my brain; it only took a few minutes. First I would get drowsy and then I would be sound asleep. In the end, though, I couldn't have been happier. It was beautiful, just as he said it would be. He took several pictures of it to add to his book. I had to spend almost another week getting straight enough to drive back. Not only had I been made simple from the brew, I was sore as hell from the needles. I wasn't worried about Consuelo being angry. It was between teaching terms so the books weren't critical. When I called, I just said I was enjoying the place and was taking a little extra time. After all, it wasn't the first time I'd gone exploring.

But the evening I returned, she knew something was different about me, something that I wasn't sharing with her and I could tell that it made her angry. I was on the receiving end of more sideways, one-eyed glances than ever before. We had a late supper about the usual time. She asked me about why I'd been delayed. I suppose I should have known better than to be evasive with her, but the tattoo was a secret I was savoring as I had the identity of my father. I just said I'd run into someone and decided to stay for a little while, hoping that she would assume it was a woman and drop the subject. She nodded, but I knew the subject hadn't been completely closed.

I was upstairs in my room later that night, getting ready for bed when the snake came out of the bag. I'd taken my shirt off and was standing at the window, admiring the street scene below when I heard her scream at me from the hall, "What in the name of God have you done to yourself!"

I whirled around, startled.

She dashed up to me, her face shivering with rage, grabbed my arm and spun me around so she could see it more clearly. "My God! Is that--that--permanent?" She touched it. Even though the moment was happening so fast and seemed so unreal, the part of my mind which recorded events noted that that was the first time she'd ever laid hands on me.

"Yes. It is. It's a tattoo. I got it done while I was there. That's why I was delayed. I met someone on the road. Watanabe-San. An artist who..." I didn't get any further.

She whirled me around again and slapped me across the face, a surprisingly hard, stunning blow. "How dare you! You are--you were-- the single most beautiful man I have ever known and now--mutilated! You're mutilated! And you chose to do this to yourself!"

I just stood there, trying to understand what was going on. But when she raised her hand again, I grabbed it and said, "No. You are not going to hit me again. Do you understand? This is something I've wanted to do for a long time. It's my body and my business. I don't have to ask your permission."

"But why?" she whispered between clenched teeth. "At least tell me that much."

I tried to calm her down by explaining a little more about the Snake, who was now working me over fiercely as he usually did when my emotions were flowing full tilt, how I had decided a long time ago that I wanted to bear his image in the same way that I'd always borne him, about the day in Golden Gate Park with R.E. when I'd decided that's what I wanted to do. That was my downfall, remembering R.E. too clearly. It gave Consuelo the opening into my thoughts that she needed for her next shot at me. I let go of her hand but remained braced. She was still shaking. Stepping back, she surveyed me and I watched something in her eyes change, a kind of focusing. Then she said, with what I swear was R.E.'s voice, "If you were a man, you would be crossing your bear instead of trying to bear this ridiculous cross. But instead you are nothing more than a cowardly child, hiding out in this house, drinking, and pretending to be some kind of pariah when you are not."

I recoiled like she'd punched me in the gut, which in a way she had. She had done what she claimed she never would, use her sight to reach into my head and yank out something to swat me with, to punish me. "Damn you, Consuelo. You don't know what you're talking about. You have no right to... I'm outta here." By then I was just as angry as she was and suddenly afraid that I might strike her. I grabbed my travel bag, which was never far from my side, no matter how content I was, a few things, a shirt, my wallet, and I ran out of the room, down the stairs, and out into the night. I walked for hours and then finally caught a bus to the nearest large town where I started the longest and deepest drinking binge I can remember. Or not remember, more precisely said. Then, one afternoon, I looked up into the sun and her familiar outline shaded me. A hand reached out.

"Going to hit me again?" I asked.

"Don't be foolish. Of course not."

I reached up and she hauled me to my feet, surprising me with the strength in her grip. She was still looking grim, but at least the dark angel she'd warned me about seemed to be under control. "So. Have you gotten this out of your system?"

"Have you?"

She nodded. Then, without looking at me, she said the two most difficult words she could have made herself say. "I'm sorry."

I nodded.

She glared at me when I remained silent.

"I didn't do anything which would require an apology," I reminded her. "I got tattooed on my own body of my own accord."

She tried to wave the image away with both slim hands. "Don't remind me about that..." It seemed that she couldn't think of a word bad enough to describe it so she changed the subject. "Get your things." I noticed then that the Mercedes was parked on the street. "Come home."

I shrugged. "If you want me to."

It was then that she dropped all pretense of being cool about this. For the one and only time in our years together, she let her feelings show plainly on her face and I knew in my bones that she loved me. She had all along, the other reason that she'd taken me in. So I didn't push the matter any further. I went upstairs, got my things together in one sweep around the room, and came back downstairs. She'd already settled my bill and was gathering her dignity back around herself like a crisp new rebozo. "I drove all the way and I'm tired now. I'll nap in the back seat while you drive."

And that was all we ever said about it. I made a point of never taking any chance on her seeing the offending art and she never mentioned the subject again. However, the brief separation and her moment of insight into my memories opened a conversational door for us that had always been closed: my past. I told her, among other stories, in the briefest form I could, about Coleman, R.E., and the night in the desert. When I was done, she smiled at me, her eyes shining. "Bravo."

***

Consuelo got sick at the end of the last autumn I lived in México. Never one for ceremony, she called Chuy and me into the bedroom one afternoon to explain that the house, most of the money, and all of the land would go to her and her family in return for caring for Consuelo for so long. A smaller amount of money would go to the church to fund the school, which Chuy would take over until she could get a new teacher trained for the job. A generous amount of cash would go to me. She also asked me to try to get her writing published in the States.

The pneumonia that took her was just as efficient as she, carrying her off later that evening. Before she went into the last deep sleep, she said she loved me, confirming verbally what we had both realized for some time. She said that love was so much more than the physical act. She had never wished to share that with me, since she was so much older, and since what she felt was "higher on the spine." That was why she had tolerated my bringing women into the house. I knew then that I loved her, too, and I said so.

She wasn't one for long goodbyes, either. After holding my hand for a moment, she said, "Time for you to cross your bear." She closed her eyes, and that was that. Bear my cross, cross my bear. Be active, not passive. She was right and I knew it.

I sat there in the dark with her for a few moments, then left to find Chuy. She was already in the hall, tears in her eyes. Time to return.

"Henceforth I ask not good-fortune,
I myself am good-fortune,
Henceforth I whimper no more,
postpone no more, need nothing,
Done with indoor complaints,
libraries, querulous criticisms,
Strong and content I travel the open road.

...

(Still here I carry my old delicious burdens,
I carry them, men and women,
I carry them with me wherever I go,
I swear it is impossible for me to get rid of them,
I am fill'd with them, and I will fill them in return.)"

Walt Whitman, *Leaves of Grass, Book VII,*
Song of the Open Road

XI.

The Last Third

Rural Mexican bus stations change only in superficial ways. The fundamentals remain the same: indigenous profiles that could have come from Palenque, sighing chillers filled with soft drinks and beer, small snack packages of candy and chips, tiny brown women burdened with shawls loaded with babies, corn, or pigs. Those were all the same. Only the tunes on the tinny radios were different. It had been a couple of decades since I'd fled the country, leaving everyone and everything I knew and loved behind. I hadn't seemed to change much either, I noticed as I glanced at my refection in the dusty station window. My hair was shorter, I was browner, but my shape was about the same. My face and eyes seemed older, or maybe it was the darker light in them. And now here I was, ready to cross over again, but this time, I wasn't running. I could take my time.

A young man about the same age I'd been when I first crossed had been trying to strike up a conversation for a short while. He kept clearing his throat softly, trying to make eye contact. I let the Snake loose for a few shakes to see if that would scare him off. It didn't. So I caged it and returned the contact, waiting for him to start. I was in no mood to make this easy.

"So, I heard you speaking Spanish earlier. You're really good."

I nodded.

"Live here long?"

I nodded again.

He went quiet. But after another ten minutes or so passed, he started again. "How do you deal with living here?"

The look in his eyes suggested it wasn't his choice, as my being there hadn't been at first, so I relented and asked, "You like beer?"

He glanced at the clock. It was about 10 A.M.

"Bienvenidos a México." I bought us a couple of bottles of Pacifico, a light brew I favored on hot mornings, and some tacos from a street vendor's cart. After we walked to the slight shade afforded by the bus station overhang and settled down on the bench, I pointed out the signs of street food you could probably trust: clean pans, bottled water jugs nearby that were used to wash them, not just tap water, the particular smell of meat that had been stored properly, and the abundance of limes and chili used in the sauce. "It helps if you're not gut-sick most of the time."

He nodded. "How can I pick up the language as soon as possible?"

"Use your ears. Talk to people. Most folks here didn't get much formal education and the Spanish is really different from the one spoken in Spain, so forget anything you might have learned in high school or college."

"But isn't that the correct way to speak?"

"Imagine you were talking to a foreigner, say a guy from Russia, and that foreigner started correcting your English with a London accent, saying you didn't speak properly, how would you feel?"

He smiled. "I see your point."

"Good. Then, you'll be okay. Just let go of any ideas you have about what Mexico is, what the people are like, and then live each day as it comes. One at a time."

We chatted a little more. I knew from the gradual exodus of half the crowd towards the street that his bus into the country would be coming soon, so I could afford to be generous with my time and attention. Then, I would have sweet solitude again for transition reverie. Sure enough, it rolled in. He was mildly apprehensive about its condition. I just nodded and pushed him towards it. "Think about the great story it'll make."

"Thanks." He started towards the bus and turned back. "I'll try fitting in."

"That's all you can do."

Not long after, my own less than standard vehicle pulled in and I climbed on board. As we rolled through the desert, I watched the images go by, letting the past and the present sort themselves out in my mind. The border grew closer and I began to worry about the actual crossing. The only identification I had on me was a twenty-year old driver's license. But it seems I wasn't the only person with the same problem. The driver pulled over that night and several people began gathering up their things. I'd lived down South long enough to know that this was the cross-on-your-own stop. I'd only taken a slightly newer backpack with me: clothes, the diary and photos, a few precious items. I didn't want to be hauling a trunk around until I knew for sure I'd be staying. So, I got off the bus and walked quietly along in the dark with the others. We stopped alongside a two-lane blacktop and everyone else went to sleep. I pondered the night sky, wondering how I'd explain myself. But it wasn't necessary. Around daybreak, a truck pulled up, we got in, a tarp came down over us, and some time later, I was on a San Diego street corner with a lot of other Braceros. I politely declined offers to pick fruit and headed for the bus station.

My initial plan had been to go back to Pacific Grove, but as I got closer, I hesitated, something I hadn't done in many years. I had changed so much in Mexico. In all of my years down south, if I wanted to do something, I never faltered or wavered, I just did it. But now, back in California, I began to feel that old uncertainty creep back. I wanted to get in touch with R.E., Raz, Amanda, Jesse, everyone again, to wrap up that last page of my own First Third, before I decided which country I'd settle down in and live out the Last Third. But what if they had changed so much they would be embarrassed by me? It's not everyone who enjoys seeing former friends crawl out of the woodwork. The mental picture of disappointment or worse, disgust, at seeing me again held me back. And the most negative thought froze me in time: what if no one even recognized me? So I fell back on the old Troy, who hemmed and hawed and hesitated. I eventually headed for Castroville and rented the smallest and cheapest place I could find. I only took it for a month, figuring that would be enough to get my bearings. Besides, the changes in prices for everything in the last twenty years stunned me.

I did venture closer and closer to old haunts, gradually circling Pacific Grove, never finding the nerve to actually enter town. The closest I got was the Thunderbird bookstore and café. I could catch up on the local newspapers, get a coffee and sandwich, and buy an occasional paperback. Then one day, paths were crossed for me once again. As I was paying my check, my eyes wandered over some cookbooks on the counter. One jumped into my attention: *Recipes from Farm Outta*

Sight. I had to smile at the title, so I picked it up and there, on the back, her face smiled back at me: R.E. I stared at it so long the cashier finally asked me if I was okay. I nodded and managed, "I used to know her."

"Wow! Lucky you," he said. "She's so great. She runs this organic farm and heirloom seed company up between Gilroy and Castroville. They grow herbs." I laid down some extra money for a copy and he included a little pamphlet about the place. Later, back in my room, I read both and smiled. She had started the enterprise some ten years ago, a place where people who are "challenged" in some way can work away from the glare of the public spotlight. There was a mailing address on the back cover. I figured a letter would be the easiest way to make contact again. If she wrote me back, good. If not, I would decamp and go back to San Cristobal. I took my time, thinking over and over about what to say and how to begin. A couple of legal pads went into the effort. People at coffee shops even asked me if I was working on a novel. I just nodded and shooed them away since the truth would take too long to explain. Finally, I just said, "Hello, R.E. I'll save you the trouble of looking at the last line to find out who this is from by saying, it's me, Troy. I'm living in Castroville now. I don't expect anything from you. It's been a long time and there's been a lot of water under lots of bridges for both of us. I read about your farm and I'm reading the cookbook now. As always, you land on your feet and are living well. I'm proud of you. Anyway, I'm doing okay. Healthy, not exactly wealthy, but comfortable, and I hope I'm a little wiser than I used to be. Wise enough not to walk up to your door without an invitation. So, if your life has taken you in directions you'd rather not share with someone you knew a long, I mean a very long, time ago, I'll completely understand. Write me at this address if you have time and you feel like it. I'd really like to see you again before I go back home to Mexico. Hope the trails have all been happy, Troy."

Three days later I got the answer. It said, "Troy, I hope you don't already consider Mexico a permanent home. Not until you've seen the Farm. Please come for a visit. Here's a map. I can't wait to see you again. Love, R.E." I was so happy, tears jumped up from my chest and straight out of my eyes. My dear R.E., straight to the heart of the matter. I got a bus ticket the next morning and set off. I could see from the route it would drop me close enough to walk in.

The Farm was a good ways off the main road. I walked past the fields of herbs and edible flowers and stopped more than once to drink in all the smells: rosemary, thyme, basil, lavender, and so many others I didn't recognize. Then I saw the building. It was two stories, with porches all the way around and covered balconies for the second floor, windows everywhere and lots of trees. As I walked up and knocked on the front door, a medium size black dog stood up under the swing on the left and eyed me. From the other side, a large black tomcat stretched and padded softly over to guard me from the right. They both sat near me without any aggression, but I felt that I was being put to the first test. Kneeling down, I offered my hand to the dog without making eye contact. It walked a little closer and sniffed without touching me. The cat remained aloof, turned its back, and started an elaborate grooming while it ignored me completely.

"You must be Troy," a man's muffled voice said from the door. I gasped after I looked up, unprepared for the sight of his ruined face. He'd been so badly burned he looked like a melted candle from what I could see. Most of his neck and the rest of his body were covered with a loose brown monk-like robe.

"Don't worry about it. It's the typical first reaction," he said, opening the door for me. His voice was muffled since he had hardly any mouth. His eyes were still there but there were no eyebrows or eyelids and the nose was just two holes in the middle of a lot of scar tissue. There wasn't a hair on his head and only little stubs of ears remained.

"I'm sorry. Nice to meet you. I'm Troy Jacobson."

We shook. His hands and arms seemed untouched by the disaster that had destroyed his face. "I know. I'm Carl Norton. R.E. said you'd be coming."

I was about to ask how he knew my face when I glanced at the wall. Over the door that led to the big main room was a picture of me. It must have been one that Jesse had taken so long ago when I wasn't aware of his being there. I was still, sitting on my favorite window perch at the Palace, smoking one, looking out at the trees. Beside the picture, there was a framed piece of paper that said:

"This enterprise is dedicated to the
memory of Troy Jacobson, who
would have done wonders in the
world if the Farm had been around at
the same time he was."

Carl nodded and waited for me to compose myself. Then he said, "She was so happy when she got your letter. She's talked about you for years." I didn't have the luxury of reading facial expression or tone of voice with Carl so I couldn't tell how he meant that, but I decided to take it as positive, or at least neutral, for the time being. He went on, "She had to go to Pacific Grove this morning to pick Mel up. She's having another crisis with her family. R.E. said you could wander around, look the place over, meet people until she gets back. Said she was sorry she couldn't be here when you arrived."

I nodded and followed him up the wide stairs to what he said was a guest bedroom. It was one of the most pleasant rooms I'd ever walked into: windows all around, smooth wooden floors that gleamed like soft butter, light blue walls, and a high ceiling. As I crossed the threshold, the shiver of flashing-forward ran my spine and I had to hold very still inside for the Snake to calm down. Carl said from the door, "Sol is out in the packing shed if you'd like to meet him and Corinna is on the phone bank downstairs."

I put my things away and wandered around the empty upstairs. Some of the bedroom doors were open, only a couple closed. They were all just as airy, spacious, and inviting as the one I was in. Then it was outside to start meeting people, as R.E. had said I should do.

Sol, a small brown Mexican man of indeterminate age, was in charge of the shipping department. He had such severe scoliosis that introducing myself to him required a lot of stooping on my part. He took my hand and said in a warm and gracious voice, "I'm so very pleased to meet you, Troy. R.E. has spoken of you so often I feel I already know you. And she said you lived in México? How lovely. I finally have someone besides Mel to speak Spanish with."

"She speaks it?"

"Well, she's learning. My pupil." He pulled up a chair. "Here. Be seated. And please don't feel we must make eye contact to converse. It's not necessary." But it was easier if I was sitting down.

"So, this is your domain."

He smiled as several other people came in. The fall harvest had been good and there were a lot of orders to go out. I watched the flow of work and offered to help, but he said, "No, no. You're a guest. Today, anyway. Perhaps, soon you will help."

As I pondered that reply, he began taking care of the special rush orders himself, sussing out the personality of the customer from the form and tucking in a small, inexpensive, surprise extra in each box. He packaged each order carefully, labeled the boxes and cartons and envelopes, and stacked them neatly to be picked up and mailed. Proud of his labor, he bragged that he could fit more into a carton, safely, while using less packing material than any one else in the business.

Later, we took a break together under the small apple tree near the storage shed, snacking on windfall fruit, talking. He told me about his name and why it was so apt: Sol, short for Soledad. His mother had named each of her children after the town in which they'd been born. He smiled, "And since I am the only one of her children who does not live near the family, I am indeed the one who is alone."

"Why, if you don't mind my asking?"

"My mother feels guilty every time she looks at me. She believes that because she often thought of an old lover while she was carrying me, the Virgin cursed her and I was born to grow into this, a question mark." He smiled even as he shared that. "Anyway, that's what a priest told her during confession." He took another bite and chewed slowly. "So, if you don't mind a question in return, how did you pass your time in the true Big Sur?"

"For a while, I taught Spanish in the back room of a church in Chiapas. Very unofficial, I had no training, but I was able to help some of them become a little more literate so it was better than nothing."

"I'm sure you did more good than you know." He paused, "Did you also attend the services in the front of the church?"

"I was with someone who, well, let's just say she was not devout. She dealt with the priests and bishops socially so that she could have access to the rooms she needed for her classes, but other than that, Sundays were set aside for sleeping late, long meals, and lots of company and conversation. I liked going inside churches in general, though, especially the smaller chapels. The smell of incense and the Ocote pine they used to light it with, the dark, cool quiet. It was so nice after being outside in the heat and the glare. I always found myself looking for the saints' replicas in the glass boxes."

"Your favorite?"

"San Pascual."

"God's kitchen boy. Ah, mi gente. So believing, so trusting in saints and their spare parts. A sliver of bone, a vial of dust. They cure anything. You know," he continued, "my mother once tried to have me cured. Of this." He pointed to his back. "She'd read about Jesus making a guest appearance in Monterrey. So, off we went."

I nodded and he returned a mischievous grin that faded to a wistful smile. He finished his snack and carefully spit all the seeds into his palm before he continued. "She took me to a small house where a long line of people were creeping on their knees through this family's living room to the retablito where they had enshrined," he paused for effect, "a burned tortilla. I don't know what anyone else was seeing, but I wasn't seeing Jesus. I had to kiss it. It was damp from all the others who'd gone before me and it was starting to smell a little moldy. Of course," he sighed, "it didn't work. And she blamed me for lack of faith. She beat me very badly and made me take the bus home again alone. I was only twelve and up to that day, quite religious. I have never set foot in a church since." He got up slowly and opened his hand where he still held the seeds. "There are miracles, though, in the world if you have the eyes to see them. Every time I send seeds to someone, I take part in the cycle of birth, nurturing, harvest, and rebirth that Christianity was originally supposed to celebrate." Someone came up and asked several questions about an order, so many Sol decided to take care of it personally. As he turned to leave, he looked back and said, "I hope this is only the first of many such pleasant discussions, Troy."

"So do I." It was one of the deepest and finest first conversations I'd had with anyone since the days at the Palace. We connected so easily I felt I'd known Sol for many years. I sat there for some time, basking in contentment. Then I decided it was time to meet the last of the three regulars, Corinna. She worked in the big downstairs office next to the common room. I could hear her voice from the door before I walked in: soft as velvet and as deep as a summer night. She smiled and nodded to me as she took a phone call.

"Zelda Flanagan Heirloom Seeds, may I help you?" She gestured to a chair next to her desk, which had been altered to accommodate her wheelchair. The left half of her face was absolutely beautiful, as breathtaking as the ruin of the other half. It was as badly burned as Carl's though the lava flow of scar tissue on her coffee brown skin seemed texturally different, not so much candle wax as jagged glassy cracks. I had braced myself more so I didn't respond to her wounds as I had to Carl's. She finished the order and then we introduced ourselves. Like the others, she seemed to have been expecting me. "So, you've been meeting everyone?"

I nodded. "Carl. And Sol."

She smiled, "Did Carl behave himself?"

"I guess so. How do you mean?"

"Well, he's a little hard to take at first. All the rest of us have learned to deal with the accidents and situations that brought us here, but he's still bitter. He got edges, that boy." The phone rang again and I got up to wander around while she took the call. She put a second one on hold while she dealt with the first.

"Can you use some help?" I asked while she caught a quick break.

"Do you know how to use a computer?"

"Uh, no."

"Well, that would be the only way to really help here, although I do appreciate the gesture. There are a couple of others who work here, but they're on lunch break right now. They'll be back in a bit, so don't worry. I'll be just fine. But, hey! Who knows? Maybe this is where you'll land."

That was the second time that someone had hinted about my stay being more than a visit. I started to ask what was going on but I dropped it for the time being as the other people who worked the phones came in, one also in a chair, and the other walking, sort of. The Snake that was riding him was far more unrelenting than the one I'd always fought. We introduced ourselves, and the three of them got to work on the phones and computers.

I was trying to find a downstairs bathroom when I wandered into Carl's workroom. The walls were covered with pastel and ink drawings and he had a pile of fresh vegetables on his desk. He nodded at me as he arranged them but didn't say anything. I walked over to the desk but he blocked my view and then said gruffly, "Look, I know you're the famous Troy, the guy R.E. talks about all the time, the guy who saved her life, blah, blah, blah. But if you think you're gonna work here with me in catalog, you got another think comin', pal."

That was the third time the topic had come up and it was not a little unfriendly, so I said flat out, "Look, everyone I've met has hinted that you're all under the impression I'm moving in. I'm not. I'm here to visit R.E. for a little while, see? I got no plans of any kind."

"I sure hope I can change your mind." I knew it was her. That whiskey voice had only grown huskier over time. I wheeled around and we threw our arms around each other. As we spun each other in a happy circle, I wound up facing Carl over her shoulder. I couldn't read his face, but I knew by his stance that he didn't like that hug one bit. R.E. let me go and she turned to Carl. "I was really hoping for a little more civility from you."

"You get whatcha get."

"Evidently," she smiled. "Look, never mind. I haven't talked to him about anything yet." Then turning to me, she said, "Let's go out to the kitchen garden and catch up, okay?"

Time had not been kind to her, as it usually isn't to redheads. She had gray streaks in her long mane, which only came to her waist now, but they were pure silver gray. Her face had taken the brunt of the sun and the years, leaving her looking a good ten years older than her calendar age.

As we walked out back, we passed a few people on the way. She kept the conversation light: business with the folks we kept running into and commentary on the garden itself. It was actually more of a forest. There was a tall rosemary hedge around three sides of it, lined with different kinds of sage and mint plants. We wandered around bushes of scented basils and huge thyme hummocks and a lot of plants that she had to identify for me. Then we came to another basil grouping towards the east end where was a strange kind of bench. It had stone legs and arms and back, but the seat part was all low mossy plants. Above the bench was a little plaque that said, "TAKE A LOAD OFF." As we settled down and the warm scent of chamomile drifted up to me, I noticed a little stone leaf-framed face peering up at me from under one of the bushes. She nodded towards it and asked, "Recognize our old friend?"

I nodded. "The Green Man. You have to wonder how long that face had been on the well bucket back at the Palace and who carved it." We sat in silence, an easy silence, then I said, "You know, it's funny. Seems like just the other day we lived there."

"Something about this garden has that effect on people. Calendar time doesn't seem to matter as much."

"I hate to start our first conversation in so long with the topic we both used to dread, but I have to know. You seem content and safe. What happened after, you know, that night on the road?"

She glanced over her shoulder then turned to face me and dropped her voice to a whisper. "Coleman didn't die that night."

"He lived?" I braced myself for the worst.

"A couple of weeks after I got to South Texas, there was a short article in the Dallas paper. The family put out the word that he tried to commit suicide, failed, and was in the care of specialists. There was nothing about anyone else being involved."

"How did they explain the shot to the knee? That man in the car saw me do it."

"The article only said he saw a man lying by the road and that he went to a local doctor's house to get help."

I sat for a moment taking it all in. "All those years of believing that I'd killed him, that the police were looking for me, for you. All that hiding out. Hard to believe it would just go away."

"It didn't go on its own. Coleman's wife Janice showed up the next morning and had a little private talk with the witness. Then she took him to meet with the doctor and the police. He said he'd been mistaken, that he'd just seen shadows. The locals were actually relieved that they didn't have to go out and look for anyone, so it was swept under the legal rug and that was that. Classic van der Veer style. Handle it quietly and in-house."

"I don't know whether to feel relieved or pissed off."

"Lot of time lost down South."

"Not sure if it was truly lost. I guess all our paths are eventually worthwhile, but yeah. I would have rather known that at least, I had choices." We sat in silence for few more minutes, and then I asked, "Specialists?"

"Yeah," she smiled, "Janice got Mazie released from the Wellness Institute and had Coleman committed there. They debated between the place in El Paso and the one in Big Sur and finally decided they'd rather have an excuse to visit the coast every now and then, so that's where they put him."

"How was she able to do that? He would never have gone without a fight, and she didn't have that much say in things."

"Dealing with him wasn't that difficult. His body survived the shooting, but his mind didn't." She paused for a moment. "Eddie asked me one time if Coleman had been sexually abused. I never knew for sure, but when you said something about the Dutchman being inside him, it seemed to unhinge him for good. And he had been injured pretty badly. He lost a lot of blood that night. As for her power, she was the de facto head of the family at that point since she was pregnant. Coleman had had her sign a lot of papers before they got married, of course. The agreement was that 100 percent of his share would go to his firstborn, not to her. She would be the conservator in charge of the whole operation until the kid came of age. I always thought he'd never actually planned to have any kids. It was just the same mean old game his father had played with everyone. I'm sure the pregnancy was an accident, one she hadn't had the chance to tell him about."

"How do you know all these details? Surely none of that was in the papers."

"Actually, Mazie told me."

"No!"

"Yeah. I was still in South Texas working with Dado when I saw her drive up. I almost lost it, I was so scared. But she came over and hugged me. Then we sat down and talked. She said they had taken care of things and that we didn't have anything to worry about. She felt no grudge against us. In fact, she thanked you sincerely for doing what she'd never had the nerve to do."

"How did she know it was me?"

"Janice told her about what the witness had said and she guessed it was you from the description."

"How did she find you?"

"I asked her about that and she said, 'Oh, R.E. Don't be silly. I am a van der Veer. We can find out anything we want to about anyone anytime, you know that.'"

"That part of the story doesn't exactly put one's mind at ease."

She nodded. "Yeah, but it was nice to know that that cloud was not hanging over us anymore. I tried all kinds of ways to find you, get in touch with you, but you really went to ground. Finally, I just gave up and hoped that the Fates would intervene and cross our paths for us again one day." She stopped and hugged me. "And they finally did."

"So, is Coleman still alive?"

"No. He passed a couple of years ago. Duncan sent me his obituary from the *Dallas Times-Herald*. I don't hear from him very often these days so I knew before I opened the envelope that it was probably bad news about someone we used to know. The family chose an old photo for some reason. It was a little sad to see that face again, to think about what he could have been and how he turned out. The article said he died of heart failure after a long illness. Who knows if that's true but that's what it said."

I wanted to know everything about everyone, but I could see that she was tired. As we stood to walk back, I said, "Strange. Seems like we should be smoking one. I haven't indulged a single time since I went to Mexico. How odd is that? The source country for so many people, yet while I was there, it was the last thing I wanted to do."

"Are you saying that because it's something you'd be interested in again?"

"It's just that being with you, sitting here and talking, it reminds me so much of the old days and that was so much a part of everything."

"Yeah. That is something that has changed. I have so many responsibilities now--this place, the people in it, raising or helping raise other people's kids, these businesses. Now I just have wine with meals and I almost never smoke anymore. Once in a while, when I'm in the city taking a break from everything. I still like to stand outside the law every now and then." She paused and I had the feeling that there was more to that part of the story, more that I'd hear later. We walked back in, lightly linking arms. Shoulder to shoulder.

I fell asleep in that beautiful guest room and woke the next morning more refreshed than I had felt in years. It already seemed so right to be there.

In the late afternoons to come, we made the garden talk a personal ritual. The second night R.E. brought along a small thermos of tea and two lovely blue ceramic mugs. At first, she didn't tell me what was in it, but after a few moments, I felt the old familiar green wave. "Ah", I smiled. "So, do you grow your own along with all the other herbs?"

"No, I wouldn't want to put all this at risk just for an old habit. I don't even keep the tea bags here. But as I said, I have a source in the City. I brew up a little now and then and bring it home for special occasions like tonight."

I sighed as the calming took over, "This is just as nice as a fumito."

She raised her eyebrows then nodded. "A little smoke. Yeah, I started getting worried about that delivery system, too."

We let a few more minutes pass then I asked, "I know what you'll probably say, but tell me about your dad."

"He only lived a year or so longer after I joined him."

I knew that he had probably passed, but it still brought a catch to my voice. "I think I missed him as much as anyone while I was away."

"I still do every day. You know, he was real proud of you, for what you did."

"Was he?" Even after all that time, I was surprised at how much I wanted his approval, his attention.

"Yeah. He said you were a man's man."

"Wow." I laughed. "That gives me shivers."

She patted my shoulder. "He said he would have been proud to have a son just like you."

"Oh, man. You have no idea how much that means to me." I could feel a cry near, so I tried to change the subject. "Anyway, after Sam went on ahead, what did you do?"

"Well, I went to Austin and got my degree in social work." She smiled and then it faded to a thoughtful look. "Then, I got married."

"Really? Who was the lucky guy?"

"You remember John? The friend of Eddie's who sewed up my face?"

"Kind of. We weren't around him much."

She nodded. "I was doing an internship in a clinic next door to his in Austin. That was where he moved after we all left Denton. At first, we were just friends and then we realized it was more than that." She smiled and said, "It was good. Real good. In fact, I think that was just about the easiest time of my life. I loved him. He was my partner, my friend. He ran his clinic and I worked for various agencies, both public and private, serving whoever seemed to need it most at the time."

"So where is he?"

She shook her head. "He died."

"Oh, no. I'm sorry. When was it?"

"We'd been together about ten years. It was real fast. Massive stroke. All those years of stress, I suppose, and smoking. Even though he was a doctor and knew it was bad for him, he just couldn't quit. It was just one of those things." She sighed. Now her voice was a little ragged. We sat in silence for a while and then she said, "Even after all these years, I still can't think about him without thinking about how much I lost that one afternoon. One minute he was there, and the next..." It was several minutes before she spoke again. "After that, I came back to California. I tried doing social work again in the City, but I couldn't go on. I was burned out. Then one weekend while I was visiting Raz and Amanda, I saw an ad for this farm. The price seemed about right. As soon as I saw the fields, I said to myself, 'Outta sight!' and then starting laughing at how Mel would roll her eyes at the Dino-Lingo."

"I take it that's any slang from any era earlier than hers?"

She nodded and smiled. "Then I thought more about that phrase. I'd just been talking with Corinna the day before. She was one of my last cases and we'd become friends. She was saying how hard it was to not only get work but to be in the everyday glare of people who couldn't get past her scars. As soon as I walked up to the porch, it hit me. Open a place where people can work without judgment about their physical selves, a safe protected shelter. And let me tell you, this place is safe! Insured up to the chimneys. Fire, earthquake, flood, you name it, we're covered." She laughed that laugh I'd missed for so long as she grinned and nudged me, "Especially for arson! You never know."

I glanced around conspiratorially, "Hush about that!" I stayed turned around briefly, admiring the structure. "How could you afford it? It's a really big place."

"Well, I was married to a doctor for nearly ten years. John wasn't one of those guys that had a huge, moneymaking kind of practice, but he did make a good living and we didn't spend much on middle class things. He always said that what counts most wasn't how much money you made, but how little you spent. The businesses have done well, so we're all in good shape. The Farm's set up so the regulars share the profits, and of course, the part timers are treated right."

"I wouldn't expect anything less from a Union Maid."

She rolled her eyes. "Old Maid, more like."

A dark-haired girl in her twenties came out then. "I thought you'd be out here. You said you'd help me with my research paper this afternoon," she said, disapproval puckering her mouth, standing so that she was beside us but still able to turn her back on us slightly. She was medium height, skinny, dressed in baggy men's shorts, a flannel shirt over a faded torn gray T-shirt, and what looked to be designer work boots. Her black hair was long in some places, almost cropped in others, and she had several rings and different items dangling from lots of holes in her right ear, but nothing from the left, though it sported just as many holes.

"Mel, I already gave you a list of all the sources you need. You know how to find them, you've got a plan for writing the paper, and I told you I'd read the draft when it's done."

"Who's the new stray?"

"Behave yourself. This is Troy."

She turned back to me, surprised. "Really? That Troy?"

I held out my hand and she shook it. "Nice to see you again," I said. "I know you'd hate to hear it, but it's the truth. Last time I saw you, you were a baby."

She screwed up her face.

"I said you'd hate to hear it."

She pouted. "I do. Anything to do with babies, I hate."

"I can dig it."

"Dig? Oh, my God. Have you two been speaking Dino-Lingo all day?" Then she shrugged. "So, you coming in to dinner?"

"In a bit." R.E. frowned as Mel slumped back inside. "She's going through some tough times. But most of them that age are. The press has labeled them Generation X and lots of folks our age look down on them, make them feel bad because there's no Vietnam, no central focus point for their hormones. They have causes, mostly personal ones. It's tough being in your 20s these days. AIDS, the economy, unreal expectations from all sides."

"Speaking of people who rag on the young, is Mack still around?"

She shook her head. "You know, I was just thinking about him. That old bulldog went on ahead not long after Dado. I still think about that day at the farm when he was railing against us all so hard, how I went on such a guilt trip. I know that all I've done, facing down Coleman, doing social work, running this place, none of it would have satisfied him. That old man was for nothing less than all-out industrial actions. Funny, in so many ways we could never satisfy the ones who went before. I suppose that's why I'm easier on kids these days than my generational peers are. I don't want to be like Mack, always trying to make people feel guilty. But these days, I'm at peace about it. I did what I could. It just took a long time to know what it was I was meant for. Maybe that's what Mel and people her age are feeling about choosing a future. They don't know. She won't talk about what she wants to do. Can't get anything out of her except moods these days."

"Carl said something the day I came here about her having another crisis with her family?"

"Yeah, she goes around and around, especially with her mom. See, Amanda wound up having six more kids."

"Oh, man! How has Raz handled all that expense?"

"Pretty well. He became the top man on the coast at doing Victorian restorations and he really cleaned up every time there was a gentrification project. And they always lived very frugally. Amanda thought Mel would fall in line and get on the baby wagon like she had. But Mel balked and dug in her heels, refusing to babysit the last two, twin girls. And when Amanda decided to take her father in after his stroke, Mel left home and lived here for almost a year. She showed up on the doorstep on acid one day muttering 'Shit and diapers, shit and diapers.' Amanda is all too glad to take on the task, though. She's close to her dad now, after her mother passed."

"So, they reconciled."

"Oh, yeah. Not long after we all split for the coast. Amanda felt guilty and got in touch. Her parents felt just as guilty so they had a big reunion in P.G. Turns out they really like Raz. So that all blew over pretty quickly."

"How long do you think Mel will stay mad?"

"Not for long, I hope, for their sake but she's welcome to stay as long as she needs to. The latest feud is her lack of commitment to any one major in school." She got up and stretched. "She's torn between psychology, music theory, and French. Problem is, she's equally talented in all three areas. Music seems to be the major draw right now, but Raz and Amanda want her to have something with more financial security."

"Does she have a band?"

"The last one was called Dr. Lector's Lunchbox." She waited for me to smile, but there was no cultural resonance yet. "You have a lot of catching up to do. Shall we call it a night?"

I nodded and we walked in. The smell of rosemary was strong that night: remembrance.

The next evening we got around to other stories. I started out by asking, "So, do you hear from Eddie at all? Whatever happened with him and Lizzy?"

"He stayed around the City and Liz for a few years, and then a weird thing happened. She began to misunderstand his attentions, and given that she was so precocious, well, she thought he was interested in her sexually. And one night, she came onto him."

"Oh, boy. How did he handle that?"

"Well, it rattled him pretty bad. He left the City as fast as he left Denton that day, just dumped his things into Mariah and took off." She paused and then she went on. "I was just finishing one of my classes in Austin late one afternoon and he walked in the door." She smiled. "When we met up again, it was like only an afternoon had passed. We just started talking. But I could tell he was confused. Hurting."

I thought about it, tried to put myself into Eddie's shoes. Of course, I couldn't. But I asked, "He didn't--I mean--not with Lizzy. Did he?"

"No. He didn't. He couldn't, but he realized that part of him wanted to. Real bad. She looked so much like Maja when she was younger. And he said that after all, she probably wasn't really his. But no, he just left. He didn't explain anything to her. As far as she knew, he was a friend of the family that she'd come on to and been turned down by. In order to explain, he'd have to tell her everything. It would've been pretty hard to take, knowing she'd just come on to someone who might be her father."

"What did he do?"

"He stayed in Austin with me for a month or so. But it was another finishing up, not a starting over, because John was already on the scene. We were still in the friendship stage, but I'm sure that Eddie saw we could have something he could never give me, a committed relationship. Still, I'm glad I had that time."

"I miss him, too."

"He was also very impressed by what you did for me. We still write to each other. He gives great letter."

I laughed at that. "That sounds a little twisted."

"I know."

"So, where is Eddie these days?"

"Last I heard, he was in Nova Scotia."

"Why there?"

"It's far away from everything. He never really got over Maja, you know. She died in Korea a few years ago. So, he just drives and drinks a lot. Still. And writes some."

"Ever published?"

"No, though he told me I could try for him if I wanted to. I want to get that book of his poems in print. He wants to, but he can't bear going through the process. For all his toughness, he's pretty soft inside."

"Yeah." Then I asked. "And Jesse?"

"Well, that's a little happier story. Texas Weather blew itself out, as you probably have imagined. Too much talent in one band, he always said, and he was right. Ty and Vance went on to front their own bands. Did real well, though neither of them tour much these days."

"Why?"

"Well, the half-life of bands is a lot shorter now than it used to be. Ty still does nostalgia tours. Calls it the dead horse circuit, but he needs the money. Had lots of kids. Three, no four wives. And Vance still plays, mostly as a sideman for other bands. Lots of guitar slingers look up to him. It's a real coup to get him on an album."

I sighed. "It's so hard to realize that people I knew are now old guys."

"Yeah. We're all old guys to some folks, but still young 'uns to others."

"So, Jesse's doing okay?"

"Actually, he's coming into his own these days. He did a lot of studio work there for a while. And then started producing, arranging albums for other bands. Got very famous at that. And last year, he came out with a solo album. It wasn't a best seller, but it's very well thought of among musicians."

"He'd like that better anyway."

She nodded. "He lives down in L.A. now, but he's thinking about leaving, building a place in New Mexico somewhere. Home studio. All that."

"So you see him much?"

"Not so much, but I hear from him. He communicates through his music rather than by letter. Albums used to show up in the mail every now and then, now he sends tapes or CDs. I can tell how he's doing by the sound of his tunes," she smiled. "And who's in the band. He's on his second wife. And he went through a lot of girlfriends."

"No doubt."

"Calls them all La Muse du Temps. In fact, that was the title cut on his solo album."

"Stan and Moe? JaeDeen and RaeAnn? They all okay, too?"

"Stan and Moe are. They avoided the plague that brought so many gay folks down because they always were mostly monogamous. Or careful. They bought a house in the Bay Area a long time ago, been raising a couple of kids they adopted. JaeDeen is on the coast, too. San Diego, last I heard. RaeAnn passed away about three years ago. Complications from diabetes."

And I finally asked something I'd been wondering about since I arrived. "So, is there anyone that you're involved with now?"

"I see this guy when I go to the City, but he's got his life there and I'm here." She smiled. "He's a lot like me. Same French-Irish-Cherokee mix. Same age, too. Strange how that's so important to me these days."

"Why?"

"Well," she smiled, "I guess I just got tired of being with people who weren't from the same generation. That was one thing about being with John. We always had to explain things to each other, all those differences."

I nodded, thinking of Consuelo. "Yeah, imagine being with someone more than twenty years older and from a totally different culture."

"You haven't said much about your time down south."

"Your dad said once that a person's story deserves time to be told, and that is most definitely one that needs time. Let's save her story for a whole 'nother night." I switched the topic back to where she'd left off. "What's your friend's name?"

She smiled. "The first time he told me, I almost fell over. It's Jake."

"That is too weird."

"Yeah. Jake MacKenna. I've explained most of my personal history, and the family's, to him, so he understands why I have trouble saying the name. I just call him J.M."

"J.M. and R.E. Does he call you that?"

"No, he calls me Zell, a short form of Zelda. We met at a book signing for my cookbook."

"You think you'll get married again?"

"That, I don't know. He's kind of wild, really. A poet. Writer. Political columnist. Says he can't stand being out in the country. And me, I'm fed up with cities in general. So, who knows? But it's fine for now." We stayed outside for a while longer, talking about other things: politics, cultural changes, music, and books. What she'd said about generational shorthand was true, and I'd forgotten how much I missed it. And I did find out about why Mel's band's name was so creepy.

***

It was the next day, smack dab in the middle of an afternoon break that the last piece of the puzzle clicked into place. I was downstairs in the study, looking through an album of Jesse's photos that he had given R.E. as a Christmas present one year. It was like falling through the rabbit hole to see the pictures again: the Palace, The Corner Room, all of us so young and sweet and so sure of ourselves. And when I came across a picture of me and Claire kissing, another that Jesse had sneaked, the dagger of memory pinned me to the chair with such an audible moan that R.E. and Corinna both came in to see if I was all right. I nodded but they knew I wasn't so they left me alone for a while.

That night, R.E. stayed quiet on our bench, waiting for me to ask, which I finally did. "So. Claire. What happened? You haven't said anything about her."

She leaned back and took a deep breath. I knew this wasn't going to have a happy ending, so I braced myself. "She did come back to Pacific Grove, just a month or so after we split that day. But since we were both long gone and no one knew where to, eventually, she went back to Austin. She and Duncan wound up getting married." She frowned. "It wasn't happy. She always worried about money so much that he had to quit the music scene and start working. Some state job that he hated."

"I thought he had that trust fund. Wasn't it enough?"

"Well, for one person, back in those times, it was fine. But as times went on and things got more expensive, it wasn't enough for a family, especially since Claire wanted to be a stay at home mom."

She paused and looked at me to see how I was taking it. "They," she paused and then went on, "had two kids, so she finally got that wish. That connection kept her corresponding with Amanda. Claire and I stayed in touch, too, but we had less and less in common as time went by."

"Are they still together?

"No. Troy, she died. It was one of those stupid things, a routine operation, some polyp they had to take out. She went under the anesthesia and she never woke up again."

I still don't know why it hit me so hard after so long, but I started sobbing. R.E. walked away and let me work it out on my own. But that was the last of the stories from the Palace. Or so I thought.

The next morning, over coffee, I asked her, "So, you've been hinting that you want me to stay for more than just a visit."

She smiled, "Yes. I started this place in honor of you, and although it's easy to see you've outgrown being whipped by the Snake, you can still fill a void here."

"How?"

"Role model. You went out in the world and you made your way. I never intended this place to be the last stop on the train route. A couple of folks have already gained a lot of skill and self-confidence and moved on. And besides, Troy," she said as she leaned over and patted my hand, "I've really missed you. You are the one of the last friends I have who still calls me R.E."

I returned the smile and nodded, but I insisted on a trial run. I moved my few things in, but I was careful not to intrude on anyone's turf as far as jobs. I was especially careful about Carl since he seemed the most resistant to my being there. He made his feelings about my not belonging plain. So, I was doubtful about R.E.'s suggestion that he and I share office space and tasks. It was rough going at first: icy silence and more than a little intentional contact with boxes and open cabinet doors. But over the following weeks, we came to a tenuous truce. He did the art and I did the words for the catalogs.

Maybe we were so edgy around each other because we're a lot alike. We both have a tendency to go to extremes in our work. His sensuous drawings and photographs bring out an almost human side to the products we sell; I tend to what R.E. calls "vegetable pornography" in the descriptions. I admit I use a few terms too often: fleshy globes, heavy melons, firm zucchini, etc. But it's because I have discovered a long-buried gardener self within. I am enamored of tomatoes ripe on the vine, full of sun-warmed juices. I lie on my back in the fields sometimes, looking up through the mini-canopy of bean leaves, watching the sun illuminate the flow of water through the veins. I have studied the evening light on a single green bell pepper and smiled at the Weston brothers' amicable argument over who actually ate *Pepper #30* for lunch after their dad had captured its curves. Participating in the cycle of birth, harvest, and rebirth that Sol so wisely knows is the basis for the mystery religions has become a deep and abiding obsession. So, when R.E. accuses me and Carl of going overboard, we defend ourselves by reminding her that we are competing with other businesses and that we are only doing our best to make our catalog stand out.

One excessive morning brought Carl and me together in a funny way. I was feeling especially energetic and positive due to a spell of glorious weather. Carl was also upbeat, or what passes for upbeat with Carl. He had one photo of Soledad's slim brown hands holding two humongous tomatoes, his thumbs resting on the blossom ends. He laughed and moved a cardboard frame around the shot until it looked as though the fruits were barely enclosed in a leafy blouse and that Sol was helping them out. I contributed to the mood by rhapsodizing about the firm, juicy globes and their willingness to ripen in the knowing gardener's hands. It all went downhill from there. By the end of the day, we'd produced two paste-up pages of the purest veggie porn ever written, as well as the two pages we were scheduled to show R.E. the next morning. However, we were having such a good time that we got them mixed up and left the prank pages on R.E.'s desk instead of the serious ones.

R.E. was already looking at the two porno pages when we walked into her workroom. My jaw dropped and Carl coughed a little in embarrassment. Turning back to us and gesturing with her coffee mug, she tried to remain boss-like but I could see that her eyes were gleaming gold as they did when she was suppressing amusement. "Guys, what's wrong with these pages?"

It was Carl who finally said, "Too much blossom end?"

R.E.'s whiskey laugh had grown even warmer through the years. "I think you hit it right on the head. As it were. Man, you know we can't use this stuff, though I do kind of like the jaunty angle on that erect zucchini."

We all laughed a little then and Carl left quickly to fetch the real pages.

R.E. smiled at me. "You're working better with him than anyone else ever has."

"He's all right."

She put her mug down and filed the paste-ups away. "I'm keeping these."

"No problems?"

"Hell, no. But, please. We do need that catalog to be ready for press on schedule. Don't want to leave customers without the stimulation only my troops can provide." As I turned to leave, she said, "I'm glad you're here."

My heart was suddenly too full for speech so I nodded and went back to work.

It was a couple of nights later, when we were planning a big get-together and reunion to celebrate my official moving-in, that R.E. dropped the last and the biggest information bombshell. She said, "Troy, there's one part of Claire's story I left out the other night. I don't know how to get around to it any other way than to just tell you straight out. You have a son."

My knees gave way and the kitchen floor jumped up to smack me in the butt. "That's impossible," I whispered.

"No, it's true. Claire was already pregnant when she blew out of Pacific Grove. Her periods were so irregular that she didn't know at first. By the time she went back to Austin, it was pretty clear."

"But you said she got together with Duncan. And that they had two kids."

"They did, but they raised three."

"And he didn't care that it--he was mine?"

"He said he didn't. His true feelings came to light much later." I couldn't say anything, so she went on, "His name is Matthew but he prefers to be called Jude, after the Beatles song. It's a name that he chose when he was a kid."

"Is he--okay?"

"Perfectly."

I gasped. "Good. Does he know?"

She shook her head. "No, we all decided not to tell him. He thinks Duncan's his father. They were never close, though, and after Claire died, Duncan and his two seemed to close ranks emotionally, so he ran away and came out here. He was only about twelve at that time. Amanda, Raz, and I took turns raising him. Summers with me, school seasons in town with them. He's a fine boy. Boy," she grinned, "I say that out of habit. He's in his twenties, now, but I still think of him as a kid. Very talented artist. Right now, he's living up in the City. He and Mel are good friends."

I took a deep breath. "How does he look?"

"He's gorgeous. Looks a lot like Claire, but with your eyes. A real lady-killer. He speaks French. When he wants to." She held out her hands to help me to my feet. "He's coming up for the party with everyone else."

We walked out towards the garden to gather a few things. The late afternoon light was soft yellow gold, my favorite moment when it seems that the world glows with Celtic clarity. It brought out all the highlights in her hair. Those iridescent eyes were glowing. She was as lean as ever from all the years of physical labor, and I knew that I loved her as much as I ever had. And I also knew we'd never act on it but that was okay. She felt my mind, I suppose, because she turned, smiled at me and said, "Of course I do, too. I always have, and I always will." Then she walked on ahead of me, down the path between the rows of rosemary and rue.

***

And so, I have come home for the last time, to live out my Last Third. I don't know if I will ever tell Jude who I really am or who his grandfather really was. He'll see the retablo one day and maybe he'll ask who the people are. That might be a moment that could open up the story. I'm in no hurry. But, whatever happens, it will be strange and I hope, interesting to get to know him.

And there are projects to be done, legacies to be printed: Eddie's poetry and the books Consuelo wrote and entrusted to me. R.E. has recently taken on a writing task of her own. She's thinking about finishing the work that her mother started so long ago: the history of the U.S. written from the point of view of the people in the margins and the footnotes, all those that went before. She isn't sure if it will be fiction or history or a combination of the two. "There are so many stories to be told," she smiled as we were looking through all of the bits and pieces she had assembled.

That's true. There's a lot of work to be done in my Last Third and I look forward to it. I'm one of the luckiest people in the world and I'm smart enough to realize that. Who knows? Maybe there's a love of my life to meet. There are voices in the yard. Party time. People to see again. People to meet. Happy trails.

"Fare thee well now
Let your life proceed by its own design.
Nothin' to tell now.
Let the words be yours
I'm done with mine, done with mine."

Bob Weir / John Barlow
Cassidy

Many thanks to Alan Trist, Elizabeth Clementson, Pamela Quick, and Stephen Gerringer for help in obtaining permission to reprint the following quotations:

www.ingramcontent.com/pod-product-compliance
Lightning Source LLC
Chambersburg PA
CBHW050551260626
47157CB00002B/522